He makes the rul...
he win her, body ...

WANTED BY
THE BOSS

Three dramatic, exciting stories from
three of your favourite authors

We're proud to present

MILLS & BOON

Spotlight

*a chance to buy collections of bestselling novels
by favourite authors every month – they're
back by popular demand!*

July 2009

The Royal Wager

Featuring

by Kristi Gold
Persuading the Playboy King
Unmasking the Maverick Prince
Daring the Dynamic Sheikh

Wanted by the Boss

Featuring

Sleeping with the Boss by Maureen Child
Cowboy Boss by Kathie DeNosky
Billionaire Boss by Meagan McKinney

August 2009

Tycoon's Temptation

Featuring

The Truth About the Tycoon by Allison Leigh
The Tycoon's Lady by Katherine Garbera
Her Texas Tycoon by Jan Hudson

Dark, Devastating & Delicious!

Featuring

The Marriage Medallion by Christine Rimmer
Between Duty and Desire by Leanne Banks
Driven to Distraction by Dixie Browning

WANTED BY THE BOSS

Sleeping with the Boss
MAUREEN CHILD

Cowboy Boss
KATHIE DeNOSKY

Billionaire Boss
MEAGAN McKINNEY

⊚™ MILLS & BOON®
Pure reading pleasure™

*This collection is first published in Great Britain 2009.
Harlequin Mills & Boon Limited,
Eton House, 18-24 Paradise Road, Richmond, Surrey TW9 1SR*

WANTED BY THE BOSS © Harlequin Books S.A. 2009.

The publisher acknowledges the copyright holders of the
individual works, which have already been published in the UK
in single, separate volumes, as follows:

Sleeping with the Boss © Maureen Child 2003
Cowboy Boss © Kathie DeNosky 2002
Billionaire Boss © Ruth Goodman 2003

ISBN: 978 0 263 87159 3

064-0709

*Printed and bound in Spain
by Litografia Rosés S.A., Barcelona*

Sleeping with the Boss

MAUREEN CHILD

MAUREEN CHILD

is a California native who loves to travel. Every chance they get, she and her husband are taking off on another research trip. The author of more than sixty books, Maureen loves a happy ending and still swears that she has the best job in the world. She lives in Southern California with her husband, two children and a golden retriever who has delusions of grandeur.

Visit her website at www.maureenchild.com.

To Wendi Heard Muhlenbruch – an artist with
flowers and the inspiration behind Eileen – may
your new baby bring you and Daren joy always.

One

Eileen Ryan faced her grandmother down in battle, even knowing that she would, eventually, lose the war. It was inevitable. Her grandmother was undefeated. If she wanted something, Margaret Mary—Maggie to her friends—Ryan, usually found a way to get it. But Eileen was determined to stand her ground. "Gran, I'm not a secretary anymore."

Sunlight danced in the small living room. The tiny beach cottage that Maggie Ryan had called home for more than forty years was packed full of her memories, but was never less than tidy. Gran sat in a splash of sunshine that gilded her perfectly styled gray hair. The older woman wore a pale peach dress, nylons and sensible black shoes. Her deeply lined features creased in a patient smile and her hands rested on the doily-covered arms of her favorite chair. She looked quietly regal—which was one of the reasons *no one* ever won an argument with her.

"Yes, but it's like riding a bike," Gran countered. "You never forget."

"You can if you work at it hard enough," Eileen told her, stubbornly clinging to her argument.

Heaven knows Eileen had certainly tried to forget everything about being a secretary. It had been three years since she'd last worked in an office. And she didn't miss it.

She'd always hated working in offices. First, there was the whole "trapped behind a desk" feeling— not to mention having to put up with a boss looking over your shoulder all the time. But the absolute worst part of being a secretary, as far as Eileen was concerned, was being smarter than the boss and having him treat her like an idiot. An old echo of pain welled up inside her and she fought it back down. Her last boss, Joshua Payton, had pretended to love her. Pretended to need her. Until he got the fat promotion that had taken him up the ladder of success and sent her back to the secretarial pool.

Well, she wouldn't be used and discarded again. She'd made her escape and didn't want to go back. Not even temporarily.

"Piffle."

"Piffle?" Eileen repeated, laughing.

Maggie's nose twitched. "It's not as though I were asking you to take a nosedive into the black hole of Calcutta."

"Close, though."

"I'm only asking you to help Rick out for two weeks. His secretary's gone on maternity leave and—"

"No way, Gran," she said, shaking her head and taking a step backward, just for good measure. Going into an office again was going backward. Revisiting a past that she'd just as soon forget.

Maggie didn't even blink. She simply stared at Eileen through emerald-green eyes and waited. And waited.

Eileen folded. She never had been able to stand tough under the silent treatment. "Come on, Gran. It's my vacation."

"Your vacation was canceled."

True. She and her best friend, Tina, had planned on two weeks in Mexico. Until, that is, Tina had unexpectedly eloped with her longtime boyfriend, leaving Eileen an apologetic message on her machine. Now Eileen had her passport in hand and no real desire to go to a fun-in-the-sun spot all on her lonesome.

Frustrating, since she'd spent so much time arranging things so that her flower shop wouldn't fold in her absence. Eileen had prepped her staff, coached her assistant and cleared her own decks to allow herself two whole weeks of a well-earned vacation. Early October was the best possible chance for her to take some time off. There was a real lull in a florist's calendar at this time of year—and as soon as October was finished, the holiday frenzy would kick in. She wouldn't have a moment to herself until after Valentine's Day.

Stress rattled through her like a freight train and even her eyes suddenly hurt. She could almost feel her time off slipping away from her. "The *trip* was canceled. I still have my two weeks."

"And nothing to do," her grandmother pointed out.

True again and darn it, Gran knew her *way* too well. Yes, she'd probably go a little nuts with nothing to occupy her time. But she was willing to risk it. "Hey, you never know. I might actually learn to *like* doing nothing at all."

Maggie chuckled. "Not you, honey. You never were one to sit still when you could be up and running."

"Maybe it's time I slowed down a little then," Eileen said, and started pacing. "I could read. Or go to the movies. Or maybe sit down at the beach and watch the waves."

Maggie waved a hand at her. "You wouldn't last twenty-four hours."

Eileen tried to placate her grandmother even while sticking to her plan to escape doing her this "favor." "Rick Hawkins is a pain, Gran, and you know it."

"You only say that because he used to tease you."

Eileen nodded. "You bet. Every time he came over to pick up Bridie for a date, he tormented me. He used to make me so mad."

"You were a little girl and he was your big sister's boyfriend. He was supposed to tease you. It was sort of his job."

"Uh-huh."

Maggie's sharp green eyes narrowed. "His grandmother is a very old, very dear friend."

"Great," Eileen interrupted in a rush. "I'll go help *her,* then."

"Nice try, but Loretta doesn't need a secretary. Her grandson *does.*"

"So what's he do, anyway?" Eileen plopped down into a chair close to her grandmother's. "With as mean as he was to me, I'm figuring he's some sort of criminal mastermind."

"Financial advisor," Maggie said, reaching up to tuck a stray curl behind her ear. "He's doing very well, too, according to Loretta."

Eileen wasn't impressed. "She's his grandmother. She's deluded, poor woman."

"Eileen…"

"Fine. So he's rich. Is he on wife number five by now?"

"Awfully curious, aren't you?"

"It's a tragic flaw."

Maggie's mouth twitched. "One ex-wife, no children. Apparently the woman was just a barracuda."

"Hey, even a barracuda doesn't stand a chance against a great white." She hated to admit that she felt even the slightest pang of sympathy for a guy she hadn't seen in years, but divorces were never pretty. Not that she would know from personal experience, of course. You had to actually get married to be able to experience divorce. And her one and only engagement had ended—thank heaven—before she'd actually taken the vows.

"Honestly, Eileen," her grandmother said. "You're making the man sound awful."

"Well…"

Maggie frowned at her. "Rick is the grandson of my very dear friend."

The solid steel guilt trap was swinging closed. Eileen could actually feel its cold, sharp jaws pinching at her flesh. Yet still she struggled. "Rick never liked me much either, you know."

"Don't be silly."

"He probably wouldn't *want* me to help him."

"Loretta says he's grateful for your offer."

Eileen's eyes bugged out. She wouldn't have been surprised to feel them pop right out of her head. "He *knows* already?" So much for free will.

"Well, I had to say something, didn't I?"

"And volunteering me was the first thing that came to mind?" Her only family, turning on her like a snake.

"You're a good girl, Eileen. I didn't think you'd mind."

"Rick Hawkins," she muttered, shaking her head. She hadn't seen him in six years. He'd come to her grandfather's funeral. Six years was a long time. And that was okay by her. The one brief glimpse of him in a business suit didn't wipe away her real memories of him. The way she remembered it, he was a bully who'd picked on an eleven-year-old kid who'd kinda, sorta, had a crush on him. There's a guy she wanted to work for. Nope. No way. Uh-uh. "I'm so not gonna do this."

Maggie Ryan rested her elbows on the arms of the floral tapestry chair and steepled her fingers. Tipping her head to one side, she studied her granddaughter and said softly, "When you were ten years old, you broke Great Grandmother O'Hara's china cup."

"Oh, God…" *Run, Eileen,* she told herself. *Run and keep on running.*

"I seem to remember you saying something along the lines of, 'I'm so sorry, Gran. I'll do anything to make it up to you. Anything.'"

"I was ten," Eileen protested, desperately looking for a loophole. "That was seventeen years ago."

Maggie sighed dramatically and laid one hand across what she was pretending to be a broken heart. "So, there's a time limit on promises in this house, is there?"

"No, but…" The trap tightened a notch or two. It was getting harder to breathe.

"That was the last cup in the set my grandmother carried over from the old country."

"Gran…" The cold, cold steel of guilt wrapped around her, the jaws of the trap nearly closed around her now. She winced.

The older woman rolled her eyes toward heaven. "*Her* grandmother gave her the set as a wedding gift. So she could bring it with her from County

Mayo—a piece of her old world. And she took it with love, knowing they'd never meet again in this life.''

If she started talking about the steerage section of the boat again, it was all over. ''I know, but—''

''She kept those cups safe on the boat. It wasn't easy. She was in steerage, you know and—''

Snap.

''I surrender,'' Eileen said, lifting both hands in the traditional pose. No matter how much she wanted to avoid working for Rick, she was caught and she knew it. ''I'll do it. I'll work for Rick. But it's two weeks only. Not a day longer.''

''Wonderful, dear.'' Gran reached for the shamrock-dusted teacup on the table beside her. ''Be at the office at eight tomorrow morning. I told Rick to expect you.''

''You knew I'd do it all along, didn't you?''

Gran smiled.

''Just so you know, I still haven't forgiven you for the whole Barbie episode.''

Rick Hawkins just stared at the tall, elegant-looking redhead standing in his outer office. Her features were wary, but couldn't disguise her beauty. Irish green eyes narrowed, but not enough to hide the gleam in their depths. Her mouth was full and lush, her eyebrows finely arched. Her hair fell in red-gold waves to her shoulders. She wore a white dress shirt tucked into sleek black slacks and shiny black boots peeked out from beneath the hem. Small silver hoops dangled from her ears and a serviceable silver watch encircled her left wrist. Her hands were bare but for a coat of clear nail polish. She looked businesslike. Dignified and too damn good.

He never should have listened to his grandmother. This could be a long two weeks.

"You were eleven," he reminded her at last.

"And you were almost sixteen," she countered.

"You were a pest." Looking at her now, though, he couldn't imagine being bothered by having her around. Which worried him a little. He'd been taken in by a gorgeous face before. He'd trusted her. Believed in her. And then she'd left. Just like every other woman in his life—except the grandmother who'd raised him after his mother decided she'd rather be a free spirit than be tied to a child.

She nodded, allowing his point. "True. But you didn't have to decapitate Barbie."

He smiled despite the memories crowding his brain. "Maybe not, but you left me alone after that."

"Well yeah." She folded her arms across her chest and tapped the toe of one shoe against the steel-blue carpet. "That's a sure sign of a serial killer in the making."

"Sorry to disappoint you. No grisly past here. Just a businessman."

She shrugged. "Same difference."

Rick shook his head. She had the same temperament she'd had as a kid. Always ready for war. Must be the red hair. And with a personality like that, this might just work. "Is the office going to be a war zone for the next two weeks, because if it is…"

"No," she said, tossing her black leather purse onto the desk that would be hers as long as she was there. "I'm just being pissy. It's not even your fault."

"For which I'm grateful."

"Cute."

"Peace, okay? I appreciate you helping me out, Eileen." He did. He needed the help. He just didn't need the kind of distraction she was no doubt going to be.

Her eyebrows went high on her forehead. "Hey," she said smiling, "that's an improvement. At least you didn't call me Eyeball."

"No," he said, giving her a slow, approving up-and-down look. The scrawny little girl with long braids and a perpetual scab on her knee was gone. This woman was a world away from the child he'd nicknamed Eyeball. "You're definitely an 'Eileen' these days."

She inclined her head in a silent thank-you and it seemed, he thought, that a temporary truce had been declared.

"It's been awhile," she said.

"Yeah." It had, in fact, been about six years since he'd last seen her. When they were growing up, he and the Ryan sisters had been thrown together a lot, thanks to their grandmothers' close friendship. But once out of high school—hell, once he and Eileen's sister Bridget had broken up, he'd stopped coming around.

And while he'd been gone, Eileen Ryan had done a hell of a job of growing up.

Damn it.

"How's your grandmother?" he asked.

"Just as spry and manipulative as always," Eileen said with a quick grin that dazzled him even from across the room. "Here I stand as living proof. Gran is probably the only woman in the world who could have talked me into taking on a job on what should have been my vacation."

"She's good."

"She is." She reached up to push her hair behind her ears. The silver hoops winked at him in the sunlight. "And she misses you. You should stop and see her sometime."

"I will," he said, meaning it. Maggie Ryan had been a second grandmother to him. It shamed him to admit that he hadn't kept up with her.

"How's your gran?"

"In Florida," he said, grinning. "To catch the space shuttle launch next week."

Eileen turned and leaned one hip on the edge of her desk. "She was always doing something exciting, as I remember it."

Rick smiled to himself. His grandmother had always been one for grand adventures. "I think she was actually born a gypsy and then sold to a normal family as a baby."

Eileen shrugged and that fabulous hair actually rippled with light and color. "What's normal?"

"Beats the hell outta me," he admitted. He'd once thought he knew what normal was. It was everything he didn't have. A regular family with a mom and a dad. A house with a picket fence and a big sloppy dog to play with. Dreams and plans and everything else he'd worked so hard to acquire. But now he wasn't so sure.

For some people, Rick thought, "normal" just never came into play. And that was okay with him now that he'd come to grips with the fact that he was a member of that particular group. He'd tried to find that normalcy once. He'd married a woman he thought loved him as much as he cared for her. By the time he'd figured out how wrong he was, she'd left, taking half of his business with her.

And his ability to trust went with her.

"So." Eileen's voice cut into his thoughts and he turned his attention back to her, gratefully. "What exactly is it you need me to do?"

"Right." Good idea, he told himself. Stick to business here. Just because their families were friendly was no reason for them to treat this situation as anything more than strictly business. Better all the way around, he thought as his gaze slipped back to her and he felt his blood thicken. Yep. A long two weeks.

Rick walked to the desk and stopped behind it. "Mainly, I need you to take care of the phones, take messages and type up a few reports for me when necessary.''

"So basically, you want me to stick my finger in a dyke and keep the place from flooding until you can get someone in here permanently."

"Well, yeah, that's one way to put it." Rick pushed the edges of his navy-blue suit jacket back and shoved his hands into his pants pockets. "With Margo out early on maternity leave, the place is falling apart and the temp agency can't send me anyone for another two weeks at least."

"Whoa—" Eileen held up one hand as she stared at him. Okay, she could admit, to herself anyway, that Rick Hawkins was a little...*more* than she'd expected. For some reason, even after that glimpse of him six years ago her mind had kept his image as he was at sixteen. Tall and lanky, with messy brown hair and a crooked smile. Well, that smile was there, but he wasn't lanky anymore. He was built like a man who knew what the inside of a gym looked like.

And his voice sounded like melted chocolate tasted.

So sure, she was female enough to be distracted. A lot. Until he'd used the words "at least". She wasn't about to let herself get sucked into giving him more than the agreed-on time.

"At least?" she repeated. "I can only do this for two weeks, Rick. Then I turn back into a pumpkin and head back out to Larkspur."

"Larkspur?"

"My shop." Her pride and joy. The spot she'd worked so hard to build.

"Oh that's right. Grandma said you worked at a flower shop."

"I *own* a flower shop. Small, exclusive, with an emphasis on design." She reached across the desk for her purse, rummaged in its depths for a second or two, then came up with a brass card case. Flipping it open, she pulled out a card and handed it to him. Pale blue linen, the card stock was heavy, and the printing was embossed. A lone stalk of delicate-looking flowers curled around the left-hand side, looping around the name Larkspur. Eileen's name and phone number were discreetly added at the bottom.

"Very nice," Rick said, lifting his gaze back to hers as he automatically tucked the card into his breast pocket.

"Thanks. We do good work. You should give us a try."

"I will." A heartbeat or two passed and the silence in the room dragged on, getting thicker, heavier, warmer. Something indefinable sizzled in the air between them and Rick told himself to put a lid on it. He'd never made a play for a co-worker before and *now* certainly wasn't the time to start. Not when he would have *two* grandmothers out for his head if Eileen complained.

"Anyway," he said, his voice a little louder than he'd planned, "two weeks will be great. I'm sure the temp agency will come through for me."

"There're plenty of temp agencies out there. Why not try a different one?"

He shook his head. "I've tried lots of them. *This* one always sends good people. Most of them don't. I'd rather wait."

"Why didn't you get someone lined up before Margo left?"

"Good question," he said wryly. "Should have. But I was so busy trying to get things done and finished before she was gone, that time sort of got away from me. And then in the last month or so, Margo wasn't her usual organized self."

"She probably had more important things on her mind."

"I suppose." His trusty secretary-assistant had left him high and dry even before her last day of work. Margo's normally brilliant brain had dissolved into a sea of pregnancy hormones and daydreams of pitter-pattering feet. He couldn't wait for her to give birth so things could get back to normal. "I'm just glad she's going to come back to work after she has the kid."

"That's a shame," Eileen said.

"Huh?" He looked at her. "Why?"

"Well, because if I had a baby, I'd want to be able to stay home and take care of it myself." Eileen set her purse down again, walked around the edge of the desk and nudged him out of the way so she could sit down in the blue leather desk chair. "I mean, I know lots of women *have* to work, but if you don't have to…"

"Margo would go nuts without something to do with her day," he argued, recalling his secretary's gung-ho attitude. "She likes being busy."

"I hear babies can keep you plenty busy."

He shuddered at the thought of Margo turning into a stay-at-home mom. "Don't say that. She *has* to come back to work. She runs this place."

"She probably will then," Eileen said and opened the top drawer, inspecting, looking around, familiarizing herself with the setup. "I'm just saying..."

"Don't say it again. You'll jinx it."

"Very mature." She shut the drawer and opened another one, poking through the pads and boxes of pencils and even a bag of candy Margo had left behind. Pulling one piece free, she peeled off the silver foil and popped the chocolate into her mouth. "Do we have a coffee pot?"

"Right over there." He pointed, looking away to keep from noticing how her tongue swept across her bottom lip as she chased every last crumb of chocolate.

"Thank God," she muttered, and hopped up again. Striding across the room to the low oak sideboard, she glanced over her shoulder at him. "Since it's my first day, I'll even get you a cup. After that though, you're on your own. I'm not a waitress. I'm a secretary. Temporarily."

Temporarily, he reminded himself as his gaze locked onto the curve of her behind as she moved with an easy sway that was enough to knock any man's temperature up a notch or two. Hell, every relationship became temporary eventually. At least this one was labeled correctly right from the start.

This could only be trouble, he told himself and wondered how in the hell he'd survive the next two weeks with Eileen back in his life.

By day three, Eileen remembered exactly why she'd left the business world for that of flowers. Flowers never gave you a headache. Flowers didn't expect you to have all the answers. Flowers didn't look great in three-piece suits.

Okay, that last one wasn't one of her original reasons for relinquishing her keyboard. But it was right up there on the list now.

The work wasn't hard. It was actually fairly interesting, though she'd never admit that out loud to Rick. And, after spending the past two years in a work wardrobe that consisted of jeans and a wide selection of T-shirts, it was sort of nice getting dressed up again. Good thing she hadn't gotten rid of her work wardrobe. Slacks, shirts, discreet pumps or her comfy boots. She was wearing makeup and doing her hair every morning, too. A big change from her usual ponytail and a quick slash of lipstick. But none of that made up for the fact that she was spending way too much time watching Rick.

She'd had a crush on him when she was a kid, of course. Well, at least until the unfortunate Barbie incident. He and Bridie had ignored her most of the time and, when forced to spend time with her, Rick had teased Eileen until she'd wanted to kick him.

But now…she turned her head just far enough to be able to look into his office through the partially opened door.

With his tie loosened at his open collar and his dark brown hair mussed from stabbing his fingers through it in frustration, he looked…what was the word? Oh, yeah. *Tasty.*

Oh ye gods.

This was a complication she didn't want or need.

She couldn't be fantasizing about Rick Hawkins. For one thing, when these two weeks were up, she'd be going back to her world, leaving him to his and never their twain would meet again. For another…he was *so* not her type. She liked the artsy guys with a slightly bohemian air that she ran into down at the beach. The guys who were tanned and relaxed, with the attitude of *why do today what can be put off indefinitely?* Those guys were safe. She knew no relationship with them was going to go anywhere. The farthest they could see into the future was the next wave. Or their next paycheck. They didn't have portfolios.

Heck, most of them didn't own a pair of shoes that required socks.

So why suddenly was she spending way too much time thinking about, and fantasizing about, Mr. Corporate Millionaire?

TWO

Rick leaned back in his chair and watched Eileen stop just at the threshold. She'd been doing that for three days now. She did the work. She was efficient, smart, organized. But she kept him at a distance. Always made sure she held herself back from him. And if he was smart, he'd appreciate that.

Instead, it frustrated him.

He hadn't expected to be so attracted to her. When his grandmother had first suggested Eileen as a temporary secretary, Rick hadn't been able to imagine it. The Eileen he'd known years ago was hardly his idea of a good assistant. But he'd been desperate and willing to try anything. Now that she was here, he could hardly think of anything else.

Probably not a good sign.

"Hello? Earth to Rick."

He blinked, coming up out of his thoughts like a man waking from a coma. "What?"

"I don't know. You called me in here, remember?" Eileen was still standing in the doorway, but now she was looking at him as if he had a screw loose. And hell. Maybe he did.

He pushed out of the chair and stood up. He'd always thought better on his feet anyway. "Yeah. I did. I'll need you to stay a little later tonight—" He broke off when the phone in the outer office rang.

"Hold that thought." Eileen turned and walked to her desk.

He deliberately avoided watching the sway of her hips. It wasn't easy.

She grabbed the receiver on the third ring. "Hawkins Financial."

Rick watched her as she reached across the desk for a pen. The hem of her skirt rode tantalizingly high on her thighs with the movement and he told himself not to look. But hell, he was male, right? And breathing? Impossible *not* to look.

Didn't mean a thing.

"Vanessa Taylor?" Eileen turned to glance at him, a question in her eyes.

Damn.

No, he mouthed, shaking his head and waving both hands. All he needed right now, was having to listen to Vanessa ramble about cocktail parties she wanted him to take her to. Never mind that he hadn't called her in weeks. Vanessa simply assumed that every man who crossed her path would become her helpless love slave. Rick Hawkins, however, didn't believe in love or slavery.

Tell her anything, he mouthed the instructions and hoped to hell Eileen was good at lipreading. He felt like a damn mime. But he couldn't risk a whisper. Vanessa had ears like a bat. She'd know he was there, then she'd insist on talking to him and he just wasn't interested.

Hell, he hadn't been interested when they *were* going out.

Anything? Eileen mouthed back, a decided gleam in her eyes. When he nodded, she smiled wickedly and said, "I'm sorry Ms. Taylor, but Rick can't come to the phone right now. The doctors have advised him to not speak until the stitches are gone."

What? Rick took a step closer.

Eileen backed up. "Oh, you didn't hear? A minor accident," she said, laughter in her eyes and feigned sympathy in her voice. "I'm sure the disfigurement won't be permanent." An instant later, Eileen jerked the phone from her ear and winced. "Wow. She slammed the phone down so hard I think I may be deaf."

Rick stared at her. "Disfigurement? I'm disfigured? Why did you do that?"

"Eh?" She cupped one hand around her ear and tilted her head.

"Funny, Ryan." He smirked at her. Pushing the edges of his jacket back, he shoved both hands into his pockets and rocked on his heels. "What's the deal?"

"You said I should tell her anything."

"Within reason."

She held up one finger and shook it. "No one said anything about reason."

Rick pulled his hands free of his pockets and crossed his arms over his chest. She kept surprising him. Which intrigued him. Which worried the hell out of him. "I didn't think I'd have to *request* reason. I'll be more prepared next time."

She chuckled.

"You enjoyed that."

"Oh yeah," she admitted, and leaned back, perching her behind on the edge of her desk. "And by the way, Vanessa?" She shook her head sadly. "Not the deepest puddle on the block. Just the word 'disfigurement' was enough to get rid of her." She studied him through amused eyes. "Swimming in pretty shallow pools, aren't you?"

Shallow? Good description of Vanessa and all of her pals. But hey, he wasn't interested in meaningful. At the time, all he'd been interested in was a dinner companion and a bed warmer. Vanessa hadn't been much good at either one. But that was hardly the point.

"Are you this mouthy with all of your employers?"

She came away from the desk. "I don't have an employer. Not anymore. I'm my own boss."

"Probably a wise move."

"What's that supposed to mean?"

"You don't play well with others, do you?"

"I've been doing a good job, haven't I?"

"Sure," Rick said, moving a little closer. Her scent reached out to him and he sucked it in. Stupid. "If you don't take into account the grumbling and the refusal to take orders and—"

"I don't need to follow orders, I know how to run an office—"

Hell, she was as easy to bait as she'd been as a kid. That Irish temper of hers was always bubbling and simmering just below the surface. And watching the temper flash in her eyes was damn near hypnotic. The emerald-green depths churned and darkened and bordered on dangerous, and still Rick was fascinated.

"But this is *my* office," he countered, egging her on. Her skin flushed, her breathing quickened and she looked like a coiled spring ready to explode. And his mouth nearly watered. Man, he was in some serious trouble here. He hadn't wanted a woman so badly in…ever.

"Oh, I know it's your office," she said, taking a step closer and leaning in for effect. "It's got your boring, unoriginal stamp all over it. Anyone else would have a little color around here. But not the great Rick Hawkins. Oh no. Let's play the corporate game. Battleship-gray all the way for you, isn't it? You're just one of the fleet. No originality at all."

"Originality?" She could say whatever the hell

she wanted about the decor. Because he couldn't
give a good damn about what the place looked like,
beyond it appearing dignified and successful. Did
she really think he was the kind of guy to carry
swatches of fabric around, for God's sake?

But he was damned if he'd stand here and be
called a lemming. He'd opened up more brokerage
accounts in the past year than any of his competitors.
He'd become the fastest growing firm on the West
Coast over the past three years and that hadn't happened because he blindly followed everyone else.

"Well, look around you," she exclaimed. "This
whole building is like a warren of rabbit holes. And
every one of you bunnies is tucked away in your
little gray worlds." She waved her hands around,
encompassing the pale gray walls, the steel-blue carpet and the generic watercolors dotted sparingly
throughout the room. "I'm willing to bet the same
interior decorator did *all* of the offices in this place.
You've probably all got the same awful paintings
hung in the same places on the same gray walls."

"Because I work in an office building I'm unoriginal?"

She nodded sharply. "Hard to be a free spirit
when you work on the *S.S. Conformity.*"

"What?" He had to laugh despite her insulting
tone. She was way over the top. Like some latter-
day hippie. He half expected her to start chanting
and calling on Sister Moon to help free his soul.

Damn, he hadn't had this much fun in a long time.

"What you need is—" She slapped one hand to her left eye and shouted, *"Freeze."*

"What?" Instinctively he took a step.

"Don't move." She gave him a one-eyed glare. "Don't you know what 'freeze' means?"

"What the hell are you talking about now?"

Slowly she lowered herself to the floor. "My contact. I lost a contact."

"You're kidding."

"Do I look like I'm kidding?" She tipped her head back to stare at him.

"You wear contact lenses?"

Her one good eye narrowed. The other was squeezed shut. "Well, to coin a phrase, *duh.*"

Rick glanced at the floor and carefully went down on his knees. "I knew your eyes couldn't be that green naturally."

"Watch where you kneel!" she blurted, then giving him a one eyed glare again, she added, "And they're not tinted lenses, if you must know."

He looked at her. "Prove it."

She opened her left eye. Just as green as the right one. Deep and pure and clear, they looked like the color of spring grass. Or, of a backlit emerald in a jeweler's display case. He stared into her eyes and, for a moment, let himself get lost in their depths. It was almost like drowning, he thought, then brought himself up short when she tore her gaze from his. He wasn't going to drown in any woman's eyes. Not again.

"So." She swallowed hard, inhaled quickly and said, "Just run your fingers gently over the carpet."

"This happen often?" he asked as he knelt beside her.

"Usually just when I'm upset."

"So, often."

She gave him an elbow to the ribs. "Cute."

"So I've been told."

"By Vanessa?" she asked.

"Vanessa was a client," he explained, his gaze searching the carpet as his fingers traced softly across the fabric. "We had dinner a couple of times, that's all."

"Apparently she's still hungry."

"Too bad," he muttered, briefly remembering just how boring Vanessa really was, "because I've had enough."

"Ooh." Eileen turned her head to look at him. "Sounds like there's a story there."

He glanced at her. She flipped her hair to one side. She smiled and something inside him tightened. Her fingers brushed his as they searched and he felt a short stab of heat that sliced right down to his insides. He'd never felt that with Vanessa. Or his ex-wife. Or anyone else for that matter.

Damn it, she was getting to him. And he couldn't allow that to happen. He had to remind himself that Eileen was just an old—not friend—not enemy, either. And certainly not old. So what did that make her? Besides, of course, a top-grade, A number-one temptation?

"Hello?" she muttered, and waved one hand in front of his face.

"Right. Story. No story. Vanessa was just..." He thought about it for a long moment. He didn't owe her or anyone else an explanation. But since she was staring at him from one good eye, he knew she wouldn't just drop it, either. Finally he said simply, "Temporary."

Her eyebrows arched. "Lot of that going around."

"Nothing lasts forever." His voice sounded tight, harsh, even to his own ears.

"Well, that's looking on the bright side." She crawled forward an inch or two.

"Just realistic." He knew that better than anyone. Love, friendship, relationships, they all ended. Usually when you were least expecting it. A long time ago Rick had decided to take charge of his world. Now *he* ended things before they got complicated. *He* was the one to walk away. He'd never be the one standing alone with a broken heart again.

Crawling carefully along the carpet, he stayed close to her. "How far can these things roll, anyway?"

"Pretty far," she said. "So, why is realistic cynical, why?"

He glanced at her. Damn, she was too close. Close enough that he could count the handful of freckles dusting the bridge of her nose. There were six. Not that he cared. "Why are you so interested?"

She shrugged. "Humor a half-blind woman."

Rick chuckled. She made him laugh. Had been since the first day she was here. And that was something he didn't do nearly often enough. He'd been too busy building his world to take the time to enjoy what he'd created. Too busy proving to everyone— including himself—that he *could* go to the top, to enjoy the trip. But somehow, Eileen lightened things up, even when she was arguing with him.

Impossible to ignore, too dangerous to pay attention to. Great combination.

He shrugged and stopped, thinking for a second he'd spotted a glint of light, like sunlight bouncing off a lens, but then it was gone. "No deep dark explanation," he said, refusing to be drawn into the long, sad history of his past relationships. Not only wasn't it any of Eileen's business, but he'd learned to let it go. No point in revisiting it. "Vanessa and I were just two ships colliding briefly in the night, then going our own way. That's realistic, not cynical. Pretending it was anything else would be a waste of time."

Colliding ships, huh? Eileen mused on his choice of words for a minute or two. If their ships had collided, then they'd probably slept together. Which meant this Vanessa had seen Rick naked. Instantly an image flashed into Eileen's mind. The same image that had been taunting her for the past few days.

She kept imagining Rick wet.

Stepping out of the shower, a skimpy towel wrapped around his waist, beads of water clinging to the hairs on his chest. Then she imagined him shaking his head and tiny droplets of water flying from the ends of his hair like diamonds. Then she imagined the towel dropping and him stepping forward to take her into his arms. The vision was so clear, so tantalizing, she could feel his wet skin next to hers. He bent his head, his mouth just a breath away from hers and then—

"Found it!"

She sucked in air like an old, wheezing vacuum. "What?"

"Your lens," Rick said, holding it out to her. "I found it."

"Right." She swallowed that gulp of air and held it in, hoping to steady herself. Jeez. Did it have to be so darn hot in the room? Right now, she felt as though a fever were racing through her body. She looked into his eyes, and those brown depths seemed to pull her in. His victorious grin set off a series of minor explosions within her and her blood pumped as if she was in the last leg of a marathon.

She'd never had this sort of reaction to a man before. Oh, the cute ones jangled her nerves, and here and there a fabulous mouth might make her a little antsy. But *never* had she fantasized so well that her whole body was tingling with heat and want.

Not even over her late, unlamented ex-fiancée. Not even with her last boss…the one with lots of promises and an exceptionally bad memory about them.

Nope. Rick stirred things up that had never been stirred before.

Oh, boy.

"Thanks," she said, and picked her contact lens up from the center of his palm. The brush of her fingertips against his skin sent another jagged spear of something dark and wicked through her body, but Eileen fought it. Otherwise, she'd be forced to roll over onto her back and shout, *Take me, big boy!*

Oh, wow.

Eileen pushed herself to her feet. "Okay, better go take care of this. Don't want to look at life like a Cyclops."

She headed unsteadily toward the door. He was right behind her, but Eileen didn't look back. The words "pillar of salt" kept reverberating inside her mind.

"Can I help?"

"No thanks," she said, waving one hand. "Been doing this for years."

"I didn't know you wore contacts."

"No reason you should, since we haven't seen each other in six years."

The hall looked impossibly long. The wall on her right was painted the ever-present gray, but the wall on her right was glass. Afternoon sunshine poured in, and five stories below them, it winked off the windshields of the cars jammed bumper to bumper on the 405 freeway. Just the thought of joining the thundering herd trying to get home made her grateful that Rick wanted her to stay later than usual.

Even if he was making her a little nervous.

"Man," Rick said from behind her, as if reading her mind, "the freeway's a mess."

"I noticed." She made a sharp right and walked into the ladies' room.

"It should be thinned out later, though. We could send out for dinner while we work."

Dinner. She wasn't sure she'd be able to swallow. Eileen looked into the mirror and stared at Rick's reflection. He was there. Right behind her. In the pale blue lounge area. Of the *ladies'* room, for Pete's sake. Two vinyl chairs sat on either side of a low table holding a bowl of fresh flowers. Eileen looked into the mirror, ignoring the furnishings to stare instead at Rick. "Dinner?"

"What? You don't eat?"

"Sure I eat. I just usually don't have men following me into the ladies' room to deliver an invitation."

He shifted his gaze from hers and looked around, as if surprised to discover where he was. Then he looked back into the mirror, meeting her gaze again with a wry, crooked smile. "Oops."

Eileen felt a *ping* bounce around inside her and realized that smile of his could still affect her. Apparently, at heart, she was still that eleven-year-old girl with a kinda sorta crush. For heaven's sake.

He jerked a thumb at the closed door behind him. "I'll, uh, see you outside."

"Good idea."

Once he was gone, Eileen let out a breath she hadn't realized she was holding. Leaning forward, she planted both hands on the slate-blue Formica counter and stared at her reflection. "This temporary job was a *bad* idea, Eileen. *Really* bad."

Three

Rick hadn't had Mexican fast food in far too long. He didn't remember tacos and nachos ever tasting quite so good. And he'd never considered having an indoor picnic on the floor of his office. But then maybe it wasn't the food, he told himself. Maybe it was sharing it with Eileen. She was annoying, irritating and more entertaining than he would have guessed.

Watching her now while she talked about some of her customers, he saw her eyes flash with humor.

"This one guy is a regular," she was saying, and paused to take a small bite of a taco. She chewed, swallowed and said, "He's got a standing order for a dozen roses once a week."

"Good husband?" Rick ventured.

"Hardly," she said with a quick shake of her head. "It's for the girl of the week. Always someone different, always a different color rose—according to their personalities, he says. But one week, he changed the order—switched to a spider plant."

One of Rick's eyebrows lifted. "Makes you wonder, doesn't it?"

"Makes me wonder how he finds so many women willing to go out with him." She sighed and leaned back, bracing her hands on the floor behind her. "His bedroom must be like an assembly line."

"And you think I'm cynical?" Rick drew one knee up and rested his forearm on top.

"Touché." She inclined her head at him, allowing him a point.

"So," he asked after a long minute of silence, "how's Bridie doing?"

Eileen smiled. "Big sister's doing fine," she said, thinking about Bridget and her ever-growing family. "Three and a half kids and a husband she drools over. She's disgustingly happy."

"Three and a half?"

"Pregnant again," she said with a slow shake of her head. "Hard to imagine, but Bridie just loves being pregnant and Jefferson—that's her husband—he's as nuts about kids as she is." Eileen met Rick's gaze. "If you guys hadn't split up, you could have been a very busy father by now."

He frowned, reached for his soda and took a long drink. "No, thanks." He set the large cup back onto the rug. "Tried the husband thing. It didn't work. Besides, I'm not father material."

"There's that sunshiny outlook on life I've come to know so well," Eileen said.

"Touché." His turn to incline his head and acknowledge her point. Then he asked, "What about you?"

"What about me?"

"You involved with anyone?" And why do you care? Rick asked himself. The answer was, he didn't. Not really. It was just a polite inquiry. Didn't matter to him one way or the other.

She sat up, dusted her palms together and gathered up her trash, stuffing it into the white paper bag. "Not lately."

Good, he thought even though he knew it would have been better if she were engaged. Married. Hell. A nun. "Hard to believe."

"Why?" She looked up at him.

He shrugged. "It's just..." He waved a hand at her. "I mean..."

She smiled. "Are you about to give me a compliment?"

Frowning, Rick crumpled up the last of his trash and snatched the bag from her hand to stuff his trash inside. "Stranger things have happened."

"In science fiction movies."

"You're not an easy person, are you, Eyeball?"

She tossed a wadded-up taco wrapper at him, bouncing it off his forehead. "Gran always said nothing good ever comes easy."

"Yeah, but who knew she was talking about you?"

Silence dropped between them. Outside the windows, the sun was setting and the low-lying clouds were shaded a deep purple and crimson. And inside, the silence kept growing, until it was a living, breathing presence in the room.

Rick stared at her and caught himself wondering what she would taste like. And he wondered if he'd be willing to stop at just one taste. That couldn't happen though. He wouldn't get involved with Eileen Ryan. Beyond the fact that she aroused too much emotion within him—there was the whole business of her being the granddaughter of his grandmother's best friend.

She wasn't the woman for a no-strings affair. She was hearth and home and family dinners. Definitely, she was *hands off*. There might as well have been a sign reading Keep Away tacked to her forehead.

If he was smart, he'd pay attention.

"We'd better finish up that contract stuff," she said, her gaze locked with his.

"Right." Rick nodded and pulled in a deep breath. "Otherwise, we could be here all night."

"Probably not a good idea," Eileen said softly, and licked her lips.

"Yeah," he said, wincing as his body tightened. "Not a good idea at all."

By Thursday evening, Eileen was regretting ever agreeing to this situation. She felt as if she was tightrope walking over a pit filled with hungry lions. One wrong step and she was nothing more than a quick meal.

What she needed was the weekend. Time to spend down at the beach, in her own cottage. Painting the china hutch she'd picked up at the flea market last month. Or stenciling the kitchen walls. Heaven knows, she'd been putting that off for months. There'd never been enough time to get around to all of the crafty things she liked to do. She was always too busy at the shop.

Which was why she'd been looking forward to these two weeks. With Paula, her new manager, in charge at Larkspur, Eileen could relax about the shop. It was in good hands.

Her full vacation was already shot, so she planned to make good use of at least the weekends. She'd have some breathing room. She needed to get herself far, far away from Rick Hawkins. She needed to keep busy enough that maybe she'd stop daydreaming about what she'd like to be doing with Rick. Eileen groaned quietly. All she had to do was get through today and tomorrow, and she'd have two whole days to decompress.

"Eileen?"

"Yessir, boss?" She turned her head to watch him come through the doorway from his office.

He frowned and looked at her as she stood up, holding onto her purse and car keys as if they were life rings tossed into a churning sea. "You leaving already?"

"It's not 'already,'" she said, scooping her black cardigan off the back of her chair. "It's after five and I'm going home." She was actually *running* home, but didn't feel the urge to tell him that. Back to her empty little cottage where she wouldn't have to look into Rick's brown eyes. Where she wouldn't have to remind herself that she wasn't interested in getting involved with *anyone* again, much less the bane of her childhood.

Slipping into her sweater, she flipped her hair out from under it, then pointed at a manila folder on her desk. "The last letters you wanted are right there. Sign them and they'll go out in tomorrow morning's mail."

"Fine, but—"

"See you later."

"Eileen."

His voice stopped her just three feet from the door. She gave that magic portal one longing glance, then took a deep breath and turned to face him. His hair was mussed, his tie loose and his collar opened. He looked far too good. If he suggested ordering dinner in and working late again, she'd have to say yes. She'd spend the whole meal drooling over him and then go home to be frustrated alone. But if he didn't ask her to stay late and have dinner, she'd be disappointed because then she wouldn't get a chance to drool over him. Oh yeah. No psychological problems *here*. "What?" She snapped out the word a little harsher than she'd planned.

"You free this weekend?"

Whoa. She reeled a little. Was he asking her what she thought he might be asking her? Not just fast-food dinner and work, but maybe a date? Maybe a movie or something else that was totally inappropriate considering they were working together? Considering their *grandmothers* had arranged all of this? Considering that she wasn't in the mood for a man in her life? Ye gods. Her stomach skittered nervously. "Why?"

"I've got some meetings."

Okay, no date. Work.

"Now that's a shame," she said, and sidled closer to the door.

"I'll need a secretary."

No way. She'd already lost two perfectly good weeks of vacation. She wasn't about to give up her weekends, too. "Rick..."

"One meeting's scheduled for late tomorrow morning, then all day Saturday. Maybe one Sunday morning."

"But I don't—"

"You'll be paid overtime."

Her fingers curled around her purse strap. "That's not the point."

"What is?" he asked, folding his arms across a chest that she'd spent far too much time imagining bare. "Too scared to go away with me?"

She laughed shortly, harshly and hoped it sounded convincing. "Yeah. That must be it—go away? Go away where?"

"Temecula."

"In Riverside county?"

"Is there another one?"

"No, but—"

Rick walked across the room, stared out the window for a long minute, then turned to look at her again. "Edward Harrington was my first client when I opened my business." Rick shrugged. "He took a chance on me. Twice a year, I go out to Riverside to look over his portfolio and discuss changes and investments."

"You go to him?"

Rick smiled. "Most independents go to their customers."

"Still. One customer's going to take all weekend?"

"No, but Edward referred me to some of his golf buddies and I see *all* of them when I go out there. I'm seeing Edward tomorrow and then the others on Saturday."

"So you work all week and then even more on the weekend."

"Uh-huh." He studied her for a long, thoughtful minute, unfolded his arms, then waved both hands at her. "You know what? Never mind. You're right."

Wary now, Eileen watched him. It wasn't like him to change tactics so suddenly. "I'm right about what?"

"I can't ask you to go."

"You already did," she pointed out.

"I take it back."

"What?" she said. Turning around, he walked back into his office. She was right behind him. Rick smiled at her hurried footsteps as she raced to catch up. "You take it back?" she asked. "What are you, in third grade?"

"Nope." He walked around behind his desk and took a seat. Keeping his gaze averted from hers, Rick shuffled through the piles of financial reports on his desk. The minute he'd asked her to go along, he'd known she'd refuse. And maybe that was how he should leave it. It'd be a hell of a lot safer. But damn it, he wanted her to go with him. Wanted her away from the office and on neutral territory. Wanted her—hell.

He just wanted her. "I'm just being logical," he said. "I can handle the work without you. And you'd hate it anyway and I don't blame you. You'd be bored."

"Bored?"

"Sure." He glanced at her. Her eyes were flashing. It was working. Damn, she hadn't changed a bit. For one brief second, he wished he'd been wrong and that she had simply said, *Okay fine. See you.* Then that feeling was gone and he was prodding her again. "Besides, like I said, I can handle this alone. I'll take a laptop with me. Type up my own notes."

She snorted.

He glanced at her. "I don't need a secretary after all," he went on, warming to his theme now that he was on a roll. Eileen was reacting just as he'd known she would. Just as she always had. Tell her she couldn't do something and there was nothing she wanted to do more. Like the time when she was ten and her gran told her that she couldn't hang on to a car bumper while on her skateboard. Naturally, she'd done it anyway, the car made a sharp right turn and Eileen had broken her wrist when she crashed into Mrs. Murphy's trash cans.

Maybe it was a mistake to challenge her hard enough so that she would come along for the weekend, but damned if he could resist the idea. He hadn't felt this kind of attraction for a woman before. And it was bloody hard to deny it.

Her green eyes were stormy and he could actually *see* thoughts and emotions pinwheeling through her mind. God, she was so easy to read. And he enjoyed it after years of looking at a woman and wondering just what the hell she was thinking behind her cool, polite mask of interest.

"You don't need a secretary?" she said. "You, who types with two fingers?"

One eyebrow lifted. "Speed won't be required. Just accuracy."

She frowned at him, turning that delicious-looking mouth into a pout that made him want to bite her. Oh yeah, it'd be much better—safer—if she told him no. Damn, he hoped she didn't. "I can handle note taking. I'll bring a tape recorder or something. You can type everything up on Monday."

"I could go with you."

"Well, of course you *could*," Rick said, watching her as she leaned both hands on the front of his desk. The high collar of her business shirt dipped just a bit and he caught a tantalizingly small peek at her chest. But just that tiny glimpse was enough to make him hard—and damn grateful to be sitting behind his desk. Clearing his throat, he continued, "I'm just saying, there's no reason to. I wouldn't want to put you out."

She pushed up from the desk, planted both hands at her hips and countered, "I'm working for you. It's part of the job."

"I can't ask you to go away with me for the weekend." He kept arguing, knowing it was in her nature to dig in her heels. She was absolutely the most contrary woman he'd ever met. She fascinated him. "Wouldn't be fair."

"Fair?" she repeated. "Now we're talking about fair?"

"Hey." Rick leaned back in his chair, gripped the arms and said, "I'm only trying to be reasonable."

"Uh-huh. Where's the meeting?" she asked, tapping the toe of one shoe against the carpet with a staccato beat.

He hid a smile at the temper already rising inside her. He should feel guilty about manipulating her into this, but he didn't. "Eileen, it's not necessary for you to go."

"I'm *going*." She glared at him. "I'm your secretary and it's my job."

"I don't think it's a good idea."

"Deal with it," she said. "Honestly, you wanted me to work for you and then when I say I am, you say no."

"Just trying to be fair."

"Well, quit it."

"Okay." He held up both hands and surrendered. "Didn't know it would mean this much to you."

"Now you know."

"I appreciate it."

"No problem." She inhaled sharply and blew it out again in a rush. "Where do you want me to make reservations?"

"The Hammond Inn will work. Their number's in the Rolodex."

"Fine," she said, and turned to leave the room.

"Get a two-bedroom suite. We can work in the living area."

Eileen stopped and looked back over her shoulder at him. His brown eyes looked rich and dark and impossibly deep. Her insides twisted suddenly and she heard herself say, "I'm not going to sleep with you, you know."

His eyes narrowed. "Don't recall asking you to."

"Okay then." She blew out a breath and nodded sharply. "Just so we're clear."

"Crystal."

She left his office and closed the door behind her. Then she leaned back against it and stared blankly at the ceiling. "What happened?" she whispered aloud. "You just gave away your weekend. What were you thinking?" She'd practically begged him to let her go along. And worse yet, now she'd be sharing a suite with the very man she was trying to stay away from.

"Yeah, you're doing great, Eileen," she told herself and headed for her desk. She had to make the reservation before leaving for the day. Sending the Rolodex into a wild spin, she muttered, "Just great."

The Hammond Inn was the perfect romantic getaway. An hour and a half away from Orange County by freeway, it was a world away in feeling. The town of Temecula had started life as a stagecoach stop…and was now an interesting collection of old and new.

Many of the original buildings were still standing in old town, but the new housing developments were springing up all over everywhere like a virus run amok. Still, there were ranches and elegant old homes studding the landscape and the Hammond Inn was a perfect example.

A gracious Victorian, it had been perfectly restored to its former glory. Its wraparound porch was studded with hand-carved pillars painted a pristine white. The house itself was bright, sunshine-yellow with white trim and dark green shutters. The wide porch held clusters of white wicker furniture, inviting cozy conversations. Hanging plants hung from the overhanging roof, dotting the porch with thick green foliage. Late-blooming chrysanthemums burst into rainbows of color along the skirt of the house and lined the long walkway from the curved drive-way. Maples and oaks, now boasting their brilliant fall colors, crouched around the house like protective soldiers decked out in their dress uniforms.

A cold wind swept through the hills, rattled the leaves and bowed the flowers as Eileen and Rick walked up the path.

"It's gorgeous," she said, turning around to get the whole picture. Trees dotted the rolling, winter-brown hills and though new housing developments were encroaching, they were still far enough away that the inn seemed secluded. Private.

Eileen shot Rick a sidelong glance and told herself to get a grip. They weren't here for romance. The inn was simply a temporary headquarters. They were here to conduct meetings with a few of Rick's clients. They all lived locally and it was much easier for Rick and her to spend the weekend at the inn rather than driving the freeway to Riverside County every day.

Although, she thought, turning back around to continue walking, if they *had* been here for romance, they couldn't have picked a better spot.

"I like it," Rick said, oblivious, thank heaven, to her thoughts. "The owners aren't the kind to organize 'fun' for their guests. They leave me alone to conduct business."

Eileen shot him a look and shook her head. "Get down, you funky party weasel."

He stopped and gave her that look she was becoming all too accustomed to. It was the sort of stare you gave someone speaking a foreign language. Conveying the thought that maybe, if you listened hard enough, you'd understand. "Party weasel?"

"*Funky* party weasel. That was sarcasm."

"Thought it might be."

Eileen waved one hand up and down in front of him. "But honestly, Rick. Look at you. You drag that gray world you work in everywhere you go."

He touched one of his lapels. "This is a blue suit."

"Whoa. Cuttin' loose."

One dark eyebrow lifted. She was getting used to that, too.

"I'm here on business," he reminded her.

"You never heard of casual Friday?"

"It's my company, we don't *have* casual Friday."

"The fact that it's your company is the point. You could have casual Friday every day if you wanted to."

"I don't."

"Hence, the gray world," she said, walking again. "Life—conformity style."

Rick caught up with her in a couple of long strides. He was really tall—he towered over her. She liked the difference in their heights. She liked that he looked serious, but his eyes sparkled. Wow. Was that a glint of humor she saw there?

"You know, some people actually dress for success."

She shrugged. "I figure, success means you can dress however you want to."

"Ah, so I should be wearing jeans and a torn T-shirt."

"Nobody said anything about torn."

She took the five, freshly swept steps to the porch and stopped at the top. Turning around to face him, she had to look down, since he'd stopped at the bottom. "I don't remember you being such a stuffed shirt when you were a kid."

"I," he pointed out as he climbed the steps to stand eye level with her, "grew up."

She clutched her heart and grinned at him. "Cut to the bone."

"You're impossible, aren't you?"

"That's been said before."

"Not hard to believe."

For several moments they stood there looking at each other. Rick broke away while Eileen was still in a sexual trance. He bounded up the rest of the steps and crossed the wide porch.

He reached out, opened the door and held it for her to pass through in front of him. His gaze dropped over her before lifting to meet hers again. "Besides, I don't see you in jeans."

She smiled at him. "You will later."

"Can't wait."

Eileen stared up into his eyes and told herself to ignore the flash of heat that sizzled in those brown depths briefly before disappearing. She didn't need this complication.

Four

Their suite was bigger than the one he usually took when he stayed here. Of course, Rick thought, usually he didn't bring his secretary with him. Margo wouldn't have come along, preferring to be at home on the weekends with her husband. As for Eileen, he probably should never have pretended—to both of them—that he'd needed her on this trip.

Just the drive on the freeway had been torturous. His hormones were doing the kind of back flips they hadn't done since he'd hit puberty and had his first fantasy about...what the hell was her name? He shook his head. Didn't matter. And it would probably be a good idea to keep the word *fantasy* out of his mind, too.

God knows, he didn't need any encouragement.

He watched Eileen walk around the big living room, inspecting the whole place, from the books lining the bookshelves, to the hearth, already set and ready for a romantic fire. An overstuffed sofa in a pale flowered fabric crouched in front of the fireplace and two matching wing chairs sat on either side of it. Gleaming wood tables held vases of fresh flowers and dozens of scented candles dotted nearly every surface of the room.

"It's gorgeous."

He nodded. She certainly was. That black skirt of hers had been driving him nuts since she'd arrived at the office. She'd left her car in the parking lot at the office so they could drive down together. And during that long hour and a half, his gaze had slipped to her bare legs often. Her dark red shirt was plain, businesslike, and yet still managed to give his heart a kick start. Her hair, though, tempted him sorely. The long, loose waves draping around her shoulders made him want to spear his fingers through it. He'd had to keep a tight grip on the steering wheel, just to defeat the urge to reach out and see if her hair felt as soft as it looked.

"Shall I set up on that table?"

"Hmm?" He gave himself a mental shake and stared at her. "What?"

"The first meeting." She checked her silver wristwatch, then looked at him. "Your Mr. Harrington should be here in about twenty minutes."

"Yeah." Edward Harrington. Client. Business.

Good. Concentrate. "Sure. Uh, set up his files there and I'll order room service for when he gets here."

"I can take care of it."

"Fine." Rick picked up his suitcase. "Which bedroom do you want?"

"Doesn't matter," she said with a shrug. "Surprise me."

Something jumped inside him, but he buried it fast. The kind of surprise he'd like to show her had nothing to do with the choice of a bedroom, but what to do inside it. "You take the one on the right. I'll take this one."

He didn't wait for a response before escaping into the bedroom and shutting the door. Dropping his suitcase, he walked across the room to the tall bureau and stared at his reflection in the silvered mirror above it. Shoving both hands through his hair, he met his own gaze grimly. "Keep your mind on business, Hawkins. Anything else is just a world of trouble."

Lightning shimmered in the distance and thunder rolled across the sky to growl like a caged tiger in the living room of the suite. Eileen hugged herself and stepped through the French doors and out onto the narrow balcony. The wind slapped at her, lifting her hair and twisting it around her head in a wild tangle of curls. She reached up and scooped it back, then tipped her face into the wind, loving the feel of it rushing past her. The scent of coming rain surrounded her and she felt as if her skin was electrified by the building storm.

In the blustery weather, no one else was outside and they had the only balcony on this side of the house. It was private, secluded.

Behind her, lamplight glowed in a pale, golden haze over the table where Rick sat, still working over the last of Ed Harrington's file. She half turned to look at him and caught herself noticing how he ran his fingers through his hair. How his tie always crooked to the right when he was tired enough to loosen it. How his eyes shone in the lamplight. How his shoulders looked broader without the confines of his ever-present suit jacket.

Her blood pumped simply looking at him and she turned around, grateful that he was still immersed in his work. Just as well, she told herself, curling her fingers around the wrought-iron railing. They'd done fine all day, working side by side. She'd listened to him advising Ed about investments and his portfolios and even though she hadn't understood a word of it, she'd had to admit to being impressed.

But now that the work was finished for the day, her brain was free to think about other things. And not one of them had anything to do with his *brain*.

Lightning flashed, illuminating the edges of the clouds overhead and tracing white-hot, jagged fingers across the sky. Thunder boomed, closer this time.

"You're gonna get wet in a minute."

Her pulse quickened as Rick stepped out onto the

balcony beside her. "I love a storm," she said over the rumble of thunder. "We don't see many of them."

"Good thing. Had to shut the computer off because of the lightning."

Eileen smiled. "Poor worker bee. Had to stop."

"There's always the battery."

She nodded. "So why're you out here?"

He shifted his gaze from her to the storm-tossed sky. "Like you said, we don't see many of 'em." He leaned forward and braced his hands on the railing. "You were good today."

"Thanks." Nice compliment but she hadn't done all that much. Typing while they talked wasn't that tough.

He sighed and looked out over the garden below and the hills beyond the inn. "Edward's never talked that much. He's been a client for two years and I've never heard him talk about his late wife." Turning his head, he looked at her. "But you had him reminiscing inside a half hour."

"He thinks you're the greatest thing since sliced bread," she said, remembering how the older man had heaped praise on Rick. "He said you took his modest savings account and fixed it so that he doesn't have to worry—" she paused and smiled "—and that his grandkids will say great things about him because he left them so much money!"

Rick grinned and shook his head. "His grandkids are nuts about him. He takes them fishing every weekend."

"And he says that you've made lots of money for all of his friends," Eileen said, as if he hadn't spoken. "They buy him coffee every morning at the doughnut shop, just to thank him for referring you to them."

"That's nice to hear." His gaze drifted over her lazily.

"He says you're the smartest man he's ever met."

"He exaggerates."

"Maybe." But Eileen had to admit, she'd seen a whole new side of Rick today. Though to be fair, she'd been seeing him anew all week. The terrible boy he'd been was gone, and in his place was a thoughtful, intelligent man who was as careful with his clients' life savings as he would have been with his own grandmother's. Plus, he looked incredibly good when his tie was loose.

Whoops. Where did that come from?

"Ed's a sweetheart," she said quickly, jumping back to their conversation. "Sweet, sad and still lonely for the woman he loved most of his life."

"He enjoyed talking about her today."

She nodded. "All I did was listen. He was nice."

"Yeah," Rick agreed, staring into her eyes with a steadiness that made her shaky. "You're pretty nice yourself."

"Wow." She waved a hand at her face dramatically, as if to ease a nonexistent blush. "My little heart's fluttering."

"Uh-huh." A wry grin touched one corner of his

mouth. "Smells good out here," he said, and slid his hand on the railing until it brushed against hers.

Her skin heated, warmth rushing through her bloodstream. "It's the rain in the wind."

"Nope," he said, turning his head to look at her. "It's more like—" he leaned in closer to her, inhaled "—flowers."

Her breath caught when she stared into his eyes.

"It's you, Eileen." His gaze shifted, moving over her face, her throat, her breasts, and back up again.

"Rick..." She hadn't expected this. Hadn't expected him to say anything about the tension simmering between them. And now that he had, she wasn't sure what to do about it.

Her body, on the other hand, knew just what to do. Her heartbeat crashed in her ears, louder than the thunder booming out around them. Heat spiraled through her body, churning her insides, fogging her brain, liquefying her knees.

He drew back and turned his head to stare out into the night and the blustering storm. "Forget it," he muttered. "Shouldn't have said anything. Just let it go."

She should, Eileen told herself. If there was ever a moment to pay attention, to take an order, now was it. She should do just what he said and forget he'd ever opened this particular can of worms.

But she wouldn't.

Couldn't.

"Don't want to let it go," she admitted, and her

words were nearly swallowed by the next slam of thunder.

He snapped her a look and slowly straightened, reaching for her, drawing her up close. "We should, though."

"Right." She laid her hands on his forearms. "We don't even like each other."

"Yeah. You're a flake."

"And you're wound so tight, in a hundred years, you'll be a diamond."

"So," he said, "we forget the whole thing."

"That would be the reasonable thing to do," she said, and swept her hands up his arms to encircle his neck.

"I want you more than my next breath," he said tightly. "Screw reason."

His mouth came down on hers just as another, bigger, slash of lightning scraped jagged fingers across the sky. Brilliant light flashed before her closed eyelids and Eileen felt the sizzle in the air. As the following thunder boomed around them, it seemed to pale in comparison to the thudding of her own heart.

Rick lifted his head and stared down at her, his breath rushing from his lungs. Behind them, the room was dark, plunged into blackness.

"Power's out," he murmured.

"Not from where I'm standing," she said, meeting his gaze, her blood quickening on the hunger she read there.

A cold, strong wind whipped past them, wrapped

itself around their bodies like a frigid embrace, then dissolved in their combined heat. Lightning flashed, thunder rolled and desire, fed by the raging storm, clawed at them. Air rushed in and out of Eileen's lungs and still, she felt light-headed, as if a fog were settling over her brain, making thought impossible. But who needed to think when your blood was racing and your stomach was spinning and all points south were tingling in anticipation?

Rick must have felt the same because he took her mouth again. Hunger roared through her as he plundered her. His tongue parted her lips and swept into her warmth, tasting, exploring, plunging again and again into her depths. She welcomed him, her tongue meeting his in a tangled dance of need.

She arched forward, pressing herself into him, and moving, rubbing her aching nipples against his chest and torturing herself with the action. Her knees went weak and she tightened her grip on his shoulders to keep herself upright. His hands moved over her body, up and down her spine. He dragged her shirt free of the waistband of her skirt and skimmed his hands beneath it. Her skin tingled, firing with his touch until she felt as if every square inch of her body were bursting into flame.

He tore his mouth from hers and shifted lower, running his lips and tongue along her throat, tasting her pulse point at the base of her neck.

Eileen groaned and tipped her head back, inviting more, silently asking for more. And he gave. His lips and tongue teased her. His teeth nibbled at her skin, sending ripples of awareness and greed dancing through her. She clung to him, digging her fingers into his shoulders and, even while her brain sizzled with sensation, she was alert enough to notice that beneath his starched white shirt, his muscles had muscles.

''I can't get enough of the taste of you,'' he muttered, his breath dusting her skin as his words quickened her pulse.

He dropped his hands to the waistband of her skirt again and Eileen hung on as she heard and felt the zipper slide down. As soon as the black fabric was parted, he shoved it down over her hips. She felt the fabric slip along her legs and pool at her feet. Quickly, eagerly, she stepped free of the skirt and kicked it aside.

Cold, damp air caressed her bare skin, but she was too hot to care. Nothing mattered but the touch of his hands on her body. The feel of his mouth across her skin. And she needed more. Needed all of him. Now. She shifted her hold on him, her hands moving around to the front of his shirt. Quickly, deftly, her fingers undid the buttons on that white conservative business shirt and once she had the fabric parted, she scooped her hands across the white T-shirt beneath. Even through the warm cotton fabric, she felt the clearly defined muscles he hid so well.

He sucked in air through clenched teeth, then let her go long enough to pull off his dress shirt, then yank off the T-shirt.

''Wow,'' she murmured, her gaze dropping to the

broad expanse of his chest. His flesh was golden-brown, still tanned from summer, and deeply cut, with each muscle defined as if by an unseen sculptor. She ran the flat of her hands across his skin, twining her fingers through the dusting of brown curls and smiling when his breath hitched. "You're hiding an awful lot under those suits and ties."

He grinned wickedly. "You ain't seen nothin' yet."

Her stomach pitched and deep within her the flames burned hotter.

Rick reached for her, his fingers tearing at her shirt buttons. Hell, why'd they have to make buttons so damn small? Impatience drove him and he damn near gave in to the driving urge to just rip the blouse off her body. But then the last of the buttons slid free and he was pushing the shirt off her shoulders and looking down at the silky, dark red teddy she wore. Lace decorated the bodice, caressing the tops of her breasts. Her nipples, hard, erect, pushed against the fragile fabric and his mouth watered. He wanted to taste her. All of her. He wanted her beneath him, he wanted her over him. He just wanted her.

More than he'd ever wanted anything.

Rick lifted both hands to cup her breasts and she wilted into him, tipping her head back, shaking that glorious hair. She moaned, her mouth opening on the sound, her tongue sliding across her bottom lip in a not too subtle message.

Lightning crackled again and the resulting boom

of thunder clapped directly overhead, rattling the windowpanes and electrifying the air. The scent of coming rain filled him, but it could have poured on them and he still wouldn't have moved. Holding her here, in the open. In the darkness with the crash of nature all around them, felt…right. He wanted her here. On the balcony.

Now.

His thumbs and forefingers tweaked her nipples, tugging, pulling, sliding over the tips, pulling the fabric taut and using it to torture her gently. She twisted, moving into him, pressing her abdomen against his erection until he couldn't stand the wait any longer. Letting her go briefly, he ordered, ''Stay here.''

He stepped into the darkened hotel suite, but in moments, he was back. While the storm raged around them, he tore the rest of his clothes off, then reached for her again.

''Just a second,'' she whispered brokenly, and tugged the hem of her red lace teddy up and over her head, baring her breasts to him. In the electrified night, her skin glowed with a creamy translucence. Dark red lace panties were all she wore and he ached to get her out of those, too.

She stepped into his embrace, and Rick's arms came around her, holding her close, pressing her body along the length of his. Bodies brushed together. Soft to hard, rough to smooth. And with each touch, the storm between them grew stronger.

''Gotta have you,'' he murmured against her

mouth as he took her bottom lip, and then her top lip between his teeth, tasting, nibbling, claiming.

"Oh yeah," she said, swallowing hard as she took a tiny bite of his neck. "Now. Please, now."

"Now," he agreed, and with one quick turn of his wrist, snapped the flimsy elastic band of her panties. The red silk dropped from her skin and lay like a forgotten flag on the balcony's gleaming wood floor.

Lifting her easily, he sat her on the narrow metal railing and she yelped at the kiss of cold iron on her bare behind. One brief spurt of panic shot through her, remembering that they were on the second story. But his hands were strong and warm, holding her safely, tightly. Then he kissed her again, taking her mouth in a long, fast, hard plunge of desire. Panic receded and the heat between them fired and exploded.

Tearing her mouth from his, she fought for air as she held tightly to his shoulders. "Now, Rick," she urged as she parted her legs for him, "I want you inside me. *Now.*"

Her hands on his shoulders speared heat through his body and it was all Rick could do to one-handedly slide the condom he'd retrieved from the bedroom into place. Then, without another thought beyond easing the turmoil raging within him, he pushed himself inside her.

She gasped and tipped her head back, staring wide-eyed up at the stormy sky.

His hands clutched her waist in a firm grip, holding her safely. Holding her to him. In and out, he rocked within her, claiming her, taking her, giving her all he could give and taking the same from her. Her hot body surrounded him, holding him as tightly as he held her.

Above them, lightning flashed again and again. Thunder roared, crashing down on them, muffling the sounds they made as they came together in an urgency that mirrored the strength of the storm.

Bodies meshed, breaths met, mouths claimed, hands gripped.

Eileen felt him slide in and out of her body and felt the quickening rush of expectation building within her. He drove her, pushing them both higher, faster, until all she could see was the lightning reflected in his eyes. Dazzling flashes of light dancing across deep brown pools of emotion, sensation and she lost herself in it—in *him*.

She felt wicked. Wild. Wanton.

Surrounded by the storm, the cold, sharp wind, scented with rain, pushed at them, enveloping them. The metal railing beneath her was cold and narrow, but Rick's hold on her made her feel safe enough to enjoy the thrill of the moment. To concentrate on nothing more than the hard, solid strength of him driving into her body.

Eileen lifted her legs and wrapped them around his waist as her climax neared. She moved into him, rocking as much as she dared, taking as much of him as he gave, offering herself and pulling him closer, deeper, within her.

The rain started.

Icy pellets of water sluiced over them in a rush.

As if the sky had reached the point of no return and hadn't been able to hold back any longer.

Eileen knew the feeling.

With rain cascading over them, she shook her wet hair back from her face and fought for breath. Her mind splintered. Her body exploded.

"Rick...Rick..." Her fingers flexed on his shoulders, her nails digging into his flesh, holding on, squeezing as he pushed her up that last, sweet climb to release. She looked into his eyes and watched him as he kissed her. His tongue swept across her lips, her teeth, moving inside, taking her breath and giving her his. She felt it all. Felt the magic build. Felt the sudden sway of her body tipping into oblivion, and then she groaned and rode the wave of completion, locked within his grasp, his mouth muffling her cries.

And before her body had stopped trembling, he plunged deep within her and stiffened, reaching his own release in time to join her on the slow slide down from heaven.

Five

His body still quivering with reaction, Rick lifted her off the railing, and keeping his body locked tight within hers, carried her inside, out of the rain.

She wrapped her arms around him and kept her legs twisted about his waist like a vise. Burying her face in the curve of his neck, she shuddered, then whispered, "Okay, *that* was impressive."

He chuckled, and holding her close, made his way carefully across the darkened living room to his bedroom. "And that was wet. I do my best work when I'm dry."

She lifted her head to look at him in the dim light. "Well heck," she said, "hand me a towel."

He gave her behind a sharp pat. "That's the plan."

"Love a man with a plan," Eileen said, keeping her gaze fixed on his as he stepped through the doorway and into his room.

Rocking her hips, she moved on him and he sucked in air through clenched teeth. Slapping one arm across her behind, he held her still. "You're killing me," he admitted.

"Oh," she said, shaking her head, letting water droplets fly, "not yet."

One corner of his mouth lifted as he eased down onto the soft mattress, his body still deep within hers. "Got your own plans, have you?"

"I'm making it up as I go along," she said, reaching to cup his face between her palms.

"You're doin' fine," he assured her. "Don't stop now."

"Don't worry about that." Now that they'd started, giving in to the tension that had rippled between them all week, Eileen didn't want to stop. She wanted more of him. She wanted to feel that building excitement within again. She wanted to experience the crashing explosion of desire and the throbbing pulse of satisfaction.

She hadn't expected this.

Hadn't planned on it.

But she was smart enough to enjoy it once it had happened.

The old quilt beneath her felt warm and soft. Cotton brushed her skin and wrapped up around her like a cocoon. She felt surrounded by warmth even though her skin had been chilled by the rain, now beating down on the roof like tiny fists in a fury. Occasional flashes of lightning were the only illumination in the room, but it was enough to see Rick's face, read his features, and know that he was feeling the same things she was.

He moved within her, hard again and she arched into him like a lazy cat waiting to be stroked. Tipping her head back into the mattress, she unwound her legs from his hips and planted both feet on the bed. Then rocking her hips against his, she opened wider for him, taking him as deeply as she could and wishing she could take him completely inside her. He was so big, so hard, she felt as though he was touching the base of her heart when he plunged inside her.

"More," she demanded, dragging her nails along his back, down his spine.

"More," he agreed and suddenly flipped over, taking her with him, until she straddled him and he lay flat on his back.

Rick watched her in the half-light and wished he'd taken the time to light some of the candles that were sprinkled around the room. Apparently there were lots of power outages around here. And a few lit candles would have been enough to let him completely enjoy the sight of Eileen atop him.

With her legs on either side of him, she braced her palms on his chest and fingered his flat nipples, stroking, caressing. She moved on him, rocking her hips and bucking, arching her back as though she were riding a half-wild horse in a rodeo.

Her skin still damp with rain, cold drops of water dripping from the ends of her hair to splatter against his body, she looked fierce and tender and free. Her head fell back and her eyes closed as she moved on him, taking him deep within her and grinding her hips against him. She drove him higher, higher than he'd expected. Higher than he'd thought possible. And the flashing need erupting inside him nearly strangled him.

He reached up, covering her breasts with his hands, his fingers and thumbs squeezing her hardened nipples. She pushed herself into his touch and he smiled, before dropping one hand to the spot where their bodies met. He fingered her center, toying with that small nubbin of flesh that held her secrets, cradled her need.

"Rick!" She groaned his name and moved harder on him, swaying, moving with a rhythm that rocked him to his bones.

"Feel it," he ordered, watching her face, seeing the pleasure streaking across her features.

"Too much," she murmured, shaking her head, biting her bottom lip.

"Never enough," he told her, and kept stroking her center as she moved on him, rocking, swaying, taking.

She gasped as her body tightened on his. The first tremors took her and she moved quickly, fiercely, heightening her own pleasure while demanding his.

"Never enough," she echoed as he erupted inside

her, then cradled her gently as they took the fall together.

Minutes, hours…heck, it could have been *days* later, for all Eileen knew—or cared—she collapsed beside him in a boneless heap. She licked her lips and tried to fight off the buzzing in her head long enough to say, ''That was… amazing.''

''In a word,'' he said, his voice nearly lost in the crash and boom of thunder.

''You know…'' Eileen took a long, unsteady breath and blew it out again before continuing. ''For a guy who looks like Mr. Uptight and Closed Off, you do some great work.''

''You're not so bad yourself,'' he said.

She smiled in the darkness, then felt that smile slowly fade away as reality came crashing down on her. ''We're gonna be sorry we did this, aren't we?''

''Probably.''

''That's what I thought.'' Eileen studied the play of slashes of light across the beamed ceiling and listened to Rick's heavy breathing in the quiet. Her thoughts raced across her mind in such a blur of speed she couldn't really nail one down long enough to examine it. And that was, no doubt, for the best. Considering that if she really stopped to think about what she'd just done with Rick, she'd probably smack herself in the forehead.

''I want you to know,'' she said, ''I'm not looking for a relationship.''

''Me neither.''

"That's good, then."

"Yeah. Good."

"Still, this is going to complicate things, isn't it?" she asked.

"You mean, am I going to look at you sitting at your desk and picture you here?" he asked. "Oh yeah."

"It's not going to be easy for me either, you know." She couldn't even imagine being in the office with him and *not* thinking about those wild moments out on the balcony. Stupid, Eileen. Really stupid. She shouldn't have done this. Shouldn't have given in to her hormones like some vapid teenager who didn't know better.

She should have remembered that men were trouble and her track record was less than stellar.

"Which is why we shouldn't have."

"True." Eileen glanced at him, and noted that he, too, was staring up into the darkness. She wondered what he was really thinking. If he was wondering how to make a graceful exit from the bed. If he'd just fire her right now and avoid the whole embarrassing after-sex scene. "I'm only in your life—your world, temporarily. Two weeks. That's it."

"Should have been simple," he said.

"Not anymore."

"Nope."

She sighed and turned onto her side. Heat from his body reached out for her and she couldn't resist touching him again. Sliding one hand up his chest, she murmured, "Just think, our grandmothers got us into this."

He chuckled, caught her hand and threaded his fingers through hers. "I don't think this is what they had in mind."

"Hardly."

"Look," Rick said, his voice gaining strength, his fingers tightening on her hand. "What happened, happened. We're adults. It shouldn't be any big thing to deal with. It was just sex."

"Amazing sex."

"That goes without saying."

"It'd be nice to hear, though."

He looked at her. "Amazing sex."

"Thank you."

"No," he countered, "thank *you*."

"Trust me," she said, a reluctant smile curving her mouth. "My pleasure."

"Yeah, I know."

"No ego problems here."

He rolled over, pushing her onto her back and bracing himself up one elbow so that he could look down at her. "It's one night. One night out of a lifetime. Neither one of us is looking for—or expects—roses and cherubs. We enjoy each other, then go back to business as usual tomorrow."

Eileen looked up at him, studying his eyes, his face, the curve of his mouth. She wanted to kiss him again. To taste him. To feel his tongue sweeping against hers. Hunger arced inside her again, fresh, greedy. She'd never felt like this before.

She'd been with a man before, of course. Her fiancé and then Joshua. But those experiences were nothing compared to what was going on inside her at the moment. She'd never felt the compulsion for more as she had tonight.

Even though she'd just been with Rick, she wanted him again. Now. Inside her. She wanted to feel his body moving within hers. Wanted to feel a part of him. Wanted to be locked within his embrace—and that was new.

A part of her wanted to explore these new sensations. And another, more wary part of her wanted to back off now, while she could still think logically. There was no future with Rick. He was just like every other man she'd ever come across. He wanted her to help him out at work. He wanted her in his bed. But, like every other male in her life, he didn't want *her*. This wasn't a relationship. This was simply two people who felt a…connection. Was that enough reason to enjoy each other? And could they keep it that simple?

"Can we do that, do you think?"

"I can," Rick said, smoothing his fingertips across her cheek, pushing her hair back behind her ear. Looking at her now made him want her again. And yet he knew he would be able to say goodbye. Because he *had* to. He wouldn't let her get close. Couldn't let her in. He'd taken one chance and got smacked for his trouble. He wouldn't be doing that again.

Rick had learned years ago that life was easier if

lived alone. Sex was one thing. Love—a relationship—was something else. Something he wasn't interested in. "So the question is," he asked, "can you?"

She shivered at his touch, the tiny bursts of heat transferring from his fingers to her skin. Could she forget what happened tonight in tomorrow's light of day? She wasn't sure. Could she give up the chance to feel more of what she already had? No way. So there was really only one answer to his question.

"Yes, I can."

"Good," he said, and pulled away from her.

"I say yes and you leave?"

He pushed off the bed and turned back to look at her again, a smile tipping one corner of his mouth. Her heart jumped in response.

"Just going to light a few of these candles," he said. "This time I want to see you."

"Oh, boy."

She looked beautiful by candlelight.

Tiny flames flickered around the room, tracing halos of golden light against the flowered wallpaper. Beyond the windows, the storm still raged, rain pelting at the glass, lightning and thunder growling and snapping, like ferocious beasts demanding entry. The four-poster bed looked wide and soft and compelling, as Eileen lay across the clean white sheets, her bare body a temptation no man could resist.

And Rick had no desire to resist her.

He couldn't remember ever feeling this hunger before. The sizzle and snap of heat that burst into life every time he touched her made him yearn to feel it again. Watching the candlelight play on her smooth, pale skin made his palms itch to touch her again.

Eileen was unlike any woman he'd ever known.

Hell, everything about her was different.

Unique.

Her attitude, her laugh, her scent. She smelled of roses and sunlight—a compelling mixture to a man too used to burying himself under mountains of work, shut away in corporate towers. She laughed at his work ethic. Teased him about taking himself too seriously and fought him when he gave orders. And he was enjoying himself far too much.

Which should have worried him—but he was too hungry for the taste of her to think about it now.

He crossed the room to her, his skin tingling in anticipation of the brush of her body against his.

She went up on both elbows, cocked her head to one side and smiled. "You know, something just occurred to me."

The pale light in the room danced on the ends of her still damp hair and glistened in the water drops like diamonds. That stray thought brought him up short. Hell, he'd never been particularly poetic before. "Yeah? What's that?"

She drew one leg up, sliding the sole of her foot up the length of her other leg in a long, slow caress that caught his gaze and stole his breath.

"Do you always go armed with condoms when you travel with your secretary?"

He stopped at the edge of the bed and dropped one hand to her calf, smiling when her eyes closed at his touch. His fingers drifted along her skin with a feather-light caress. "Nope. Remember when we stopped for gas?"

"Uh-huh," she murmured as his hand slid higher, higher, past her knee, up along her thigh.

Rick smiled, remembering the impulse that had told him to buy a couple of the dusty packages of condoms he'd found on a back shelf. "Stop-and-shop gas stations carry a lot of items these days."

She dropped backward onto the mattress and arched her hips as his fingers brushed the juncture of her thighs. She sucked in a gulp of air and released it from her lungs slowly. "Thank heaven, you're a careful shopper."

He watched her through narrowed eyes. Flickering light played across her features as she practically vibrated under his touch. "One of my many gifts."

"What's another?" She lifted her hips into his hand, her breath hitching as his fingertips stroked her center.

"You're about to find out." Rick's heartbeat pounded in his ears. Blood rushed through his veins, creating a heat that made him feel as though he were standing in the center of a roaring fire. His breathing strangled, he gave into the urges riding him and grabbed her legs. Pulling her quickly around, he turned her abruptly on the mattress and yanked her toward him.

"Hey!" She grabbed at the sheets beneath her as if holding on.

"Shut up, Ryan."

"Excuse me?" She lifted her head to stare at him.

Tugging her to the edge of the bed, he spread her legs with a gentle touch, then sank to his knees in front of her. "I said shut up."

"What the he—" She stared down at him. "Rick…"

He looked at her and his breath stopped. Candlelight danced in her eyes and brushed her skin with a soft golden haze. She looked beautiful and wild and lush enough to steal a man's soul.

If he let her.

Rick wouldn't.

He just had to have her.

"Trust me," he whispered, his voice a hush, lost in the fury of the storm beyond the cozy, softly lit room.

Lifting first one of her legs and then the other, Rick laid them across his shoulders, then scooped his hands under her bottom. Her body trembled and she arched her hips, squirming as if trying to free herself. But she wasn't trying hard.

"Rick, you don't have to—" She reached one hand out to him.

"Like I said—shut up, Ryan." He locked his gaze with hers as he took her. His mouth covered her center. Her eyes went wide, her mouth dropped open and air rushed from her lungs in a whoosh.

She watched him take her, and feeling her gaze

on him fed his own hunger. He licked her soft flesh and she whimpered, threading her fingers through his hair and holding him to her as if afraid he'd stop. She needn't have worried. He couldn't stop. The feel of her body melting beneath his touch inflamed him. Her sighs filled him. He tasted her, dipping his tongue within her tender flesh, sending her higher than she'd ever been before.

One hand kneaded her bottom while he swept the other around to dip first one finger, and then two, into her depths. She shuddered, lifting herself into his mouth.

"Rick, that…feels…so…*good*. Don't stop. Don't ever stop."

Her broken voice, her breathy words, carried on the next clap of thunder, and he instinctively gave her more, pushing her farther, faster.

Eileen moved with him, rocking her hips, reaching for the wonder she knew was waiting for her. She watched him, unable to tear her gaze from the sight of him taking her so intimately. His gaze burned into hers. Candlelight flickered over his features and he looked dark, dangerous and too damn good.

He lifted her bottom off the bed and she was dangling in his grasp, his mouth the only stable point in her world. His hot breath dusted her most intimate flesh and his fingers and tongue worked her body into a frenzy of sensation that pooled in her center and spiraled throughout her insides. Her heartbeat drummed in her ears. Her breath staggered. She couldn't hold out much longer. Couldn't make it last, despite wanting his mouth on her forever. The end was crashing down on her and she rushed to meet it.

She cupped the back of his head, holding him to her as she cried out his name. He kept kissing her until the last of the tremors subsided and, when she thought she might shatter, he eased her back into the middle of the bed.

Her vision blurred as she looked up at him, kneeling between her legs. "You're just full of surprises, aren't you?"

"I try."

"Well, you're doin' fine," she assured him, and told herself that it didn't matter if her heartbeat was somewhere around three hundred. If she died of a heart attack right now, she'd meet death with a satisfied smile on her face.

"Glad to hear it." He grinned and leaned over to snag another condom from the bedside table. As he tore the foil packet open, he looked back at her. New desire shimmered in his eyes, sending a wicked spiral of want and need spinning through her. Surprise and pleasure shifted inside her, opening her to more sensations, making her wonder where this was all leading. Making her stop and think. Which she didn't want to do at the moment.

Thankfully, Rick splintered her thoughts and sent them packing when he asked with a wink, "Ready to go again?"

Six

In the candlelight, his skin gleamed like polished oak. Every well-defined muscle stood out in sharp relief and all Eileen could think of was that she wanted to trace every inch of his body with her fingers. Her lips. She wanted him as she'd never wanted anyone before. She couldn't seem to get enough of him. And that thought shimmered briefly in her mind before she set it aside to explore later.

There would be plenty of time for thinking once the sun came up and their one-night bargain ended. For now... there was Rick. Nothing else.

"Sleep," she said, "is vastly overrated."

"Is that right?"

"Oh yeah," she said, and squirmed slightly on the bed, scooting closer to him, feeling the brush of his hardened body against her core. "It's a known fact. You don't need more than twenty minutes sleep a night to function at your best."

"That's a relief," he said, pulling the condom from the packet.

"Wait," she said. "Let me." She snatched the condom from his grasp. Half sitting up, she covered the tip of him with the pale latex, then slowly, sinuously, rolled it down along his length.

He sucked in air with a hiss.

Her fingers folded around him and squeezed gently.

His eyes closed and a muscle in his jaw twitched.

She touched him, sliding her fingers up and down the hard, solid length of him, then stopped to boldly cup him. His eyes opened and the candlelight reflected in those dark depths made him look dangerous again as he pulled her hand away.

"That's it," he muttered, and leaned over her. He grasped both of her wrists in one tight fist, holding her hands against the bed, high over her head. She writhed and twisted beneath him on the bed, moving into him, lifting her hips, inviting him in.

Rick surrendered to the fury pulsing within. Desire scratched at him. Need howled inside him. Hunger raged in him. And when he pushed himself into her body, it all escalated. His heartbeat raced, his blood pumped and his breath staggered in and out of his lungs. All he could hear was her sighs. All he could feel was her breath as he lowered himself to kiss her. She nibbled at his mouth and planted her feet on the mattress to rock her body against his.

She was all.

She was everything.

And for tonight, she was *his*.

Releasing his grip on her wrists, he groaned when she dragged her nails along his back. Then she pulled his head to her breasts and he pleased her, suckling, drawing, pulling at her nipples, first one, then the other. The scent of her drove him wild, the taste of her created hungers he'd never known before.

They moved together, two shadows in the candlelight. And while the storm raged beyond the windows, two souls found something neither of them had been looking for.

Dawn arrived sooner than they would have wanted.

"Storm's over," Eileen said, knowing Rick was lying beside her, wide-awake.

"Yeah, looks like."

Rain dripped from the eaves, sounding like a clock, ticking away the last seconds of an incredible night. The first brush of daylight softened the room, obliterating the light from what was left of the candles. Most of them had guttered out in their own wax hours ago. The last few were unnecessary now.

Eileen winced and shifted position, tugging the edge of the quilt up over her breasts. Though why she was bothering with modesty at this late date was beyond her. There wasn't one square inch of her body that Rick hadn't seen, tasted or explored.

She slapped one hand across her eyes and tried not to think too much about everything they'd done together in the dark.

"Regrets?" he asked, his voice a low rumble close to her ear.

She thought about that for a long minute. Did she regret any of it? Could she? He'd made her feel things she'd merely read about. He'd made her body sing. No. She didn't regret it. She was only sorry their agreement had been for one night only. Though it was probably safest that way. She wasn't going to get involved here and she knew darn well that if she kept sleeping with him, her heart *would* make the leap whether she wanted it to or not. So in the spirit of self-preservation, she'd stick to the bargain despite the clamoring of her hormones. "No. No regrets."

"You had to think about it, though," he teased her.

Turning her head on the pillow, she looked at him. In the early morning light, he looked just as good as he did in candlelight. "What about you?"

He slid one hand up her body, across her rib cage to cup one of her breasts.

She sucked in a gulp of air.

"No regrets," he said, and leaned in close enough to kiss her. Then he pulled away, rolling onto his back to stare up at the ceiling.

"So," Eileen said, feeling the loss of his hand on her body, "now we get up, get showered and move on."

"Right," he said.

Boy, that had sounded like a good idea the night before. Now though…she sat up and swung her legs off the edge of the bed, before she could do something really dumb like suggest that they pretend it wasn't morning yet. "Night's over, so we're finished."

"Exactly. Back to business."

"Right," she said. She was achy all over. Muscles she hadn't used in ages were shrieking at her. And still, it was all Eileen could do to keep from turning back around and jumping on to him. She stood up and walked across the room toward the door, snatching up the complimentary plush white robe on the bench at the end of the bed. Slipping into its warmth, she belted it at the waist and paused in the doorway to look back at him. "I'll go over to my room, hop in the shower and then meet you in the living room for breakfast in an hour or so?"

He went up on one elbow, his dark brown hair falling across his forehead to give him a rakish air he wouldn't have once he was back in one of his blasted suits. Her palms itched to smooth across his chest again. To feel his heart beating beneath her touch. She curled her fingers into fists and shoved her hands into the robe's pockets.

"An hour," he said tightly, and watched her go.

* * *

Standing under the pulsating jets of hot water, Eileen struggled to clear her mind. To push the night's memories into a dark corner, where they couldn't sneak out to taunt her. But it was no use.

Hot, needlelike punches of water beat on her body in staccato bursts from the shower massage and reminded her of his hands on her. Of his mouth. Of his touch. Of the fires he could stoke with a look.

And she ached for him.

At the slide of the curtain rings on the metal pole, she turned in time to see him step naked into the shower behind her. "Rick—"

He grabbed her and pulled her close, sliding her water-slick body along his. "Sun's not all the way up yet. Night's not over."

She stared up at his taut features, swallowed hard and said, "Works for me."

Turning her around, Rick pressed her back up against the shower wall and lifted her off her feet. Steam from the shower rose up like a soft fog, enveloping them in a small, private world. Water pounded on his back like a heartbeat. She wrapped her legs around his waist and he entered her with one quick lunge that stole his breath. He'd tried to stay away. But hearing the water, knowing she was naked and wet and warm, was simply too much of a temptation to ignore.

Now he moved within her, racing toward the ecstasy that had become familiar during the long night. Burying his face in the curve of her throat, he gave himself to her and took all she had to give.

* * *

An hour later, they were in her bed, having breakfast. Wrapped in the thick terry robes, they shared strawberries, Belgian waffles and hot coffee.

"When does your first client get here?" Eileen asked, biting into a fresh ripe strawberry direct from the inn's greenhouse.

Rick checked the bedside clock. "About an hour."

She nodded. "Probably a good thing, huh?"

He looked at her and all he could think was that he wanted to taste her strawberry-stained mouth. His body stirred and even he was amazed. He should be exhausted, yet he felt more awake, more alive than he ever had before. She was like a jolt of pure electricity. She kept his body humming and his blood pumping and he hadn't had nearly enough of her yet. "Yeah," he murmured. "A good thing." Pouring more coffee into both their mugs, he said, "There are three meetings today and one tomorrow morning."

"Okay."

"If you want to, later we can go out. There's an Indian casino near here. We can catch a show."

"Sounds good."

Rick winced at the stiffness in her voice. Hell, in *his* voice. "Look, we don't have to be this polite and formal with each other," he said, hating the distance springing up between them, even though he knew it was for the best. No point in dragging this on, right? Not when he knew damn well he'd be saying goodbye to her in another week. And he *would* say goodbye.

That's what he did.

He didn't stick around and give women the chance to leave him. Not again. Not ever again. "We had a good time," he said. "Now it's over."

"Right," she said, and relaxed back against the headboard. "We're adults—neither one of us is committed to someone else. No reason we can't walk away. We can do this."

He smiled at her. "Just as well we're not going to be having another night like last one."

"Why?" She cradled her coffee cup between her palms.

Rick grinned and took a sip of the hot, rich brew. "When Mrs. Hammond brought the breakfast tray up here, she asked me if I'd heard anything unusual during the night."

Eileen's eyes went wide. "Unusual?"

"Uh-huh. Seems that just before the rain started, she heard a loud yelp."

She clapped one hand across her mouth. "Oh, God."

He chuckled and shook his head. "Don't worry. She thought a coyote had gotten hold of some small animal."

"A *coyote?*"

"Yeah. Apparently, you hit just the right note to sound like a dying rabbit."

She bounced a pillow off his head.

* * *

"Okay, this no more sex thing just isn't working out."

"Yeah, I noticed." Rick rolled to one side of her and lay on his back, struggling to catch his breath.

Lying naked on the braided rug in front of the fireplace, Eileen winced and reached beneath her. She pulled a ballpoint pen out from under her bottom. "That's what that was."

"Huh?"

"The pen your last client lost?" she asked, holding it up. "I found it."

Rick chuckled, then shook his head. "What the hell are we doing, Eyeball?"

"Beats me, Hawkins." Holding the stupid pen, she let her hand drop, falling across her abdomen. "But if we don't figure it out soon, we're gonna end up killing each other."

The last client had only left the inn an hour ago and already, Eileen and Rick were naked and exhausted. Sexual heat still shimmered in the air and Eileen felt the first stirrings of need building within her again. Much more of this and they'd be too weak to drive home.

They'd made it through the long day, though the tension between them had been thick enough to chew on. Eileen had taken notes, typed them up and helped Rick draw up the paperwork for two of his clients to diversify their stock holdings. She'd made small talk and tried to avoid meeting Rick's gaze. She'd felt him watching her as his clients came and went. She'd smiled and visited with the older men who, each in turn, told her what a great catch Rick Hawkins would be. How smart he was. How rich.

Of course, when the talk had turned in that direction, Eileen had actually *seen* shutters drop across his eyes. As if he was distancing himself from the conversation, even though he had to know the men had only been teasing. She'd had the urge to tell him that he was safe. She wasn't interested in a "great catch" or any other kind of catch. But in front of his clients, that hadn't seemed appropriate— and once she and Rick were alone…well, the subject hadn't come up.

"Well," he said finally, "our one-night bargain is shot."

"Pretty much," she agreed.

"Do we make a new one-night agreement?"

"That would technically be a *two*-night bargain."

"Fine. Two nights. Whatever."

She turned her head to look at him. "Whoa. Lack of sleep making somebody cranky?"

"No." He met her gaze. "It's not sleep I'm craving."

Eileen's stomach flip-flopped, then did a slow whirl. "Me neither, big boy," she admitted, then added, "but before this turns into the Lost Weekend, we'd better have some ground rules."

He rolled onto his side and propped his head on his hand. "Rules are good."

Eileen chuckled. Now there was a statement on his personality. "Figured you'd say that."

She too went onto her side and lay facing him. Flames danced in the hearth behind him, sending ripples of light around the room and gilding the ends of his hair until he looked almost as if he were wearing a halo.

Rick Hawkins? A halo?

Okay, rules were definitely in order!

Idly he reached out one hand to stroke her breast. Eileen hissed in a breath and let it out again. "First," she said, a little more loudly than she'd planned, "no strings."

"Agreed," he said, his now-narrowed gaze focused on hers. "I'm not looking for anything permanent."

"Ditto." She caught a flicker of surprise in his eyes and addressed it. "What? You think every woman you meet is trying to lure you into a bear trap?"

One dark eyebrow lifted, managing to convey a world of comments.

"You can relax on that score, Mr. Wonderful," she assured him. "You're completely safe."

"No strings means what, exactly?" he prompted, ignoring her last statement.

"I guess it means we enjoy what we have while we have it," Eileen said, and gulped when his talented fingers tweaked her nipple. Closing her eyes briefly, she opened them again and stared directly into his. "When one of us has had enough, it's over. Deal?"

"Deal."

"Shouldn't we shake hands on it?"

A corner of his mouth tipped up. "Oh, we can do better than that."

The rest of the weekend was a blur.

A good blur, but a blur.

On Sunday afternoon, Eileen walked into her house, left her small, rolling suitcase in the foyer, then dropped onto the worn overstuffed sofa. Its soft down-filled cushions came up around her like a warm hug. Propping her feet up on the mission-style coffee table, she scraped both hands across her face and tried to figure out how she'd work a temporary affair into her world.

God, she hadn't planned on this. Who would have guessed that Rick Hawkins would be the man who could light up her insides like a Christmas tree? And who would have thought that a two-week favor to her grandmother would turn into...she dropped her hands onto her lap. Turn into what? What exactly had happened? One red-hot weekend?

Because if that's all it turned out to be, a part of her would be sorry. She didn't really want to get involved with anybody, but on the other hand, it had been a long time since she'd been with a man. A long time since she'd felt...close, to anyone. And damn it, she'd enjoyed it. Not just the sex, she thought, though she had to admit, Rick had a real gift in that area, but it was more than that. It was laughing with him. Talking to him. It was midnight meals and napping in front of the fire. It was long walks on windswept hills and hearing him try to explain the securities market.

It was a lot of things she hadn't expected.

She hadn't felt anything remotely like this since just before she'd broken off her engagement to Robert Bates. Frowning, Eileen grabbed one of the green plaid throw pillows and hugged it to her chest. He'd been her college boyfriend. Pre-med when she met him, they'd made plans for the future. Eileen had planned their wedding, their marriage and even how many kids they'd have—three—two boys and a girl. And then at graduation, Robert had suggested they not get married right away. Instead, he wanted her to go to work. They could live together, he'd said, and she could support him while he finished med school. *Then,* if the time was right, they'd get married.

Sighing, Eileen let her head fall back against the cushions. "But the time was never going to be right," she muttered, remembering the look of surprise on Robert's face when she came home early from work one night. Of course, the girl he was on top of was pretty surprised, too—but it was Robert's expression that had stayed with her. Not hurt, not defeated or even guilty. Just angry. Angry at *her* for not being at work, like the good little cash cow he'd expected her to be.

She'd grabbed up as many of her clothes as she could and walked out, leaving Robert and his floozy right where she'd found them. That was the last time she'd trusted her heart to anybody. And she'd vowed then that she wouldn't do it again.

"But this is different," she argued to the empty room. "It's not my heart involved here...just my hormones."

Her own words echoed in the quiet and even *she* didn't quite believe them. But she would. All she had to do was keep reminding herself that this whole situation was temporary.

"Yeah," she said, pushing up from the couch. "That'll work."

Seven

Seven

"**Y**our grandma called," Eileen said as she poked her head into Rick's office Monday morning.

He looked up. "What line is she on?"

"No, *called,*" she repeated. "Past tense." Leaning against the doorjamb, she folded her arms over her chest and looked at him. "She said to tell you she didn't have time to talk. She booked a last-minute Fall Foliage train trip and she still had to shop for clothes."

Rick smiled to himself. His grandmother would never change. She treated life like an adventure. She never bothered to plan something out. She thought there was no fun in anything if it wasn't spontaneous. Hence, her trip to watch the space shuttle launch. And apparently, fall leaves. "When's she coming back?"

Eileen laughed shortly. "She wasn't sure. But she did say she tried to get my gran to join her."

"Is she?"

"No." She straightened up and walked across his office to stand in front of his desk. "When Gran takes a trip, she likes to go to the auto club and stock up on maps months in advance. Half the fun, she says, is planning her route."

"Your grandmother plans, and mine's a free spirit," he murmured, leaning back in his chair to study her. "Ever think we were switched at birth?"

"Possibility. I used to plan things. I gave it up."

"How'd you sleep?" he asked, his voice dropping a notch or two, until the sound of it scraped along her spine and sent a shiver of expectation rattling through her.

"Fine. You?"

"Great."

"Good."

"Good," he said, his gaze locked on hers and burning with unspoken words. "I missed—"

She held her breath.

"—breakfast in bed," he finished.

"Me too."

"With you, I mean," Rick said, standing up and moving around the edge of his desk. "I missed a lot of things. Missed hearing you breathing in the dark."

"Rick…"

"I missed reaching for you and finding you there, hot and ready."

"Yeah well," Eileen admitted after inhaling sharply, "I kind of missed being reached for."

"So what're we gonna do?"

"I guess we're gonna keep this going for a while, huh?"

"Is that what you want?" he asked.

"Depends. Is it what you want?"

He took her hand and yanked her close enough that she could feel his hard strength pressing into her abdomen. "You tell me."

"Okeydoke, then." Her body burst into flames. She knew because her mouth was suddenly dry. "After work. My place?"

"After work," he repeated, and reluctantly released her. "But for now," he said as he walked back to his desk chair, "I need to see the Baker files."

"You bet," she said, and turned around, headed back to the outer office. She felt him watching her with every step.

Two hours later, Rick was closeted with a client and Eileen's phone was ringing.

"Hawkins Financial."

"Hello, honey!"

Eileen smiled into the phone. "Hi, Gran."

"How's it going?"

She opened her mouth, then closed it again, pausing to think. Hmm. How to describe what was going on around here. "It's going…fine." Safe, boring and as far from the truth as she could get. But what else was she going to tell her grandma? That Rick was the best sex she'd ever had?

Good God.

Right after recovering from her heart attack, Gran would drag Eileen to St. Steven's and stretch her out prostrate on the altar. Nope. Sometimes a comfortable lie was better than the truth.

"Good. I knew everything would work out as soon as you were able to let go of the whole 'Rick was mean to me' issue from your childhood."

"Issue?" Eileen pulled the phone from her ear and stared at it for a moment through thoughtful, narrowed eyes. Then she snapped it back and asked, "Have you been watching that talk show again?"

"Dr. Mike is a very smart man," Gran said.

"Oh," she said dryly, "I'll bet." Gran's favorite TV psychologist had an answer for everything from hair loss to potty training and wasn't the least bit shy about sharing them. And women like her grandmother ate it up.

"He's simply trying to help people face and confront their fears." A long pause. "You might think about watching him sometime, dear."

Eileen sighed and pulled her hands back from the keyboard. Giving the closed door to Rick's office a quick look, she said, "I don't have any fears to confront, Gran. But thanks for thinking of me."

"Commitment-phobic people always claim that."

"What?" Her eyes bugged out and Eileen

slapped one hand over them to prevent another contact lens search.

"Dr. Mike says that people who are afraid to get hurt should just jump in and take the risk anyway. It's healthy."

"Dr. Mike can kiss my—"

"Eileen Ryan!"

"Gran." Instantly apologetic, Eileen remembered where she was and lowered her voice. "I'm sorry. But seriously, stop trying to cure me by watching television. *And,* I don't need a cure. There's nothing wrong with me, anyway."

"Nothing a husband and kids wouldn't fix," her grandmother argued.

Eileen's chin hit her chest. Gran had been singing the same song for years. "Not everyone is going to live happily ever after, you know? Not everyone wants to."

"Yes, but *you* do. I know you're lonely, Eileen. Do you think I don't notice how you watch Bridie and her family? Do you think I don't see that sheen of tears in your eyes when you hold the baby?"

Eileen huffed out a sigh. Fine. So she felt a little sorry for herself sometimes. Who didn't? Did that make her a potential customer for Dr. Mike? No, she didn't think so. What it made her was human. Sure she envied Bridie's happiness a little. But Eileen was happy, too. Her life was just the way she wanted it.

And the phrase, *methinks you protest too much,*

floated through her mind before she had a chance to cut it off at the pass.

"Look, Gran," she said quickly, "I've gotta go. Rick needs something." A small lie, she plea-bargained with the gods as they no doubt made a little black mark on her soul. Lying to sweet old ladies didn't go down real well in the world of Karma.

"Fine, fine, I don't want to keep you," Gran said in the tone that clearly said she wasn't ready to hang up yet.

"I'll call you later."

"Come for dinner."

"I—*can't,*" she said, remembering that she'd be busy after work. "But I'll call. Promise."

"All right, but I really think you should—"

"Gotta go, Gran. Seriously." Eileen bent over her desk, still talking while she lowered the receiver toward its base. "Honest. Gotta go." Her grandmother was still talking. "Bye."

Then she hung up, knowing that she'd be paying for that one later.

Sitting back in her chair, Eileen thought about everything Gran had said. Lonely? Sure, she was lonely sometimes. Wasn't everyone? But on the whole, she liked her life. It was good. Full. And just the way she wanted it. She liked an empty house. The silence. The time to herself.

So why then was she so glad that Rick would be coming over to the house after work?

* * *

The small beach house was just the way he imagined Eileen's place would look. Craftsman style, the front of the house was all wood and aged stone. It had to be at least sixty years old, with charm in the hand-carved porch railings and the stone balustrades.

He parked his luxury sedan at the curb and paused beside his car to take a good look at her place. Just a few blocks inland from the beach, the house was surrounded by greenery and fall flowers. Painted a bright sunshine-yellow with forest-green trim, the cottage looked warm and inviting. White wicker furniture on the porch invited a visit and the porch light gleamed with a soft pink glow. Naturally Eileen wouldn't have just a plain old white bulb in there. She'd go for color.

Reaching into the car, he pulled out the bottle of iced chardonnay he'd brought along, then started up the rosebush-lined walk. He caught himself wondering what colors those now bare roses might be in the summer. But as soon as the thought entered his mind, he dismissed it. He wouldn't be around long enough to find out anyway.

Rick smiled to himself as he climbed the five front steps. The cement had been painted. Somehow, Eileen had laid out a pattern and then painted the porch and steps to look like a faded, flowered Oriental rug. It looked great, but he couldn't help wondering how she'd ever thought of it. Who the hell painted rugs on cement?

The front door opened.

Eileen stood in the open doorway. Her hair was loose, falling around her shoulders in soft red-gold waves. She wore a short white tank top with slender straps and a pair of faded denim shorts. Her feet were bare and her legs looked impossibly long. His mouth watered and he forgot all about the faux rug on the porch. Forgot about the new client he'd picked up over lunch. Forgot about the wine in his hands. All he could focus on was her.

And heaven help him, what she did to him.

"Hi."

She smiled and his breath left him. Her eyes lit up and her features brightened and his blood pumped a little faster. "Hi back," he said.

"That for me?" She indicated the wine.

"Yeah."

"Want some now?" she asked, stepping back to let him in.

"Not thirsty," he said, entering the house, then closing the door behind him.

"Me, neither," she said, taking the wine from him long enough to drop it onto the nearby couch.

"Good," he muttered, and grabbed her, pulling her close, wrapping his arms around her and holding on as if his grip on her meant his life. And maybe, just for the moment, it did.

She went up on her toes and met his kiss coming in. Her lips parted, her breath left her, rushing to him, and his tongue swept into her mouth, instantly demanding, plundering, pushing her back to the brink she now knew so well.

He tore his mouth from hers and laid down a path of hot, damp kisses along the column of her throat. She moaned softly, holding on to his shoulders and arching into him. His hands lifted the hem of her shirt and swept beneath the fabric to cup her breasts, his fingers teasing, tweaking, caressing.

She hissed in a breath through clenched teeth and held it, as if afraid she wouldn't be able to draw another. Rick nibbled at her neck, tasted the frantic pulse beat at the base of her throat, and felt his own heartbeat kick into high gear and match the wild rhythm of hers.

Lifting his head, he continued to palm her breasts, rubbing the tips of her nipples just to watch a glassy sheen dazzle her eyes. "Bedroom?"

She licked her lips, blinked a couple of times, then tried to focus on his face. Lifting one hand, she pointed. "Thataway."

"Let's go," he said, and bent low enough to plant one shoulder in her middle. Then he stood up, draping her across one shoulder.

"Hey!" Both hands on his back, she pushed herself up. "What's with the caveman routine?"

He gave her behind a friendly swat. "Quicker this way."

"Okay then," she said, and let herself drop against his back while he crossed the room in a few long strides. "As long as there's a good reason."

Rick moved through the living room without even looking at it. Right now, he wasn't interested in the decor. All he was interested in was Eileen. And find-

ing that sweet satisfaction he'd only ever found with
her. He needed her, damn it.

He didn't want to.

Hadn't planned to.

But in the space of one long weekend, she'd become... important. His grip on her tightened in response to that thought, but he didn't linger on it.
Didn't want to consider what ramifications might be
lurking behind that one little word, *important.*

He glanced through one open doorway. Green
tiles, parrots in jungle shower curtain. Bathroom.

''Turn left,'' she said, as he paused in the hallway.

He did.

''No, the other left,'' she corrected, pushing herself up again. ''*My* left. This upside down and backward trying to give directions thing sucks.''

''You're a backseat driver, too, aren't you?''

''Only trying to help.''

He walked into her bedroom, noted the queen-size
bed covered with a pale blue-and-white quilt, and
ignored everything else. A small, beside lamp was
on, sending a pale yellow light spreading across the
blanket. Bending down, he flipped her onto the mattress and she laughed when she landed and bounced
a couple of times.

''There's just nothing like a Neanderthal,'' she
said, stretching like a cat on the bed.

''Glad you approve.''

''Oh, yeah.''

Eileen watched him through eyes already hazy

with a building passion that swamped her with sensation and expectation. He looked...different. He wore a black sweater over dark blue jeans and the casual clothes made him seem more—reachable, somehow. The suits that were such a part of him were almost like a well-cut wall he wore around him, keeping the world at bay. Tonight he'd apparently stopped by his own house to change before coming over. And as much as she appreciated the new him, she wanted him out of those clothes. Now.

As if he heard her thoughts, he tore his sweater off and threw it aside. The glow from the lamp defined his broad chest and Eileen's insides shivered. As he stripped off his jeans, her breath came fast and hard and her body went warm and damp and ready.

He came to her then, kneeling on the bed beside her, lifting her from the mattress slightly to yank her tank top up and over her head. Then he bent to her breasts, taking first one nipple, then the other into his mouth, teasing, tasting, taking them both to the beginning of another wild, fast ride.

Eileen gasped and fought for breath. She ran her fingers through his hair, then skimmed her hands down to stroke his shoulders, his back. He lifted his head, looked into her eyes and admitted, "I missed you, damn it. Even though we worked together all day, I missed you."

"Yeah," she said, and slid one hand around to cup his face in her palm. "I know. I feel the same way."

"Which means…"

"Heck if I know," Eileen said and sucked in a gulp of air when he dropped one hand to the waistband of her shorts. She held that breath while he undid the button, pulled down the zipper, then drew the shorts and her panties down her legs. She kicked free of them, then said, "I just know I want you. Really bad."

His lips curved into a smile that shook her to her toes. "Back atcha, Eyeball."

She laughed as he shifted to cover her body with his. She opened for him, welcoming him as he pushed himself within her. Still smiling, she rocked her hips against his and gave herself up to the wonder he created inside her. She looked up into his eyes and found more than desire written there. She also saw warmth, humor and tenderness.

Sensations spiraled through her and as her peak hovered close, she realized that she and Rick had crossed a border at some point. They'd moved beyond simple passion and hunger to a realm where things could get a lot more complicated.

There was something more here than desire.

How much more, she didn't know.

Then his body pushed her higher, faster and she forgot to think. All she focused on was the moment. This time with him, when it was just the two of them in the soft light, bodies claiming each other, breath mingling in the quiet.

When the first dazzling sparks shot through her bloodstream, she held on to him tightly, digging her short nails into his shoulders. Her voice broke on his name and a moment later, he stiffened against her, finding his own release and following her into the haze of completion. Eileen wrapped her arms around him and held him tightly as together they fell.

Two days later, they were together again in her room, as they had been every moment when they weren't at work. Something was happening between them, but neither of them was willing to admit it, much less talk about it. Instead, they wrapped themselves in the staggering sensations that surrounded them. Losing themselves in the magic. Finding more than they'd bargained for. More than they wanted to claim.

Rick worried that they were getting in too deep, but he couldn't seem to stay away from her. In a rational corner of his mind, a small voice warned him to start distancing himself. To start pulling away, retreating from Eileen and the dangers she represented.

But he couldn't do it.

Not yet.

He would, though. He *had* to. Because no matter what, he wouldn't be drawn into a situation where a woman had the power to crush him again. But there was time. There was still time to enjoy what he'd found before having to give it up.

For now, though, he moved inside her again, rocking his body into hers, driving her and himself to the very edge. Then with one last thrust, Rick felt her body flex around his, watched her eyes widen and heard her whisper his name as the tremors took her—and only then did he allow himself to find the completion he needed so desperately.

Minutes later, he rolled to one side of her, groaned and said, "Damn it."

Eileen gasped, struggling for air as she fought to get her heartbeat back under control. She turned her head to look at him, a satisfied smile on her face. "Rick, what could possibly be wrong?"

His expression tightened as his narrowed gaze locked with hers. "The condom broke."

Her eyes went wide and, even in the dim light, he saw her skin blanch. *"Uh-oh."*

"That about covers it." Dread pooled in the pit of his stomach, but there was still a chance. "Tell me you're on the pill."

"You want me to lie at a time like this?"

"Damn."

"Hey," she said, reaching for the quilt to cover herself, "until you, I hadn't been with anyone in a couple of years." She drew the quilt up over both of them. "I wasn't going to be taking pills when there was no need for them."

"Okay, then." Pushing one hand through his hair, he gritted his teeth and asked, "Let's figure this out. When was your last period?"

Eileen shifted her gaze to the ceiling and tried to focus. Hard to actually think when your body was still churning. But she tried. Thinking back, she counted, mentally tripping over her body's calendar. Then she recounted. And did it one more time. *Oh, God.*

She hesitated, then realized that there was no easy way to say it. "It was, uh, *due* three days ago."

"Uh-oh."

Eight

"How long does it take, anyway?"

Eileen shot Rick a dangerous look. "Three minutes, okay?" She'd already told him that several times, but, apparently, it wasn't getting through. But then, she could sort of understand that. She, too, was feeling a wild mixture of panic and fear and expectation and even, if she was completely honest and why the hell not, since only she would know... *excitement.*

She was about to find out if she was going to be a mother, for Pete's sake. A mother. Her. She'd given up on that particular little dream when she'd found Robert doing the horizontal cha-cha with the bimbo of the week. Eileen loved being an aunt to Bridie's kids, and she'd long told herself that that was enough. That she didn't need to actually give birth to feel complete. But she obviously hadn't believed herself because here she stood, hoping she was pregnant and terrified to admit it.

She pulled in a long, deep breath, let it out slowly, then repeated, "Three minutes."

"Longest three minutes of my life," Rick muttered, and paced the confines of the short hallway outside the bathroom.

"Well, contrary to public opinion," she said as she watched him turn and pace in the other direction, "snapping people's heads off does *not* make time fly."

He stopped and looked at her over his shoulder. "Sorry. It's just…"

"Yeah, I know." Eileen leaned one shoulder against the doorjamb and somehow resisted peeking in the bathroom door at the pregnancy test wand laying on the counter. She'd know soon enough. And when she knew…that would be the time for panic. And decision making. And maybe, for scraping Rick up off the floor.

No, she thought, as she watched him shoving both hands through his hair with enough force to yank every hair out of his head, that wasn't totally fair. He could've split, told her it was her problem to deal with and just disappeared. But he hadn't. Instead, right after discovering the broken condom, he'd gotten dressed, driven to the drugstore and bought a pregnancy test kit. Now he was waiting out the results with her.

Of course, she knew darn well what answer he was hoping for. She could all but see him issuing fervent prayers to the gods of fortune.

"Just because one broke doesn't mean the others were faulty," he said, and she was pretty sure he was talking to himself more than her.

But she answered him anyway. "Condoms aren't a hundred percent effective anyway."

"Thanks for that."

She shrugged and folded her arms across her chest. "I'm just saying—"

"That maybe a stop-and-shop gas station wasn't the *best* place to buy protection?" he finished for her.

Eileen smiled. Her stomach was in knots, her hands were shaking, hence the folded arms thing, after all, why should she advertise her own case of nerves? "The point is, there's no use in rehashing now. Or saying what if. The deed is most definitely done."

"I know," he said, and turning around, leaned back against the wall, his gaze fixed on the bathroom doorway.

When the timer went off, both of them jumped. He took a step, then stopped, letting her go into the room before him. Eileen hit the stop button on the timer first, since the incessant ringing was drilling a hole through her head. She picked up the wand carefully, as if it might explode if handled roughly. Glancing back at him as he came up behind her, she said, "We look together?"

He nodded. "Together."

Staring down at the tiny window where the results were displayed, she saw the tiny pink plus sign. Her stomach fisted. She heard his quick intake of breath. Her fingers tightened on the plastic. "Since it's pink, do you suppose that means it's a girl?"

If he could have figured out how to do it effectively, Rick would've kicked his *own* ass. Stupid, he thought. Stupid and careless and now...caught.

From his chair at the two-person table, he watched Eileen move around the small homey kitchen. She'd already made a pot of coffee and now she busily brought cups and a plateful of homemade chocolate chip cookies to the table. She hadn't said a word in fifteen minutes and the silence was beginning to stretch a little thin. Although, Rick thought, he really couldn't blame her for not speaking. Hell, he couldn't think of anything to say, either. An apology didn't seem right, but congratulations was clearly out of the question, too.

When she finally sat down opposite him, she poured a cup of coffee for each of them, picked up a cookie and proceeded to nervously turn it into crumbs.

Rick reached across the table and covered her hands with his. "We have to talk about this."

Her gaze lifted to his and he tried to read the emotions darting across the meadow-green surface of her eyes. But they shifted and changed so quickly it was impossible to nail one down.

"Look Rick," she said after a long minute, "I know you're trying to help, but honestly, I don't want to talk about it right now."

"But we have some decisions to make." Hell, they had a ton of decisions to make.

She smiled, shook her head and leaned back in the chair. "I'm not deciding anything tonight."

"Eileen, this is serious."

"Really?" She took a bite of her cookie, chewed it and swallowed. "You mean being pregnant isn't a joke? It's not all fun and games? Wow. I'll alert the media."

"Funny."

"Didn't mean to be." She ate the rest of her cookie and reached for another one.

"Is chocolate really the answer?"

"Chocolate can solve just about anything."

"Not this."

"I said, just about. Besides, it's worth a try."

He pushed his chair back and the legs scraped against the worn linoleum with a screech. Standing up, he came around the table, reached down and grabbed her hands, then pulled her to her feet.

Her eyes looked bruised, worried and that ate at him. If she hadn't come to help him out—to do him a favor, they never would have connected again and she wouldn't be standing here pregnant.

With *his* child.

That last sentence bounced around the inside of his heart and cracked the edges of it just a little. A child. He'd never expected to be a father. Well, certainly not after his wife had left him. When he first got married, he'd convinced himself that he was in love. That he and Allison would build a family together. But then in a few short months, he'd discovered that Allison had had her eye on his bank account, not their future.

When she left, his dreams had died. And out of the ashes, he'd built a new company and a new life for himself. If that life was a little lonelier than he'd once imagined he would be, at least it was a fair trade-off. He'd never have to watch another woman walk out of his life.

Now, suddenly, the rules had changed on him again. Now there was a tiny life inside Eileen that existed because of *him*. Whether or not they'd wanted this to happen, it *had*. And he wouldn't brush it aside. Wouldn't walk away. He'd be damned if he'd abandon his own child as his parents had done to him.

And since walking away wasn't an option, there was only one thing left.

"Eileen," he said, staring down into the eyes that had haunted him since first seeing her walk into his office more than a week ago, "marry me."

She blinked, shook her head and blinked again. *"What?"*

"You heard me."

"I know what I think I heard, but pregnancy must affect your hearing." She tried to pull away from him, but he held her tight. "You're just reacting— you're not thinking rationally."

He laughed shortly and let her go. "You? Teaching me about rational?"

"Somebody has to." Eileen reached up and scooped her hair back from her face. She felt trapped. Standing with her back to the wall, the fridge on one side of her, the table on the other and Rick blocking the way out, she suddenly couldn't catch her breath. Pent-up emotions charged through her body, closing her throat and sheening her eyes with tears she didn't want to cry.

She needed time to herself to figure this out. To deal with everything that was crowding her mind and her heart. She was pregnant. She had a baby inside her. Living. Growing. Oh, my.

"Marry you?" she repeated, and pushed him out of her way so she could walk past him, "God, Rick. I'm about ten minutes pregnant and you want to plan a wedding?"

"It's the right thing to do."

"Sure," she said over her shoulder as she stalked into the living room, "if you're living in a movie from the fifties."

He was right behind her. And suddenly, her living room seemed a lot smaller than usual.

Grabbing her forearm, he turned her around to face him. "Eileen, that's *my* baby you're carrying."

"Rick, it's too soon to talk about this." She needed quiet. She needed to think. To feel. To plan. Good God. She, Eileen Ryan, needed a plan? The woman who hadn't planned anything in years? If she wasn't so scared, she might have laughed at the idea.

"Fine," he said, and let her go, taking a step backward as if to keep himself from reaching for her again. "It's too soon. But—" he waited for her to meet his gaze before continuing "—I have to know you'll talk to me before you decide anything."

His features were taut, strained, and Eileen knew he was feeling the same turmoil racing through her, so she smiled as she reached up to cup his face in her palm. "I promise. Just…give me a little time, okay?"

A few hours later, Eileen let herself into Larkspur, shutting the front door quietly behind her. Instantly she was enveloped in the commingled perfume of flowers. The scents of chrysanthemums, roses, sweet peas and dozens of others filled the small shop.

Strings of tiny white lights outlined the two large windows that fronted Pacific Coast Highway and threw shadows around the small showroom. Galvanized buckets of water crouched in the center of the room, holding the flowers that didn't need refrigeration to retain their freshness. Across the room were the glass refrigerator cases, where the roses, orchids and other more fragile flowers stood waiting their chance to be admired.

She hit the overhead light switch and a bank of fluorescent lights flickered to life, dropping shadows around the room. Eileen walked into the back room where the florist supplies were kept. Glass vases in varied shapes and sizes and colors were stacked on a series of shelves. Nearby, there was florists tape and shears and green foam and everything else required to build the fantasy flower arrangements Larkspur was known for.

Everything was neat as a pin. The floor was freshly swept and the cuttings from the day had been carried out to the trash can behind the shop.

Flipping on the radio, Eileen listened to a slow, sad song about love and loss. Then she shrugged out of her sweatshirt and reached for one of the vases. Working with the flowers always relaxed her, gave her a chance to think. To let her mind wander while her hands were busy.

And boy, did she need to think.

Rick's apartment was dark. Empty. He stood with his back to the room, staring out a bank of windows at the ocean below. Off shore, oil derrick islands were lit up like a tropical paradise and a few boats bobbed in the harbor, their running lights twinkling on the dark surface of the water.

The quiet was starting to get to him. But he was used to being alone and he couldn't remember it bothering him much before this past week and a half.

Now, whenever he was in this place, all he could think about was leaving it. Going to work, where he'd see Eileen—or better yet, going to her house, where he could be with her. Being there, in her house, he felt…alive. There was warmth there. And laughter. There were long hours cuddled together on her couch watching old movies. There was music, drifting from her neighbor's backyard and the sound of kids playing hoops down the street.

Here…he turned from the windows and raked his gaze across the narrow, sparsely furnished room. After his divorce, he'd moved into this apartment, thinking it was a temporary thing. Then the days and weeks and months had slipped past and he'd stopped thinking about moving. Stopped living—beyond his work. Until Eileen.

Fear chewed at his insides, though he didn't want to admit it even to himself. When she left, as he knew she would, she'd not only be taking the warmth he'd only just discovered—she'd be taking his child.

He couldn't allow that.

Taking a sip of his twelve-year-old Scotch, he felt the fiery liquid spill heat throughout his body and knew it wouldn't last. The chill gripping him since leaving Eileen was bone deep.

And it was only going to get worse.

The ball whizzed past his opponent's ear and Rick winced as the man ducked. "Sorry."

"Man, who're you trying to kill?" Mike Taylor asked. "Me? Or just a poor innocent ball?"

"Neither," Rick said, and stalked to the sidelines where he'd dropped his towel and a quart-sized bottle of water.

The early morning game of racquetball wasn't going so well. He'd thought that a quick game would clear his head. That working up a sweat would somehow help him clear things in his mind. But it wasn't working. Hell, he wasn't even winning. Usually he was way ahead of Mike by now. Instead, he was six points behind and fading fast.

Wiping his face with the towel, he slung it over his left shoulder and watched his friend approach. He and Mike had been college roommates. And that was the only thing they had in common. Rick studied the market and Mike built custom motorcycles for the idle rich. He was so damn good at it, he'd become rich himself—though far from idle. He still built the bikes himself, preferring to stay in the "pit" as he called it.

"So what's goin' on?" Mike reached out for his bottle of water and unscrewed the cap.

"Nothing."

"Sure." Mike took a long drink, then capped the bottle again. "You never play this bad, man. Something's on your mind."

Rick looked at his old friend for a long minute. "I asked Eileen Ryan to marry me."

Mike was so damn impassive, Rick wasn't really sure his friend had heard him. Until he said, "Are you nuts?"

"Entirely possible," Rick muttered.

"Thought you swore off marriage after Allison left you bloody and broke."

"I did."

Mike snorted a laugh and slung his towel around

his neck. "Proposing's a weird way to avoid marriage, man."

"She's pregnant."

Mike's blue eyes went wide as he scraped one hand across his jaw. "You sure it's yours?"

That was the one worry that had never crossed his mind. Eileen was too honest and outspoken to lie about something like this.

"Yeah, I'm sure."

Mike nodded. "Is she keeping the baby?"

"Don't know." Rick shifted his gaze toward the plate-glass wall that divided this racquetball court from the one beside it. The gym was crowded, with everyone trying to get in a workout before heading off to their jobs. But he wasn't paying attention to the people surrounding him. Instead, his mind was focused, as it had been all during the sleepless night, on Eileen. And his child.

He'd never wanted to be a father, but now that the baby existed, he couldn't stand the idea of losing it. And if she decided to end this pregnancy, there wasn't a damn thing he could do about it. His hands fisted helplessly at his sides.

He didn't want a wife.

But he damn sure wanted his child.

By the end of the week, Rick was holding on to his unraveling temper with a tight fist. Somehow or other, Eileen had managed to avoid him for the last few days. Oh, she showed up for work every morning, right on time. She was polite, efficient, and completely shut him out anytime he tried to talk to her about what was happening. About the baby. About them. Hell. About anything other than work.

Rick had tried to give her space. He'd swallowed his impatience and buried his concerns. He looked into her soft green eyes and read no welcome there, so he didn't force the issue. He hadn't stopped by her place after work, even though it was killing him to stay away. He missed her, damn it. He'd driven down her street and paused long enough to look at her lamp-lit windows, but he hadn't stopped, not sure if he'd be welcome or not. And to be honest, he didn't think he'd be able to stand it if she opened the door and told him to leave.

But he'd waited as long as he could. Today was the last day she'd be working for him. By Monday, he'd have some anonymous temp in the outer office and Eileen would be back in her flower shop—as far away from his world as if she were on Saturn.

So it was now or never. Standing up from behind his desk, he crossed the room and stood in the open doorway leading to the outer office. Eileen had been here only two short weeks, but her presence had been made known. There were sweet-smelling flowers in a glass bowl on her desk, colorful throw pillows on the plain, dark blue couch and a small watercolor in a pale yellow frame hung near the file cabinets. With just a few minor changes, she'd lightened up his reception room—made it more welcoming for clients.

Just as, simply by being *her,* she'd made changes in his life.

He used to be content to spend his evenings alone, mapping out the next day's work. He'd focused all of his energies on the business that had been his whole life. Now, when he wasn't with Eileen, he was thinking about her. He couldn't sleep at night because her image kept him awake. His bed felt empty and the quiet was deafening. He'd never considered having a family—now he was worried about a baby that wasn't even the size of a pencil eraser.

His gaze locked on Eileen as she sat with her back to him, the phone held to her left ear. Morning sunlight drifted through the tinted windows and lay over her like a gentle haze. She almost seemed dreamlike. But Rick knew, only too well, just how real she was.

"Okay, Paula," she was saying. "I'll be back at the shop on Monday."

Monday, he thought, realizing that was just a few days away. When she wasn't here, in the office every day, how would he get her to talk to him? How would he prevent her from slipping out of his life and taking his child with her?

"That's great!" Eileen's voice hit a high note. "The Baker wedding? That's terrific."

Joy filled her voice, and when she laughed it was like music. Rick leaned against the doorjamb and folded his arms over his chest, just enjoying the sound of it. When she was gone, the emptiness she'd leave behind would be impossible to fill. Damn it, she hadn't even left him yet and he already missed her.

Eileen half turned in her chair to reach for a pad and a pen. That's when she spotted him. "Um, Paula? I'll call you back later, okay?" She smiled into the phone, shifting her gaze from his. "Yeah, I'll do that. Okay. Bye."

He waited until she hung up. "Paula?"

"She's the manager of my flower shop."

Rick didn't give a good damn who Paula was, but at least Eileen was talking to him. "Problem?"

"No," she said, and turned away, rummaging through her desk aimlessly. Finally she grabbed another of the chocolates Margo had left behind and quickly unwrapped it. Popping it into her mouth, she bit down hard and said, "Actually, it's good news. We landed a big wedding."

"Congratulations."

"Thanks." Her fingers twisted the scrap of silver foil candy wrapper.

She wouldn't even look at him and the tether on Rick's temper strained to the breaking point. "I'm the boss here," he said. "You can't ignore me."

She glanced at him, then away again. "I'm not ignoring you, I'm *overlooking* you. There's a difference."

"Funny, feels the same."

"Yeah, I guess it would."

He came away from the doorway, walked up behind her and gave her chair a spin hard enough to turn her around.

"Talk to me," he said.

She nodded and stood up to face him. She was close, really close. Trapped between the chair and his body. Typical Eileen, she didn't try to run, just stood her ground. She reached up, and for a split second he thought she was going to touch his face and his heart stopped. But all she did was tuck her hair behind her ears, displaying her simple silver hoop earrings. They winked at him in the sunlight. "You're crowding me," she said, then reached out and casually pushed against his chest until he stepped back out of her way. "I appreciate you not pushing me this week, Rick."

"It wasn't easy."

"I can see that," she said, and lifted one hand to briefly touch his cheek. "You look like you're ready to implode."

He blew out a breath, pushed his suit jacket back and shoved his hands into his pants pockets. "Close."

"Well, don't. Everything's fine. Or—" she thought about it for a moment "—*will* be fine. I'm keeping the baby."

Rick's heart started beating again. Now that he knew that, the rest would fall into place. It would be all right. "So you'll marry me."

Nine

Eileen blinked at him. In the past few days, she'd thought about little else but the baby inside her and the panicked proposal he'd made. She was positive it had been nothing more than a knee-jerk reaction to a situation neither of them had been prepared for. In those first few hours, she'd actually considered what it might have been like if he'd *meant* that proposal. If he'd really loved her. If they'd met, and fallen in love and *then* slept together and *then* got married and *then* got pregnant.

Briefly she'd entertained the image of she and Rick and baby made three, all living happily ever after in her tiny cottage in Laguna. But reality had reared its ugly head in time to splinter that vision and remind her that a temporary affair wasn't exactly the best basis for a marriage even if Rick *had* meant the proposal.

And of course he hadn't. It was a knee-jerk reaction. Which said a lot, she guessed, about his character. But she didn't want to be the good deed he was forcing himself to do.

"You have to stop saying that," she said.

"I want to help."

"Helping is doing the dishes, not proposing."

"I don't do dishes."

Eileen smiled. "Cute, but I'm still not marrying you."

Frustration rippled across his features and was gone again in the next instant as he tried a different approach. "What about the baby? Are you…"

She dropped one hand to her flat belly in a protective gesture that he noted with one raised eyebrow. "I'm going to raise it myself."

"I'm glad." Then his features tightened and his eyes narrowed. "But it's my child, too."

"Yes, but right now, it's more mine than yours."

"And I have no say in anything."

"I didn't say that, exactly."

"I won't be shut out, Eileen."

Eileen bent down to open the bottom desk drawer and pull her purse from its depths. Flipping back the leather flap, she dug into the big, dark brown bag and rummaged around for her keys. While she searched, she talked. "We both went into this saying no strings. Remember? And either one of us could end it whenever we were ready?"

"That was then," Rick said tightly. "This is now. It's not just us anymore. There's a baby involved. And strings don't come any bigger than that."

Her fingers curled around her car keys as she pulled them slowly from her bag. Lifting her gaze to his, she fought down a pang of something she really didn't want to look at too closely. But how could she not? Once again, she wasn't wanted for *herself*. Rick didn't want to marry her because he was crazy in love. Not even because he couldn't live without her in his bed. Nope. He only wanted her because she was carrying his child. Admitting that to herself stung, but better that she face the truth, which was that *nobody* needed that kind of marriage.

"True. But a baby isn't enough of a reason to get married."

A harsh laugh shot from his throat, but no humor shone in his eyes as he scraped one hand through his hair. As if he couldn't stand still, he stalked off a pace or two, then spun around and came right back. "Funny. That's what my parents thought, too."

Eileen winced at the echo of old pain coloring his voice. His eyes were filled with shadows that tore at her even as she sensed the emotional distance he was keeping between them. He didn't want her pity, but she couldn't help the tide of sympathy that rose up inside her. "Rick..."

"They didn't bother to get married. They didn't bother to raise me, either." His jaw tightened and as he continued speaking, Eileen could almost *feel* him pulling away from her. "They handed me off to my grandmother and went their separate ways."

"Rick, I'm sorry."

His gaze snapped to meet hers. "I don't need your pity, thanks. What I want is to be my child's father."

Eileen reached out and laid one hand on his forearm, somehow wanting to reassure the boy he'd once been—along with the man standing in front of her. "You will be. You just won't be married to its mother."

A few hours later, curled up on her couch, Eileen tried again, as she had for the past few days, to come to grips with what had happened. In the course of a couple of short weeks, she'd reconnected with Rick, found the lover of her dreams and wound up pregnant. That had to be some sort of record.

Dipping her spoon into the monster-sized chocolate sundae she'd made for herself, she scooped up the whipped cream and chocolate sprinkles and savored the rich, smooth taste. Wouldn't you know, she thought, that she'd set *this* kind of record? "You couldn't just jump rope for a hundred and eighty-seven days straight?" she muttered.

She stabbed her spoon into the ice cream and remembered the look on Rick's face when she'd walked out of the office, leaving him alone. She'd chanced one last look at his face—saw the loneliness and resignation in his eyes, and had almost gone rushing back to him. Almost.

But she'd remembered the one important point.

He didn't want her for her.

He wanted her for the baby within her.

Disappointment welled up like a wave surging toward shore. Maybe if he'd proposed differently. Maybe if he'd told her that what they had was more than physical. Maybe if he'd—

A knock on the door had her jumping and twisting in her seat to stare at it. *Rick?* Her stomach skittered nervously and she was torn between pleasure and impatience that he'd show up at the house to plead his case again. She didn't want to keep saying no, but she couldn't very well say yes to a man who didn't actually *want* her, could she? More brisk knocking sounded out and Eileen told herself she'd just ignore it. After all, just because someone dropped by didn't mean she had to pay attention.

"Eileen Honora Ryan!" Her grandmother's voice rang out loud and clear. "You open this door right this minute."

Scrambling, Eileen set the sundae on the coffee table and raced around the edge of the couch. Grabbing the doorknob, she turned it and yanked the door open, narrowly missing being rapped on the nose by Maggie Ryan's knuckles. "Gran? What's wrong?"

The older woman's face was flushed, cheeks pink, eyes flashing. She pushed into the house, shooting Eileen a look that she hadn't seen since junior high when she'd toilet-papered her history teacher's house. "Gran?" Her gaze followed the older woman as she stomped into the living room, turned around and glared.

"What do you mean you won't marry Rick Hawkins?"

Eileen closed the door, barely managing to keep from slamming it. *Big mouth.* And a dirty fighter. Going behind her back to her grandmother was cheating and he knew it.

"He told you."

Her grandmother sniffed, put both hands on her hips and tapped the toe of one shoe against the braided rug. "He did the honorable thing. He came to your family, explained the situation and told me he wants to marry you."

"Because of the baby."

"Precisely."

"No way." Eileen swallowed hard, but she wouldn't give in on this. "I'm not going to marry a man who doesn't want me. All he's concerned about is the baby. This isn't about *me* at all." She reached up and tightened the rubber band around her ponytail. Then she shifted a quick look at her grandmother before looking away. "It's Robert all over again, Gran. Robert wanted me so I could support him and Rick wants the baby."

Gran's eyes softened. "Ah...I think I understand."

"What?" Eileen kept a wary eye on her grandmother. An abrupt change of heart like that could only mean she'd thought of a better plan of attack. It paid to keep on your toes around Maggie Ryan.

"Well, if you didn't love him, you'd marry him."
Her grandmother shrugged slightly. "He's a rich,
handsome, kind man, with whom you *obviously*
share an…affection. So, if your heart weren't involved, you'd accept his proposal, because you'd
risk nothing." She smiled and folded her hands at
her waist. "But caring for him, you risk pain. So
you must actually love Rick—or at least be *falling*
in love with him."

She swayed a little, as if she'd taken a direct hit.
Love? No one had said anything about *love*.

"That's ridiculous." Eileen walked around the
couch, plopped down and reached for her sundae
again. Love? She liked him. A lot, actually. He
made her laugh. He was fun to talk to. He was smart.
And kind. And—enough, she ordered herself. She
wasn't in love with a man who didn't love her back.
She wouldn't do that. Not again. Taking a huge bite
of her sundae, she winced as an ice cream headache
instantly throbbed between her eyes. Great. Now
even her snack was ruined. She set the ice cream
back on the table and squinted at her grandmother
as she rubbed her forehead.

"I'm not in love with him and I'm not going to
marry him just because you and he think it's a swell
idea."

"I raised you better than this, Eileen." Simple
words, spoken in a soft, disappointed voice. "Your
baby deserves better."

"My baby will have me, and you, and Bridie."

Her sister Bridget would be delighted to be able to love a baby she didn't have to deliver herself.

"And a father? What about the baby's father?"

The father? When Eileen caught up to him, the baby's father was going to pay for spilling his guts to Gran.

Rick knew before he even answered the door that it would be Eileen. When he'd gone to see Maggie after work, he'd realized that he was setting himself up for a hell of a fight with Eileen. But even being prepared, he was taken aback by the dangerous glint in her eyes as she glared at him before stomping past him into the living room. She stood in the middle of the lamplit room, the night beyond the windows black and empty.

As empty as he'd felt since the moment she'd walked out of the office. Out of his world.

"That was low, Hawkins," Eileen said as she whirled around, strawberry ponytail flying to smack her across the eyes. "Going to Gran was really low."

"Yeah, I know." He closed the door and walked into the room, hands stuffed into his pants pockets so he wouldn't be tempted to reach out and grab her. "Desperate times…"

"You fight dirty," she snapped, interrupting him. "I'll have to remember that."

"You left me no choice." He'd have used whatever weapons he had at his disposal to convince her.

He couldn't let this go. Couldn't walk away and pretend everything was fine.

"But going to Gran? I wouldn't have thought you'd—" she said, letting her gaze sweep the sterile room. He looked at it through her eyes and watched her note the plain, unadorned furniture. The barren walls, lack of anything even remotely homey. "This place is awful."

"Yes, I went to your grandmother—and the place isn't that bad."

"The decorator ought to be shot."

"There was no decorator."

"*You* did this?" She turned in a half circle, and he watched her, as she shook her head in disbelief. "It's like a hotel room—no wait. Hotel rooms have color." She looked at him again. "You're taking this little gray world of yours *way* too far."

"I'm not here a lot."

"Good thing. You'd stick your head in the oven."

"It's electric."

"Probably safer that way." She shook her head again and then got back on track. "Anyway, the point is, I'm not going to marry you just because you sicced Gran on me."

"Damn it, Eileen," he said, stalking closer, unable to keep his distance, or his temper. "I don't want my child born a bastard."

She flinched and pulled her head back to stare at him openmouthed. "That's an ugly word. And an outdated one."

He barked a laugh that scraped his throat and tore at his heart. "It's so easy for someone like you."

"What?"

"Your grandmother raised you and Bridget. But your parents were married. They loved you guys. The only reason you didn't grow up with them is because they died."

Eileen blanched a little at the old yet still painful memory.

"Your parents loved you two. They were *married.* Committed to each other and their children." Rick, on the other hand, knew just how cruel other children could be. "You don't know. That word's not so outdated," he muttered, his hands fisting in his pockets.

Her voice dropped too, as she said, "Our child will be fine. Loved. It won't matter—"

His gaze snapped to hers. "It'll matter to *me,*" he ground out. "And trust me, it'll matter to him, when kids start calling him names."

"They won't."

"They will." Staring into her eyes, he swallowed a hard knot of bitterness choking his throat. "You don't know what that's like, Eileen. But I do. I remember. And I won't let a child of mine experience the same damn thing."

"Rick—"

"Being married to me wouldn't be so bad," he said, rushing to convince her. Hell, he was a rich man. He could give her whatever she wanted. "I could help you expand your flower shop..."

"I don't need—"

"You were talking about that wedding job you
got earlier—" he said, warming to his theme now.
If he couldn't get her to marry him for the child's
sake, maybe she'd marry him if he could show her
what he could do for her. Hell, Allison had married
him for his money. Why not Eileen?

But no. Eileen was nothing like Allison. She
wouldn't care if he was broke or a gazillionaire. She
was smart and funny and so damn independent she
didn't *need* him at all. Money wouldn't convince
her. But maybe he could talk her into marrying him
just for the sake of their child. Of course, he knew
she wouldn't stay with him. She'd never stay. Not
forever. But before she left, they could be married
and give their child a name. Protect it from the hurts
other kids could, and would, deliver. "I could help
there, too. Finance you and you could go into the
wedding planner business. You'd be good at it."

"Rick," she said on a sigh, "I like my business
just the way it is."

He kept talking though, pointing out all the ways
that being married would be a good thing. Which
wasn't easy, since he'd hardly had a stellar experience with it himself.

Eileen listened, but more importantly, she *heard*
him. He was talking so fast, she was pretty sure even
he wasn't sure of everything he was saying. But she
understood. It wasn't *just* the baby motivating him.
It was more. She knew why he was so determined
to marry her. Whether he knew it or not, he did care

for her. Oh, he'd never admit it, but he did. It was there in his eyes. Along with the fear that she was slipping away from him.

As had everyone else in his life.

Except for the grandmother who'd raised him, no one he'd cared about had ever stayed.

His parents.

His ex-wife.

Now he was sure *she* was leaving, too.

So he was protecting himself and his child the only way he knew how. Her heart ached for him as understanding dawned and a million thoughts careened through her mind at once. Maybe Gran was right, she thought. Maybe she *did* love him. If she didn't, she could marry him with a clear conscience—make it a sort of business deal.

But since she *did* care, she *couldn't* marry him? Okay, next stop…therapy. She was getting too confused. He wasn't offering her love, because he didn't believe in it. He wasn't offering to be with her always because he believed she wouldn't stay.

So all she could do now, she told herself, was say yes. Because the only way she could convince him that she would stay was by marrying him and proving it to him. The only way he would allow himself to love her was if she could show him that it was safe.

One of them had to take a chance.

And it looked as if it was going to be her.

"Okay," she said, cutting into his speech.

"Okay?" He looked at her, suspicion in his eyes.

Clearly this wasn't going to be easy. But with the decision made, Eileen suddenly knew it was exactly the right thing to do.

"I'll marry you," she said. "On one condition."

Wary, he asked, "What?"

"That it's a *real* marriage. In every way."

He pulled his hands from his pockets and reached for her. Dropping both hands onto her shoulders, he looked down into her eyes and nodded. "A real marriage. For as long as it lasts."

"Well, there's that optimistic outlook again," she said as his arms came around her. Eileen laid her head on his chest, closed her eyes and hoped to hell she was doing the right thing.

The wedding itself was short and sweet. What it lacked in magic, it more than made up for in kitsch.

Plastic ribbons dotted the "pews" and elevator music streamed from the overhead speakers. Happy couples were lined up in the lobby, waiting their turn at the "altar"—a silk-flower-bedecked wicker arch at the end of a narrow red-carpeted aisle. The minister was short and round, with wire-rimmed glasses and a long white beard. Actually, he could have passed for Santa, except for his Hawaiian shirt, faded jeans and sandals.

Both grandmothers were there along with Bridie and her husband. They'd left all three kids with his mother so they could enjoy a long weekend alone in Las Vegas.

Everything was as it should be. Until "Santa"

asked, "Do you take this man to be your lawfully wedded husband?"

Eileen experienced a moment of sheer, undiluted panic. Everything inside her was screaming for her to rethink this situation. It was only two weeks since Rick's hasty proposal and she was sure they were rushing blindly into something that had every possibility of ripping their bleeding hearts from their chests and stomping them into the ground.

She swallowed hard and glanced over her shoulder at her family. Gran, calm and regal as always, looking confused in her dark blue suit with a flashing silver pin on the lapel. Bridie, her red hair shining in the overhead lights, clung to her husband's arm and made wild gestures with her eyes, as if telling Eileen to say *something*. Rick's grandmother, one long, silver braid laying across her right shoulder, chanted quietly.

"Eileen…" Gran whispered the word loudly, as if trying to snap Eileen out of a trance.

"Is everything all right?" Rick's grandmother's hushed stage whisper carried over the numbingly generic music.

All right? Eileen thought. Probably not. She had the distinct feeling that this wedding was going to create more problems than it solved. So what was she doing here?

Eileen looked at the minister, then shifted her gaze to Rick. Her stomach did a slow roller-coaster ride. One look from him turned her insides to jelly and stole her breath. His dark brown eyes met hers, and she saw a mixture of sorrow and acceptance glimmering in their depths. He *expected* her to back out. He was already prepared for her to change her mind and walk away. Heck, a part of him was *waiting* for her to leave him standing alone at the altar.

And that, more than anything, convinced her that she was doing the right thing. "I do," she said.

A flicker of surprise lit his eyes as he slipped a four-karat stone, deep set into a platinum band, onto her finger. Eileen blew out a long breath as she experienced the weight of that ring on her hand. Promises she'd never thought she'd make echoed over and over in her mind. She tried to figure out how a temporary job had slowly worked into a lifetime commitment—and she wondered if it had been *meant* to work out this way. Was she, all those years ago, when Rick Hawkins had been teasing her and cutting off Barbie's head, already destined to reach this day? Had she always been meant to find a future with Rick? Or was it all just a quirk of fate?

She watched the play of light across the surface of the diamond while the minister droned on. And silently she promised the child within her to make this marriage work. To find a way to convince Rick Hawkins that she loved him.

The world went suddenly still.

It was as if time stopped.

She *did* love him.

It wasn't affection. It wasn't just caring.

She was in love. For the first time in her life. With a man who was convinced she already had one foot out the door.

Ten

Time started up again when the minister said, "You can kiss her now, son."

Rick turned her face up to his and lowered his head until they were nose to nose. She held her breath and felt the soft brush of his on her cheeks. Unexpectedly, tears rose up behind her eyes and she blinked frantically to keep them at bay.

While the music played and their families applauded, he whispered, in a voice low enough that only she could hear, "Thanks for this, Eyeball," just before he kissed her.

The moment his lips touched hers, Eileen's heart quickened. Here was magic. Here was thunder and lightning and a rush of blood that made her head swim. Love swelled inside her and she reached up, wrapping her arms around his neck. The warm, solid strength of him pressed against her, felt good... right. She gave herself up to the kiss that seared her soul and stirred up longings for more. Eileen wanted his love. Not just his name. Not just his child.

She wanted him to love her.

To believe in the life they could build together.

And she knew she was in for the fight of her life.

Ignoring their audience and the cluster of couples waiting to be married, Rick took his time about kissing her. He parted her lips with his tongue and she melted into him, savoring the flash of fireworks in her bloodstream and the thundering pound of her heartbeat. Clinging to him, she gave him all that she had, pouring her heart and soul into the kiss—hoping he would feel it, sense it, and know that she wouldn't leave him. Ever.

"Okay folks," the minister said gruffly. "I've got five more couples to marry before dinner, so let's move it along, huh?"

Rick broke the kiss, lifting his head to stare down at her. And just for a minute, Eileen saw something in his eyes that made her feel better about this wedding.

While she accepted congratulations and hugs from her grandmother and sister, she clung to the *hope* she'd read in his eyes and told herself that it was, at least, a start.

At night, Las Vegas sparkled like a black bowl full of precious gems. Ruby, emerald, sapphire and diamond lights lit the darkness until it was as bright as day, yet still disguised the city in a cloak of beauty.

Tourists streamed up and down the sidewalks as traffic stalled on the strip. On one street, you could find the Eiffel Tower, downtown New York and a slice of Italy. You could visit the pyramids, Medieval Europe and the Caesars of Rome. All along the street, crowds of people moved in a hurry, clutching plastic buckets filled with quarters and nickels and what was left of their dreams. Would-be millionaires stepped off curbs into traffic, following the lure of the next casino.

But the view from a penthouse suite was all lights and glory.

Eileen turned away from the window and faced Rick as he closed the door behind the room service waiter. Now that they were alone, their families off and playing somewhere in Sin City, the silence was nearly deafening.

"Hungry?" he asked, lifting the silver dome off one of the plates on the rolling tray.

She hugged herself, rubbing her hands up and down her upper arms. "Not really."

He set the dome back. "Me, neither." Instead, he grabbed a bottle from its silver ice-filled bucket and twisted the wires around its neck. "We'll have some of this instead."

"I probably shouldn't have any." Too bad, she thought, because if there was ever a time when she really wanted a drink, it was now.

"No problem," he said, tearing the wire cage off and tossing it onto the cart. "It's sparkling cider."

Eileen laughed shortly. She shouldn't have been surprised. Of course Rick would remember that she shouldn't have wine—and being him, Mr. Organization, naturally he'd arrange for something appropriate. Warmth trickled through her. "Cider?"

He shrugged. "How bad can it be?"

"Guess we'll find out." While he took care of the bottle, she shifted her gaze to the room. It was huge. A one-bedroom suite with a gigantic living room, it perched on the thirtieth floor of the Sandalwood hotel. Twin sofas sat facing each other, with a wide, low table boasting an arrangement of fresh, fragrant roses in between. A gas fireplace, flames dancing on the faux hearth, was on one wall and a wide entertainment system on the other. A bank of floor-to-ceiling windows opened onto the night and even this high up, the lights from the city below stained the room with a soft glow, making lamplight unnecessary.

Eileen shifted her gaze to the door on the far wall, through which lay the bedroom, where the king-size bed had already been turned down for them by the maid. Her stomach skittered as the image of Rick and her rolling across that wide mattress rose up in her mind. Silly really, but she was nervous. Rick had seen and explored every inch of her body already, so there was no reason for her to be a shy bride, but apparently logic had little to do with how she was feeling.

The cork popped, bounced off the ceiling and
landed on one of the couches and Eileen jumped,
startled. Slapping one hand to her chest, she blew
out a breath and told herself to get a grip. But in
another minute or two, Rick was walking toward
her, carrying two crystal flutes, filled with the sparkling cider. And just like that, her heart jumped
again.

Handing her one of the glasses, he touched his to
hers with a quiet *clink* and said, "Here's to us."

She stared up into his eyes and wished he'd meant
that. Wished he'd believed that this was the beginning for them instead of the beginning of the end.
She wished he could believe that they could build a
family. That with love, anything was possible. But
all she could hope for was that he'd learn. That
she'd be able to convince him that a future was possible. That it was safe to love her.

But Rome hadn't been built in a day, so she
would take it slow and try not to lose patience.
Though she had the distinct impression that Rick
was going to be a lot tougher work than any old
Romans had ever had to deal with.

"Right. To us." She nodded and took a long
drink, letting the fizzy cider slide down her throat.
Her gaze locked on the simple gold band she'd
placed on his finger and in the pit of her stomach,
worry fizzed along with the cider.

Rick watched the flashing change of emotions
charging across the surface of her eyes. And not for

the first time since she'd walked back into his life, he wondered what the hell she was thinking. Was she already regretting agreeing to this? Was she already mentally packing her bags?

And why did it matter?

They were married now. His child was protected. No one could ever call him a bastard. Even if Eileen walked out on him tonight, the marriage certificate would be a shield for his child.

But damn it, he didn't want her to leave.

Just the thought of Eileen walking out of his life was enough to open up a black hole of emptiness inside him. When Allison had left him, Rick had survived. She'd hurt him. Disappointed him. But she'd left his heart intact.

When Eileen left, she would take his heart with her.

But for now, she was here and she was his wife. And tonight, was their wedding night.

Taking her glass from her, he set them both aside on a nearby table. Then turning back to her, he cupped her cheek in his palm and asked, "Did I tell you how beautiful you looked today?"

One corner of her mouth lifted. "I don't think so."

"You do," he said, and let his gaze slide down and back up her body, appreciating her beauty now as much as he had when she'd first entered the chapel. The lemon-yellow dress she wore looked like sunshine. Bright and warm, the fabric fell into a full skirt that stopped just above her knees and swirled around her with every step. The neckline was wide, displaying her collarbones and the fine column of her throat to perfection. He'd taken one look at her and felt a flash of something red-hot surge through him. She tossed her head, sending that gorgeous hair of hers into a rippling arc around her head and he'd wanted to go out and find a dragon to slay for her.

As she walked up that short aisle toward him, Rick had told himself to enjoy the sight of her, the picture she made. The anticipation and joy in her face, despite her obvious reservations. He told himself to carve this memory and any others they might make, deeply into his brain, so that they'd always be there, just a dream away.

She smiled at their families as she moved to join him and, when she took her place beside him, an unexpectedly sharp, sweet sting of regret shot through him. Regret that this moment couldn't last.

Already Rick knew that this marriage would end, so it was hard to hold on to any rays of hope, no matter how tempting. Hadn't he been crushed by misplaced hopes before? Hadn't he decided long ago to not be led down the path of impossible dreams?

And yet, when he slipped his ring onto her finger, he realized sadly that he was closer than he'd ever been to *real* love.

But it was too tenuous to hold on to and he could already feel it slipping through his fingers.

She was going to leave.

If not today, then soon. So he couldn't allow himself the luxury of loving her.

But he could give in to the desire raging through him. The need to touch, to caress, to claim.

His thumb moved over her mouth, and his body tightened. Mind racing, pulse pounding, breath staggering from his lungs, Rick watched as her eyes closed and she turned her head into his caress. His fingers touched her smooth, soft skin. In the reflected light of the neon world thirty stories below them, her flesh looked like golden honey and he hungered for her as if it had been years rather than weeks since he'd last touched her.

"I need you," he said softly, not really sure if he'd spoken the words aloud—because they were repeating over and over inside his mind, like a tape stuck in permanent rewind.

"I need you, too," she said, and moved into him, pressing her body along his, inflaming them both.

"Now." Rick took her face between his palms, letting his fingers spear through her long, loose hair at her temples, and the red-gold strands lay across his skin like cool silk.

He kissed her, taking her mouth, plundering her warmth and drawing it deep inside him, where the cold still lurked in the dark corners of his heart. He held her, pressing her tightly to him, as if he could pull her into his body, making her a part of him.

She moved in even closer, as if sensing his need and sharing it. She cupped the back of his head in her palm and kissed him back, showing him her hunger, her need, and Rick reveled in it. Her hands slid across his back, stroking, caressing and all he could think was that there were too many clothes in the way of claiming her.

Reaching behind her, he undid the zipper of her dress and as the fabric spilled away, his fingertips wandered down her spine. She wore no bra and her panties were nothing more than a tiny piece of elastic with a scrap of lace attached. In seconds, they were gone, the elastic snapped in his eagerness to touch her. To hold her. To claim her one more time. To feel all of the things he'd only discovered in her arms.

''Rick—'' She broke the kiss with a gasp and breathed his name in soft exhale of breath that staggered him. Then she scooped her hands around to his chest and pushed his suit jacket down and off. Her fingers tore at the buttons of his shirt and he stepped back to help her, because she was taking too long and he needed to feel her skin flush with his. Shared heat, soft to hard, smooth to rough.

Yanking his shirt off, he laughed when she grinned, and a flash of something warm and hot and desperately dangerous pushed through him. She was more, so much more than great sex. So much more than the woman who carried his child. She was light and heat and smiles and laughter. She was everything he'd always dreamed of and everything he knew he couldn't have. And he wanted her more desperately than he'd ever wanted anything in his life.

He tore off the rest of his clothes, then grabbed her close again, sliding his hands up and down her body, pressing her tightly to him. ''You feel so good,'' he murmured as he dipped his head to kiss the curve of her shoulder.

Her head fell back, exposing her throat, and she

said on a sigh, "You feel wonderful against me, Rick. I love it. I love how you kiss me." She lifted her head and met his gaze. Running her tongue across her bottom lip, she admitted, "I love how you feel inside me. I love what you make *me* feel."

His blood roared in his ears. Heart pounding against his chest, he couldn't breathe and didn't care. She was all that mattered. The next touch. The next kiss. The next taste of her.

He was hard and ready and wasn't willing to wait another second for her. Dragging her down to the lush carpet in front of the wide windows overlooking the strip, Rick scraped his hands up and down her body. He kissed her, plunging her depths, tasting, caressing, exploring her secrets and taking all she had to give.

Eileen held on tightly and met his tongue stroke for stroke. As his hands fired her blood and scorched her body, she planted her feet on the thick, soft carpet and lifted her hips in a silent plea. She wanted him within her. Needed to feel him fill her.

His hand swept down and cupped her and she groaned tightly, as tiny ripples of expectation shimmered through her. "Yes," she whispered, sliding her hands across his chest, smoothing, stroking. "Touch me, Rick. Touch me."

"Always," he murmured, and then he did. Dipping first one finger and then two into her depths, he stroked her, setting a rhythm that tantalized her even as he reached deeper and touched her soul. She felt the connection and hoped he felt it, too. Hoped he knew that she was giving him all that she was. Hoped he could believe in her.

And then her thoughts splintered as his thumb stroked her most sensitive spot. "Rick, I...need..."

"I know, baby," he whispered, his breath dusting warm across her face. "I know."

"Be in me," she said, and locked her gaze with his. "I need you to be inside me."

His jaw tightened, but he shifted, moving to cover her body with his and in seconds he was within her, claiming her, taking her higher, faster, than she'd ever been before. She moved with him, rocking her hips, finding the rhythm he set and she stared up into his eyes as the first explosion shuddered through her. Eileen called his name and held him tightly as she rode the wild wave of sensation cresting within. Moments later, he joined her and together they drifted slowly back to solid ground.

When the world stopped spinning and she thought she could gather enough breath to speak, Eileen said softly, "Happy wedding, Rick."

He lifted his head to stare down at her. "Same to you."

And if a small corner of her heart ached because she was in love with a man who would never believe that, she didn't let him know it.

Eleven

One month later, Eileen still wasn't sure if she'd done the right thing or not. Oh, she was married. She had pictures of the event to prove it.

She just wished she *felt* married.

But that wasn't easy when your brand-new husband insisted on treating you like a temporary roommate. A roommate he had great, amazing, mindboggling sex with, of course. But still, there was no closeness out of their bed. He was hardly ever at home, spending most of his days—even the weekends at his office. And she couldn't even see him there, since the temp agency had, true to their promise, sent a substitute secretary until Margo returned. Between Eileen's work at Larkspur and his hours at the office, the only time they ever saw each other was in bed. And once the sex was finished, he went to sleep, turning from her even as he prepared for her to leave him. There was no late-night cuddling and whispered conversations about the future. How could there be, she asked herself, if he didn't think they were going to *have* a future?

Eileen had tried to remain cheerful. She'd been right there, every day. Trying to prove to him that she wasn't leaving. But she could see it in his eyes that he didn't—or couldn't—trust her to stay.

"How's the new house coming?"

"What?"

"Hello?" Bridie grinned and grabbed a cookie for herself.

The scent of cinnamon sugar filled Bridie's kitchen and felt cozy and warm. As November drifted into December, the weather was cold and dreary, but being here, Eileen thought, really helped dispel the chill she carried inside her.

"Your new house," Bridie prodded. "How's it coming?"

The new house. Another sore spot. Eileen frowned. Rick had bought the huge Spanish-style house on a bluff overlooking Pacific Coast Highway without even consulting her. He said he'd wanted to surprise her. But the plain truth was, she thought, he was just trying to give her a gilded cage. By buying her a big house, he'd hoped to keep her there. To give her something she couldn't have gotten for herself.

But the house wasn't a home. It wasn't cozy and

small like her old cottage. It was empty and sterile and, so far, not exactly the land where dreams were made. She rattled around in the big place by herself more often than not and couldn't even convince him to help her pick out furniture.

"It's not," she finally said, blurting out the truth, before she could talk herself out of it.

"What do you mean?"

Eileen grabbed one of her sister's homemade snickerdoodle cookies and leaned back in her chair. "I mean, we don't even have any furniture. It looks like a warehouse. The few pieces I brought with me from the cottage hardly fill up a corner of it."

"For Pete's sake, Eileen. Take some time off work and furnish the place."

She crumbled the cookie slowly, watching each crumb drop to the table and bounce. "I don't want to do it alone, Bridie. It's *our* house. Or supposed to be. He should be a part of it."

"But..."

"But..." Eileen wanted to unload on her sister. God knows, she needed to talk to someone about this. But at the same time, she felt almost disloyal talking about Rick behind his back. Damn the man, couldn't he see that she loved him? Couldn't he see that he was pushing her away by not reaching out to her? Did he care?

As if sensing Eileen needed a change of subject, Bridie shifted gears. "I still can't believe you're married to my old boyfriend."

Eileen was grateful. She didn't want to think about her troubles right now. For this one moment, she wanted to enjoy being in her sister's happy home. This was what it should be like, she thought. This was how she and Rick should be living. With clutter and laughter and the sound of kids in the background. Instead, she had emptiness and silence.

Leaning forward, Eileen grabbed another cookie and this time she took a bite. "Gee thanks. What does that make Rick, the ultimate hand-me-down?"

Bridie's big blue eyes rolled. "Oh please. Let's see, he broke up with me in senior year of high school, so I'm thinking...*no*."

"That's right," Eileen said, straightening in her chair as memories drifted through her mind like stray clouds across the sky. While her brain worked, her gaze shifted, scanning her sister's tidy blue-and-white kitchen as if looking for something. Idly she noted the kids' drawings stuck to the refrigerator doors, the small fingerprints left on the sliding glass door leading to the screened-in patio and crayons and coloring books scattered over the freshly waxed floor.

But she wasn't really seeing any of it. Instead, she was reaching back in her memory and discovering something she'd long forgotten. "You didn't break up with him, did you? *He* left you."

"Yeah," Bridie said. "And just before homecoming, too, the rat." Grinning, she added, "Lucky for him, I've decided to be a good sport and forgive him."

Excited, Eileen shook her head and leaned forward, bracing her arms on the polished oak table. "No, don't you get it? He broke up with you *before* you could break up with him."

Confusion filled her sister's eyes. "And this means…what, exactly?"

Eileen opened her mouth to speak but was cut off when a red-haired toddler burst into the room, tears streaking her tiny face.

"Mommy, Mommy," three-year-old Becky ran across the floor and slammed into her mother's right knee. "Jason won't let me fly with him."

"Honey, Jason can't fly. He—" Bridie's eyes widened as she jumped up. *"Fly?"* Already headed out to the backyard, she shouted, "Be back in a minute," and rushed out of the room.

Becky climbed up onto Eileen's lap, stole a cookie and leaned back against her. "Boys are dumb," she said around a bite of cookie.

Eileen stroked her niece's soft-as-silk hair and kissed the top of her head. "I'll remind you of that in about ten years."

But the little girl wasn't paying attention. She'd already slid off her aunt's lap and stretched out onto the floor, grabbing up her favorite purple crayon. While she watched her niece, Eileen smiled to herself, patted her abdomen and whispered, "No flying for you unless we're on a plane, deal?"

Then her smile slowly faded as thoughts of Rick poured back into her mind. Years ago, he'd broken up with Bridie to avoid having her break up with him. And Eileen had to wonder if his first marriage hadn't ended because he'd held back from Allison, too. Just as he was doing now, with her.

Oh, he hadn't actually *left* her. But he might as well have. He was hardly ever home—in that cavernous, impersonal house he'd bought for her. He kept himself at an emotional distance. He wouldn't be drawn into conversations. He didn't even want to talk about the baby or make plans, as if he already knew he wouldn't be a part of any plans Eileen might make.

He cared for her, she could see it in his eyes. He still turned to her at night, drawing her to him, giving her his body but not his heart. But otherwise, he moved like a ghost through her life.

There, but not connected.

Present, but not a part of anything.

Physically there, but emotionally distant.

He kept walls up around his heart in an attempt to protect it. But he didn't even realize that in building the walls, he was shutting love out, never letting it in. He was already cutting her out of his life so that when she left, he wouldn't be hurt.

And she didn't know if she could find a way past his defenses.

Two days later, nothing had changed and Eileen's legendary impatience was near implosion point. And she simply couldn't wait one more day to have her say. Waiting, trying her limited store of patience, wasn't helping. Maybe nothing would, a quiet, sad voice whispered in the back of her mind.

But she had to try.

And since he was leaving for a four day business trip to San Francisco, it was now…or wait some more.

She chose *now*.

Eileen was dressed and waiting in the kitchen when Rick came downstairs. She heard him long before she saw him, since his footsteps on the uncarpeted oak staircase echoed in the stillness.

The whole house was like an echo chamber. Wide front windows with a view of the ocean. Empty rooms. Unadorned floors. Nothing on the walls.

It felt abandoned.

She'd stewed about this for two days. Her dreams had been filled with it. And now it was time to make a stand. It was time to force Rick to talk to her. To make him see and admit, at least to himself, that he was shutting her out.

He came around the corner from the living room and stopped dead when he saw her. He wore a dark blue suit, pristine white shirt and a bloodred tie. His aftershave, a spicy mixture, drifted to her from across the room and she had to take a deep, calming breath to keep from rushing at him, throwing herself into his arms.

She knew he'd welcome her embrace.

There was nothing wrong with the physical side of their relationship, except for the fact that that was all they had going for them at the moment.

He set his garment bag down in the doorway, then shoved his hands into his pants pockets. "I thought you were going into the shop early today."

At least he listened to her when she talked. That was something.

"I called Paula," Eileen said. "She's going in to accept the deliveries." She took a long sip of her coffee, swallowed it, then set her cup on the counter. "I asked her to help me this morning, because I needed a few minutes with you before you left. We have to talk."

As if someone had hit a light switch, she actually *saw* those now-familiar shutters slam down over his eyes. He didn't have to physically back up for her to see him put more distance between them. "Can't," he said shortly. Checking his gold wristwatch briefly, he looked back at her. "Have to leave to catch my flight and—"

She interrupted his flow of excuses. They weren't good enough anymore, and she wouldn't let them stop her. "Rick, you can't just ignore me."

He walked past her toward the coffee pot. Pouring himself a half a cup, he glanced at her. "Nobody's ignoring you, Eileen."

He was so close his aftershave seemed to surround her. And yet, he was further away from her than ever. "Okay, poor choice of words." She reached up and tightened her ponytail before dropping her hands to the edge of the cold, gray—yes, *gray,* God, was everything in his world gray?—

granite counter. Steeling herself, she blurted, "You're not ignoring me. You're placating me."

"What?"

At least she had his attention. She swallowed hard. Now all she had to do was keep it. "This house for instance."

He took a drink. "I thought you liked the house."

"I do, but that's not the point."

He took another sip of his coffee and looked at her over the rim of the cup. "Then tell me what is."

Eileen just stared at him for a couple of heartbeats. Was he really that obtuse? "You bought this place without even telling me."

He stiffened slightly. "We already went over this. I wanted to surprise you."

Yeah, they'd gone over it. When she'd freaked out over his buying a house on a hill in Laguna as casually as most men bought a new shirt. She'd been bowled over by the beauty of it and hurt by the fact that he hadn't even included her in the decision to buy it. But it was hard to *stay* mad at a man for buying you a darn mansion. Even if she did miss the coziness of her cottage. "Congrats. It worked."

A muscle in his jaw twitched. "What're you getting at, Eyeball?"

The use of her old nickname should have warmed her. It didn't. It was simply something he tossed her, like throwing a hungry dog a meatless bone. He used it to pretend they were close. To somehow assure himself that everything was fine. It wasn't. She sighed, tipped her head back and looked him squarely in the eye. "We have to talk."

Rick's stomach fisted.

Every muscle in his body tightened as if waiting for a blow. He'd been expecting this. But even he was a little surprised that this moment had arrived only one short month after their wedding.

Watching her, his heart turned over. Her red-gold hair, in the ponytail she wore when she was going to work at her flower shop, swung like a metronome behind her head, ticking off her movements. It bounced when she walked and seemed to swing even harder when she was mad. It was a soft, shining indicator of her moods. And he loved the way it moved with her. She wore jeans and an old sweatshirt with a faded Santa lying in a recliner emblazoned across the front.

Everything about Eileen got to him.

Living with her, being with her all the time had been both heaven and hell. Hearing her voice in the darkness, having her no more than an arm's reach away during the long nights was more happiness than he'd ever known. She sang—badly—in the shower, cried at television commercials and thrived on the most appalling fast-food diet he'd ever seen. When happy, she laughed with a wholeheartedness that made him envy her joy. She'd stormed back into his life and turned it all upside down.

And realizing it was all going to end, knowing that she'd never stay, haunted him day and night.

He wanted to enjoy what time they might have

together, but every instinct kept urging him to pull back. To keep his heart distant. Safe. She smiled and he hungered for more. She sighed and turned into him in her sleep and his soul ached.

But if nothing else, her lack of interest in their home was the clincher for him. Eileen was a nester. Yet she hadn't done a damn thing in, or to, the house. No pictures on the walls, no pillows, no plants. Not even a bunch of flowers graced the sterile rooms. The monstrous house was exactly the opposite of her cozy cottage. She'd made it pretty clear that she considered this place a stopgap measure on her way to other things.

But if it was all going to end now, then he'd rather it was a clean break. He couldn't imagine a life now without her in it—didn't want to try—but if she was going, he thought, *go now*.

Before her leaving would kill him.

"Fine," he said, taking a deep gulp of coffee, letting the hot liquid burn his throat. That searing pain could at least distract him from the sound of his own heart breaking. "Talk."

"Wow." A breath shot from her lungs. "Feel the warmth."

His back teeth ground together. "Eileen…"

She held up one hand to silence him. "Are you my husband?"

"Excuse me?" Not the opener he was expecting.

"My husband," she repeated, and just for good measure, grabbed one of his hands and moved her fingers wildly in his palm as if using sign language to communicate. "Are you my husband, or are you just a close personal friend and a snuggling room-mate?"

He pulled his hand free of hers, then, with his hand at his side, he rubbed his fingers together, just to savor the warmth of her touch. "Where are you going with this?"

"No, the real question," she said, "is where have you been? Where are you now?"

Rick pushed away from the counter, needing to be mobile. "I'm standing right here. Being in-sulted."

Her face brightened, but there was no humor in her eyes. A sure sign that things were about to get rough. "Then this is an occasion! It's the first time you've been here. With *me*. Since we got married."

Okay, he wasn't going to take that. He was here. Day and night. He knew, because he'd gotten used to living with tension as white-hot as a live electrical wire. "What're you talking about? We both live here."

"No," she countered with a slow shake of her head that sent her ponytail into a wide wave. "*I* live here. You just haunt the place."

Stalking past him, she crossed the kitchen floor, her heels clacking on the terra-cotta tile. That po-nytail swung back and forth furiously and, despite the anger churning in the room, Rick couldn't keep his gaze off it. When she whirled around to face him, the emotion in her eyes tore at him.

Then she spoke and for a minute he was lost.

"You broke up with Bridie."

He stared at her for a long moment, then shook his head as if to clear it. How'd they get from talking about *them* to talking about his breakup with her sister more than ten years ago? *"What?"*

"My sister. Bridget."

"I *know* who Bridie is," he snapped. "What I don't get, is what the hell you're talking about."

"You really don't, do you?" she asked, anger sliding from her as easily as rainwater rolling down a glass window pane.

"Enlighten me."

"Gladly." She planted both hands at her hips and met his glare without flinching. "Your senior year, you broke up with Bridie right before homecoming."

"And this is important…why?"

She smiled, but it was a sad, small twist of her lips that tugged at his heart. "God, Rick. You were doing it back then too, and you still don't realize it."

There was only so much psychoanalyzing he was willing to put up with. "I don't know what you're talking about," he said, walking to the sink to set his coffee cup down on the shining, cold stainless steel.

"You broke up with Bridie to keep *her* from breaking up with *you*."

Something pinged inside him. Recognition?

No.

"I broke up with Bridie because I couldn't afford a girlfriend."

"No, you couldn't," she said, her voice a low, strained whisper. "Just like you can't *afford* a wife, now."

He snapped her a look, then slowly turned to face her. "You've got me all figured out," he said quietly. "Let's hear it."

"Okay." She shoved her hands into her jeans pockets and rocked back and forth, her tennis shoes squeaking on the clean tiles. "You were afraid of caring too much for Bridie, so you broke up with her." Just like now, you're terrified to love me, so you pretend I'm not here."

"That's it." That was a little too close to home. His insides twisted into knots and his heart ached as though a giant fist was squeezing it. Rick held up both hands. "I don't have time for this. We'll talk when I get back from San Francisco."

She stepped in front of him when he crossed the room to pick up his garment bag. Pulling her hands free of her jeans, she slapped both palms against his chest to stop him. "No, we won't talk—because you *don't* talk."

"Yeah?" he countered, trying not to feel the warmth of her hands, spreading down, into the chill of his soul. "What do you call *this?* What we're doing now?"

She ignored that.

"This isn't right," she said. "It isn't enough."

"What's not enough?" he spoke up quickly,

fighting a losing battle yet unable to surrender just yet. "I married you. Committed to you."

"You won't even commit to a *couch,* Rick."

He reached up and scraped both hands through his hair. "I told you, buy the damn furniture. Get whatever you want. You have the credit cards, go crazy."

She gave him a shove that didn't budge him an inch, then dropped her hands and stepped back. "Don't you get it? This is supposed to be *our* house. If I furnish it, it's *my* house. I want you *here,* Rick. I want this place—*me*—to matter."

"Damn it, Eileen, you *do* matter. You're carrying my child."

A short, harsh laugh shot from her throat as a single tear escaped her eye and rolled down her cheek. "This isn't about the baby. This is about *us.* Or the us we might have been."

Cold radiated from his heart and spilled throughout his bloodstream. He just managed to keep from shivering in reaction. "God. You're telling me we go from no furniture to divorce court?"

Sadly she shook her head and wiped away her tears with an impatient swipe of her hands. "The empty house is a metaphor. Don't you understand? Don't you see? *We're* empty, too, Rick. And we always will be until you let me in. But you won't do that, will you?"

He reached out to her, then let his hand drop to his side, his fingers curling tightly into a helpless fist. Holding her wasn't the answer, because he could never hold her tightly enough to keep her. Heart aching, breath strangling in his chest, Rick muttered thickly, ''Can we just talk about this when I get back?''

''Heck, why bother to come back, Rick? Why should *I* be here?'' She looked up into his eyes and Rick felt himself falling into those green depths and wanted, desperately, to let himself go. To give in to the need to be a part of her. To be held deep within her body, her heart. To finally find a place—a heart—he could call home. But pain was a good teacher and it held him tight in its grip. Memories flooded his brain, reminding him just what it was like to lose the very thing you valued most. And that reminder was enough to keep him from reaching for her, burying his face in the curve of her neck, inhaling the sweet, floral scent of her.

''This is an empty house, Rick,'' she said, her voice low and harsh, as though she were having to push each word past a throat clogged with emotion. ''And it'll always *be* empty because that's the way *you* want it.''

He flinched as if she'd struck him. But this blow was sharper, deeper than if she'd slapped his face. That would only have been physical. This cut him right down to his bones.

''You don't want to take a chance,'' she said, reaching around him to pluck her car keys off the counter. ''You *want* to shut yourself off until no one can reach you.'' Her gaze locked on him again and he read the sorrow written there. ''Well, that's safe,'' she said, ''but it's lonely as hell. Are you *trying* to be alone for the rest of your life?''

All Rick heard was her saying *Why should I be here?* She was leaving, then. Just as he'd known she would. It was over. And why did it hurt so much? Why was pain radiating through his body with strength enough to cripple him? He'd protected himself to prevent this much pain. He'd held back. Hadn't admitted even to himself just how much he cared.

And now he never would.

He'd never let himself think the word *love,* because knowing he'd loved her and lost her...would finish him off.

She turned then and headed for the front door.

Rick followed after her, listening to the sound of her footsteps pounding through the silence like a heartbeat frantically beating its last.

She had stepped through the front door and was halfway down the walk before he spoke.

''I *knew* you'd leave.''

Twelve

In her car, Eileen slapped the dashboard, completely disgusted with herself. "Damn it. I *did* leave!" She'd fallen right into his expectations. Done exactly what he'd believed from the first that she would do. She'd fulfilled his predictions, despite her intentions. "I can't believe it. What was I thinking?"

Naturally she didn't have an answer to her own idiocy. She reached up and scrubbed both hands over her face as if she could wipe away the memory of the last few minutes. "I walked out on him. Left him standing in that big, empty house all alone. Stupid, stupid, stupid."

Gran used to say that one day her impatience would get the better of her. Well, as much as it irked her to admit it, Gran had been right. She'd given in to her frustration, her fury and she couldn't take any of it back now. Even if she tried, he'd never believe her.

From now on, every time he looked at her, he'd see her walking away from him and he'd never stop waiting for it to happen again.

It didn't really matter whether she'd had reason enough to do it or not.

She shouldn't have walked out.

But as long as she had, she wouldn't go rushing back in all apologies and promises. She'd already made a promise to him. At their wedding. But he hadn't believed that one, so why would he believe one now?

No. She'd sit here a minute or two. Wait. See if he came after her. If he was willing to fight for her. For *them*.

Seconds crawled past and stretched into minutes and the only sound was her own breathing and the wind pushing at the car.

He wasn't coming.

And she couldn't go back inside.

Not now.

"For Pete's sake, Eileen," she snapped as she fired up the ignition and gave the house one last look. "You *married* him, hoping to teach him you *wouldn't* leave." She threw the Jeep into first gear. As she pulled out of the driveway and turned into the street, she muttered, "Nice job."

* * *

On the last night of his business trip, Rick was like a man possessed. He couldn't keep his mind on the job. Didn't have the patience to deal with crotchety clients only worried about the fluctuations in the market.

"What the hell does the market matter?" he groused as he flopped onto the hotel bed and reached for the phone. "Nothing matters," he said, answering his own question as he got an outside line and punched in the phone number to the big house in Laguna. "Nothing matters but Eileen."

He'd been gone four days. And wondering where she was. What she was doing. What she was thinking. Because he'd done a hell of a lot of thinking since she'd walked out the door that last morning.

She was right.

About everything.

He'd broken up with Bridie and others like her, over the years, to prevent *them* from breaking up with *him.* It was a pattern he hadn't even seen. It hadn't made sense then. Or now, for that matter. But he didn't want to make the same mistake again— not when, this time, there was so much more riding on it than a homecoming dance.

Over and over again, his brain had replayed the image of Eileen striding away from him. Again and again he heard the sound of her car's engine firing up.

He hadn't gone after her.

He'd stood there, stupidly watching her drive off.

Yet…in his dreams, it was different. In his

dreams, he'd chased after her. He'd caught her before she opened the car door. He'd pulled her into his arms and told her he loved her. Asked her to stay. Asked her to love him. To be with him. To never leave.

And in his dreams, she smiled.

And came back to him.

But dreams weren't reality and when he woke, he was in a hotel. Alone.

Across the room, the muted television flickered wildly, and light played in the shadows of his otherwise darkened hotel room.

He listened as the phone in the empty house on the bluff rang and rang and rang. She wasn't there. She'd left and she wasn't coming back. He could picture the empty house. The big rooms. The silence. And he knew that without Eileen in his life, no matter where he lived, he would be surrounded by emptiness. Silence would follow him through the years. He would watch his child grow up with the love of its mother and Rick would know, always, that he might have shared in it all. Might have been a part of something wonderful. Instead, he would be on the outside, as he'd always been, looking at love, wanting it, but never having it.

And always knowing that it could have been different, if he hadn't been too much of a coward to take a risk with his heart.

He hung up, setting the receiver back into its cradle. Then, looking into the mirror over the generically ugly dresser, he stared into his own eyes and

said, "So what're you gonna do about it, you idiot?"

No-brainer.

Hopping off the bed, he stalked to the closet,
snatched up his suitcase and started throwing things
into it. With any luck, he could catch an early flight
home. And if his luck was *very* good…he'd find
Eileen still willing to talk.

It was raining.

Her car was in the driveway.

Rick's heartbeat sputtered erratically as the wind-
shield wipers pushed at the sheet of water crashing
onto the car. He stared at a blurred image of her
jeep and told himself not to get his hopes up. He
hadn't expected to find her here. He'd thought he'd
have to track her down at Larkspur and somehow
force her to listen to him.

But this was better.

He should tell her here, in the place he'd wanted
them to call home.

Pulling in behind her, he parked his car, jumped
out and ran to the front door. By the time he hit the
front porch, he was drenched. He could hardly
breathe. Desperation fueled him. He knew now. He
could admit it now. When it was too late, he could
finally make himself say it and believe it. He loved
her. Completely. And this was perhaps his last
chance to convince her of that.

He unlocked the door and stepped into a strange
place.

Standing on the marble tiles in the foyer, Rick swiped his soaking wet hair off his forehead and out of his eyes. Quietly he closed the door behind him, without ever taking his gaze off the room in front of him.

Area rugs were sprinkled across the wide expanse of knotty pine flooring. Lamps stood on highly polished oak tables, sending puddles of golden light into the room, banishing the shadows. A fire burned in the wide, stone hearth, flames snapping and dancing across the wood stacked behind a black wrought-iron screen. Two floral-patterned sofas in a dark burgundy fabric sat facing each other, with a huge oak table supporting a bowl of fresh flowers between them.

Paintings, dozens of them, hung on the walls and under the wide front windows stood a multitiered plant stand boasting ferns and flowered plants that spilled onto the floor.

Rick held his breath, tears sheening his vision until he blinked them back and rubbed one hand across his mouth. He took one hesitant step into the room, almost afraid to move, lest it all be an hallucination that would dissolve on his moving.

But it remained.

All of it.

From the kitchen, the delicious scent of bubbling pasta sauce reached for him. His mouth watered. But it wasn't the promise of food delighting him.

It was the promise of so much more.

But where was Eileen?

He stopped to listen, straining to hear something that would lead him to her. And that's when he heard it. A radio, playing softly. Old Blue Eyes was crooning about a summer wind.

Leaving a trail of water in his wake, Rick headed for the stairs, and before he'd taken more than two steps he was running. He hit the first carpeted tread and, grinning, he grabbed the banister and kept running, taking the stairs two and three at a time.

In the long hall, he kept moving. Blood racing, heart pounding, head spinning. He glanced into rooms as he passed and where there was once just cavernous, empty places, there was now, a *home*. Fresh flowers everywhere, there was furniture and rugs and paintings and…everything he'd hoped for. Everything he'd ever wanted.

And following the sound of the music, he stopped at the threshold of the nursery and saw the woman who had given it all to him, despite his own stupidity. Her back to him, she swayed to the music and the crooner's smooth-as-silk voice. Rick's heartbeat steadied, but he felt that organ swell to the point of bursting as he looked around the room where his child would live. Clouds dotted the blue ceiling. A mural of a garden colored one wall and the white furniture was offset by the multicolored linens and the pillows tucked into a rocking chair just waiting for a mother and her child.

"You came back."

She stopped struggling to hang the picture of a mother bunny and looked over her shoulder at him.

"Boy, am I glad to see you," she said with a grin. "I need a tall person to hang this."

His throat closed and, instead of trying to speak, Rick walked across the room, took the picture from her and carefully hung it from the nail in the wall.

"There. Finished." She looked up at him. "Doesn't it look great?"

"Great doesn't even come close," he murmured, and grabbed her. "You're here. I can't believe you're here. God, Eileen. I need you so much. I—" Pulling her to him, he enfolded her in his arms and held on tight, just in case she might change her mind at the last minute and make a run for the door.

He couldn't hold her tightly enough. Couldn't feel her close enough. And he suspected he'd never be able to hold her tight enough to satisfy all of the hungers within him.

She hugged him, then pulled her head back to look up at him. "Surprised?"

Scooping one hand up to cup her cheek, Rick let his gaze move over her, assuring himself that she was real—and here—in his arms. "Oh, yeah."

"Good. Then my work here is done."

One brief flash of panic flared inside him. "Don't leave."

"What?"

"Don't leave, Eyeball. Don't ever leave me."

"I'm not going anywhere, Rick," she said, and her voice softened on the tears clouding her eyes. "I love you, you big dummy."

He laughed and it felt good. Everything felt good.

For days, he'd held his pain close. Nurturing it. Telling himself it was what it was. But now, as he looked into her eyes and saw the love shining there, he knew pain would never be able to touch him again.

"I love you," he said, and waited a beat for the words to register in her eyes. "I'm not afraid to say it anymore. But I was. God, Eileen. I thought I loved you too much."

She smiled up at him and his world straightened up and felt right again.

"There's never too much love."

"I think I know that now," he said. "But I just love you so much it terrified me to think of losing you. And God, then I almost chased you away."

She shook her head and held his face between her palms. "Not a chance, Rick. I'm not going anywhere."

"I know," he said, feeling years of cold drift away in the rush of warmth spilling into his soul. "I knew the minute I saw the house. What you'd done to it. And a part of me knew before. I was just too scared to believe." His hands moved up and down her arms, and back up to her face, her hair. He couldn't seem to touch her enough.

"I called here last night. I wanted to talk to you—needed to talk to you—but no one answered and I—"

She placed her fingers across his mouth. "They painted the nursery yesterday and the smell made me sick, so I stayed at Gran's."

"The nursery," he repeated, savoring the words. The images they painted. He and Eileen. Their child. And the others that would follow. He could see them now, moving through the years together.

And he thanked God for granting a fool one more chance at love.

Eileen lifted her arms to encircle his neck and, smiling up at him, she said softly, "Welcome home, Rick. Welcome home."

Then she kissed him and Rick knew that at last he'd finally found home. Here, with Eileen, his temporary secretary and forever love.

Epilogue

Five years later...

"**D**addy, where's mommy?"

"Shh," Rick whispered as his four-year-old son Ryan climbed up onto the couch beside him. "You'll wake the baby."

Ryan reached out one chubby hand to pat the infant asleep and sprawled across her daddy's chest. "Kerry's not sleepin'."

"She will be if we're quiet," Rick said, smoothing his son's hair back off his sweaty forehead. The little boy had been running all over the backyard with his puppy until the little dog lay in a crumpled heap of exhaustion on the rug. Ryan, however, was harder to exhaust. His other sister Katie, two years

old and a bigger handful than her older brother had
ever been, was, thankfully, fast asleep in her room
upstairs.

And if Rick could just get Ryan to lower his
voice, he had high hopes for getting Kerry down for
a nap, too. But at six months old, the baby was
determined to not miss a thing and rarely closed her
big green eyes.

In a stage whisper that could have been heard
from outside, Ryan leaned in and asked, "When's
Mommy comin' back?"

"In a while," Rick told him and felt love rush
into his heart for this child and the others he and
Eileen had been blessed with. He had so much now.
So very much. "She went shopping, remember?"

"To buy me somethin'?" Ryan flopped into
Rick's side and idly played with his sister's tiny
hand.

"Probably," Rick admitted, smiling. With Christmas right around the corner, Eileen had taken off
for some quality time at the mall with her sister. But
Rick didn't mind. There was just nothing he liked
better than being with his family.

"When's she comin', though?" Ryan tipped his
head back to look up at his daddy. "Are we worried?"

Rick leaned over and kissed the top of his dark
blond head. "No, we're not worried," he said, smiling. "Mommy's having fun with aunt Bridie."

Ryan nodded. "Cousin Jason says he's gonna
teach me to fly."

Rick rolled his eyes and made a mental note to talk to his nephew. "No flying for you, buddy. Okay?"

"'kay. When's Mommy comin'?"

Rick sighed and Kerry squirmed on his chest, lifted her head and gave him a drooly smile that tugged at his heart. "So much for nap time, huh?" he asked, laughing just as the sound of a car engine came to him. "Hey, bud. Mommy's home."

"Yay!" Ryan shrieked, jumped off the couch and clattered across the floor to the front door. Rick was just a step or two behind him, cradling his now wide-awake infant daughter in his arms.

He opened the door and watched Ryan race outside to greet his mother. It was enough for Rick to stand on the porch and watch that gorgeous redhead climb out of her Jeep and scoop her son up into her arms for a big kiss. In a splash of sunlight, she turned and grinned at him and Rick counted his blessings again.

"Hey," Eileen called out, "I need some help with these bags."

He nodded and walked down the steps to join her. Handing her the baby, Rick leaned in for a quick kiss.

"Miss me?" she teased, smoothing the baby's wispy red-gold hair back from her forehead.

"Always," he said.

"But we wasn't worried," Ryan chimed in.

"No?" she asked, still smiling.

"No," Ryan said with confidence, "cause my daddy says that Mommy's always come home."

Eileen's features softened and her mouth curved as Rick leaned in for another kiss. Their mouths met in a promise of more to come later.

Then, with his son tugging at his pants leg, Rick winked and said quietly, "Welcome home, Eyeball."

*   *   *   *   *

Cowboy Boss

KATHIE DeNOSKY

KATHIE DeNOSKY

lives in deep southern Illinois with her husband and three children. She is ecstatic about being able to share her stories with others. Highly sensual stories with a generous amount of humour, Kathie's books have appeared on the bestseller lists. She enjoys going to rodeos, travelling to research settings for her books and listening to country music. She often starts her day at 2:00 am so she can write without interruption, before the rest of the family is up and about. You may write to Kathie at PO Box 2064, Herrin, Illinois 62948-5264, USA or e-mail her at kathie@ kathiedenosky.com.

To Carolyn Columbo-Baziluk, Jack Van,
Mona Smith and Harrison Norris.
Thank you for teaching me the beauty of
reading books and the skills needed to
write them.

And a special thank-you to Helen Galloway
for inspiring me to reach for the stars.

One

Cooper Adams had stared death square in the face and lived to tell about it. But his recovery from a run-in with the meanest, nastiest rodeo bull the good Lord ever blessed with the breath of life, couldn't compare with the uphill battle he faced now.

He turned to glare at the old man standing next to him. "Whiskers, what on God's green earth ever possessed you to buy this dump? And with *my* money."

"Now, Coop, don't go gettin' your nose outta joint." Obviously unperturbed by Cooper's disgusted tone, Whiskers Penn flashed a toothless grin. "Like I told you on the phone, the Triple Bar might not look like much right now, but it's got a lotta maybe in it."

Cooper snorted. "Yeah, *maybe* the house and

barns won't fall down with the first stiff wind that
comes along.''

He stared at the house that had been purchased
with his hard-earned money. To say the place had
seen better days was an understatement.

Huge strips of peeling paint flapped in the breeze.
The windows—what few that weren't broken—were
so coated with dry Texas dust they were opaque. And
the back porch roof sagged ominously on one end
from a broken support post. But that wasn't the worst
of it. There were so many shingles missing, Cooper
had no doubt the place leaked like a sieve when it
rained.

He pushed his tan Resistol back off his forehead
and planted his hands on his hips as he mentally
calculated how much money it would take to make
it livable. By the time he hit the five figure mark, he
cringed. There went the second truck he'd planned
to buy before winter.

Damn! He'd counted on being moved in by the
time his brother-in-law, Flint McCray, got back from
taking Cooper's sister Jenna and their boys to Disneyworld. That was only a week away and Cooper
still had the pastures to fence before Flint brought
the cattle over from the Rocking M.

"Well, I'm gonna mosey on up to Amarillo,"
Whiskers said, checking his watch. "I oughtta have
just enough time to pick up them fencin' supplies
you wanted.''

Cooper nodded. "While you're at it, pick up a
couple of rolls of heavy plastic.''

The old man chuckled. "You thinkin' on coverin'
some of them places where the shingles are missin',
are ya?''

"And the windows," Cooper said, nodding. "The weather report said it's supposed to start raining and continue through the week. I don't want the interior damaged any more than it already is before I can get around to making repairs."

"I coulda told you it was gonna rain without havin' to listen to a danged old weather report," Whiskers said, limping toward Cooper's pickup. "My joints are painin' me somethin' fierce and it's put a real bad hitch in my get-along."

Cooper watched the bowlegged old cowboy slowly climb into the truck and start the engine. Pulling the truck to a stop beside Cooper, Whiskers grinned. "Looks like you're about to get some company."

Turning, Cooper watched a red truck bounce down the narrow road leading to his new home—such as it was. The truck bottomed out in a pothole deep enough to bury a full-grown mule before coming to a stop beside some fence posts holding up some broken boards—the corral. Something else he'd have to fix.

"Probably the authorities coming to condemn this place," he said, glancing at the old man.

Whiskers gave Cooper an ear-to-ear toothless grin that made the hair on the back of Cooper's neck tingle. "Don't shame me, boy. Just be sure you mind your manners, ya hear?"

"Howdy!" A burly looking man of about fifty got out of the red truck and started removing luggage from the back. "Name's Bubba West. I'm your neighbor to the east."

"What the hell's going on here?" Cooper demanded.

"Looks to me like somebody's fixin' to stay a spell," Whiskers said, sounding a little too innocent. He cackled as if he found something highly amusing, gunned the engine, then pulled around the red truck before Cooper could stop him.

When the dust settled, Cooper frowned. Had Whiskers finally gone around the bend?

He dismissed that idea immediately. He'd known the old geezer for over five years and, if anything, Whiskers's mind got sharper with age. No, he definitely had something up his sleeve and wanted to make a fast getaway. Cooper just didn't know what that something was, or what it had to do with him. He did, however, know that as sure as the sun rose in the east, he wasn't going to like it when he found out.

Cooper opened his mouth to stop Bubba, but the sight of a young woman exiting the passenger side struck him speechless. He'd been so preoccupied with what Whiskers was up to, Cooper hadn't noticed there was a second person in the truck. But he sure as hell noticed now. When she turned to say something to Bubba, her long, wavy auburn hair brushed the middle of her back and drew Cooper's attention to the best-looking backside he'd seen in years. Maybe ever.

Tall and slender, she wasn't skinny like those pencil-thin models he'd seen in magazines and on television. No, this was a woman with enough curves to drive a man to the brink of insanity. Her hips flared just enough to draw attention to the narrowness of her waist, tight little rear and long blue-jeans clad legs. Shapely as hell legs. The wrap-around-a-man-and-take-him-to-heaven kind of legs.

Cooper gulped hard and shook his head to clear it. He couldn't hear what she'd said to Bubba, but it was clear the suitcases were hers. Cooper started to protest, but she moved to face him and he couldn't have formed words if his life depended on it. She wasn't just attractive. The woman was downright gorgeous.

Her full mouth and sensuous lips curving in a slight smile, made his mouth go dry. But it was her eyes that damn near knocked his size thirteen boots right off his feet. Big, brown eyes stared at him expectantly and made him want to do something stupid like slay a dragon or move a mountain for her.

"See ya 'round, neighbor," Bubba said with a wave. When had the man stopped pulling bags from the truck and climbed back into the cab?

Brought back to his senses by the growl of the powerful engine turning over, Cooper tried to stop him. "Hey—"

But it was too late. Bubba was already turning the truck around and heading back down the lane, leaving a cloud of Panhandle dust swirling in his wake.

Cooper and the woman stared at each other for several long seconds before he finally managed to make his feet move toward her. "I'm Cooper—"

"I'm Faith—"

They both stopped to stare at each other.

Laughing, Cooper extended his hand. "Let's try this again. I'm Cooper Adams."

She smiled and placed her hand in his. "And I'm Faith Broderick."

As soon as her soft skin came into contact with his callused palm, heat streaked up his arm, then headed straight to the region south of his belt buckle.

He quickly released her hand. To his satisfaction, she had trouble meeting his eyes and seemed to take a great interest in the strap of her shoulder bag. He took it as a sign she'd been as shaken by the contact as he'd been.

Feeling a little better just knowing he wasn't the only one affected, he asked, "What can I do for you, Ms. Broderick?"

She glanced toward the lane leading to the main road. "Was that Mr. Penn I saw leaving in the black truck?"

Her voice was so soft and sexy that Cooper found himself having to swallow several times before he could force words past the cotton coating his mouth and throat. Nodding, he said, "Whiskers went up to Amarillo for fencing supplies."

"Oh." She suddenly looked uncertain. "Did he say when he'd return?"

Cooper smiled in an effort to reassure her. "He should be back before dark. Is there something I could help you with?"

"I don't think so." She shook her head and gave him a smile that damned near knocked the breath out of him. She nervously fingered the strap on her shoulder bag. "I really should talk to Mr. Penn. Did he give you any instructions before he left?"

Cooper laughed. "He's never been at a loss for telling me what to do or how to do it. And out of respect for his age, I listen, then do what *I* think is best."

Her smile faded. "He lets you get away with that?" she asked, clearly incredulous.

"Oh, he can get kind of mouthy about it sometimes." Cooper shrugged. "I just let him spout off and ignore most of it."

"I've never had a boss that lenient," she said, shaking her head. "It's going to take some getting used to."

He suddenly felt like they were carrying on two completely different conversations. "You think I work for Whiskers?"

"Don't you?"

Cooper frowned. "No. When he's not trying to run my life, he works for my brother-in-law, Flint McCray."

She shook her head as if she didn't believe him. "When he hired me, Mr. Penn said he needed someone to keep his house and do the cooking for the Triple Bar Ranch."

"He did what?!" Cooper felt like the ground had dropped from beneath his boots. He glanced at the suitcases. He'd forgotten all about them once she'd treated him to her sexy smile.

She placed her hand to her chest and started backing away from him. Well, hell. The last thing he'd meant to do was scare her.

"Look, Ms. Broderick, I'm sorry if I frightened you. I certainly didn't mean to. But I'm the owner of the Triple Bar Ranch." He glanced over his shoulder at the house. "And as you can see, I won't be needing a housekeeper for quite some time."

The ringing of his cell phone stopped Cooper from saying anything further. Releasing the clip on the side of his belt, he snapped it open and punched the talk button.

Before he had the chance to say a word, Whiskers's voice crackled across the line and into his ear.

"Coop, I'm bettin' your purty sore at me and Bubba 'bout now."

Cooper glanced at Faith. She looked like a skittish colt—ready to bolt at the slightest provocation. And if she didn't stop fiddling with the strap on her shoulder bag, she'd twist the damned thing clean in two.

Instead of the tongue-lashing he wanted to give Whiskers, Cooper said tightly, "You could say that."

Whiskers chuckled. "I figured you would be. That's why I'm gonna mosey on back to the Rocking M and wait for Flint and Jenna to get back from vacation. It'll give you time to cool off and get to know that little gal. I'll come back down to the Triple Bar when Flint brings the cattle next week."

Cooper glanced at Faith and tried to give her a reassuring smile, but he was pretty sure it looked more like he was about to lose his dinner. He turned his back to her and lowered his voice to a whisper. "And just what am I supposed to do with Faith Broderick in the meantime?"

The old man laughed. "Now, boy, if you don't know what to do with a purty woman on a deserted ranch, there ain't no hope for you."

The cell phone began to beep, signaling the battery was about to go dead. "Whiskers, you've got my truck and we're twenty miles from the Rocking M," Cooper said, starting to realize the gravity of what the old geezer had done. Careful to keep his voice low, he asked, "What the hell are we supposed to do for food?"

"I've already seen to that." Whiskers sounded so damned proud of himself that Cooper wanted to reach through the phone and shake him. "Everything you two are gonna need is already inside the house or the barn. I even seen to puttin' your clothes in there 'fore I left.''

''But there's no electricity.'' Cooper hated sounding desperate, but the battery on the cell phone wouldn't last for more than a few seconds longer and Whiskers knew damned good and well there was no way to charge it.

''You don't need 'lectricity, boy,'' Whiskers said, laughing. ''Now, treat that little gal like the lady she is and I'll see you in a week.''

Before Cooper had a chance to say anything more, the cell phone went completely silent. He looked at the display screen. Nothing. He slowly snapped the useless apparatus shut and barely resisted the urge to throw it as far as he possibly could.

Instead he clipped it to his belt and reviewed the facts. He was stuck on a deserted ranch with a woman he didn't know, had no transportation and no means of communication. He turned to face her. And worst of all, he had to break the news of their situation to her.

If Cooper could have gotten his hands on Whiskers at that very moment, he'd have cheerfully choked the stuffing out of the meddling old goat.

Faith watched Cooper Adams turn to face her. He didn't look at all happy. ''Is something wrong?'' she asked, apprehension forming a tight knot in her stomach.

He shifted from one foot to the other, then removed his cowboy hat to run a hand through his thick, dark blond hair. He stared off into the distance as if he couldn't quite meet her questioning gaze.

Placing his hat back on his head, he finally faced her. "Uh...it seems that we might have a slight problem."

The knot in Faith's stomach clenched even tighter and her knees began to tremble. Cooper clearly had something he didn't want to tell her and, if the expression on his handsome face was any indication of what was running through his mind, she wasn't going to like hearing what he had to say.

She walked over to the pile of luggage and sat down on one of the larger suitcases before her trembling legs failed her completely. "What is it?"

His broad chest expanded as he took a deep breath. "It seems Whiskers has decided to stay up at my sister and brother-in-law's ranch. He won't be returning until Flint gets back from vacation and brings my cattle over from the Rocking M."

Faith felt a tension headache coming on. Although she wasn't from Texas, she'd read enough to know that some ranches were spread out over several hundreds, sometimes thousands of acres, and were miles apart.

"When will that be?" she asked, feeling her life begin to spin out of control.

He ran a hand over his face before his bluer-than-sin gaze met hers. "In about a week."

Her heart skipped several beats. Not good. Not good at all. "If you would be kind enough to take me to Amarillo, I'll..."

She'd what? There was nothing for her there, nor was there anything for her back in Illinois. Nothing but small town gossip and the constant reminder of all her failings. Her head began to pound. How could her carefully laid plans have taken such a wrong turn?

"Ms. Broderick, that's the biggest part of our problem," Cooper said, breaking into her thoughts. "When Whiskers drove off in my truck, he took our only means of transportation with him."

Faith looked around. There wasn't a vehicle in sight. Not even a tractor. She glanced at the cell phone clipped to Cooper's belt. "Use your phone to call someone. I'm sure Mr. West would—"

"The battery's dead."

She gulped. "Then charge it."

He shook his head. "Can't. The electricity hasn't been turned on."

Her head pounded harder. "You mean we're stuck here for the next week with no way to leave and no means of communication?"

He nodded, his grim expression verifying her fears. "That's exactly what I mean."

Faith swallowed her rising panic and rubbed her throbbing temples with her fingertips. Why had Mr. Penn lied to her about owning the ranch? And why had he stranded her here with the sexiest cowboy she'd ever seen?

Whiskers Penn and her late grandfather had been friends since they were boys, and when her grandmother told Faith about the job, she'd vouched for his integrity. That's why Faith had contacted him and taken the position. Whiskers had her grandmother's approval—not an easy thing to obtain—and it had seemed an easy way to leave the past behind and start rebuilding her life.

But in her haste to do that, she'd apparently repeated her mistake. She'd trusted in basic goodness and honesty. She'd been so desperate to make a fresh start that she'd jumped from one bad situation to another. And once again, she'd been burned. Would she never learn that she had to stop trusting people and taking everything they said as the truth?

Disgusted with herself for once again being so gullible, she asked, "Why would Mr. Penn do something like this?"

"Because the old geezer has a streak of mischief in him a mile wide," Cooper muttered. He folded his arms across his wide chest. "Whether we like it or not, Ms. Broderick, we're both going to have to get used to the idea of being stuck here for the next week."

Cooper glanced at his new home, then back at Faith. The place was way too small for his peace of mind. Hell, every time they turned around they'd be bumping into each other. The thought of his body brushing against hers sent a flash of heat straight to his loins.

Shaking his head to clear it, he swept his hand toward the house. "We might as well go see what the inside looks like."

She gave him one of those you're-feeding-me-a-line looks, before asking, "If what you say is true—if this place does belong to you—then why don't you know what the interior of your own home looks like?"

He sighed heavily. "Because I was fool enough to buy it, sight unseen."

"Why would you do that?" she asked, skepticism written all over her pretty face. "Even I'm not *that* gullible."

Cooper shook his head. He'd asked himself the

same thing about a hundred times in the last half hour. "After I retired from bullriding, I started doing commentary for a few rodeo companies. But I'm tired of living like a nomad. When I made the decision to find a place to settle down, I was out on the circuit and didn't have time to get back before the auction. And Flint and my sister were away at a horse show."

"So you had Whiskers make the bid?" she guessed.

He nodded. "Unfortunately, I trusted Whiskers when he said it needed a little work, but that it was a good deal." Cooper blew out a disgusted breath. "You can bet I won't make *that* mistake again."

She glanced at the bags around her, then rose from her perch atop one of the biggest suitcases he'd ever seen. Why was it that men could stuff everything they'd need for a month in a single duffel bag, but women needed at least a six-piece set of luggage for an overnight stay?

"I suppose it would be a good idea to start moving my things," she said, grabbing a suitcase in each hand. "It looks like it's going to start raining any minute."

Cooper glanced up at the clouds building overhead, then at the monstrous pile of luggage. Hefting as many bags as he could carry at one time, he started for the house. If they hurried, they might get everything transferred to shelter before the sky opened up and poured.

Fat raindrops suddenly began to raise little puffs of dust as they hit the dusty soil.

Then again, maybe they wouldn't, he decided as they jogged toward the house. By the time they covered the distance to the sagging porch, water was coming down in sheets and, instead of soaking into the ground, it started to form little rivulets of mud.

Dropping the load in front of the door, Cooper turned and sprinted back to what remained of the pile. Scooping up the last three bags, he ran through the downpour and up the porch steps, careful to avoid cracking his head on the sagging eaves of the roof.

Faith had already entered the house, which was fine with him. The sight of her cute little backside bobbing as she ran to the shelter of the porch had already sent his blood pressure up about fifty points and activated his imagination more than he was comfortable with. Considering their situation, having his thoughts stray in an erotic direction was pure insanity.

As he stood there trying to figure out how they'd get through the next week without him walking around in a constant state of arousal, a crash, followed by a woman's bloodcurdling scream brought him back to his senses. The sound sent a chill straight up his spine and made the hair on the back of his neck stand on end.

"What the hell?"

The old wooden screen door suddenly flew open and before Cooper knew what was happening, Faith Broderick came flying out, vaulted the pile of luggage and wrapped herself around him tighter than a piece of shrink-wrap on a hot plate.

Two

Faith felt Cooper's arms close protectively around her a moment before he stumbled back down the steps to sit down hard in the muddy yard. Instantly drenched by the pouring rain, she parted the wet waves of her hair to find their faces only inches apart.

Time stood still as she sat on his lap, straddling his lean hips, feeling the rock hardness of his thighs beneath her bottom. Staring at him, she felt she just might drown in his deep blue eyes. His firm lips parted and she wondered how they would feel on her own. Would they be hard and demanding, or gentle and coaxing?

Despite the chilling rain beating down on her, Faith felt an inner heat warm her all the way to her toes. Even soaking wet the man was gorgeous and made her think of things she had no business dwelling on. And that wasn't good, considering for the next week they would be stranded together on a deserted ranch.

"Are you all right?" he finally asked, his voice sounding so darned intimate and sexy that her temperature rose another couple of notches.

His face was so close she could feel his warm breath on her cheek, see the tiny scar just below his right eyebrow that she hadn't noticed before. His arms held her securely against his broad chest and the feel of his body pressed to her sensitive breasts made her insides feel as if they'd turned to pudding.

Not at all comfortable with the feeling, she scrambled to her feet. "I, uh…yes. Yes, I'm fine." She hated her breathless tone and the fact that her knees didn't want to support her.

Water dripped from his tan cowboy hat as for several long seconds they continued to stare wordlessly at each other. "Come on," he finally said. Rising to his feet, he took her by the hand to tug her along. "Let's get out of this rain."

Faith had forgotten all about the downpour and the fact that they were both soaking wet. She'd been too fascinated by the sight of his soaked western shirt molded to his perfect torso and broad shoulders. Her ex-husband had worked out at the gym for years and never managed to build the type of rock hard muscles that Cooper Adams had. But then, she'd learned the hard way that Eric hadn't spent as much time at the gym as she'd been led to believe.

Back under the shelter of the sagging porch roof, she noticed Cooper's eyes darken to pools of navy as he stared at her. When she realized the exact direction of his gaze, Faith quickly crossed her arms over her breasts, her cheeks burning. Thoroughly drenched, her pale yellow T-shirt might as well have been transparent. It clung to her breasts like a second skin and her flimsy lace bra left little or nothing to the imagination. A fact that Cooper seemed to find quite fascinating.

He cleared his throat. "What the hell happened in there?" he finally asked.

It took her a moment to realize what he meant. Remembering the reason for her flight from the house, she shuddered. "There's some kind of hideous creature in the kitchen."

He sighed heavily. "What did it look like?"

"Well, I...I don't know exactly," Faith admitted.

"You didn't see it?"

She shook her head. "I didn't stick around long enough to find out how horrible it looked."

He propped his hands on his hips and stared down at her. "Then what makes you think it was horrible?"

"Because when I knocked over a box full of pans it made an awful hissing sound." Irritated by Cooper's questions and the amusement dancing in his eyes, she glared at him. "I wasn't about to stand there and let it bite me."

His lips twitched, and she had no doubt he was trying to keep from laughing out loud. She wanted to punch him. Why did men feel so darned superior when it came to a woman's fears of creepy things?

"Well, we can do one of two things," he said solicitously.

She glared at him. "And what would that be, Mr. Adams?"

"We can either stand here and debate the issue while we freeze our butts off in these wet clothes, or we can go inside and change.'' He shrugged and reached for the screen door. "I'm opting for warm and dry. How about you?''

The temperature had to have dropped a good ten degrees with the onset of the rain and the October breeze had picked up enough to blow water in from the open side of the porch. "But what about…the animal…in there?" Faith asked, her teeth beginning to chatter. She wasn't about to go back inside the house until the creature had been dealt with.

He let go a long, resigned sigh. "Where did you see the damned thing?''

"I told you…I didn't see it. I only *heard* it.''

He rolled his eyes. "Okay. Where did you *hear* this hideous beast?''

"In…the kitchen,'' she said, shivering as much from the memory of the sound, as from her wet clothing. "By…the boxes in the center…of the room.''

Cooper opened the door and stepped into the dim light of the kitchen. In truth, he was damned glad to put some distance between himself and Faith Broderick. When she'd come flying out of the house and jumped into his arms, the feel of her soft body clinging to him, her long legs wrapped around his waist, had just about sent his blood pressure into stroke range. But it was the sight of her wet T-shirt that had almost done him in completely. He'd been left with more than a clear image of the size and shape of her breasts, and when her nipples tightened from the chilled air, his eyes had damned near popped out of his head. How was a man supposed to ignore a sight like that? Or forget about it?

He shook his head. He couldn't do either. And he

had a feeling the next week was going to be sheer hell.

Glancing around, he decided whatever Faith had heard must have moved on. As he turned to tell her the coast was clear, a movement on top of the boxes in the center of the room caught his attention. He stepped closer and the little lizard let loose with a loud hiss.

As frustrating as their situation was, Cooper couldn't help but chuckle at the turn of events and his own foolishness. When he'd first laid eyes on Faith, he'd thought he might like to move a mountain or slay a dragon for her. It appeared he'd get to do both. He'd already moved that mountainous pile of luggage, now he'd get to play the white knight and get rid of her dragon.

You've got to get out more, Adams.

When a man started suffering the "white knight" syndrome over a lizard and a pile of beat-up suitcases, it was a sure sign he'd been too long without the warmth of a woman.

"Here's your 'hideous creature,'" he said, pushing open the screen door.

"What is that thing?" she asked, drawing back as he walked past her to the edge of the porch.

"It's just a little old horny toad." He released the reptile, then turned to face her. "He didn't mean any harm."

"I...I'll have...to take...your word...for that," she said, shivering violently.

She had to be chilled to the bone and damned uncomfortable in those wet clothes. Stopping himself from wrapping her in his arms, he reached for the screen door instead. They were little more than strangers and he had a feeling she wouldn't buy that he was trying to lend her his warmth any more than he would.

Placing his hand at her back, Cooper ushered her through the door, then quickly put distance between them before he did something stupid. "Where do you want me to put your bags?" he asked, preparing to relocate Mount Samsonite to its next location.

"Put them in…the living room for now," she said, shivering as she looked around the kitchen. "Before I start unpacking anything…we'll have to clean."

Cooper took that to mean she intended for him to do a critter check of the house and get rid of any more unwanted guests.

Once her suitcases had been moved and he'd located the duffels Whiskers had left for him, Cooper retrieved a couple of towels. Walking back into the kitchen, he handed her one of the plush bath sheets. "You'd better get dried off and put on something warm."

She eyed him warily.

All things considered, he guessed he could understand her reluctance to strip down even with him in one room and her in another. She had no way of knowing he could be trusted not to violate her privacy, or that he was about as harmless as that little lizard he'd pitched out earlier.

Wanting to put her mind at ease, he squarely met her uncertain gaze. "You don't have to be afraid of me, Faith. You've got my word, I'll stay in here while you change."

The sound of his deep baritone saying her name sent a shiver up Faith's spine and had her scurrying into the living room to find dry clothes. Cooper might not think of himself as the threatening type, but she knew better. Physically, she had no doubt he would keep his promise. How she knew that, she wasn't sure. She just did.

But the fact that he practically oozed virility from every pore of his skin was what had her concerned. She didn't want to find Cooper Adams attractive, didn't want to think of him as honorable or trustworthy. In fact, she didn't want to think of him at all. Her peace of mind depended on it.

But the memory of his body pressed to hers, the smell of his clean masculine skin and the integrity she'd detected in his deep blue eyes wouldn't allow her to forget.

She peeled her wet clothes off and vigorously ran the towel over her skin in an effort to rub away a fresh wave of goose bumps that had nothing to do with being chilled, and everything to do with thinking about Cooper Adams.

Faith selected a black sweatshirt and matching sweatpants from one of her suitcases. Certain her choice would be as appealing to a man as a burlap bag, she pulled them on, along with a pair of thick socks. Digging around in the suitcase containing her shoes, she slipped on a pair of cross trainers, combed the damp waves of her hair into a semblance of order, then ventured back into the kitchen.

"At least Whiskers brought something to heat the house with," Cooper said, looking up as she entered the room. He finished lighting a large kerosene heater, then straightened and started unbuttoning his shirt. "I'll change, then help you go through the boxes to see what kind of food the old geezer left for us."

She nodded. She couldn't do anything else. As he parted the front of the garment, the sight of well-defined ridges on his stomach and perfectly sculpted pectoral muscles struck her completely speechless. He pulled the sleeves from his arms and she swallowed hard. His biceps were moving in really fascinating ways as he shrugged out of the shirt. She remembered how securely those arms had held her to keep her from being injured when they landed in the yard and how safe she'd felt with them wrapped around her.

Oblivious to what the sight of all that masculine flesh and sinew was doing to her, he turned and headed for the living room. A long white scar ran down from just below his shoulder blade to curve around his left side, but it didn't even come close to detracting from the sexiness of his broad shoulders and narrow waist. But when she noticed his tight rear encased in those well-worn jeans, Faith caught her breath. Lord have mercy, except for the scar, the man's body was absolutely perfect.

She shook her head to chase away her foolishness. He was nothing more than a good-looking, well-built man. And she'd learned the hard way that men couldn't be counted on for anything but a truckload of grief.

If she intended to get through the next week with any sanity left, she'd have to remember that. She'd also have to keep her gaze from straying anywhere below Cooper's chin, in order to avoid panting over his gorgeous body.

As soon as he entered the living room, Cooper blew out the air trapped in his lungs and ran a hand

over his abdomen. He'd never had a problem with a
bulging stomach. But when he'd noticed Faith staring
at him like a hungry dog after a juicy steak, he'd
damned near suffocated trying to tighten his already
flat belly.

What the hell had gotten into him? He'd never in
his life felt the need to impress a woman with his
physique. He hadn't needed to. From about the age
of fifteen he'd pretty much had all the female attention he wanted or—for that matter—could handle.

He frowned. It had to have been a case of temporary insanity. That's all it could be. He'd been
working so hard lately, he hadn't had the time to
think about a woman, let alone be with one. And
finding himself stranded on a deserted ranch with a
beautiful female after a long dry spell wasn't going
to make the next several days any easier. Not by a
long shot.

Satisfied that he'd discovered the reason for his
irrational behavior, Cooper shucked his muddy jeans
and toweled himself dry. He could tell she didn't like
the attraction any better than he did. But that didn't
change the fact that it was there. They just had to
ignore it.

That might be easier said than done, though. Faith
had put on a sweat suit, and Cooper would bet his
last dollar it was an attempt to lessen her appeal. He
chuckled. She had no idea that even if it was baggy
fleece, she made black look good. Real good.

When his body reminded him of the way she'd
felt sitting on his lap, he shook his head. That line
of thinking was not going to help the situation one
damned bit.

Pulling on a dry set of clothes, he forced himself

to look around his new home. If anything could douse a case of the hots and get his mind back on track, it was all the work he had ahead of him. Cooper wandered into one of the three bedrooms and discovered that he'd get a lot of the repairs done while they were stranded.

Whiskers had planned quite well and thought of just about everything. New panes of glass for the broken windows were propped against the walls awaiting installation, gallon buckets of paint for both the inside and outside of the house were stacked in one corner and several squares of shingles to fix the roof were stacked in another. A tool belt with a hammer, tape measure and caulking gun, along with several boxes of nails and an assortment of handsaws were piled on top of a stack of plywood resting on sawhorses. Two large rolls of heavyweight plastic with a note attached rounded out the supplies.

Fencing supplies in the barn. Have a good time. Whiskers.

"Crazy old coot," Cooper muttered, relieved to find the other bedrooms had double beds with comfortable looking mattresses. At least, he'd get a good night's sleep after working himself day and night trying to get the place livable.

"Did you find candles or something we could use for light?" Faith called. He listened to her poke around in the kitchen, opening drawers and closing cabinet doors.

"I'll check," he said, grabbing a roll of plastic and the tool belt. He tucked them under his arm and walked back into the kitchen. When Faith raised a brow, he explained, "After I help you find some type of light, I'm going to tack up some of this plastic to keep the heat in and the rain from blowing through the broken windows.''

He put the tool belt and plastic to one side, opened the boxes and started pulling items out. Handing Faith a handful of candles and a camping lantern, he turned back to the cartons. ''Looks like Whiskers left us a camp stove for cooking,'' he said, setting the item on the counter.

''Tell me he left a can opener in there somewhere,'' she said, eyeing several cans. ''If he didn't, we're in bigger trouble than he is.''

''You planning on giving him a piece of your mind?'' When she nodded, Cooper laughed and held up a can opener. ''He's off the hook on this one, but you'll have to stand in line. I have first dibs on his ornery old hide.''

''How long have you known Mr. Penn?'' she asked, taking the can opener and several other kitchen utensils he'd removed from the boxes. She placed them on the counter. ''Does he do things like this very often?''

Cooper handed her a bag of rags and a spray bottle of all-purpose cleaner he'd found at the bottom of the box. ''Not really. Not since…''

His voice trailed off as he thought of the last time Whiskers had pulled a stunt like this. It had been with Cooper's sister Jenna and Flint McCray. The old geezer had purposely glossed over the news of a storm warning in order to strand them in a remote line shack. And Whiskers had even tried to get Cooper to help him. Cooper gulped as he stared at Faith's back. Jenna and Flint had just celebrated their fifth wedding anniversary.

When Whiskers called to say he was on his way

to the Rocking M, Cooper had been so angry he
hadn't given much thought to the old man's reasons
for stranding them. Now that he'd calmed down,
Cooper knew exactly what the old goat had up his
sleeve. Whiskers was trying to get them together for
a trip down the aisle.

"Not since when?" Faith asked, spraying the
cleaner and wiping down the insides of the cabinets
with the rags.

"Not…" Cooper had to clear the gravel from his
throat before he could finish speaking. "It doesn't
matter. Let's just say it's been a long time and leave
it at that."

She stopped cleaning and turned to look at him.
"Do you think his age has something to do with his
behavior?"

"Could be," Cooper hedged. "If you can handle
things from here, I'm going to get this plastic put
up."

When she nodded, he hastily picked up the items
he needed and headed into the other room. He wasn't
about to tell her that the only thing wrong with
Whiskers's mind was a misguided belief that he
needed to play matchmaker and see everyone he
knew blissfully hitched.

Two hours later, Faith looked around to find all
the boxes of food had been unpacked and put away.
After Cooper had finished putting plastic over the
broken windows, he'd helped her by storing the
canned goods in the cabinets she'd cleaned. Then
he'd tinkered with the hand pump and finally gotten
enough water to warm on the camp stove for her to

wash the few dishes and cooking utensils they'd found.

"Looks like Whiskers thought of just about everything," he said, pulling a blue graniteware coffeepot from one of the cartons. "At least we can start the morning off with a cup of instant daylight."

"Why do you call it that?" Faith asked, smiling at his relieved expression.

"Because one sip of my coffee and the cobwebs are instantly cleared out of your head for the rest of the day," he said proudly. "Wakes you right up and gets the blood to pumping."

Laughing, she took the pot from him and plunged it in the soapy dishwater. "It sounds a little stronger than I care for. I think I'll pass."

"Where's your sense of adventure?" he asked, grinning back.

"I lost it..." She checked her watch. "...about three hours ago."

He nodded. "I can understand. I guess it was pretty disappointing to find this place in the shape it's in." He frowned. "I know I wasn't too happy about it."

"Oh, I was just beside myself," Faith said dryly. "And then when I found out that I was going to be stranded here for the next week with no electricity it was almost more happiness than I could handle."

Cooper chuckled. "Yeah, I guess that did take care of any expectations you had about taking the job."

Faith marveled at Cooper's good-natured attitude. "But I would imagine my disillusionment pales in comparison to yours. My money didn't pay for this place. Yours did."

His grin made her feel warm all the way to her

toes. "Well, I will admit that I felt a little discouraged when I first saw it."

"A little?"

Faith could well understand how he must have felt. Her reaction upon seeing the place had been far from thrilled. But to know that your hard-earned money had gone to pay for something that needed as much work as this place did, had to have been extremely disheartening.

His laughter filled the room. "Okay. You got me on that one. I took one look and felt like I'd taken a sucker punch to the gut. But after I changed clothes, I looked through some of the rooms and it's not as bad as I first thought. There are three good-sized bedrooms, a big office and a room large enough to put in a whirlpool."

"Oh, a long soak in the tub sounds heavenly," she said, closing her eyes.

"Having inside conveniences period, would be nice," he agreed. "Especially with it raining cats and dogs."

Surely she hadn't heard him correctly. Opening her eyes, she stared at him. "Are you telling me there are *no* bathroom facilities at all?"

He nodded. "None."

She opened and closed her mouth several times as she tried to digest what he was telling her. "Then how...I mean, where are we—"

"Outside," he said, apparently aware of her concerns. "There's an outhouse about fifty yards—"

"An outhouse?!" She hated having to discuss something so intimate with a stranger, but it couldn't be helped.

He nodded. "Look, I know it's not the best of

conditions, but that doesn't mean we can't think of this as an adventure. Try pretending you're on a camping trip.''

''Right.'' She was beginning to realize just how isolated and primitive their situation was. ''Did you find a can of bug spray in any of those cartons?'' she asked suddenly.

''No.'' He looked at her like he thought she might be close to losing it. ''Why do you want bug spray?''

''Spiders.'' She shuddered. Even the word gave her the creeps and sent a chill snaking up her spine. ''I can't stand them.''

''Oh, right. I guess there might be a few that have taken up residence in there.''

''Exactly.'' There was no way she'd step foot anywhere that a spider might be lurking about just waiting to pounce on her. She shuddered. And if the spiders around here were like everything else in Texas, they'd be the size of a Volkswagen.

He walked over to the door and looked out. ''The rain's let up to a steady drizzle, but I don't think it's going to stop for a while.'' Turning back, he gave her a lopsided grin. ''I'll make you a deal. I'll go out and take care of any eight-legged varmints in there, if you'll cook supper.''

''Deal,'' Faith said, smiling back at him and extending her hand to seal the bargain.

The minute he took her hand in his, warmth streaked up her arm to spread throughout her body. His gaze caught hers and she could see by the darkening of his eyes that he'd experienced a similar reaction to their touch.

Faith jerked her hand back. ''If you'll show me how to light the stove without blowing myself up,

I'll start dinner,'' she said, hating the breathless tone of her voice.

He stood, staring at her for endless seconds before nodding and showing her how to operate the camp stove. Then, without a word, he walked out into the cool, October rain.

Three

Cooper watched Faith slowly push back from the makeshift table he'd constructed of plywood on sawhorses. "If you'll get 'Old Faithful' to spout forth some more water, I'll get these dishes washed," she said, sounding tired.

"Nope." Shaking his head, he got up from the crate he'd been sitting on and walked over to the pump. "You cooked. I'll take care of cleaning up."

"That's not necessary, Mr. Adams," she said, gathering their plates to stack them on the cracked countertop. "I'm used to—"

"The name's Cooper," he said, grasping the handle to see if he could coax water from the ancient pump. The first thing he intended to do when he had a means of transportation was to find the nearest hardware store and buy plumbing supplies. "You've had a hell of a day and I'm betting you're pretty tired. Besides, you fulfilled your end of the deal. You cooked.''

''But the agreement—''

''I know what the deal was,'' he said, pouring rain water he'd collected in a bucket into the apparatus to prime it. It had to be the ultimate irony that you had to have water to get water from old hand pumps, he decided as he moved the metal lever up and down several times until water finally belched forth from ''Old Faithful.'' Filling a large pot, he set it on the camp stove and lit the burner before turning to face her.

The combination of fatigue and nerves had taken their toll. She'd yawned several times in the last half hour and a hint of dark circles had appeared under her beautiful brown eyes.

''Where did you say you're from?''

''Illinois.'' She covered her mouth against another yawn.

''When was the last time you slept?''

''Night before last.'' She yawned again. ''I was too excited about the trip to sleep last night.''

He whistled low. ''You have to be dead on your feet. Why don't you get ready and go to bed? While you finished cooking supper, I found some sheets and made both beds. All you have to do is crawl in and crash.''

''But—''

''But nothing.'' Cooper placed his hands on her shoulders and turned her away from the counter. He quickly turned her loose and did his best to ignore the heated sensation running from his palms, up his arms and gathering in his gut. ''Get some rest.''

He watched her eye the door. ''Is it still raining?''

"No."

"Did Whiskers leave a flashlight?"

"Yes, but why do you—" When she jerked her thumb in the direction of the outhouse, understanding dawned. "Oh, yeah. Sorry."

Handing her the requested light, he busied himself with the dishes as she quietly opened the door and stepped outside. Why did he feel the need to shelter this woman? What was there about Faith Broderick that made him want to take care of her?

Several times throughout the afternoon and evening he'd detected a quiet reserve about her, a sadness she couldn't quite hide. Maybe that was why he'd felt his protective instinct rear its head.

He'd developed that particular trait when he'd been responsible for watching out for his sister, Jenna. After their mother abandoned the family for greener pastures, their dad had lost interest in life, leaving Cooper with no choice but to finish raising himself and his sister. But he'd learned to tamp down any more of his sheltering tendencies with other women. Jenna had pointed out time and again that he tended to be on the overly protective side, and that women didn't particularly care for that these days.

Nope. He wasn't going to get involved or try to help Faith with whatever bothered her. She'd probably tell him to mind his own business anyway.

The back door suddenly flew open, breaking into his thoughts. White as a sheet and trembling uncontrollably, Faith slammed the door and leaned back against it.

"What's wrong?" he asked, rushing over to her. He could tell something had terrified her and without a second thought, he wrapped her in his arms. So much for his internal pep talk.

Sagging against him, she shook her head. "I'm not going back out there."

"Why? What happened?"

"Didn't you hear it?" she asked, her voice shaky.

"Hear what?"

She pushed back from his chest to meet his gaze. "Something out there is howling like a wounded banshee."

Confused, Cooper stared down at her. "I didn't hear…" He stopped in midsentence. He had heard something, but he was so used to it, the sound hadn't really registered. "Coyote," he said, hoping his smile reflected reassurance instead of the physical awareness streaking through his body. "That was just an old coyote yipping at the moon. He didn't—"

"Don't tell me. I know. He didn't mean any harm." She pushed from his embrace. "The creatures I've encountered so far might not mean to hurt me, but they've certainly succeeded in scaring the living daylights out of me."

He let her go. She'd felt way too good nestled against him. And that wasn't going to make the next week any easier. No siree.

She stood for a moment, staring at the door, then turned to walk into the living room. Realizing she hadn't had time to reach her outdoor destination, he tried to think of the least embarrassing way to offer his assistance.

"I'm going that way," he said, taking the flashlight from her. He was proud of himself for managing to sound nonchalant. "Want to tag along?"

A blush tinted her pale cheeks, but after a moment's hesitation, she nodded.

Ten minutes later, Faith stepped back onto the porch. She truly appreciated Cooper's consideration for her privacy when they'd reached the outhouse. He'd stood several yards away, making her feel a little better about his accompanying her. But not much.

She was still embarrassed beyond words over her recent behavior. Normally she took things in stride and let very little frighten her. Hadn't her ex-husband always called her the strong one in their relationship—The Rock?

The only explanation she could think of for her uncharacteristic fear had to be exhaustion. And not just from the trip to the ranch, or the disillusionment she'd felt at finding herself stranded here with the sexiest man she'd ever seen.

No, it had more to do with the emotionally draining events of the past year than anything else. She wished she had a nickel for every piece of small-town gossip and all the instances of humiliation she'd suffered when everybody in the community learned that her husband had left her to marry her best friend. If she did, she'd be a very rich woman and wouldn't be seeking employment on a run-down ranch in the Texas Panhandle.

But she'd lived through it, held her head high and ignored as much of it as she could. Only her grandmother knew the true extent of how badly she'd been hurt by her husband and *former* best friend.

Faith shook her head and put it out of her mind. Now was the time to move forward, not to look back.

No one here knew the circumstances surrounding her divorce, or that her judgment had been seriously flawed. As far as she was concerned, they'd never find out either.

Taking the battery operated lantern from the middle of the plywood table, she walked into the living room and eyed her suitcases. "Have you decided which bedroom you're taking?"

"Doesn't matter to me," Cooper said, following her into the room. He pushed his hat back on his head, then jammed his hands in the front pockets of his jeans as he rocked back on his heels. "Take the one you want and I'll take what's left. I'll move your luggage in the morning."

"All right."

She gathered her nightgown, slippers and robe into one arm, traded him the lantern for the flashlight and walked down the short hall to enter the first bedroom she came to. Stopping short as the beam of light flashed across the bed, she bit her lip to keep a hysterical giggle from escaping. Life just kept getting more bizarre with each passing minute.

Leaning back around the door, she called, "Uh…Cooper, we have a slight problem."

"What's wrong? Did you see another critter? I swear I checked—"

"No." She couldn't keep from laughing. It was just too unreal to be believed. "I think this problem is a lot bigger."

"What makes you think that?" he asked, walking toward her with the lantern. The light cast his features into sharp relief and accented the frown furrowing his brow. He was the best-looking man she'd seen in years. Maybe ever.

Shaking her head to dispel the wayward thought, she pointed into the room. "Unless I'm mistaken, that's chunks of the ceiling on top of my bed."

Shouldering past her, he raised the lantern to get a better look. Pieces of plaster and dust covered the entire double bed. He suddenly let loose with a string of curses that all but turned the air blue and ended with a threat to do bodily harm to Whiskers Penn.

When he stopped cursing, he looked thoroughly disgusted. "The roof must have leaked, water collected behind the plaster—"

"And it gave way," Faith finished for him, unable to stop giggling.

He eyed her like she might be suffering from hysteria. "Do you feel all right?" he finally asked, ushering her into the bedroom that would have been his. "Maybe you should lie down."

Nodding, she wiped the tears at the corners of her eyes. "I'm fine, but this whole day has been a disaster."

He stared at her a moment longer, then threw back his head and laughed with her. "It has been like something out of a bad movie, hasn't it?"

"So what do we do now?" she asked, yawning.

"Nothing." He sat down on the side of the bed and took off his boots.

What on earth was the man up to? she wondered.

Cooper stood up in the middle of the bed and poked at the ceiling. "This one's fine," he said, stepping back down on the floor. "No signs of weakness, so you should be safe from any more falling plaster. You take this bed and I'll bunk down in the living room."

"But—"

"Don't argue." He walked to the door. "You need sleep," he said, his low sexy drawl sounding like a caress. "Good night."

"Nite."

In the silence that followed the quiet click of the door, Faith felt the last traces of her energy drain away. Her arms and legs suddenly felt like lead weights and she was too tired to think about this latest turn of events, let alone how to deal with it.

Slowly changing into her nightgown, she crawled between the cool sheets. She tried to free her mind and forget everything about the entire day. But as soon as she closed her eyes, a tall, sexy Texan with eyes bluer-than-sin and a voice that made her feel all warm and fuzzy inside, filled her mind and beckoned her into the welcome respite of sleep.

Cooper whistled an off-key version of a popular Garth Brooks song while he propped the ladder against the side of the house. He hoped like hell the ladder didn't sink in the mud. But while there was a break in the weather, he needed to get plastic on the east side of the roof. He'd much rather be slapping shingles in place, but the way the clouds were gathering up in the northwest, he'd be lucky to get the sheeting nailed in place before the sky opened up and poured again.

Once he climbed onto the roof, he quickly unrolled the plastic and began nailing it down. Halfway through the task he realized someone was calling his name. Peering over the edge of the roof, he spotted Faith standing with her doubled fists propped on her shapely hips, a scowl on her pretty face. She'd pulled on the baggy black sweat suit and it looked as if a lover's hands had been tangled in her long auburn hair. He didn't think he'd ever seen a woman look quite so sexy.

"Morning," he said, grinning down at her.

"What in all that's holy do you think you're doing?" she demanded, her voice still husky from sleep.

"Fixing the roof."

She didn't smile back. "What time is it?"

Cooper checked his watch. "It's a little past seven. I could tell how tired you were last night. That's why I didn't wake you for breakfast. I thought I'd let you sleep in."

"And just how did you think I'd be able to sleep with you banging on the roof above my head?" she asked, giving him a look that clearly stated she didn't think he had enough sense to pour water out of a boot with the directions on the heel.

"Uh, sorry about that." He ran his hand across the back of his neck. He hadn't even thought about waking her. "I'm used to Whiskers being around. He can sleep through anything. And I wanted to get this plastic on before it rained again."

Fat raindrops began to make little plopping noises on the heavy plastic and the wind suddenly picked up. The end of the sheeting he hadn't yet tacked down began to flap wildly. Cooper lunged to keep the wind from tearing loose the end he'd already nailed in place. In the process, he lost his grip on the hammer. He watched it slide down the roof, then heard it drop to the soft dirt below.

"Damn," he muttered. How was he going to hold the plastic and climb down for the hammer?

"Lose something?" Faith asked.

Her voice sounded close. Too close.

He glanced over his shoulder and his heart came up in his throat. She'd just finished climbing the ladder and was crawling on all fours up the slope of the roof toward him.

"What the hell do you think you're doing, lady?" he demanded, holding his breath until she was sprawled out on top of the plastic beside him. She was afraid of harmless critters, but she'd scaled a ladder to lend him a hand? Maybe she was more gutsy than he'd first thought. "You could fall and break your neck."

"You're very welcome, Mr. Adams," she said, handing him the hammer. "Now hush and get this thing nailed down while I hold it. I'd like to get off the roof before we both get soaked."

Taking the tool from her, Cooper quickly nailed the sheeting. "Okay, it's done," he said, pounding the last nail into place. "Thanks."

"No problem." She sat up and began to make her way toward the ladder, but hadn't gone more than a few inches before she started sliding on the wet plastic. "Ooh…"

Cooper quickly reached out, circled her waist with his arm and hauled her to him. "Careful, darlin'. We'll have to take this slow or we'll both wind up flat on our backs on the ground."

He closed his eyes and took a deep breath. His heart felt as if it was in his throat as he held her close. What would have happened if he hadn't been able to catch her before she slid down the slope of the roof? With no transportation and no way to call for help, it could have been disastrous.

The heat of her slender body pressed to his chest,

the feel of her breasts resting on his forearm and the scent of her peach shampoo where her hair tickled his nose, quickly turned his thoughts from what had almost happened to what he'd like to have happen.

Cooper suddenly felt as if he'd already taken a dive off the roof and landed on his head. Damn but the woman smelled good. Felt good in his arms.

"What do we do now?" she asked, sounding breathless.

He threw the hammer over the side of the roof, shifted her to sit between his thighs, then wrapped both of his arms around her middle. "We're going to take this real slow and scoot our way over to the ladder."

He felt her spine stiffen at the intimate contact of her bottom resting so intimately against the most vulnerable part of him, but placing her hands on his forearms, she nodded.

Slowly, carefully maneuvering them toward the ladder, Cooper felt his lower body awaken to the fact that a delectable, feminine rear was rubbing against it. His problem must have registered with her, too, because she stopped scooting to glare at him over her shoulder.

"Mr. Adams—"

"I don't like it any more than you do," he lied, interrupting what he figured to be a strongly worded warning. He wasn't about to tell her that he was having a hell of a time fighting the urge to throw caution to the wind and seduce her right here on the roof. She'd probably throw him over the side herself if she found out.

"There's nothing I can do about it," he tried explaining. "You're a beautiful woman and I'm a flesh and blood man, not a damned saint."

Faith's cheeks burned. It seemed that every time she turned around she found herself in Cooper's arms. How on earth did she manage to get herself into these predicaments anyway? More than that, why was her body responding to his?

As soon as he'd caught her from sliding off the roof, tiny currents of electrical impulses had streaked through her to form a coil deep in the pit of her stomach. The feel of his changing body pressed to her backside tightened the coil and reminded her that she hadn't been held by a man, loved by a man, for well over a year.

Giving herself a mental shake, she took a deep breath in hopes of steadying her voice and nerves. "Let's just get down from here and out of this rain."

"Works for me," he said, tightening his hold on her and carefully scooting them both toward the edge of the roof. Reaching their destination, he lifted her to lie beside him. "I'm going down first. If you slip on the wet rungs, I'll be there to catch you." He lifted his hand to brush her cheek with his knuckles. "I promise I won't let you get hurt."

His statement set off alarm bells deep within her soul. But his warm breath feathering over her cheek, sent shivers of excitement down her spine. She watched his blue gaze darken to navy and his lips part as he stared down at her. The warning signals seemed to fade considerably.

"I want to kiss you," he said simply.

"That wouldn't be wise."

He shook his head. "Probably not. Would you stop me if I did?"

The alarm bells went completely silent, and instead of nodding that she would stop him, she shook her head.

"Do you want me to kiss you, Faith?"

"Yes."

Yes? Had she lost the last of what little sense she had left? They were stretched out on a rooftop, it was raining buckets and she'd just told him she wanted his kiss.

Faith watched Cooper push his hat back, then slowly, deliberately move closer. She could tell he was giving her the chance to change her mind, to call a halt to this insanity. But she found she really did want his kiss, wanted to feel his firm lips pressed to hers, wanted to know the taste of him.

Her breath caught and she closed her eyes as his mouth descended to hers. Warm, firm and oh so exciting, the contact caused sparkles of light to flash behind her closed lids and she felt as if the roof shifted beneath her.

Cooper coaxed her to open for him and she couldn't have stopped herself if her life depended on it. She wanted his kiss, wanted to feel his tongue mate with hers. Heaven help her, but it had been so very long since she'd tasted a man's desire, felt his body respond to hers.

He slid his hand from her hip, beneath the tail of her sweatshirt and up her ribs to the swell of her breast. Cupping the weight with his large hand, he teased the hardened tip with his thumb. "You're not wearing a bra."

"I...didn't have time...to put one on," she said, her head spinning from the sensations his touch created.

"I'm glad," he said huskily.

His callused palm felt absolutely wonderful on her sensitized skin and she couldn't stop a small moan from escaping. The long forgotten sound of her own passion startled her. What in the name of heaven was she doing? Had she completely lost her mind?

She had to spend the next week with this man. Falling into his arms, welcoming his kiss, spelled disaster at any time. But the day after her arrival? It was pure insanity.

"Please let me go," she said, pushing against his chest.

He allowed her to sit up, but didn't let go of her arms. "Don't be upset, darlin'. A little kiss among friends never hurt anyone."

Faith felt as if she'd been dumped into a tub of ice water. She knew better than anyone how deadly a kiss among friends could be, how it could destroy lives. Two years ago, her husband's affair with her best friend had started with a friendly little kiss under the mistletoe at the staff Christmas party where they all worked.

Cooper had said that he wouldn't let her get hurt and she had no doubt he would keep her safe physically. But there were other types of hurt. She had firsthand knowledge of how emotional pain lasted longer and left deeper scars than any physical injury ever could.

The warning signals were practically screaming at her to run as hard and fast as she could. To put as much distance as possible between herself and Cooper Adams.

Pulling from his grasp, Faith scooted herself to the ladder and began her descent to the ground. She had a feeling he was completely unaware of the effect he had on women, of how his very presence charged the atmosphere with enough electricity to light a small city. The fact that he'd turned that energy her way, scared her to death.

"Faith, wait a minute," she heard him call from above.

She ignored his request and continued to scurry down the ladder. She needed to put distance between them. She had to get her equilibrium back.

No sooner had she thought of regaining her mental balance, than her foot slipped on the wet rung and she fell the last few feet to the ground. She landed hard on her right foot, but ignoring the numb, cold feeling that followed, she started for the house. She'd only taken a couple of steps when a searing pain shot through her ankle and up her calf. Crying out, she stumbled and would have fallen if not for the two strong arms scooping her up and cradling her to a wide chest.

She gazed at the man holding her. Cooper's bluer-than-sin eyes were filled with nothing but kindness and concern.

Tears blurred her vision and she buried her face in the side of his neck. Would she never stop making a fool of herself in front of this man?

Four

When Cooper scooped Faith into his arms, she pressed her face to the side of his neck and her shoulders shook with silent sobs. It just about tore him apart.

She'd scared the living hell out of him when she'd jerked from his arms and started down the ladder. Visions of her falling and being seriously injured had flashed through his mind and he'd immediately started down after her. But when she fell, he'd swear he aged a good ten years.

Any way he looked at it, he was responsible for her falling. He'd known how jumpy she'd become after feeling his body respond to hers. But like a damned fool, he'd reacted with his hormones instead of his good sense. He'd given into the temptation that had eaten at him since he first watched her get out of Bubba's truck. And she'd gotten hurt because of it.

"It's going to be okay, darlin'," he said, shouldering open the kitchen door.

"Please put me down."

"No."

"I can walk," she insisted. Her warm breath on the side of his neck caused him to clench his jaw so tight he thought he'd most likely crack a couple of teeth.

She might be able to walk, but Cooper wasn't real positive that he could for all that much longer. "Are you sure?" he asked.

When she nodded, her silky hair brushed the side of his jaw. His blood pressure shot up several points and his lungs refused to take in air.

Setting her on her feet, he asked, "Are you certain you're okay?"

"Yes." She started to limp toward the living room, but in her haste she bumped into the edge of their makeshift table.

Cooper caught her before she fell and swung her up into his arms once again. She pressed her face to his shoulder and Cooper felt every one of his protective instincts spring to life, as well as every one of his hormones.

Heading straight for the bedroom she'd used the night before, he gently placed her on the rumpled sheets. He tried not to think about how her slender body had felt pressed to his chest, or how much he'd like to crawl into bed next to her, take her into his arms and…

Stepping away from the bed, he started backing his way out of the room. "I'll be right back."

"Don't bother," she said, throwing her arm across her eyes. "I'd rather die by myself."

Apprehension tightened his gut. He hadn't thought she'd been injured *that* seriously. "Die? I thought you said—"

"Of humiliation," she said, sounding disgusted.

Cooper was relieved to hear her sense of humor had returned. "You're embarrassed?"

She nodded, but kept her eyes covered with her arm. "You probably won't believe this, but I'm normally a very sensible, very 'together' person." She paused to take a deep, steadying breath. "And I'm never clumsy."

"Never?"

She lifted her arm to glare at him. "Never."

Cooper wisely suppressed his smile. At least her spirit was intact. "I'm going to get the first-aid kit. I'll be right back."

Turning, he retraced his steps to the living room to rummage through one of the duffel bags Whiskers had left for him. When he found the white metal box filled with medical supplies he always carried, he returned to the bedroom and sat down on the bed beside her.

"Let's get this shoe off and see what we've got here," he said, carefully lifting her leg to rest it on his knee.

He pushed the bottom of her sweatpants up to midcalf and tried not to notice the feel of her satiny skin beneath his palm. Now was not the time for a case of the hots, he reminded himself. That was what had gotten them into this mess in the first place. If he hadn't acted like a seventeen-year-old with a perpetual hard-on and scared the hell out of her, she wouldn't have been injured.

Easing the cross-trainer from her foot, he carefully peeled the sock off and examined her ankle. He was relieved that there was very little swelling. He'd seen enough injuries in his many years on the rodeo circuit to tell that it was most likely a mild sprain and not broken.

"Can you wiggle your toes without pain?" he asked, running his hands over the delicate bones on the top of her foot.

She moved them without hesitation. "I'm fine. Now, go away, Adams."

He chuckled. "I can't."

"Why not?" she demanded, lifting her arm to look at him.

"I haven't finished taking care of your ankle."

Faith gritted her teeth and tried to concentrate on something—anything—besides the feel of Cooper's strong hands stroking her arch, massaging the sole of her foot. "There's nothing to do," she said through gritted teeth.

"We need to put ice on it to keep the swelling down," he insisted, reaching into the white metal box.

Relieved that he'd stopped his sensual assault on her foot, she laughed. "And just where do you expect to find ice without a freezer or electricity to operate it?"

He grinned triumphantly and held up a small plastic bag. "Modern medicine is a wonderful thing."

Faith watched him grasp the bag in both hands and apply pressure in the middle with his thumbs. A slight pop followed, then he shifted it back and forth several times as if he was mixing the contents. When he placed the bag on her ankle, it was extremely cold.

"Chemical cold-packs are a staple of any well-stocked first-aid kit," he said, his smile so smug that she felt like punching him.

His hand still rested on her shin and she wasn't sure whether the shiver that ran up her spine was from the intense cold of the ice-pack, or the feel of his hand heating her skin just above it. Either way, she was beginning to understand the sensual combination of fire and ice.

Concentrating on the cold bag against her skin, she grimaced. "How long do I need to keep this on here?"

"About thirty minutes."

"My ankle will be frozen solid."

"No it won't." His low, sexy chuckle sent her temperature up another notch. To her relief he gave her shin a gentle squeeze, then closed the box and set it on the floor. Rising to his feet, he reached for the pillow beside her, folded it in half and propped her foot on top of it. "If you need me—"

"I'll let you know."

She wished he'd take his disturbing presence into the other room and let her regain at least a scrap of her common sense. With the exception of her injured ankle, she was extremely warm and getting warmer with each passing second.

Nodding, he started for the door, but turned back. "How do you like your coffee?"

"With cream," she said automatically.

He grinned. "Will powdered creamer do?"

"That will be fine. But you don't have to—"

"Yes, I do," he said, his expression turning serious. His gaze drifted to the floor and he ran his hand across the back of his neck. When he raised his head to look at her, the remorse in his eyes startled her. "I'm really sorry you got hurt, Faith. It's my fault and I intend to make it up to you."

She opened her mouth to tell him that it wasn't necessary, but he didn't give her the chance. He simply turned and left the room, ending any further discussion of the matter.

How could she tell Cooper, without making the situation even more embarrassing, that she hadn't been running from him, but from herself? How could she explain that she'd wanted to be held by a man again, to once again feel as if she were desirable? Even if it was just for a few moments.

She shook her head. She couldn't. There were some things that were better left alone. And explanations about her recent past and the reasons for her panic when he'd kissed her were among them.

When he returned holding a package of breakfast muffins in one hand and two coffee mugs in the other, he grinned. "I know it's not the healthiest of breakfasts, but it's about all we have."

"It's fine." Sitting up, she leaned back against the headboard and took one of the mugs from him. "Thank you." Faith took a sip of coffee and made a face. "You…weren't kidding when you said you make your coffee strong."

Cooper grinned. "Instant daylight." His expression turned hopeful. "I tried to tone it down a little by putting in an extra scoop of creamer. I hope it helped."

"Thank you. I can only imagine what it would taste like without it," she said dryly. She took another sip from the cup, then added, "But if you don't mind, I'll make the coffee tomorrow morning."

He opened the package of muffins, then held it out to her. "We'll see how you're getting around first."

"I'll be fine," she said firmly. She selected one of the delicious-looking blueberry muffins. "I'd be even better if you'd remove that ice-pack. My ankle is freezing. How much longer before we take it off?"

He laughed. "You're as impatient as Ryan and Danny."

"And they are?"

"My nephews." He checked his watch. "I'll wrap your ankle with an elastic bandage after you finish eating."

"How old are your nephews?" she asked, noticing a deep fondness reflected in his voice.

"Ryan's eight, he's Flint's son from his first marriage, and Danny's three. But don't tell them that." Chuckling, he shook his head and reached for the first-aid kit. "They think they're grown and ready to conquer the world."

Faith's chest tightened. She'd always wanted to have a son one day. But like so many of her other dreams, it just wasn't meant to be.

She finished the last of the muffin. Delicious before, it suddenly tasted like sawdust. "They sound like typical little boys," she said, her chest tightening at what she would miss.

"Oh yeah." He grinned as he removed a beige roll from the metal box. "My sister is never sure what she'll find in their jeans pockets when she puts them to bed at night. One time she found a small frog in one of Danny's pockets and another time she reached into Ryan's pocket and pulled out a garter snake.''

''Oh dear heavens!'' Faith shuddered at the thought of what that must have felt like. ''I'll bet that was a shock.''

''It just about sent Jenna into orbit. And believe me, she's not the type to scare easy.'' The rich sound of his laughter sent a shiver up Faith's spine. He had the sexiest laugh. ''Jenna screamed so loud that her husband, Flint, damned near broke his neck trying to get upstairs and the guys down at the bunkhouse grabbed their shotguns and came running to see what was wrong.''

Faith nodded. ''I'd have done the same thing.''

Cooper grinned. ''For a long time after that Jenna made Flint go through the boys' pockets before they came in from playing outside.'' He laughed and shook his head. ''But that doesn't stop us—them—from sneaking in a critter or two from time to time.''

''Us?'' She smiled. She could tell he was very close to his family and instinctively knew that he loved children. ''It sounds to me like their uncle might have helped them get some of those forbidden pets into the house.''

''Me?''

''Yes, you,'' she said, laughing.

''Well, I might have helped run interference when they found Peewee.''

''And what is Peewee?''

''A box turtle.'' He removed the cold plastic bag from her ankle, then lifted her leg from the pillow to rest it on his knee. ''They kept him hidden in a shoe box in the closet until I could get to town to buy an aquarium.'' He turned his head to look at her and grinning, admitted, "By the time Jenna discovered that they had Peewee, we already had everything set up."

He placed the rolled bandage to her foot and began wrapping her ankle. The warmth from his hand as he touched her chilled skin raised goose bumps along her arms.

"You sound like you're just as much of a boy as they are," she said. She cursed the breathless tone of her voice. She had to keep her mind off his disturbing touch. It was the only way she would manage to keep her sanity for the next several days.

"Yeah, in a lot of ways, I guess I am a big kid." His mouth turned up in a smile so sexy, Faith barely resisted the urge to fan herself. All she could think about was how wonderful those firm male lips had felt on her own.

Searching for something to keep her mind off the heat streaking through her body, she asked, "Do you get to see them often?"

"I'm with the boys every chance I get." He finished wrapping the elastic bandage around her ankle, then attached the metal clamps to hold it in place. "Now that I'm going to be living around here, I'll get to see them even more, which is fine with me. I love little kids."

"It shows."

Cooper placed her foot back on the pillow and closed the first-aid kit. He'd liked touching her, feeling her smooth skin beneath his callused palms. He wondered if the rest of her felt the same.

Damn! Thinking along those lines could spell disaster. If he intended to keep even a scrap of what little sense he had left, he'd better keep his distance.

He tried to think of something to say that wouldn't send his imagination into overdrive. "How about you? Do you have any nieces or nephews?" he asked, deciding that should be a nice safe topic.

She took a sip of her coffee. "I used to, but I lost my aunt status when the divorce was final."

Cooper barely managed to keep his mouth from dropping open. He couldn't believe any man in his right mind would let a woman like Faith get away. "How long were you married?"

She glanced down at her hands, then back at him. "We were together for four years."

He noticed the sadness in her eyes and wondered what had happened. Did she still love the man?

Cooper couldn't tell. But he'd bet every dime he had that the break-up of the marriage hadn't been her idea. The thought of someone hurting Faith in any way caused a burning in Cooper's gut that had him wishing for five minutes alone with the jerk. By the time Cooper was finished with him, the guy would wish he'd never been born.

"What happened?" he asked when curiosity got the better of him.

"I guess we just grew apart," she said, shrugging one shoulder. Her expression turned guarded. "He ended up going his way and I went mine."

Cooper could tell there was a lot more to the story than Faith was telling. But, he reminded himself, it was her story to tell and none of his business. If she wanted him to know more, she'd have explained further.

"What about a brother or sister?" he asked, trying to find a more pleasant subject—one that would erase the shadows in her pretty brown eyes. "Maybe one day they'll make you an aunt again."

"I was an only child," she said, smiling sadly. "I would have liked having a brother or sister, but shortly after I was born, my parents decided that family life wasn't for either one of them." She shrugged. "They divorced and went their separate ways. I was raised by my maternal grandmother."

"I'm sorry, I didn't mean to pry," he said, rising to his feet. If he didn't get out of there, and damned quick, he'd end up reaching for her, offering her comfort and…more. "I'll be in the kitchen. If I can coax a little water out of Old Faithful I'm going to peel some potatoes and use some canned beef to make a pot of stew. If you need anything—"

"I'll let you know," she said, handing him her coffee mug.

Her fingers brushed his and a jolt of electricity ran straight up his arm, then made a beeline to the region below his belt buckle. He swallowed around the cotton coating his throat. He had to get out of there before he did something really stupid like lying down beside her, taking her into his arms and kissing her until…

Without a word, he turned and walked straight to the kitchen. Setting the package of muffins, coffee mugs and first-aid kit on the counter, he opened the back door and walked out into the chilling rain. It was the closest thing he could find to a cold shower.

Armed with a broom, dustpan and garbage bag, Faith limped into the bedroom where the ceiling had fallen the night before. Cooper had brought her lunch, then saying something about checking out the

barn, disappeared outside. And that was just fine with
her. The more she was around him, the more she was
reminded of how it felt to be wrapped in his strong
arms, how his firm lips pressed to her own made her
yearn for more.

She took a deep breath and shook her head to dis-
lodge that train of thought. The reason she was up
moving around in the first place was so she could
get her mind off Cooper Adams. The more she found
out about him, the more she liked him. And that was
dangerous. She'd learned the hard way that where
men were concerned, her judgment was extremely
faulty.

But what woman wouldn't like a man like Cooper? He was kind and considerate. He loved children,
placed a great deal of importance on family and
didn't take himself too seriously. And he was, without a doubt, the sexiest man she'd ever encountered.

''What do you think you're doing?''

She jumped at the harsh sound of Cooper's voice.
She'd been so lost in thought that she'd failed to hear
him enter the house.

Turning, Faith found him standing in the doorway.
Pushing the brim of his cowboy hat back, he planted
his fists on his lean hips. Her heart pounded and her
breath caught. The man was absolutely gorgeous and
she wasn't certain if her accelerated pulse was due
to being startled or because of his presence.

''I was hired to clean,'' she finally managed to say.
She plucked the largest pieces of plaster from the bed
to drop into the garbage bag. ''And that's what I'm
doing.''

''I'll take care of this mess,'' he insisted, stepping

forward to take the bag from her. "You need to stay off that foot."

"We both know that it's only a mild sprain and nothing that requires bed rest." She gathered the four corners of the sheet and prepared to lift it off the bed.

"That's too heavy for you," he said quickly dropping the garbage bag to take the bundle of dust and plaster from her. "While I dump this outside, why don't you finish stripping the bed?"

"Deal." She started to stick her hand out for him to shake, but thought better of it. All things considered, touching him in any way probably wouldn't be wise. Instead she asked, "Do you think you could get some water out of Old Faithful? I'd like to wash these sheets this afternoon."

"Sure thing. I found some rope in the barn that I'll string up in the living room," he said helpfully. "You'll be able to drape them over it so they'll dry."

"Thank you. That should work perfectly."

She waited until he carried the sheet out of the room, then forced her mind back to the chore of removing the rest of the linens from the bed. That done, she took the broom, and began to sweep up some of the dust covering the floor. She leaned down to pick up a piece of plaster by the foot of the bed and froze. Just inches from her hand sat a small brown mouse, his beady eyes staring hungrily at her fingers. Her panicked cry was instantaneous and completely involuntary. If there was any creature she feared more than a spider, it was a mouse.

Cooper had just finished shaking the last of the dust from the sheet and opened the back door to enter the house when Faith's scream sent a chill up his spine and caused the hair on the back of his neck to stand straight up. His heart pounding against his ribs like a jackhammer gone berserk, he ran toward the bedroom where he'd left her.

Had more of the ceiling fallen? Possibly on her? Or could he have misjudged the seriousness of her injury and she was in extreme pain?

He skidded to a halt just inside the bedroom, his eyes widening at the sight before him. There stood Faith in the middle of the bed, the broom held more like a weapon than a household tool.

"What happened?"

She pointed a shaky finger at the floor. "Please get rid of it."

"What?" he asked, looking around. He didn't see anything. Had she seen another horny toad, or maybe a field spider?

"Mouse," she said, shuddering visibly.

If he'd been certain she wouldn't reach out and whack him with the broom she held, he'd have laughed out loud. But he was pretty sure Faith wouldn't see the humor in the situation. At least not at the moment.

"It's probably long gone," he said, continuing to scan the floor for the furry little critter. "You know, he's more afraid of you than you are of him."

"Not likely," she said with an unladylike snort.

Moving around the room, Cooper glanced up from his search. "He was just trying to find a nice cozy home for the winter. He didn't mean any—"

"Don't you dare say it," she warned.

"Why?"

"Because if you do I'll be sorely tempted to smack you with this broom."

Deciding it would be in his best interest to refrain from telling her that the little critter was harmless, Cooper continued to look for the mouse. Just when he was ready to give up, the tiny animal scampered out from under the bed and headed straight for his boot.

"Don't kill it," she said quickly.

"Okay." He threw the sheet he still held over it, then quickly squatted down to trap the mouse in the folds. "Any idea of what you want me to do with it now that I've caught the little guy?"

"Take it outside and turn it loose," she said, her voice sounding quite firm about the matter.

"What good will that do?" he asked, scooping up the mouse inside the sheet.

"He'll still be alive and I won't have to share the house with him," she said, sounding a bit more calm now that the mouse had been restrained.

Cooper couldn't help it. This time he threw back his head and laughed.

"What's so funny?" she asked indignantly. "There's nothing wrong with the catch-and-release method of dealing with mice."

"The damned thing will probably beat me back inside the house," he said as he rose to his feet and prepared to take it outside.

"There's a good chance he'll go somewhere else," she said, sounding hopeful. "Besides, I don't want it dead. I just don't want to occupy the same space with it."

Carrying the mouse several feet away from the house, Cooper released it, then watched it turn around and make a beeline straight back to the house. When it disappeared beneath the back porch, he shook his head and sighed heavily. He'd bet every dime he had that the furry little critter made its presence known again and ended up causing him more than a little grief in the bargain.

Five

"**Y**ou know, I can really sympathize with the pioneer women who helped settle this country," Faith said, draping the last sheet over the rope clothesline that Cooper had strung across the living room.

Along with the rope he'd found in the barn, he had discovered a washboard and washtub. It wasn't the most efficient way to launder clothes, but she'd be the first to admit that it was effective. The sheets were once again a nice, pristine white.

"Pioneers didn't have it easy, that's for sure," Cooper agreed from across the room. He'd been working on a window facing and from his muttered curses, it sounded like he could use some help.

When the board he held clattered to the floor for the second time, she walked over to where he stood. "I'm finished hanging the sheets. Is there something I can do to help?"

"I'd really appreciate it if you held this while I get the nail started," he answered, leaning down to pick up the board at his feet.

She watched him lift the window facing into place, then position it where he wanted. He'd rolled up the sleeves of his chambray shirt to just below the elbows and she found the flexing of his forearms absolutely fascinating. Never in her entire life had she seen anything quite so sexy.

"Faith?"

"What?"

"I asked if you're ready?" he repeated. Taking the nail from the leather pouch hanging from a belt around his waist, he gave her a curious look. "Are you all right?"

"Y-yes," she said, trying not to blush at being caught staring at his impressive sinew. She placed her hands where he indicated and to avoid the distraction of those muscles, made a point of looking down at her feet.

Out of the corner of her eye, she caught movement to her left and turning her head, watched a furry brown mouse head straight for her foot. When it raced over the toe of her shoe, then started climbing up the leg of her sweatpants, she couldn't help it, she let loose a startled cry.

Holding the nail with thumb and forefinger, Cooper had just drawn back to hit the nailhead with the hammer when Faith screeched like a cat with its tail caught in a door. His aim thrown off by her unexpected outburst, he missed the nail and brought the hammer down on the end of his thumb.

Normally, he did his best to watch the cuss words he used around a lady, saving the worst ones for when he was extremely frustrated, and always alone or with other guys. But the pain shooting through his thumb and up his arm loosened his tongue, and he couldn't have stopped the colorful string of words flowing from his mouth if his life depended on it. He dropped the hammer, cradled his hand to his chest and all but turned the air blue with creative phrases, while Faith danced around the room whooping and hollering like a sugared-up five-year-old trying to do a rain dance. Even with a sore ankle, she managed to put on an impressive display, and he stopped cursing to stare at her in complete awe.

"What the hell was that all about?" he demanded, when the pain in his rapidly discoloring thumb settled down to an aching throb.

She stopped prancing around and stood in the middle of the room, searching the floor as if she'd lost something. "A mouse...tried to crawl...up my leg."

It figured, he thought disgustedly. He'd known the minute he released that mouse and watched it cross the yard to run back to the house that it would end up causing him a butt-load of trouble.

He was extremely relieved to hear she'd been too preoccupied with getting rid of the mouse to notice his less than polite language. "I'd say after all that noise and the little jig you just danced, he's off somewhere having a mouse coronary about now," Cooper said dryly.

She shuddered, then looked at him for several long seconds before asking, "What happened to you?"

Apparently she'd noticed the way he held his hand protectively against his chest.

He shrugged one shoulder and held his thumb out for her inspection. The movement caused the throbbing to increase. He tried not to grimace from the pain, but failed miserably. "I missed the nail."

"Let me see," she said, rushing over to him. She took his hand in hers. "I caused you to hit your thumb, didn't I? I'm so sorry."

Her touch took his mind off some of the pain and he watched as she gently examined it. How could he tell her without making her feel worse that was exactly what had happened? He'd just as soon cut his tongue out first.

Shaking his head, he lied, "My aim was off. It would have happened anyway."

"Where's your first-aid kit?" she asked, her soft hands still holding his.

"I-in…" He cleared his suddenly dry throat. "In the kitchen. Why?"

"This should be iced down to prevent more swelling." Still holding his hand in hers, she led him into the kitchen. "Do you have another ice-pack?"

Nodding, he swallowed hard. At the moment, she could have led him toward a cliff and certain death, and he would have followed her without so much as batting an eye.

She urged him to bend his arm so that his hand was held high, then pointed toward the plywood table. "Sit down on that wooden crate and rest your elbow on the table. I want you to keep your thumb upright."

He started to tell her not to worry about it, that it had only been a glancing blow and that the throbbing had already started to ease down. Instead, he seated himself on the crate and dutifully elevated his hand.

Watching her prepare the ice bag, it suddenly occurred to him that he was seeing the "real" Faith—

calm, efficient and in complete control—for the first time since her arrival. As soon as she realized he'd been hurt, she'd collected herself and taken charge. He could also tell she loved every minute of it. But then, so did he.

"I can't tell you how sorry I am that I caused you to injure yourself, Cooper," she said, gently placing the bag over his thumb.

He barely managed to gulp back a groan. Her soft, warm hands holding his were enough to heat his blood, but hearing her velvety voice say his name sent it racing through his veins with the force of a record breaking flood.

"It's no big deal," he assured her.

"After having Percy in my class, you'd think I'd be over my aversion to mice," she said, sounding disgusted.

"You're a teacher?"

Nodding slowly, she sat down across the table from him. "I taught first grade."

"For how long?"

"Six years." She glanced down at her hands for a moment, then back at him. "When one of my students was getting ready to move to another state, he donated Percy to the class. Percy was a white mouse and really quite tame." She shuddered. "But he was still a mouse."

He wanted to ask her why she'd quit teaching—what had prompted her to leave her job and move to the Panhandle to seek employment as a housekeeper. But it was clear by the way she'd rushed on with her story about the mouse that she didn't want to go into it.

"And I'll bet that mice are right up there with

spiders on your list of creepy things you'd like to avoid,'' he said, grinning.

She looked relieved that he wasn't asking more questions about her change of career. ''Absolutely,'' she said with a smile that damned near stole his breath.

He took the ice bag off his thumb and placed it on the plywood tabletop. He had to get away from her before he pulled her onto his lap and kissed her senseless. ''I guess I know what I'll be doing while you fix supper.''

A puzzled frown creased her forehead. ''What's that?''

Rising to his feet, he grinned. ''I'll be on a mouse safari.''

''You won't—''

Cooper shook his head. ''I won't hurt it. If I'm able to find him, I'll catch him and take him out to the barn where he can't terrorize you.'' He grinned. ''Maybe with him out there my thumbs will be safe.''

The next morning, Faith made sure to keep an eye on what was around her feet as she washed the few dishes they'd used for breakfast. Cooper had searched high and low yesterday before dinner, and later on during the evening, but hadn't found the mouse. He'd joked that it might have made the wise choice to move on and find another place to nest for the winter rather than risk taking part in another ''mouse dance.''

But Faith knew better. The little critter was probably biding his time just waiting for another opportunity to run around and scare the living daylights out of her.

She dried the last of the dishes, placed them in the cupboard, then walked out onto the back porch. The sun had finally peeked out from behind the clouds this morning and she wanted to enjoy it while it lasted. With rain forecast for the rest of the week, there was no telling when it would appear again.

Noticing Cooper over by the barn, she walked down the steps and crossed the yard. "What are you working on now?"

"I'm trying to get this corral repaired before Flint brings cattle over here next week," he said, without looking up. "I'll need a couple of holding pens until I can get the pastures fenced."

He'd removed his shirt to work and Faith found herself thoroughly mesmerized by his shoulders and upper arms. Her ex-husband Eric had belonged to a gym for over ten years and hadn't come close to the muscle definition that Cooper had.

She waited for the sadness and regret to tighten her chest, as it always did when she thought of her ex-husband. But to her surprise, the feeling never came.

Maybe her grandmother had been right. Maybe moving away from the constant reminder of her shattered dreams was helping her to release the past and get on with building another life for herself.

Cooper turned to face her and the sight of his bare chest and rippling stomach struck her momentarily speechless. Cooper Adams was a hunk from the top of his wide-brimmed cowboy hat to the soles of his big boots. Glancing down at the worn leather, she fleetingly wondered if the old saying about the size of a man's feet and another part of his anatomy held true for Cooper. If so…

Good heavens! Had she taken leave of her senses?

"Was there something you needed?" he asked, looking about as sexy as any man possibly could.

She gulped. It wasn't so much a matter of what she needed as much as it was what she wanted. She *needed* him to put his shirt back on before she did what she *wanted* and reached out to touch his gorgeous body.

"Uh…no," she finally managed to say. "I just thought I'd enjoy the sunshine for a few minutes."

Pushing the brim of his hat back, he glanced up at the sky. "That's probably a good idea. I don't think it'll last more than another couple of hours." He pointed to a bank of clouds slowly building on the horizon. "It's my guess the next storm front will hit just before lunch."

"Will you be able to finish this before it starts raining?" she asked, trying not to stare at all that delicious looking masculine skin.

He raised his arms over his head to stretch. "Probably not. But I intend to get as much done as I can."

Faith stepped over to one of the fence posts and made a show of examining the aged wood. It wasn't that she was interested in the type of post it was or what condition it was in. She had no idea what she was looking at, nor did she care. But she had to get her mind off Cooper and the disturbing thoughts that were invading her obviously addled brain.

When he'd stretched, his muscles had flexed in the most fascinating ways and the action had drawn attention to his lean flanks and the fact that his snug jeans rode low on his narrow hips. It also revealed a thin line of dark brown hair just below his navel that disappeared beneath his waistband. She suddenly felt warm all over. And that wasn't good.

Shaking her head to dispel the image, she concentrated on what he'd said. He needed to get as much of the corral repaired as he could before it started to rain. Since she was his only source of help, there didn't seem to be any other choice.

She took a deep breath. She'd just have to ignore the fact that he had a body to die for.

"What can I do to help?" she asked, turning back to face him.

Cooper picked up the hammer and thought about the last time Faith had offered assistance. It was probably just his imagination, but he'd swear a tiny twinge of pain ran through his sore thumb.

He glanced at the northwestern horizon, then back at the corral. Damn! The clouds were building faster than he'd anticipated and the rain would be moving in within an hour or less.

"You don't mind?" he asked. "This isn't even close to the housekeeping you were expecting to do."

She grinned. "Oh, don't worry. I expect to be well compensated for the extra work."

Even though he hadn't hired her, technically as owner of the Triple Bar, Cooper was responsible for paying her wages. He didn't quite know how to tell her, but he wasn't exactly flush with cash. Oh, he had enough to get the ranch up and running, and he'd be able to get by easy enough until it started paying off. But it sounded like she was expecting a lot more than was usual for a housekeeper's wages.

"Exactly what did Whiskers promise you in the way of a salary?" he asked cautiously.

She named an amount that was about average for taking care of the cooking and household chores. "But Mr. Penn will be paying me dearly for the extra work I do around here." She grinned and he noticed the mischief twinkling in her luminous brown eyes. "One whisker at a time."

Cooper threw back his head and laughed. "Tell you what I'll do. I'll supply the tweezers and hold him down for you."

"You've got yourself a deal, cowboy," she said, giving him a smile that damned near knocked his socks off. "Now tell me what to do so we can get this fence up before it starts raining."

He picked up one end of a fence rail. "Do you think you can hold this while I nail it to the post?"

There was no denying it. He felt a definite twinge in his thumb that time. He ignored it. The mouse was somewhere inside the house and his thumbs should be safe. At least he hoped they would be.

"I'll do my best," she said, stepping forward to support the board he'd positioned on the post.

Thirty minutes and five fence posts later, Cooper pounded the last nail into place, then straightened from his bent position. "Thanks."

"I'm glad I could do something useful," she said, sounding as if she meant it.

"This would have taken me twice as long without your help," he said, wincing as he stretched out his sore muscles.

"What's wrong?" she asked, sounding genuinely concerned.

He rubbed the scar on his left side. "One too many wild bulls."

"I remember you mentioned that you rode bulls."

He nodded. "Until about five years ago. That's when I met up with two-thousand pounds of pissed off beef called The Shredder." He chuckled. "By the time he got finished with me, there wasn't a doubt in my mind why he'd been given that name."

"Was he the reason you have that scar on your back?" she asked, walking over to where he stood.

The concern in her voice, the look of compassion in her eyes, damned near knocked the breath out of him. But when she stepped behind him and started massaging his back, he lost the ability to breathe at all as her fingers gently worked at the knotted muscle just below his left shoulder blade.

She'd asked him something, but for the life of him he couldn't remember what it was. "What did you say?"

"I asked if that was the reason you have this scar on your back," she said patiently.

She traced his blemished flesh with her fingertips and he had to clear his throat before he could manage to get his vocal chords to work. "Uh, yeah, after tangling with him I decided I'd tempted fate enough."

"It looks like it was pretty serious," she said, her hands burning a trail everywhere they touched. "How long were you hospitalized."

"Uh, almost two weeks," he answered. He had to find something—anything—to take his mind off the way her talented little hands were making his body respond. Trying to remember the intense pain he'd suffered, he said, "I lost my spleen...and my heart stopped twice before they got me into surgery."

"My God, Cooper." Her hands stilled. "It sounds like you're lucky to be alive."

He gritted his teeth and tried to ignore his rapidly changing body. "That's what I'm told."

She flattened her hands on his shoulders and trailed them down to the small of his back. "I'd have to agree. You're very lucky," she said softly.

His body tightened and he had to force himself to take a breath. The kind of "lucky" he'd like to be would probably get him a good smack across the face.

Thankful she couldn't read his mind, he tried valiantly to hold himself in check. And he might have, had it not been for the feel of Faith's soft lips brushing against the blemished flesh just below his shoulder blade. But the moment she kissed his scar, a spark ignited in his gut and the heat quickly spread to his groin. He was hard as hell and wanted her with a fierceness that damned near knocked him to his knees.

Spinning around to face her, he placed his hands on her shoulders. "Faith?"

"Cooper, please..." Her guileless brown eyes reflected the same heat that had him hard as hell and wanting to throw caution to the wind.

"This isn't smart, Faith," he said, trying desperately to talk sense into both of them.

"I know," she agreed, sounding as short of breath as he felt. "Nothing can come of it."

She couldn't have put it more plainly if she'd drawn him a picture. Faith wasn't interested in a dust-covered cowboy with nothing but a run-down ranch and a pocketful of dreams.

A pang of disappointment knifed through him. But instead of turning her loose and walking away as far as his legs could take him, he pushed his hat back, then brought his hands up to tangle in her thick auburn hair.

"What the hell. I never was the brightest bulb in the lamp," he muttered, drawing her forward to lightly brush his mouth over hers.

Her lips were soft and receptive, and he couldn't have stopped himself from deepening the kiss any more than he could stop water from rushing over Niagara Falls. Her sigh of acceptance encouraged him and Cooper parted her lips to slip his tongue inside.

When he felt her hands tentatively come to rest at his waist, he reached down to take them in his own and bring them up to his shoulders. Wrapping his arms around her, he pulled her forward and held her to him as he once again tasted and explored her sweet mouth.

Faith knew she was playing a fool's game—that her assessment of men had proven too flawed in the past for her to ever trust it again. Unfortunately, with Cooper she couldn't seem to stop herself. She'd only meant to be helpful when she massaged the knotted muscles in his back, only wanted to help him relieve the pain of the old injury. But the temptation of his warm flesh against her palms had quickly built a fire inside her that was too strong to deny.

His arms drew her closer and the feel of his hard arousal pressed to her stomach made her knees weak and caused her disturbing introspection to dissipate.

Bringing her arms up to circle his neck, she told herself it was only for support, to keep herself from falling in a heap at his feet. But the truth was she wanted to be close to him, wanted to once again feel feminine and desired.

He lifted the tail of her shirt and skimmed his hand up her ribs to the swell of her breast. His callused palm cupping her, his thumb teasing her hardened nipple sent ribbons of desire swirling through every cell in her body. When had he unhooked her bra?

She didn't know and didn't care. His tongue stroking hers, his hands caressing her sensitive breast with such mastery, felt absolutely wonderful. Never in their four-year marriage could she remember the same degree of pleasure from Eric's touch that she experienced from Cooper's.

When he lifted his head to nibble kisses along her jaw to her ear, she moaned. "This is insane."

"You got that right," he said, his warm breath sending a shiver coursing through her.

"We can't—this can't go any farther." She wasn't sure if she was trying to convince herself or Cooper.

"It won't," he said, resting his forehead on hers. "I told you when you first arrived that you had nothing to fear from me." He took a deep breath, refastened her bra and took his hand from beneath her shirt. "And as much as I'd like to deny it right now, I'm a man of my word. Nothing is going to happen that you don't want happening, Faith."

She started to tell him that he wasn't the one she didn't trust, that it was her lack of judgment that scared her witless, but the words died in her throat.

A truck was slowly easing its way down the bumpy lane that led to the ranch.

And for the life of her, she couldn't figure out why she felt nothing but sadness at the thought that they now had a way off the ranch.

Six

"**I**s that your brother-in-law?"

Cooper glanced over his shoulder to see what had distracted Faith. He mentally cursed a blue streak as he watched a silver truck navigate its way around the many potholes in the dirt road leading to the house.

"No," he said, releasing her.

At any other time, Cooper would have been more than happy to have Brant Wakefield show up. Not only would the man pitch in and help finish the repairs on the corral, he was one of the best friends Cooper ever had. Hell, if not for Brant's skills as a rodeo bullfighter, Cooper would be pushing up daisies in some graveyard instead of standing there holding the most desirable woman he'd ever known.

But Brant's arrival represented a way for Faith to leave the ranch—to leave Cooper. And although having a way off the ranch was exactly what he'd wanted two days ago, it was the very last thing Cooper wanted now.

"Who is it?" she asked.

"Brant Wakefield." Turning to face the approaching truck, Cooper made it a point to stand in front of her while she straightened her shirt. "He's an old friend of mine."

"Well, whoever he is, I'm darned glad to see him," she said, stepping to Cooper's side.

"Me, too," he lied. He reached over to smooth her silky auburn hair where he'd run his fingers through it.

"Should I go inside and find a mirror?" she asked as she tried to finger-comb it into place.

He smiled. "You look beautiful."

"No, I mean—"

"You look just fine," he assured her.

He wasn't about to tell her that her perfect lips were swollen from his kisses or that her cheeks still wore the blush of passion. That would send her running into the house for sure. And, although it was none of the man's business what went on between himself and Faith, Cooper did want Brant to know she was off limits.

"Coop, you old dog, how have you been?" Brant called as he slowly got out of his truck.

"Looks like I've been doing better than you, Wakefield," Cooper said, pointing to the brace on his friend's knee. "What was the name of the bull and whose butt did you end up saving?"

Grinning, Brant limped over to where Cooper and Faith stood. "You think you know it all don't you, Adams?"

"Am I wrong?" Cooper asked, returning the man's good-natured grin.

"Nope." Sighing, Brant reached down and rubbed his knee. "I had another run-in with Kamikaze."

Cooper whistled low. "He's one of the worst for trying to hook a cowboy when he's down."

"You got that right," Brant said, nodding. Turning his attention on Faith, he asked, "And who is this lovely lady?"

Without thinking, Cooper slipped his arm around her waist, then making the introductions, added, "Brant and I go way back. He was the bullfighter who kept The Shredder from finishing me off once he had me down."

"It's nice to meet you, Mr. Wakefield." She shook his friend's hand. "Now, if you'll excuse me, I'll let you two gentlemen catch up on old times while I go inside and make sandwiches for lunch. You will be staying, won't you, Mr. Wakefield?"

"Sure thing, Ms. Broderick." The grin Brant sent Faith's way had Cooper grinding his teeth. "And call me Brant."

"Only if you call me Faith," she said, turning toward the house.

As she walked away, Cooper swallowed hard. He'd be damned if the woman didn't have the sexiest walk he'd ever seen. If given the chance, he could watch the sway of her sexy little hips all day long and never get tired of seeing it.

"Nice view, isn't it?" Brant asked from his shoulder.

"Best I've ever seen," Cooper answered without thinking. He could have cut out his own tongue. He might want Brant to steer clear of Faith, but he could do without the man's good-natured ribbing.

"So how long have you two been together?"

"She's my housekeeper."

He watched his friend survey the sagging porch and the plastic covering most of the windows and roof. "Sure. Whatever you say, Coop." Brant leaned one shoulder against the fence. "Then you wouldn't mind if I—"

"Leave her alone, Wakefield," Cooper warned. Turning, he yanked his shirt off the top rail of the corral and shoved his arms into the sleeves. "You've got more than enough women to keep you occupied. You don't need to add another."

When he looked up, Cooper cringed at his friend's ear-to-ear grin. "You're a damned liar and we both know it," Brant said, laughing. "You've got a case of the hot and bothereds for the lady that just won't quit. So you might as well 'fess up."

Jamming the tail of his shirt into the waistband of his jeans, Cooper shook his head. "You irritate the hell out of me sometimes, Wakefield."

Brant threw back his head and laughed. "That's what Morgan and Colt keep saying."

"They're right, too," Cooper said, grinning. Maybe if he got Brant to talking about his family, he'd drop the line of questioning about Faith. "How are those ornery brothers of yours?"

Brant shrugged. "Same as ever. Morgan's still trying to find out who inherited old Tug Shackley's ranch so he can buy them out and expand the Lonetree to the west. And Colt's joined the Professional Bull Riders."

"I thought he was riding broncs," Cooper said, gathering his hammer and sack of nails.

"That didn't work out." Brant shrugged one shoulder. "He said he didn't get the same rush out of riding horses that he did from riding bulls."

Cooper nodded. "I felt the same way when I was riding." He watched Brant rub at the brace on his leg. "You never did answer my question. Whose butt did you save from Kamikaze?"

His friend's easy grin disappeared immediately. "My dumb brother's."

"Colt?"

Brant nodded. "Most guys have the sense to turn out when they draw that black-heart beast," he said, referring to a cowboy's decision to let the bull out of the bucking chute without making the ride. "But not Colt."

"I understand how he felt about a turn out. I've only done it a couple of times myself." Cooper shook his head. "It's not easy paying your entry fee, then standing by to watch the gate swing open without you on the bull's back."

"I agree. But with some bulls it's a matter of survival." Brant stared off into the distance. "I'm just glad I was in the arena that day."

"You got a busted up knee out of the deal. What did Colt get?"

"He walked away without a scratch," Brant said, grinning.

Cooper wasn't surprised. Brant was one of the best bullfighters he'd ever seen.

"The sandwiches are ready if you two would like to come inside and have lunch," Faith said, stepping out onto the porch.

"We'll be right there," Cooper called as he and Brant started toward the house. Glancing up at the sky, he noticed that the bank of clouds he'd been watching earlier had changed directions and gone due south. "By the way, what do you have planned for the rest of the day, Wakefield?"

"Far as I know, I don't have anything going," Brant said with a shrug.

Grinning, Cooper slapped his friend on the back. "You do now."

Faith watched the two men finish the last of the sandwiches she'd made. "I guess that answers my question," she said dryly.

Cooper wiped his mouth with a paper napkin. "What's that?"

"Whether or not you two like peanut butter and jelly sandwiches," she said, smiling.

Both men laughed. "In the early days, when we both started out on the rodeo circuit, we lived off peanut butter and jelly sandwiches," Cooper said.

"Don't forget the times when we'd get a little money ahead and could afford baloney and cheese," Brant added.

Cooper grinned. "Or when we'd scrape up enough change from the floorboard of your truck to get a burger at one of the fast-food joints."

Brant chuckled. "Yeah, it felt like we were dining at a five-star restaurant."

Faith enjoyed listening to the men talk about their days together on the rodeo circuit. But she couldn't seem to stop herself from comparing the two.

Physically, they were both tall, handsome beyond words, and had physiques that could cause women to stop dead in their tracks to stare. Both were easy-going and friendly and had blue eyes. But that was where the similarities seemed to end.

Although Cooper had dark blond hair, while Brant's was black, that wasn't what Faith found so different about the two men. It was her reaction to them that had her baffled. When she'd shaken Brant's hand when he first arrived, she'd experienced none of the warm tingling sensations that she did with Cooper. All Cooper had to do was walk into a room and her heart would start to flutter. And when she looked into his gorgeous blue eyes, she felt as if she might drown.

Heat flowed through her and she decided it would be in her best interest to concentrate on something besides Cooper and the way he affected her.

"Did you ever ride bulls, Brant?" she asked, careful to avoid Cooper's warm gaze.

"Good lord, no!" He looked shocked. "I've got more sense than that. I've always been a bullfighter."

"I thought that was a Mexican or Spanish sport." She rose from the table to clear away their plates. "I didn't realize they had it in rodeo, too."

Cooper shook his head. "It's not that kind of bull-fighting, darlin'. Brant puts himself in front of the bull to distract him while a cowboy dismounts and gets out of the way."

"That sounds dangerous," she said, hoping she didn't sound as breathless as she felt. Whenever Cooper called her "darlin'" in that sexy drawl of his, it seemed hard to take in air.

"It's not that bad," Brant said.

"Don't let him fool you," Cooper said, shaking his head. "There are dozens of cowboys who owe

their lives to this man, including me. That's why
you'll never hear a bullrider have anything but praise
and gratitude for the job he does.''

''Aw, shucks, Coop. I never knew how much you
cared,'' Brant said, grinning mischievously.

Laughing, Cooper stood up. ''Don't let it go to
your head, Wakefield. You've already got an ego the
size of Texas and I'll be damned if I'm going to be
responsible for making it bigger. I'm surprised you
find a hat that fits now.''

''You're just jealous 'cause I get all the girls,''
Brant said, winking at Faith.

''Like that little blonde down in Tucson?'' Cooper
shot back.

Brant groaned. ''You would have to remember
that.''

''That's just the tip of the iceberg.'' Cooper
opened the door and walked out onto the porch.
''There was that time over in Albuquerque that
you…''

Faith watched the two men file out the door, their
good-natured jibes fading as they walked toward the
corral. It was clear to see they were the best of
friends and had been for a long time.

A lump formed in her throat and tears threatened.
Until a year ago, she'd had a friend like that. Charlotte Turner and Faith had grown up next door to
each other and they'd been as close as any sisters
could ever be. She'd been able to trust Charlotte with
everything.

Or so she'd thought.

But having her oldest and dearest friend use her
deepest secret fear that she'd never be able to have
a child against her had been almost more than Faith

could bear. Charlotte had purposely become pregnant with Eric's baby because she knew how important having his own child was to him, and because she'd fallen in love with him.

Sniffling, Faith grabbed the broom and began to sweep the worn hardwood floor. Thinking about her best friend dredged up some of the best memories of her life, as well as the most painful.

But more than anything else, it proved that her judgment of people never had been reliable.

Thunder rumbled in the distance as Cooper folded his arms across his chest and proudly gazed at his newly repaired corral. With Brant's help, Cooper had replaced three fence posts, the rest of the missing rails and hung a new gate. By his calculations, they'd been able to accomplish in a few hours what it would have taken him and Faith at least a full day.

Cooper pulled his shirt on, then began collecting the tools they'd used. "Thanks for the help, Wakefield. I owe you one."

"Hey, man, I had the time and you needed the help," Brant said, grabbing his own shirt from the top of a post. He looked around. "By the way, what's the deal here? I thought you told me you'd bought a ranch that needed a little work. This place looks like it will take a month of Sundays to get into shape."

"One word," Cooper said sardonically.

Brant chuckled. "You don't have to tell me. It was Whiskers, wasn't it?"

By the time Cooper finished explaining the purchase arrangement for the property and about the scheme the old man had cooked up to strand Cooper and Faith together, Brant was laughing so hard he had to wipe the moisture from his eyes. "He sure is a crafty old buzzard."

"I was thinking more like a mean old goat," Cooper said, grinning. He spotted a roll of screen wire and an idea began to form. "I have one more project I need your help with before you leave."

"Besides taking you and Faith back to civilization?" Brant asked.

Cooper's stomach clenched into a tight knot. He'd purposely avoided thinking about them having a way off the ranch. But whether he wanted to or not, the subject had been broached and there was no turning back.

"Faith will probably take you up on the offer." He felt as if someone had punched him in the gut as soon as he said the words. Taking a deep breath, he added, "But I think I'll stay and see what I can get done around here before the cattle arrive."

Brant gave him a wicked grin. "That'll give me a good hour or more to get to know Faith on the way to Amarillo."

Cooper knew that he was being baited, but he couldn't stop himself. "I'm warning you—"

"I get the message, Adams." Brant laughed. "I just had to see how far gone you are."

"I'm not—"

"Save it," Brant said, holding up his hand. "I wasn't born yesterday. Even I'm smart enough to see that you're a goner." He smiled knowingly. "And unless I miss my guess, the lady has it just as bad for you."

"You've got it all wrong, Wakefield."

Brant folded his arms across his chest and stubbornly shook his head. "I don't think so. What do you want to bet she stays here with you when I take off?"

Cooper glared at the man. "Did that bull kick you in the head while he was tearing up your knee?"

"Nope." Brant's grin sorely tempted Cooper to reach out and strangle the man.

"Look around, Wakefield. What woman in her right mind would want a man with a run-down ranch and just enough money to get by?"

"A woman in love."

"Now I know that bull kicked you in the head," Cooper said disgustedly. "You just don't remember it."

His friend's answering laughter irritated the hell out of Cooper. "Just wait and see what happens when I take off tomorrow morning. If Faith doesn't stay here with you, I'll come back next week and help you fence every pasture this place has. And we both know how much I hate stretching barbed wire."

"You'll help anyway," Cooper said with confidence.

Brant grinned. "I know. But I had to have something to bargain with. Now what was that project you wanted me to help you with?"

"You're never going to believe this."

"Try me."

"We're going to build a cage for a mouse," Cooper said, tossing Brant the roll of screen wire.

"You're right," Brant said, shaking his head. "I don't believe you."

The next morning, Faith poured coffee for the two men to have with their muffins. "I'd like to thank both of you for building that cage and confining the mouse,'' she said, remembering how they had searched most of the evening before they finally found the annoying little animal. ''Maybe now I can get something done, instead of watching what's around my feet.''

''No, problem,'' Brant said, cheerfully. He devoured the banana-nut muffin and reached for another. ''Cooper said it tried to run up your leg the other day.''

She shuddered. ''I'm afraid I really put on a show that day, didn't I, Cooper?''

When he nodded, but didn't say anything, she wondered if she was making the right decision. He'd been strangely quiet all morning.

Deciding there was no better time than the present to find out, she cleared her throat. ''Cooper, I have something I need to ask you.''

He slowly set his coffee cup on the plywood tabletop. ''What do you need?''

You, a traitorous little voice in her muddled brain whispered. She wasn't sure where it had come from, but she fully intended to ignore it.

''If you don't have a problem with it, I'd like to stay until your brother-in-law brings the cattle.'' Rushing on before he got the wrong idea, she explained, ''I have a score to settle with Mr. Penn.''

She knew her excuse was as flimsy as tissue paper and that she'd lost every ounce of sense she possessed. But she'd lain awake half the night, thinking about leaving the Triple Bar Ranch—leaving Cooper—and she'd come to only one conclusion. She was going to stay with him. Then she'd tossed and turned the rest of the night, trying to rationalize her decision. Getting even with Mr. Penn was the only plausible excuse she'd been able to come up with.

Relief flowed through her when she watched a slow smile turn up Cooper's firm lips. "That would be fine with me, darlin'," he said. His sexy baritone sent shivers along every nerve in her body and she suddenly felt warm all over.

Brant's chuckle turned to a cough when boots shuffled under the table. "I won't be leaving until after lunch," he said, reaching down to rub his shin. "Let me know if you change your mind."

"I doubt that will happen," Cooper said, his gaze holding hers captive. "Faith deserves to take a strip off Whiskers's hide for what he's pulled."

She glanced away in time to see Brant look from her to Cooper, then grinning like the Cheshire cat, rise to his feet. "All righty then. It's settled. Come on, Coop. Let's get that junk cleaned out of the tack room before I take off."

Four hours later, Cooper and Faith stood on the porch waving as Brant pulled away from the house. Cooper liked having his best friend around most times, but this wasn't one of them. He was more than glad to see the backside of Brant's pickup truck as he drove away.

The way he saw it, he had three, maybe four days left with Faith before Flint and Whiskers arrived. He knew it was pure insanity, since nothing could ever come of the attraction between them. But he wanted to spend as much time with her as he could before she walked out of his life for good.

"Brant is very nice," she said congenially. "I'm

glad he was able to help you get the corral and barn ready for the cattle.''

''I can't think of anyone else I'd rather have in my corner when the chips are down,'' Cooper agreed. But he didn't want to talk about Brant, or corrals or cattle.

Taking her by the hand, he started down the porch steps. ''Come on, darlin'. I have a surprise for you in the barn.''

Faith gave him a grin that damned near knocked him flat. ''It's not another one of your harmless critters, is it? Because if it is, I'd just as soon pass on the opportunity.''

''Nope. This is something I think you're really going to like. Brant and I found it while we were cleaning out the tack room.'' When they reached the barn door, he covered her eyes with his hand. ''Now keep in mind that it isn't perfect and probably not what you're used to. But it's better than what we have.''

''So you're trying to tell me to keep an open mind?'' she asked, laughing.

He chuckled. ''Something like that.'' Leading her to the room in the middle of the barn, he took his hand from her eyes. ''So what do you think?''

''Is that what I think it is?'' she asked, her face breaking into a happy smile.

''Sure is.'' He rocked back on his heals. ''It's an honest to goodness, antique bathtub. After I get it scrubbed up, I'll carry it up to the house so you can take a real bath instead of having to make do with a wash pan and a sponge.''

Her reaction was everything he'd hoped it would

be. She threw her arms around his neck and planted a kiss on him that had him deciding to poke around the barn a little more and find other treasures that would make her happy.

Seven

Humming along with the classical music coming from the battery operated CD player she'd found buried in one of her suitcases, Faith lifted the last pot of hot water from the camp stove. She poured it into the old-fashioned bathtub, then added cool water to get the temperature just right. Sprinkling in a generous amount of the bath salts she'd brought with her, she inhaled deeply as the scent of roses filled the room. It smelled heavenly. She couldn't wait to immerse herself in the water and soak until it turned her completely pruny.

Gathering her long hair, she twisted the length of it, then used a large toothed clip to secure it to the back of her head. While the water had heated on the stove, she'd taken off her clothes, put on her fluffy pink terrycloth robe and collected everything she'd need. There was only one thing left to do before she lit the candles she'd arranged by the tub, stripped off her robe and slipped into the water. She needed to find some way to secure the back door to keep Cooper from accidentally walking in to find her lounging in the tub.

It wasn't that she didn't trust him to respect her privacy. She did. But he knew nothing about it. She hadn't decided to coax water from Old Faithful and indulge herself until after he'd gone outside. She was a bit bothered by the fact that she'd be bathing in one corner of the kitchen, but that's where the kerosene heater was and the other rooms were simply too chilly to even consider.

She took a deep breath and looked around. What could she use to secure the door? It didn't have a lock. When she'd first arrived, she'd found that odd and very disconcerting. But the more she thought about it, the more she decided that it probably hadn't been necessary for the occupants who had lived there so many years ago. The house was quite a distance from the main road and completely hidden from view. And neighbors certainly weren't a problem. Besides herself and Cooper, there wasn't another living soul for miles and miles.

In her search to find a way to block the door, she spotted several large packing cartons that they hadn't yet emptied. Perfect. They should be heavy enough to insure her privacy.

She lifted the towel she'd hung over the window in the door to make sure Cooper was still down by the barn. When a rusty bucket came sailing out of the big open door to land on the rapidly growing pile of things to be hauled away, she breathed a sigh of relief. He was too intent on getting the barn into shape to stop anytime soon.

Smiling, she turned and shoved the heavy boxes against the door, lit the candles and slipped off her robe. She stepped into the bathtub and sat down. It was short and narrow and she had to bend her knees a bit, but the water felt wonderful when she sponged it over her arms and upper chest. As she washed herself with the soft mesh puff, she decided it was quite possibly the most luxurious bath she'd ever taken. She smiled. Compared to washing off in a washpan like she'd had to do for the past few days, it felt positively lavish.

Resting against the high back of the tub, Faith allowed the soft scent of roses and the soothing music of Chopin to surround her. She closed her eyes in sheer pleasure. A trip to an expensive spa couldn't make her feel any more relaxed and pampered than she did at that very moment.

When the sound of thunder echoed across the land, Cooper tossed another piece of junk on the pile outside the barn door and looked up. The clouds had gathered while he'd been inside cleaning out the feed room and within the next few minutes the sky was going to open up and pour. Unless he wanted to dodge lightning bolts, he'd better knock off work and head for the house.

Dusting off his hands on the seat of his jeans, he glanced toward his new home. The place wasn't much right now. But it would be. He'd make sure of it. It already looked better, since he and Brant replaced the broken support post on the back porch. At least now he didn't have to duck his head when he reached the top step.

A sense of pride filled his chest, then spread throughout his body. For the first time in his life, he had a place of his own—a place that wasn't portable. Having been raised on the rodeo circuit, even as a child his home had been a camper on the back of a pickup truck. His family had traveled like nomads from one rodeo to another while his dad chased his dreams, first as a steer wrestler, then as a bullfighter.

But Cooper had finally made the decision to put down roots and it felt good. Damned good.

He just wished that Faith hadn't shown up to see the ranch the way it looked now. He'd have preferred her arrival a little later, after he'd made some much needed repairs and renovations. Maybe then…

Cooper shook his head. No sense worrying about that now. She'd just the same as told him she wanted no part of him or his run-down ranch. Besides, now was not a good time to be thinking about a wife. When he did find a woman to share his life, he'd have a ranch to be proud of and something more to offer her than a leaky roof and bathroom facilities that involved a fifty-yard sprint and a flashlight after dark.

His steps heavier than they'd been only moments ago, he walked to the house and up the porch steps. The sound of music caused him to stop short. Where had she come up with something to play music? He shook his head at his own foolishness. She'd probably unearthed it in one of her suitcases. He chuckled. He wouldn't be surprised at anything she found in Mt. Samsonite. Hell, as big as some of those pieces were, he wouldn't be surprised if a family of four could be housed quite comfortably in one of the damned things.

But as he listened to the classical music he shook his head again as he reached for the doorknob. She liked that lofty stuff, while he preferred the down to earth sound of country tunes. It was just one of many ways they were different, and additional proof that a woman like Faith could never be interested in a cowboy like him.

He twisted the knob, but stopped short when the door refused to budge. Glancing up, he grinned at the towel covering the window in the door. Women liked curtains, and it appeared that Faith had been busy using whatever she could find to fashion some.

But why had she locked him out of his house? Deciding that she probably wanted to surprise him with the little feminine touches she was making to his home, he tapped on the glass.

"Faith?"

Nothing.

The music from her CD player was pretty loud. She probably couldn't hear him.

Knocking on the wooden frame, he put a little more force behind his effort and managed to push the door open a couple of inches. A soft flowery scent drifted through the crack. "Faith, let me in," he called.

Still nothing.

What was going on? Could she have fallen while she was hanging things over the windows? Was she hurt?

His mind ran through a half dozen different scenarios—all of them ending with Faith injured and lying unconscious somewhere inside the house.

Placing his shoulder against the door, he shoved with everything he had and suddenly stumbled into the room amidst a pile of large boxes.

"Faith?" he shouted as he pushed himself to his feet.

Candlelight in the far corner of the kitchen drew his attention and he felt as if someone had punched him in the gut. There she sat in the old bathtub, naked as the day she was born, and looking more beautiful than any woman he'd ever had the privilege to lay eyes on.

She blinked owlishly in an obvious effort to get her bearings, and it was clear to see she'd fallen asleep while taking a bath. When her eyes focused on him, she let out a startled squeak and to his immense disappointment, quickly tried to cover herself. But the old tub was small and there was no way for her to sink lower into its depths.

"What are you doing in here?" she asked, her cheeks turning a very pretty rose color. "I thought you were clearing junk out of the barn."

He had to fight with everything he had to keep from grinning. She looked so danged cute sitting there with her silky auburn hair piled on top of her head, trying to hide her full breasts behind that puffy little bath thing.

The urge to smile died and his mouth felt as if he'd swallowed a mouth full of desert dust when he noticed how little the bath puff covered. Her coral nipples were drawn into tight buds and he couldn't have looked away if he'd wanted to. Which he didn't.

Fully clothed, Faith was beautiful. But nude, her satin skin glistening in the candlelight, she was a vision of everything a woman should be—soft, sensual and seductive beyond words.

Heat streaked through him and his lower body tightened predictably. "It...uh, started raining," he said, shoving his hands in his front pockets to relieve some of the pressure of his suddenly tight jeans.

He could tell she'd noticed his arousal, but instead of looking away, she seemed as fascinated by his body as he was by hers. He took a step forward.

A sudden flash of light illuminating the room, followed closely by a loud clap of thunder caused them both to jump and brought Cooper back to reality. What the hell did he think he was doing? He'd told her he could be trusted not to put the moves on her and he'd keep his word if it killed him. The way his lungs refused to take in air and his heart pounded against his ribs, he decided that it just might, too.

Turning around, he forced himself to take a deep breath as he headed toward the door. "I'll be out on the porch," he said through gritted teeth. "Once you've dressed, let me know and I'll empty the bathtub."

Faith waited until Cooper shoved the boxes out of the way and slammed the door behind him before she grabbed the towel beside the tub and stood up. What in heaven's name had gotten into her?

Her cheeks burned and she bit her lower lip to hold back an embarrassed sob as she vigorously rubbed the moisture from her skin. Heaven help her, but she'd wanted him to see her, wanted him to want her as badly as she wanted him. And if the bulge in his jeans and the hungry look in his eyes were any indication, he did.

Thank goodness the intrusive sound of the storm

had brought her back to her senses. But how was she ever going to face him again? Was she so desperate to be held, to once again feel desired, that she had practically issued Cooper an invitation to make love to her?

Quickly pulling on her extra baggy, blue sweatshirt and jeans, she mopped the floor where she'd splashed water out of the tub when she'd jerked to a sitting position. She blew out the candles and lit the lantern. The overcast sky outside had caused the room to be darker than usual and they would need the light in order to see. But the candles were too romantic, too intimate, too seductive.

Deciding she couldn't delay calling Cooper inside any longer, she opened the door. "You can come in now."

She didn't look at him as he crossed the room and began bailing water from the bathtub. She couldn't. Her mind was trying to sort through her tangled emotions. Humiliation still heated her cheeks at the way she'd shamelessly acted when he'd stood there staring at her. But it was the thrill she'd felt when she'd seen the hungry desire for her in his deep blue gaze that scared her senseless.

Once he'd hauled the last of her bath water outside, he walked over to Old Faithful and began working to coax water from the spout. "If you don't mind, I think I'll take a bath and shave while there's still light," he said.

Nodding, she turned to leave the room. "No problem. I'll stay in the living room until you're finished."

"You know, there's nothing to be embarrassed

about,'' he said, setting a large pot of water on the camp stove to heat.

Good grief! Was she that transparent?

Without looking at him, she shook her head. "Please, let's just forget—"

He surprised her by wrapping his arms around her from behind and pulling her back against him. "Darlin', I could live another hundred years and not forget the sight of your beautiful body," he said close to her ear.

His low, deeply impassioned statement sent a shiver up her spine and created a pang of longing in her chest that threatened to suffocate her. "Cooper, I can't—"

"It's all right, darlin'," he said, holding her close. "Like I've told you before, you can trust me. I give you my word that nothing is going to happen that you don't want happening."

It wasn't that she didn't trust him. And it certainly wasn't that she didn't want him. She did. But she couldn't trust herself not to start longing for the things she knew she'd never have.

Stepping from his arms, she started to walk away.

"Faith?"

"I'll be in the living room," she said without turning to face him. "Let me know when you've finished dressing and I'll start dinner."

Cooper dried the plate Faith handed him and placed it in the cabinet. He hated the sadness shadowing her pretty brown eyes, hated the silence between them. She hadn't said more than a handful of words in the past two hours.

"Thanks for supper," he said, trying once more

to start a conversation. "There's not a whole lot of ways to fix Spam on a camp stove, but that was really good."

"You're welcome," she said, turning to wipe off the counter. "Would you mind emptying the dishpan for me?"

As he dumped the water outside he wondered how he could get them back to the easy companionship they'd shared for the past few days. He could tell she was no longer embarrassed by his walking in on her while she took her bath. But he couldn't understand the sadness that had taken its place. If anything, he'd have thought she'd be hopping mad that he'd barged in like a charging bull.

He shook his head. There were some things about women he just didn't understand and probably never would.

The rain dripped off the porch roof and he shook his head. If the weather would cooperate, he'd take her out and show her some of the things he'd found in the barn. Things that were sure to make her smile, like the hula girl lamp or the castle made out of hundreds of glued together bottle caps. But since the storm showed no signs of letting up, that was out of the question.

Opening the door, he reentered the kitchen deep in thought. What could he do to lift her spirits?

Looking around, his gaze landed on the CD player still sitting on a box in the corner and he felt a smile slowly lift the corners of his mouth. "Faith?" When she glanced up from the book she'd started reading, he asked, "Would you mind if I used your CD player?"

"Of course not." She got up from the plywood

table to remove the classical disk she'd been playing while she bathed. "Are you going to listen to it in here?"

"No. I think I'll take it into the living room," he said, reaching for the handle.

As he picked up the unit and headed toward the front of the house, he purposely didn't ask if she'd like to join him. He had a few things to take care of first.

Setting the player on a wooden crate, he pushed all of the packing cartons into one corner and took down the rope clothesline. Fortunately, the room was large and they would have plenty of room to move around.

By the time he finished, it was getting dark outside. "Where did you put the candles?" he asked as he walked back into the kitchen.

She glanced up from the book to give him a curious look. "On the counter by Old Faithful. Why?"

"It's getting dark outside and I need a little light to keep from stumbling over something and breaking my neck," he said, grinning.

"Would you like to use the lantern?" she offered.

The last thing he wanted was the brighter light. "No. You need it for reading."

Faith watched him collect all of the candles, then stroll back down the hall. Why on earth did he need so many?

As the sound of lively country music filtered in from the front of the house, she shrugged and turned her attention back to her book. The less she thought about Cooper Adams, the better off she'd be. But when she found herself reading the same page for the third time, she closed the book and abandoned any pretense of trying to read.

Her initial embarrassment at her reaction when he'd found her naked had given way to deep sadness. He wanted her and she wanted him. But if they made love, she couldn't trust herself not to fall head over heels for him. And, if the longing that held her tightly in its grip was any indication, she was already well on her way to doing just that.

Something deep inside told her that Cooper was exactly the man he appeared to be—honest, hardworking and loyal to a fault. But she'd trusted her instincts once before and been proven devastatingly wrong.

She'd misjudged her husband and best friend, and hadn't even suspected they were having an affair. The first that Faith knew of anything going on between them had been when Eric asked for a divorce to marry Charlotte because she was pregnant with his child.

"Faith, darlin', are you all right?" Cooper asked from her shoulder.

Looking up, she noticed the concern on his handsome face. She'd been so lost in her disturbing memories, she hadn't noticed that he'd walked back into the room.

"I'm fine."

"Are you sure?" he asked. "You looked like you were a million miles away."

"I think I was," she admitted, shaking off her dismal mood and forcing a smile.

"Are you back now?" he asked. He grinned and her heart skipped a beat.

"Absolutely," she said, feeling a little breathless.

How could she think about the past with Cooper standing so close?

"I'm glad. I have somewhere I want to take you for the evening," he said.

Lightning flashed and thunder rumbled. Where could he possibly take her with it raining cats and dogs outside?

Taking her by the hand, he pulled her to her feet. A warm tingling sensation immediately raced up her arm from the contact. "Would you do me the honor of joining me in the front of the house, ma'am?"

Laughing at his mischievous expression, she followed him down the hall. "What's this all about?" she asked, raising her voice to be heard above the music coming from the CD player.

When they came to the end of the hall, he moved his arm in a sweeping gesture and leaned down to whisper in her ear. "I'm taking you to the Triple Bar Dance Hall, ma'am."

Her eyes widened and she brought her hand up to cover her startled gasp. He'd lit every candle they had to cast a soft glow over the cleared room and draped a sheet over a packing carton for a table. Two small wooden crates had been arranged on either side of the table for seating and a single taper stuck in a longneck beer bottle served as the centerpiece.

Tears blurred her eyes and she had to blink several times in order to hold back the threatening flood of emotion. She'd never seen anything more romantic or touching in her entire life.

"Do you like it?" he asked, sounding hopeful.

She nodded and had to swallow around the lump in her throat before she could speak. "Cooper, this is the nicest thing anyone has ever done for me."

Raising up on tiptoes, she placed a kiss along his chiseled jaw. "Thank you."

Looking sexier than any man had a right to look, he touched the back of his hand to her cheek. "I'm glad you like it." He gazed down at her for endless seconds before his expression changed to a teasing grin. "It looks pretty crowded in here tonight, but I think I see a table over there," he said, pointing toward the box.

He obviously wanted to lighten the conversation, which was fine with her. "I believe you're right," she said, playing along.

They crossed the room and once he'd seated her, Cooper made a show of looking around. "The waitress must be taking a break. I guess I'll have to go up to the bar to get something for us to drink. What would you like?"

She pretended to think for a moment. "I'll have whatever you're having," she finally said.

Grinning, he tipped his hat. "I'll be right back."

In no time at all he was seating himself on the crate opposite her. He placed two juice boxes on the table, then stuck narrow straws in the tops. "I got myself a beer, but I thought you might like wine."

"Nice choice," she said, smiling back at him.

The song that had been playing ended and another one began.

"Would you like to dance?"

"I'm afraid I'm not very good at country dancing," she said, shaking her head.

He rose to his feet and took her hand. "Come on, it's easy. I'll teach you."

She stood up and followed him into the middle of

the room. "I have to warn you, I'll probably step all over your feet."

"That's going to be kind of hard to do, since we'll be doing the Stroll," he said, laughing.

"Stroll?"

Nodding, he draped his arm across her shoulders. "It's a Texas tradition." He instructed her where and how to hold his hands, then how to do the steps.

They'd made a full circle of the hardwood floor before she realized that she was actually doing the dance correctly. "This is fun and not nearly as hard as I thought it would be," she said, laughing.

He grinned as they started around the room another time. "I told you it was easy."

By the time the CD ended and the changer switched to another disk, Cooper had not only taught her the Stroll, he'd taught her the Two-Step and a couple of line dances as well.

"This is really fun," she said, breathlessly.

"Ready to take a break?" he asked, leading her over to the table.

She sank down onto the crate she'd used for a chair and took a sip from her juice box. "Cooper, do you mind if I ask you a question?"

"Shoot," he said, taking a long draw on his straw.

"Why do you wear your hat while you're dancing?" She paused. "In fact, I don't think I've seen you take it off more than once or twice since I've been here."

He shrugged. "No self-respecting Texan would be caught dead dancing the Two-Step or the Stroll without it," he said as if it were the most reasonable explanation in the world. "In fact, there are only a couple of things a Texan will do without wearing his hat.''

She could just imagine what one of them was. His sexy grin told her she was right.

"Have you ever tried not wearing your hat when you dance?'' she asked, hoping he didn't notice the heightened color she was sure tinted her cheeks.

"Nope.''

"Why not?''

He slowly set his juice box down and the grin he sent her way curled her toes. "It's like Samson and his hair. With it, he's a hell of a man. Without it, he's nothing but a scrawny little wimp. Same thing holds true for a cowboy. With his hat on, he's a dancing fool. Take it off and he has two left feet.'' Grinning, he leaned over as if sharing a secret. "Besides, it looks real good.''

She laughed and shook her head. "That hat is your security, isn't it?''

"Something like that.''

When a slow song began he took her hand in his, then stood and pulled her to her feet. "Ready to try a slow one?''

The scent of his clean, masculine skin, the feel of his warm palm pressed to hers, made the ability to speak impossible. Nodding, Faith willingly followed him onto their private dance floor.

He reached down to take her hands and place them on his wide shoulders. Then, positioning one of his thighs slightly between her legs, he wrapped his arms around her waist and drew her close.

Moving them around the floor, he gazed down at her and the edge of his hat brim rested on the top of her head. It seemed to lend an intimacy that took her breath.

Lightning illuminated the room and thunder crashed. She barely noticed.

"Cooper?"

"What?"

"What are we doing?" she asked, her tone nothing more than a throaty whisper.

"We're dancing," he said, his gaze never wavering from hers.

"No, I mean—"

He placed his index finger to her lips. "Just dancing, darlin'."

She tried concentrating more on the song and less on the man holding her to his hard body. Big mistake. The words were every bit as provocative as their dancing. Maybe more so.

Cooper's hands roamed the length of her back and every cell in her body tingled to life. Resting her head against his shoulder, she had to remind herself to breathe.

When he cupped her breast and teased the tight tip with his thumb, her knees threatened to buckle and she couldn't for the life of her seem to draw in air. His muscular thigh between hers and the friction it created as he guided them around the floor sent heat streaking through her veins to pool in the lower part of her stomach.

The weather outside seemed to be intensifying, but it was nothing compared to the storm raging within her own body when he cupped her bottom with his other hand and pulled her closer. He pressed his arousal against her stomach and nuzzled the sensitive skin of her neck. Sparkles of light flashed behind her closed eyes and her heart felt as if it turned a cart-wheel inside her chest.

As the song ended, she started to pull back. He held her tightly to him.

"Just let me hold you a little while longer, dar-lin'," he said, his tone husky.

It was pure insanity on her part, but that was ex-actly what she wanted him to do. "Cooper?"

"Whenever you tell me to let you go, I promise that I will," he said, brushing his lips against hers.

His mouth settled over hers and anything even re-sembling a thought escaped her. She was too caught up in the warmth of his kiss, the teasing of his tongue as he parted her lips and slipped inside to stroke her own.

The longing she'd fought from the moment she'd met him welled up inside her and created an aching need that only Cooper could cure. She wanted him more than she'd ever wanted any man in her entire life.

"Faith?"

Pulling back, she stared up at him for endless sec-onds before conceding defeat to the desire that she'd felt from the moment she'd first seen him. The way he'd said her name, the hunger in his deep blue eyes told her more than words that he wanted exactly what she wanted.

He'd told her there were very few reasons why a cowboy removed his hat. She was absolutely certain she knew what one of them was.

She took a deep breath and smiled. "Cooper, take off your hat."

Eight

Cooper's heart slammed against his ribs, then took off in overdrive at Faith's request that he take off his hat. "Are you sure?" he asked. The last thing he wanted was for her to have regrets tomorrow morning.

She reached up and removed his Resistol. "The only regret I'll have is if we don't make love," she said softly.

He searched her face for any indication that she had even a shadow of a doubt about making love with him. When he found none, he pulled her against him and buried his face in her silky auburn hair. He'd bet good money that Faith didn't trust easily. But the confidence in him that he'd seen in her luminous brown eyes had damned near brought him to his knees. He'd make this the most memorable night of her life, or die trying.

Releasing her, he walked over to the CD player and changed disks. When the classical music that she'd been playing while taking a bath filled the room, he blew out all but one of the candles, then took her by the hand.

He used the remaining candle to light their way as they silently walked into the bedroom and, setting it on a box in the corner, took her into his arms. Her body fit against him perfectly and lowering his mouth to hers, he let her know without words how much her trust meant to him.

Her lips clung to his a moment before she opened for him to deepen the kiss, and her eagerness excited him more than anything he could have ever imagined. She was letting him know that she wanted him as much as he wanted her, that she was as caught up in the magic as he was.

When he slipped his tongue inside to explore and tease, she whimpered, then wrapped her arms around his neck to thread her fingers in the hair at the nape of his neck. Her warm touch, the sound of her desire and the sweet passion he tasted as she tentatively met his invasion, sent his blood pressure soaring and caused his lower body to throb with need. He'd never in his life been this turned on by a single kiss.

Shifting to relieve the pressure of his suddenly too tight jeans, he reached down to cup her bottom and lift her into the cradle of his hips. He wanted her to know what she did to him, wanted her to realize the power she held over him.

He brought his hands up to the tail of her sweatshirt and sliding his palms along her ribs, cupped her full breasts. "You aren't wearing a bra," he said, feeling her already tight nipples bead even further against his palms.

She slowly shook her head. "I was in such a hurry to get dressed, I...forgot."

"I'm glad." He gently circled his thumbs over the tight nubs.

She closed her eyes and he felt a tiny tremor course through her. "Mmmm."

"Feel good?"

"Y-yes."

"It's going to feel even better," he promised, reaching down to pull her shirt over her head.

She lifted her arms to help him and once the garment lay on the floor at their feet, he sucked in a sharp breath. He'd caught a glimpse of her breasts that afternoon when she'd tried to hide behind that puffy little bath sponge. But it was nothing compared to the unrestricted view he now enjoyed.

Supporting the weight of them with his hands, he lowered his mouth to first one puckered coral bud, then the other. "So soft. So sweet." He raised his head. "You're beautiful."

"So are you," she said, sounding breathless.

Raising his head, he smiled. "Guys are too flat and angular to be beautiful."

"You are." The sincere expression on her pretty face just about knocked his size thirteen boots right off his feet. "Please take your shirt off, Cooper."

He couldn't have denied her if he'd wanted to. Which he didn't.

Tugging his shirt from his jeans, he grasped the tails and pulled the chambray open with one quick jerk. He'd never been more appreciative of snap closures on a shirt than he was at that very moment.

When she placed her soft, warm hands on his chest, heat shot straight to his groin and his heart thumped so hard that he wouldn't have been surprised if it cracked a couple of ribs. As she ran her palms over the rise of his pectoral muscles, her fingers tracing his own puckered nipples, Cooper took deep breaths and tried to slow down his libido. But when she explored the ridges of his stomach, her fingers dipping slightly below the waistband of his jeans, he stopped breathing altogether.

Groaning, he took her hands in his and shook his head. "If you keep that up, you're going to give me a heart attack."

"I like touching you," she said. Her smile sent his temperature up another ten degrees.

"And I like touching you, darlin'," he said, bending down to take off her shoes and socks. He caught her gaze with his and held it as he unsnapped her jeans and pulled them and her panties over the flare of her hips and down her slender legs.

Careful to keep his attention on taking off the rest of his clothes, he didn't allow himself the pleasure of looking at her until after he'd pulled off his boots and socks, then shucked his jeans and briefs. He knew the limit of his control. He also knew he'd just about reached it.

Straightening to his full height, he tossed his clothes on top of Faith's and turned to face her. The air in his lungs stalled and his mouth went bone-dry. Candlelight painted her satiny skin with a soft glow and highlighted her firm, uptilted breasts, trim waist and the curve of her gently rounded hips.

Lightning flashed and thunder boomed, but they barely noticed.

At the sight of Cooper's powerful body illuminated by the streak of light from the storm, Faith's breath caught and her pulse pounded in her ears as loudly as the thunder crashing outside. His wide shoulders and sculptured chest tapered down to narrow hips and lean flanks. Her gaze skipped lower and she swallowed hard. Proud and strong, his manhood rose from a mat of dark brown curls. He certainly validated the old adage about the size of a man's feet being an indication of the size of his other parts.

Her gaze flew to his and he must have sensed her hesitation. "Don't worry, darlin'," he said, stepping forward to take her into his arms. Nuzzling her neck, he whispered close to her ear, "We'll fit together just fine."

The feel of skin against skin, male hardness pressed to female softness, sent electric currents of pure desire sizzling along every nerve in her body. "It's been quite a while," she admitted, wondering if that throaty voice could really be hers.

Placing his index finger beneath her chin, he tilted her head up to meet his dark blue eyes. "You trust me, don't you, Faith?"

"Yes."

His reassuring smile made her feel as if she'd melt into a puddle at his feet. "We're going to take this slow and easy and I'm going to love you in every way a man can love a woman."

Her stomach did a back flip and a shiver of anticipation slithered up her spine at his candor. But before she could tell him that was exactly what she wanted, he lowered his mouth to hers. His tongue slipped between her lips and set off a hot, dizzying current of pure electrified desire flowing to her most secret places. All thought ceased as she reveled in the man holding her to his strong body.

Breaking the caress, Cooper trailed moist kisses down the slope of her breast, then took her tight nipple into his warm mouth. Ribbons of tingling need wove their way around her and formed a tight coil in her lower stomach. Her knees trembled and she had to clutch his arms to keep from falling.

"Easy, darlin'," he said, raising his head to look at her.

The heated passion she saw in his eyes, the promise of complete fulfillment and his request for her trust, released something deep inside of her and at that moment she knew for certain that she'd fallen hopelessly in love with him.

"Cooper, please—"

Apparently he understood her unspoken plea because he led her over to the bed. "I need to get some protection," he said, turning back to the pile of clothes on the floor.

"It's not necessary," she said, quietly.

He hesitated. "You're protected?"

A deep sadness swept through her as she nodded. She couldn't bear to tell him there was no need for any type of prevention, that she was unable to have children.

Taking her into his arms, he lowered her to the bed and stretched out beside her. He gathered her to him, and gazing down at her, tenderly covered her lips with his. His callused palm smoothed over her skin with such infinite care, it brought tears to her eyes and she forgot all about prevention or her inability to become pregnant. He erased all that with his touch, his mind-numbing kiss.

He slid his hand down her side to caress her hip, her inner thigh making her quiver with need. But when he cupped the curls at the apex of her thighs, his finger dipping into the soft, moist folds to stroke and tease, spirals of sheer ecstasy swirled through her. The feelings he drew from her were so intense that she gripped the sheet beneath her and arched into his touch.

"Feel good, darlin'?" he asked, raising his head to look down at her.

When he entered her with his finger to test her readiness for him, the coil in her belly tightened and turned into a sweet ache. She squeezed her eyes shut and fought for sanity as waves of sensation flowed through her.

"Cooper, please—"

In answer to her broken plea, he spread her thighs with his knee and levered himself over her. She felt the tip of his strong arousal probe her and she tensed in anticipation of his invasion.

"Open your eyes, Faith." When she did as he commanded, he held her gaze with his. "Just relax. We're going to take this slow and easy."

The blaze of need in his dark blue eyes took her breath. But she could tell he was holding himself in check, making sure that she was as ready for their lovemaking as he was.

"Trust me to take care of you?" he asked.

She nodded without hesitation. At that moment, she trusted him more than she'd ever trusted anyone.

Slowly, gently, he pressed forward with such care she thought she'd die from the ecstasy of it. When he had filled her completely she felt him quiver inside of her as he held himself in check. Her heart swelled with love as she realized Cooper's sacrifice.

He remained perfectly still, and she instinctively knew he was giving her time to adjust to him, to the exquisite stretching of her body by his. He was placing her above his own needs. He was taking care of her.

Cupping his face with her hands, she smiled up at him. "Love me, Cooper."

A groan rumbled up from deep in his chest and he shuddered against her. "Darlin', it will be my pleasure." He pulled his hips back, then eased forward. "And I give you my word it'll be yours, too."

His rhythmic thrusts created an inner storm in Faith that rivaled the weather outside and she wrapped her arms around him to keep from being lost. The heat spiraling through her burned higher and brighter, tightening the feminine coil until it clouded her mind to anything but the love she felt for him.

A flash of lightning momentarily lit the room and seemed to charge the atmosphere with urgent anticipation. Time stood still as Cooper's body built the tempest to a crescendo and she wasn't sure if the sound in her ears was the thunder outside or the pounding of her own heart. As she gave herself up to the whirlwind of her climax, the hot tide of passion washed over her as wave upon wave of fulfillment surged through her soul.

Moments later, she heard Cooper groan deeply, then shudder as spasms overtook him and he released his essence deep within her. When he collapsed on top of her, Faith tightened her arms around him, reveling in the differences between his body and hers, anchoring him to her as his own storm subsided.

His breathing eased and he levered himself up on his elbows. "Are you all right?" he asked, brushing a strand of hair from her cheek.

"I feel incredible." She closed her eyes and stretched. "That was the most beautiful experience of my life."

"Mine, too." He rolled to his side and gathered her to him. "The next time—"

"There's going to be a next time?" she asked, her body tingling to life at the promise in his blue gaze.

"Oh, yeah."

"And when would that be?"

He chuckled. "Just as soon as I recover, darlin'."

"And how long do you think that will take, Mr. Adams?"

He brushed her lips with his. "In about five seconds, Ms. Broderick."

Wrapping her arms around his neck, she waited a few moments, then grinning, informed him, "Time's up, cowboy."

Cooper rolled over to put his arm around Faith, but he met empty air. He opened his eyes to see where she was, but the bright shaft of sunlight streaming through the windows quickly had him squeezing them shut. Cursing, he threw back the covers, sat up and swung his legs over the side of the bed.

"Burning daylight is not the way to get things done around here," he muttered as he reached for his clothes.

He stopped suddenly and listened to the country

music drifting in from the other part of the house. He didn't even try to stop the satisfied grin he was sure split his face from ear-to-ear. Faith was playing one of the CDs they'd danced to the night before—the one he'd played just before they'd made love.

The memory of their lovemaking, of her supple body taking him in, draining him of every ounce of energy he possessed, sent heat coursing through him. They had come together several times during the night and still he burned for her. He shook his head. How was he going to get any work done around the ranch when all he wanted to do was take Faith in his arms and love her until they both dropped from exhaustion?

He shook his head. He had a feeling he could make love to her for the rest of his life and still never get enough of her, never satisfy the need she created in him.

Taking a deep breath he abandoned that train of thought. He had nothing to offer her but the promise he'd one day make a success of the ranch. And that wasn't enough. A woman like Faith deserved a whole lot more than he could give her.

But he refused to dwell on that. They had until Flint and Whiskers showed up and that's what Cooper intended to concentrate on.

Lost in thoughts of all the ways he planned to love her during the few short days they had left together, he stopped short at the sound of male voices coming from the kitchen. Damn! Flint and Whiskers had arrived earlier than they were supposed to. And although that's exactly what Cooper had wanted four days ago, it was the last thing he wanted now.

Taking a deep breath, he slowly walked into the

kitchen to find his brother-in-law and Whiskers sitting at the plywood table having coffee with Faith.
He wanted nothing more than to draw back and
punch the hell out of both of them. When they left
to go back to the Rocking M later in the day, they'd
be taking Faith with them, taking her away from him.

"Would you like a cup of coffee, Cooper?" Faith
asked when she glanced up to see him standing in
the doorway. The glint of panic he detected in her
expressive eyes ripped right through him.

"Thanks," he said, nodding. He dragged a crate
from the corner and sat down. When she placed a
mug on the table in front of him, he smiled. "By the
way, I just finished putting up that rod in your bedroom closet," he said, hoping she'd catch on.

What went on between the two of them when they
were alone was nobody's business but their own. He
didn't give a damn about himself or what others
thought of him. But he was determined to protect
Faith, and if that meant telling lies the size of Texas,
he'd gladly do it.

Looking relieved that he'd fabricated a plausible
explanation for his not being present to greet Whiskers and Flint, she smiled. "Thanks. Now I can hang
up some of my things."

"Whiskers, don't you have something to say to
Cooper and Faith?" Flint spoke up, his expression
determined.

The old man cleared his throat. "Well, I reckon
as how I don't have a whole lot of choice."

"Whiskers," Flint warned.

"Tarnation, Flint, let me do this my own way,"
Whiskers grumbled. Turning to Faith, he said, "I'm
mighty sorry for strandin' you here with Coop. I

don't know what got into me. It was a mean thing to do and I shouldna done it.''

Cooper watched Whiskers hang his head for effect and almost burst out laughing. He'd seen Whiskers in action before and knew beyond a shadow of doubt that the old man didn't mean a word of what he'd just said. It was Cooper's guess that once his sister, Jenna, had gotten wind of the incident, she'd threatened to turn the old man's room at the Rocking M ranch house into a playroom for the boys if he didn't apologize. And since Whiskers thought the sun rose and set on Jenna, Cooper knew the old guy would walk barefoot across hot coals if that's what it took to get back in her good graces. He also noticed that the apology hadn't included him.

''No, you shouldn't have done that to either of us, Mr. Penn,'' Faith agreed. ''But what's done is done.'' She patted Whiskers's arm reassuringly. ''We'll just forget about it as long as you promise not to do anything like that again.''

Whiskers's head popped up so fast, Cooper thought he might have wrenched his neck. ''You got my word, Miss Faith,'' he said, giving her a toothless grin.

Cooper and Flint both coughed at the same time to cover their laughter. It was the biggest load of bull they'd ever heard the old geezer dish out.

''Where are Jenna and the boys?'' Cooper asked, once he'd recovered.

''At home,'' Flint said, rising to his feet. ''The boys caught colds while we were at Disneyworld and Jenna's got some kind of stomach flu. She thought the way the weather's been with all the rain it would be best if they stayed home.''

"Damn. I really wanted Faith to meet Jenna," Cooper said without thinking.

As soon as the words left his lips, Cooper could have bitten his tongue in two. Flint and Whiskers both knew how close Cooper was to his sister, and that it was extremely significant that he wanted her to meet Faith.

"We'd better get those cattle unloaded and in the corral," he said, to cover his blunder. He stood up and reached for his hat, but it wasn't on the peg where he always hung it before he went to bed at night.

"Where's your hat, Coop?" Whiskers asked, his eyes twinkling merrily.

"I think you left it in the living room last night," Faith said, starting down the hall. "I'll get it for you."

As soon as she left the room, Whiskers chuckled. "Only one reason I know of that would keep a man from hanging his hat on the peg before he goes to bed at night."

Cooper gave both men a hard stare. "I was tired."

Laughing, Whiskers patted Cooper's shoulder as he passed by him to go outside. "Yeah, and I'm still a young buck with piss and vinegar runnin' through my veins."

"Come on, Whiskers," Flint said, grinning. "Let's get started unloading the trailer before you get both of us into trouble."

The door had barely closed behind them when Faith walked back into the room. "Thank you," she said, handing Cooper his hat. "I appreciate the excuse you gave them for not being around when they arrived."

"How long had they been here before I got up?" he asked, jamming his hat onto his head.

"About five minutes," she said, looking relieved.

Reaching for her, he pulled her to him. "How do you feel this morning, darlin'?"

She wrapped her arms around his waist and laid her head against his shoulder. "Absolutely wonderful."

"I'm glad." He kissed the top of her head. "I feel pretty damned good myself."

"Cooper?"

"What, darlin'?"

Faith hesitated. In the past few days, he hadn't mentioned anything about her staying with him after Whiskers and Flint brought the cattle. And she really couldn't think of one good reason to remain on the Triple Bar, other than she didn't want to leave him.

Sighing, she decided there was no good way to broach the subject, nor was she willing to run the risk of having him say no if she asked him if he wanted her to stay. "You'd better get out there and help them with the cattle before they come looking for you," she finally said.

"There's really nothing for you to do here in the house," he said, leaning back to give her a look that all but melted her bones. "Why don't you come outside and see what's going to pay the bills around here one day?"

"Sure," she said, heartened that he wanted her to see a part of what he was working to build.

When they walked out into the yard, she saw a long stock trailer filled with red, white-faced cattle hooked to the bed of an extended cab pickup truck. It was backed up to the corral that Cooper and Brant had repaired, while another truck with a shorter trailer connected to it was parked close by.

"Coop, where you want me to tie the horses?" Whiskers called.

"I've got a couple of stalls ready in the barn," Cooper answered. Faith watched him help Flint lower the tailgate on the longer trailer. "Put them in there."

As Whiskers led two beautiful reddish brown horses into the barn, a stream of about a dozen cows and calves trotted out of the trailer and into the enclosure. Standing by the fence, Faith was fascinated by Cooper's efficiency. It was easy to see he'd worked around livestock all his life.

"You're going to have trouble with that one," she heard Flint say as he nodded toward a calf standing by itself on the far side of the corral.

"Why's that?" Cooper asked, closing the gate. He rested his forearms on the top of the fence and gazed at the calf Flint had indicated.

"Her momma got stuck in the mud down by the creek last night and by the time my men found her this morning, it was too late." Flint walked to the cab of his truck and removed a bucket with a long nipple attached to the side and a large bag of some kind of animal food. Handing it to Cooper, he added, "They've been trying to get her to feed, but haven't had much luck."

"It was that heifer that dropped her calf out of season," Cooper answered.

Faith wasn't sure how he could tell which cow was missing. To her they all looked alike. But that didn't matter. As an idea began to take shape, she stepped up to where the two men stood. "What will you have to do to take care of her?" she asked.

"I'll have to mix up calf formula and feed her once every few hours." Cooper shook his head. "Damn. I don't have time to be raising a bucket baby right now."

She bit her lower lip as she gathered her courage. She knew that she'd have to leave in the near future, but not yet.

Trying not to sound as if his answer would mean the world to her, she asked, "Would it help if I stayed around for a while longer and took care of the calf for you?"

Nine

Sucking in a sharp breath, Cooper's pulse took off at a gallop. Faith had a way to escape the primitive conditions they'd been forced to live in the past few days, but she was willing to stay?

"Are you sure you want to do that?" he asked, hoping with all his heart that was exactly what she wanted. "It's going to demand a lot of your time."

She smiled. "My dance card's pretty crowded, but I think I can make room for one little red calf."

Her reference to dancing sent a fair amount of adrenaline surging through his veins. She was letting him know that she was staying, not because she wanted to care for an orphaned calf, but because she wanted to be with him. He felt like picking her up, taking her inside the house and making love to her for the rest of the day.

"Darlin', you've got yourself a job." Grinning, he

handed her the feed bucket. "Welcome to mother-hood."

For a split second, he could have sworn that a deep sadness clouded her eyes, but it was gone as quickly as it appeared. "I think I'll name her Penelope," she said, turning to stare at the little calf.

He frowned. "Penelope?"

"Don't you like it?" she asked, her expression hopeful.

"It's not that I don't like it. It's fine." He shrugged. "But normally a rancher doesn't name his cattle."

"That doesn't matter," she said, smiling. "Penelope's special. She's named after my grandmother." She laughed and the sound was like music to his ears. "They both have the same color hair."

Her enthusiasm and sweet smile had him deciding that she could name every animal he owned if she wanted to and he'd readily go along with it. "Then Penelope it is," he said, smiling back.

"How old is she?"

"She was born about five weeks ago," he answered.

Turning on him, her stormy expression surprised him. "She's only a month old and she's still in there with all those big cows? No wonder she's standing there shivering. She's just a baby and scared to death. Go get her."

It appeared Faith was taking this mothering thing pretty seriously. "Where am I going to put her until I get another stall in the barn ready?"

"I don't care, but she's not staying in there."

Whiskers walked up and slapped Cooper on the

back, his toothless grin wide. "While I was puttin' the horses up, I nosed around—"

"Why doesn't that surprise me?" Cooper asked dryly.

Snorting, the old man raised his chin a notch and finished, "You could put her in the tack room."

Cooper looked over at Flint for help. But the smirk on his brother-in-law's face and his noncommittal shrug made Cooper want to punch him.

Resigned, he opened the gate and motioned for Flint to follow him. "You take the left side and I'll take the right."

In no time, they had the calf cornered and gathering her into his arms, Cooper carried Penelope out of the corral.

"Will she be all right in the tack room by herself?" Faith asked, sounding genuinely concerned. She reached out and gently ran her hand along the calf's red hide.

Cooper stared at her a moment as he watched her soothe the frightened animal he held. Faith would be a wonderful mother some day. He only wished he could be the father of her babies.

A pang of deep longing tightened his chest. He'd always planned on having a wife and kids one day, and she was just the type of woman he'd always wanted. But the timing was lousy. There was way too much to do to this place, too many repairs to be made.

His steps heavier than they'd been only moments before, he walked toward the barn. He couldn't ask Faith to saddle herself with a man who had nothing to offer her but hard work and a truckload of promises. She deserved better than that. A hell of a lot better.

Settling Penelope in the tack room, he went back outside and found Flint and Whiskers preparing to climb into the cab of Flint's truck. "I appreciate your bringing the cattle and horses." Giving Whiskers a pointed look, Cooper added, "And for returning my truck."

"You don't have to thank me." The old geezer had the audacity to give Cooper a toothless grin as he added, "I been thinkin' it all worked out right fine."

Cooper knew Whiskers wasn't referring to returning the truck as much as he was about taking it in the first place.

"If you get tired of the primitive conditions, you're both more than welcome to stay at the Rocking M," Flint offered.

Cooper glanced at Faith to check for her reaction to the offer, but an almost imperceptible shake of her head quickly had him grinning and shaking his own head. "Thanks, but I don't want to waste thirty minutes just driving over here. It's time I could be getting something done." He held up the new cell phone battery Flint had handed him earlier. "Besides, now that I can make calls, I'll be able to get the power company out here to hook up the electricity as soon as I get the house rewired."

Flint nodded as he got into the truck. "If you change your mind, you know where we are."

"Did you mention Sunday dinner, like Jenna said?" Whiskers asked, getting in on the passenger side.

Flint snapped his fingers. "Damn, I almost forgot.

Jenna said to tell you to be over at our place by noon Sunday.''

Cooper grinned. "We'll be there. Tell the boys I'll take them on another critter hunt if they're over their colds by then.''

"I'll tell them," Flint said, his grin wide. "But I've got better sense than to tell Jenna.'' Starting the engine, he and Whiskers waved as they drove away.

Draping his arm around Faith's shoulders, Cooper waited until the truck disappeared from sight before he pulled her into his arms. "I'm glad you decided to stay,'' he said, brushing his mouth over hers.

She smiled as she wrapped her arms around his waist. "Penelope needs me.''

He smiled down at her. "Is the calf the only reason you decided to stay?''

"No.''

"What's the other reason?''

"I haven't finished my work for the day.''

"Work?''

Nodding, she stepped from his arms and started walking toward the barn. "After I take care of feeding Penelope I have to—'' She stopped to glance at him over her shoulder, and giving him a smile that sent his blood pressure out of sight, finished, "Make the bed.''

Faith stirred the warm water into the powdered calf formula, then tested it on her arm to see if it was too hot. Confident that the milk was just right, she eyed the gallon bucket with the nipple on the side. It wasn't full, but it still looked like an awfully large amount for one little calf.

"Cooper, are you sure this isn't too much?" she called down the wide barn aisle.

Poking his head around the side of the stall he was cleaning, he shrugged. "Flint said they were having trouble getting her to eat, but if she starts nursing like she's supposed to, it'll be about right." He walked toward her. "I almost forgot to tell you, you'll have to be careful to brace the bucket when you start to feed her. You won't be able to just hold it by the bail."

"Why?"

He grinned. "Because she'll butt her head against the bucket just like she would against her momma's udder and you'll wind up with calf formula all over you."

"Ouch," Faith said, wincing. She could just imagine how a poor mother cow would feel. "Why do calves do that?"

"It helps get the cow's milk started," he explained. He lifted the bucket. "Come on, I'll show you how to hold it to keep her from knocking it out of your hands."

He carried the bucket down to the tack room where he'd confined Penelope, then showed Faith how to hold the bucket to steady it. "She's still a little skittish about people," he said, walking slowly over to the corner where the little calf stood shivering nervously.

Faith heard him murmur soothing words as he caught the calf and guided her to where Faith stood holding the pail of milk. "Come on, sweetheart," she said, adding her encouragement.

She watched Cooper kneel down and take hold of the nipple. He squirted a little milk toward Penelope and as soon as it landed on her nose, the calf ran her tongue out to lick it off.

"That's it, little one." He squirted more milk onto the calf's nose. "You're hungry, aren't you?" Grinning, he looked up at Faith. "Once she gets the taste and figures out where it came from, she should hit that bucket like a defensive tackle trying to break through the line."

It took several squirts for Penelope to realize where the milk came from, but when she did, she took the nipple into her mouth and butted the pail so hard Faith almost dropped it. "You were right about her butting against it," she said, laughing. "Will she drink all of this at one time?"

"Probably." He stood up and scratched Penelope's red back while she noisily sucked on the nippled bucket. "If the cow was around, she'd nurse whenever she wanted. But now that you're her momma, she'll have to get used to a schedule."

Faith's chest tightened when he referred to her as Penelope's mother. He had no way of knowing how long she'd wanted to be a mother, how she and Eric had tried to have a baby for over a year with no luck. She stared down at her bovine charge and blinked back tears before Cooper noticed. At least she'd get to mother something, even if the baby in question had a long tail that wiggled every time she ate.

"If you two will be all right, I'll go finish getting her stall ready," Cooper said.

"We'll be fine." Faith watched the level of milk in the bucket descend as Penelope butted against it and sucked noisily on the nipple. "Is there a lot left to do?"

He shook his head. "I just need to put down a fresh bed of straw."

"Where did the straw come from?" She hadn't seen Flint or Whiskers unload anything but the horses and cattle.

"Whiskers wasn't joking when he said he'd thought of everything." Cooper chuckled. "There's about twenty bales of straw stacked in one of the other stalls and about two weeks supply of horse and cattle feed stored in the feed room." He walked to the door. "When Penelope gets finished eating let me know and I'll carry her down to her new home."

Faith watched him go, then looked down at the calf he had coaxed into eating. Cooper was the most gentle, caring person she'd ever known. The patience he'd shown as he worked to help Penelope learn to find nourishment from the bucket had amazed her. And if she had any doubts about her feelings for him, they'd just been erased.

She was completely and hopelessly in love with Cooper Adams.

Faith bit her lower lip to stop its nervous trembling. She knew nothing could ever come of a relationship with Cooper. He deserved to have a family and she refused to deprive him of it. But she had a few more days to store up a lifetime of memories. And that was exactly what she intended to do.

She just hoped when the time came for her to leave that she was able to go without leaving her entire soul behind.

Cooper had just finished spreading straw over the dirt floor of the stall when he felt something tickle the back of his neck. Reaching up, he brushed his hand across his nape. When he felt the tickling again, he turned to find Faith standing behind him holding a straw in her hand.

He grinned. "Oh, so you want to play, huh?"

"How do you know that was me?" she asked innocently as she started backing away from him. "It might have been a spider that spun his way down from one of the rafters, tickled your neck, then climbed back up."

"Was it?"

Laughing, she took another step backward. "No, but it could have been."

When she turned to run from the stall, he caught her around the waist and pulled her to him. "Have you ever seen a tickling spider, darlin'?"

"No."

"Then I guess I'll have to show you one," he said, running his fingers over her ribs.

She giggled and squirmed to break free of his grasp. "Cooper—"

"What?"

"Stop…tickling me."

Her wiggling threw them both off balance, and making sure he held her so that he took the brunt of the fall, they landed in the soft bed of straw. With her sprawled across his chest, their legs tangled together, his body responded with a speed that made him dizzy. In a matter of seconds he was fully erect, his veins pulsing with need.

She must have noticed the change in his body because she stopped laughing to stare down at him. He watched as the teasing light in her eyes faded and a hunger that matched his own began to replace it.

"Faith?"

She stared down at him for several long seconds, then giving him a slow, sexy smile that damned near caused him to have a heart attack, she said, "Your hat came off when we fell."

He hadn't even noticed. Seeing it lying a few feet away, he smiled back at her. "So it did."

She ran her finger down his nose, then traced his lips. "Should I get it for you?" Her finger dipped into his mouth. "Or do you want to leave it where it is for a while?"

His grin faded and he sucked in so much air, he thought his lungs might explode as he caught on to her meaning. Was she really asking him if he wanted to make love here in the barn?

He needed to make sure he wasn't reading things wrong. "Well..." He had to stop and clear his throat in order to make his vocal chords work. "What do you think, darlin'?"

She appeared to give the matter some thought, then leaning down, whispered in his ear, "I think you'd be more comfortable with your hat off, Cooper."

The sound of his name on her velvet voice, the look of hunger in her pretty brown eyes and the feel of her soft body draped over his, sent a shaft of deep need straight to his groin. At that moment, he didn't care if he ever wore his hat again.

Cupping her cheeks with his hands, he drew her head down to his and pressed his mouth to hers. Her softness created a warmth in his chest that spread throughout his body and he moved to deepen the kiss. But Faith had other ideas.

When she slipped her tongue inside to stroke and tease his, the heat ignited into a flame that threatened to consume him. She was arousing him in ways he'd never believed possible and he had to shift to relieve the discomfort his jeans suddenly caused him.

As her lips moved over his, her hand busily worked at unsnapping the grippers on his shirt. With a pop that sounded like a cannon going off to his heightened senses, first one snap, then another gave way.

She lifted her head and the smile she gave him made him wonder what she had planned next. He didn't have to wait to find out. Leaning over, she began pressing kisses to his newly exposed skin, and with each touch of her lips a tiny charge of electricity shot straight up his spine. But when her tongue darted out to circle his flat nipple, he thought he might just end up being electrocuted from the current coursing through him.

"Darlin', you're killing me."

Her throaty laughter sent a shaft of desire coursing through every cell in his body. "You want me to stop?"

He swallowed hard in an effort to moisten the cotton coating his throat. "Hell no!"

Smiling, she rose to her knees and reached for his belt. "Are you sure?"

When he nodded, she worked the leather strap through the metal buckle, then eased the tab of his fly down. Her fingers brushed against the cotton fabric covering his arousal and he jerked as if he'd been zapped by a cattle prod.

"I can't stand much more of this," he said through gritted teeth. Unable to lie still any longer, he sat up. "It's high time I evened the score."

"What did you have in mind?" she asked, her voice sliding over him like a sensual purr.

"This," he said, pulling her sweatshirt over her head. She was wearing the lacey bra he'd seen through her wet T-shirt the day she'd arrived on the Triple Bar. He ran his finger along the edge of the cup. "You know, as good as you look in this, I like you better out of it."

"You do?"

He nodded and unhooked the closure at the valley of her breasts. Pulling the straps from her shoulders, he tossed the scrap of lace on top of his hat, then filled his hands with her.

"This kind of beauty shouldn't be covered up," he said, lowering his head to take one coral nipple into his mouth. Running his tongue over the tight peak, he tasted her, then sucked the tight bud until she moaned with pleasure. "Does that feel good, darlin'?"

"Mmmm."

"Want me to stop?"

"No." She reached out to trace her fingers over his own puckered flesh. "How does that feel?"

"Good." He closed his eyes as a shudder ran the length of him. "Damned good." When her fingertips skimmed down his chest and belly to the waistband of his briefs, his eyes popped open. "What are you doing now?"

Her smile just about turned him wrong-side out. "Last night you explored my body, now it's my turn to explore yours."

At her urging, he rose to his knees, his heart pounding like a jackhammer against his ribs. "Darlin', there's something you should know."

"What's that?" she asked.

His breathing felt as if he'd been running a marathon and he had to concentrate hard on what he was trying to tell her. "At this stage of the game, I don't think I can stand a whole lot of exploration."

"I'll keep that in mind."

Faith held his gaze with hers as she lifted his hands to place them on her shoulders, then slowly shoved his jeans down to his knees. He felt her fingers slide beneath the elastic band of his briefs and the anticipation of her touch had him gritting his teeth for control. It took everything he had not to rip both of their clothes off and end the sweet torture. But when she gently eased the cotton fabric over his arousal, pushed them down to his thighs, then took him into her soft warm hands, his head felt as if it might come right off his shoulders.

She traced his length and measured his girth while her palm cupped him. The rush of desire that coursed through him made him dizzy.

But when she stroked him, he took her hands in his and shook his head. "Darlin', much more of that and we'll both be sorry."

Passion colored her porcelain cheeks as without a word, she stood up and removed her jeans and panties. He could tell she was as turned on as he was.

When she once again knelt down in front of him, Cooper laid back against the straw. She started to take off his boots, but he wrapped his arms around her and drew her on top of him. Kissing her, he let her know he didn't want to waste time dispensing with the rest of his clothes.

She seemed to understand as she straddled him and guided him to her. He watched her body take him in, felt her melt around him. Closing his eyes, he struggled to hang onto what little control he had left.

Everything in his being was demanding that he thrust within her, to race toward what he knew would be a soul-shattering climax. But taking deep even breaths, he willed his body to slow down. He refused to complete his satisfaction unless he was assured that Faith achieved the same degree of pleasure.

When she rocked against him, he opened his eyes to gaze up at the woman who held him so intimately. She was the most beautiful woman in the world and her body caressing his as she moved was quickly shredding every good intention he possessed.

Grasping her hips, he held on as she rode him to the edge of no return. The red haze of passion surrounded him, blinding him to anything but the intense sensations Faith was drawing from him. Never in his entire life had he felt anything as overwhelming. She possessed him body and soul.

Her moan of pleasure came a moment before he felt her inner muscles quiver then squeeze him as her body urged his complete surrender to hers. His muscles contracted as he thrust into her one final time, and groaning, he gave himself up to her demands as he emptied his seed deep inside of her.

In that moment, he knew without a doubt that he'd surrendered more than just his body to her. He'd just given her all of his heart and soul.

Ten

Seated next to Cooper as he drove the distance between his ranch and the Rocking M, Faith became more apprehensive with each passing mile. She should have made her excuses and stayed behind at the Triple Bar while he visited his sister and her family.

She glanced over at his handsome profile and her chest tightened. Her reluctance to attend the gathering had nothing to do with not wanting to learn more about the man she loved, and everything to do with her self-preservation.

She'd desperately tried to deny the pull between them, tried not to fall in love with him. But Cooper had made it impossible. He was kind, considerate and the most caring man she'd ever met. How could she not fall hopelessly in love with him? Or want to know everything about him?

But the day would come when she'd have to leave the Triple Bar ranch—leave Cooper—and the more deeply involved she became with him and his family, the harder it would be for her when it was time to go. And there was no doubt that she'd have to leave.

Cooper wanted things that she could never give him. It would be unfair to him if she stayed and he gave up those dreams for her.

"You're awfully quiet," he said, reaching over to take her hand in his. "Is something bothering you?"

She shook her head. "I'm just a little tired," she lied.

He grinned and her insides felt as if they turned to melted butter. "I shouldn't have kept you awake so long last night."

His reference to their lovemaking caused a flutter deep in the pit of her stomach. "I'm not complaining," she said, trying not to sound as breathless as she felt.

"Good." He kissed the back of her hand. "Because I intend to keep you up late tonight, too."

Her heart rate increased and the fluttering in her stomach increased. She needed to lighten the moment or she might just go into total meltdown right there in the cab of his truck.

"You're insatiable," she said, laughing.

"When it comes to you, I am," he admitted. The look in his eyes seared her and she suddenly felt like fanning herself.

He steered the truck off the main road and as they passed under a wrought iron sign with Rocking M on it, she noticed a black horse grazing contentedly in the neatly kept pasture to their right. "That's a beautiful animal,'' she said, hoping to distract Cooper's attention.

"That's Jenna's stallion, Black Satin,'' he said, slowing the truck for her to take a better look. "A few years back he was the national reigning horse champion.'' He laughed. "Now he's just the well-kept boyfriend of about twenty-five brood mares.''

"Your sister raises horses?''

He nodded. "That's how she and Flint met. He owned Black Satin and hired Jenna to train him. But since she's the only person who can do anything with Satin, Flint gave him to her for a wedding present.''

"Your sister sounds like she's a very accomplished horsewoman.''

"She sure is,'' he said, sounding proud. Smiling he added, "You two will get along great.''

Faith could tell that Cooper was close to his sister and that it was extremely important to him that she meet the woman. Her apprehension increased. He wasn't just taking her to a casual family gathering, he was taking her to get his sister's stamp of approval. Her hands grew cold and a tight knot began to form in her stomach. She had a feeling she was in way over her head.

"We're here,'' Cooper said, parking the pickup beside an SUV with the Rocking M logo painted on the side.

Lost in thought, Faith failed to notice their approach to the big two-story ranch house. "They have a beautiful home,'' she commented as he helped her from his truck.

He frowned. "It's a far cry from the Triple Bar, isn't it?''

She knew he was comparing the two places and

finding his sorely lacking. "One day the Triple Bar will be just as nice, if not nicer than this ranch," she said, touching his cheek. "Just remember that."

He turned his head to kiss her palm. "Thanks, darlin'."

Before she could respond, two little boys burst through the back door, bounded down the steps and raced across the yard to greet them.

"Uncle Cooper, you've got to hear what we did in Florida," the older one said. "It was awesome."

"Yeah, awestrom," the little one said, excitedly. He hurled himself at Cooper and giggled delightedly when his uncle swung him up into his arms.

"Faith, I'd like for you to meet my nephews." Cooper ruffled the oldest one's tobacco brown hair. "This is Ryan. He's eight."

Ryan wiped his hand on the seat of his pants, then stuck it out for her to shake. "Nice to meet you, ma'am."

"It's nice to meet you, too, Ryan." She smiled as she shook his hand, marveling at how much he looked like his father, Flint.

"And this little bundle of energy I'm holding is Danny. He's three," Cooper said, shifting the toddler to sit on his arm.

She could see the love in Cooper's eyes, the pleasure of being with the little boys. He would be a wonderful, loving father one day.

Danny's little blond head bobbed up and down with excitement. "Uncle Coopa, I went to Frorida and made a sandcrastle."

"Sandcastle," Ryan corrected.

"That's what I said," Danny insisted. "Sand-crastle."

"Most of the time he talks pretty good for a little kid," Ryan explained to Faith. "But he still has trouble with some words."

Thoroughly charmed by both children, Faith smiled. "He's lucky to have a big brother like you to help him out."

"Ryan? Danny?" A pretty blond haired woman stepped out onto the back porch. Spotting Cooper, she grinned. "I should have known you were the reason the boys almost knocked the door off its hinges trying to get outside."

Cooper grinned. "Hey there, little sister. How's life treating you these days?"

"Mom's been real sick," Ryan said, looking worried.

Descending the steps, she walked over to where they stood. "Remember, your dad and I explained this to you the other night," she said patiently as she put a reassuring arm around the child's shoulders. "It's just a temporary thing. I'm going to be fine."

"What's up, sis?" Cooper asked, his grin immediately turning to concern. "Flint mentioned you had some kind of stomach thing when he was over at the Triple Bar the other day."

She nodded. "That's what I thought. But it looks like it's going to last longer than just a few days." Her smile was radiant. "It's nothing that another seven months won't cure."

Faith watched Cooper's easy expression return. "Really?" When she nodded, he put his free arm around her shoulders to hug her. "Congratulations, sis. Will I be getting a niece this time?"

"That's what we're hoping for." Turning to Faith, she smiled apologetically. "I'm sorry. We're being rude. You must be Faith.'' She pointed toward Cooper. ''I'm Jenna McCray, this big lug's sister.''

''I'm pleased to meet you,'' Faith said, nodding. It was completely ridiculous, and she felt ashamed of herself for feeling the way she did, but she couldn't keep a tiny twinge of envy from running through her when she'd learned of Jenna's pregnancy.

''Uncle Cooper, are we gonna hunt for critters?'' Ryan asked, expectantly.

''Wanna hunt kitters,'' Danny agreed, nodding his little blond head.

''It just so happens that Faith found one over at my house the other day and I caught it for you guys,'' he said, setting Danny on his feet.

''Cooper,'' Jenna warned.

''Don't go getting all riled up, sis,'' he said, reaching into the bed of his truck. ''I built a cage for it.''

Faith shuddered when she saw him remove the cage containing the mouse. ''That's one little creature you can have with my blessings.''

Jenna laughed. ''I see we feel the same way about these things.'' To Cooper she said, ''You'll have to find a place for it out in the barn. Under no circumstances is that thing coming inside the house.''

''But, Mom,'' Ryan protested. ''He's just a little guy.''

''Wittle guy, Mommy,'' Danny chimed in.

''It's the barn or nothing,'' Jenna said firmly. Faith couldn't have agreed more with her. She hadn't wanted the little critter in the same house with her either.

Cooper handed the small cage to Ryan. ''You

heard your mom, guys. We'll have to find a place in the barn.''

Jenna hooked her arm through Faith's and turned toward the house. "While Cooper and the boys find a place for the mouse, why don't we go inside and get acquainted? I've got several stories to tell you about that brother of mine.''

Faith smiled. She liked Cooper's sister immediately and couldn't wait to hear what the woman had to say about the man Faith loved.

Two hours later, Cooper sat at the big dining room table watching his sister whisper something to Faith. Whatever it was, both women seemed to find it quite humorous.

Even though he had a feeling their amusement was at his expense, it pleased him no end to see that Faith and his sister had hit it off. "What's so funny?" he asked, grinning at the two women who meant the most to him.

Faith gave him a smile that made him glad the tablecloth covered his lap. "Nothing you'd be interested in," she said, giggling.

"Nothing at all." Jenna agreed. She laughed as she wiped Danny's hands and face, then lifted him out of his booster seat.

"Uh-oh, boy," Whiskers said, scooting his chair away from the table. "When womenfolk pack up like that and start to teeheein', you better watch out." He shook his head, his eyes twinkling merrily. "Ryan, you and Danny come with me into the family room and we'll turn on the football game." He shot Cooper a toothless grin. "I have a feelin' when your uncle finds out what your momma's told Miss Faith, it ain't gonna be real purty.''

Both women laughed as if Whiskers had hit the nail on the head.

Cooper frowned. ''I can't think of anything—''

Flint chuckled. ''Let this be your first lesson about women, Coop.'' He reached over to cover Jenna's hand with his where it rested on the top of the table. ''They have minds like steel traps and never forget anything.'' He grinned. ''And you can bet it's something you'd rather forget.''

Faith and Jenna laughed again, making the hair on the back of Cooper's neck stand straight up. Surely Jenna wouldn't mention…

''You didn't,'' he said, narrowing his eyes on his sister.

Jenna's eyes danced as she asked, ''Does Fort Worth ring a bell, big brother?''

Heat crept from beneath his collar, spread up his neck and burned his cheeks. Jenna had told Faith about the time he'd been bucked off, then lost his pants when the bull hooked a horn in his hip pocket and ripped his jeans damned near off of him. He'd left the arena with his jeans in shreds and had to cover his butt with his hat in order to keep from offending anyone's delicate sensibilities.

''One of the Dallas television stations ran the clip on their evening news,'' Jenna said, laughing. ''Then it was picked up by the network.''

''Oh, no!'' Faith was laughing so hard that she had to wipe tears from her eyes.

Jenna nodded. ''The film clip was chosen as a Picture of the Week and broadcast on one of the national news shows.''

When Cooper groaned, Flint threw back his head and laughed. "I told you it would be something you'd like to forget." He rose to his feet to start clearing the table. "Face it, Coop. That little moment in the spotlight will haunt you until the day you die."

His face still feeling like it was on fire, Cooper gladly helped his brother-in-law clear the table. It was either that or strangle his sister for sharing the most embarrassing moment of his life with Faith.

After they'd carried the plates and serving bowls into the kitchen, Cooper returned to the dining room while Flint went into the family room to see how the Cowboys were doing against the 49ers.

"Where's Faith?" he asked when he found Jenna sitting at the table alone.

"Ryan and Danny wanted her to see their turtle."

"Good." He sat down in the chair beside her. "You and I need to talk."

"That's why I'm still sitting here," Jenna said, shifting to face him.

Before he had a chance to think about what he was going to say, he blurted, "I'm in love with her, sis."

"I can tell."

He grinned. "Is it that obvious?"

Smiling, she nodded. "And she's in love with you."

Warmth spread throughout his body at the thought that Faith cared as much for him as he did for her. "You think so?"

"I know so." Jenna wrapped her arms around his shoulders to give him a huge hug. "I'm happy for you, Cooper. She's a wonderful person and I'm looking forward to having her for a sister-in-law. It looks like Whiskers's meddling worked out for the best.''

Pulling away from her, Cooper shook his head. ''I'm not so sure it will work out.''

Jenna looked puzzled. ''Why? You both love each other.''

''This isn't a good time right now for me to be thinking in terms of forever,'' he admitted. ''The ranch isn't even close to being what I want it to be.''

''So what does that have to do with anything?'' she asked, clearly puzzled.

''Think about it, Jenna. I don't have a thing to offer Faith right now.'' He shook his head. ''Hell, the house doesn't even have plumbing.''

''And you think she hasn't already noticed that?'' his sister asked dryly. Her expression turned serious. ''Cooper, you're forgetting something here.''

''What's that?''

''Faith has lived there with you for the past week and a half. She knows exactly what needs to be done to the ranch. And she's still there.'' Placing her hand on his shoulder, Jenna smiled as she stood up. ''Don't you see? It doesn't matter to her. She loves you for you, not for what the ranch will be one day.''

''But I wanted to—''

Jenna shook her head. ''Build it together, Cooper. Let her help you and it will become her dream, too.''

When Jenna walked into the kitchen, he thought about what she'd said. Maybe she was right. Faith had seen the ranch at its worst and had turned down the opportunity to leave, not once, but twice.

And she believed in him and his ability to turn the Triple Bar around. It hadn't been more than a couple of hours ago that she'd told him his ranch would be just as nice if not nicer than the Rocking M one day.

His chest tightened. He loved Faith more than life itself and there was no doubt in his mind that he wanted to spend the rest of his days with her. Now all he had to do was find the perfect time to ask her to share his life, his dream.

"Cooper, do you think we should be getting back to the Triple Bar?" Faith asked as she and Jenna walked into the dining room together. "Penelope will be wanting to eat by the time we get back."

Leaning over, Jenna kissed his cheek. "You take care, big brother." Then in a soft whisper, added, "See what I mean? Let her work with you and the reality will be far better than the dream could ever be."

"Do you need my help?" Cooper asked, setting the bucket of warm water on the bench in the feed room.

Faith laughed and shook her head. "Penelope and I have a very effective system worked out. I hold onto the bucket for dear life and she drains it." Faith measured out the amount of formula, then poured it into the nursing bucket. "If you have something you need to do, go ahead. We'll be fine."

"Thanks," he said, brushing a kiss across her forehead. He gave her a smile that curled her toes, then without another word, he turned and disappeared through the doorway.

She stirred water into the powdered milk and wondered what demanded his immediate attention this time. There was no telling. After observing the work he put into the daily care and feeding of the cattle and horses, it could be one of a dozen different chores.

Shrugging, she carried the nippled bucket to Penelope's stall. She didn't mind that he was too busy to talk to her while she fed the calf. It gave her time to reflect on her day at the McCray ranch.

Even though she'd been reluctant to meet Cooper's family, she'd really enjoyed getting acquainted with them. She'd told herself to keep her distance and not form any attachments—that it would just make things that much harder for her when the time came for her to go back to Illinois. But they'd made it impossible not to care for them. Jenna had been so nice and friendly that Faith felt like they'd been friends for years. And the boys were such adorable little imps, she couldn't help but fall in love with them.

Lost in thought, Faith almost dropped the bucket when Penelope butted against it. Looking down, she was amazed to see that the calf had drunk almost all of the formula.

"Looks like she was pretty hungry," Cooper said, walking into the stall.

Faith glanced up. "Did you get your chores done?"

"I finished those before we left this morning," he said, smiling.

She looked down at the bucket. "I'm finished feeding Penelope. Did you need my help with something?"

He nodded and the sexy grin on his handsome face nearly melted her bones. Taking the bucket from her, he took hold of her hand, led her out of the stall, then secured the door to keep Penelope from getting out. "I need you to come with me."

"Where are we going?" she asked, laughing.

"You'll see." They remained silent as they walked through the early evening twilight to the house, but when they reached the back steps, he stopped and set the nursing bucket on the porch. "Close your eyes, darlin'."

"Why?"

His grin made her heart skip a beat. "Because I want to surprise you."

"What on earth have you got up your sleeve this time?" she asked, breathlessly. The last time he'd made a request like this, she'd ended up learning to dance. Her heart fluttered when she thought of how that evening had ended.

"Do you trust me, Faith?" he asked. His low voice sent a shiver up her spine and caused her knees to wobble.

"You know I do," she said without hesitation. It still amazed her how easily she'd placed her trust in him. Maybe it had been the integrity in his deep blue eyes, or his gentle, caring manner. She wasn't sure. But she knew beyond a shadow of doubt that Cooper would never do anything to hurt her in any way.

"Then close yours eyes, darlin'."

When she did as he requested, he took her hand and carefully guided her up the steps and into the house. She could tell they were moving beyond the kitchen and down the hall.

"Where are we going?" she asked as he led her through the house.

He came to a stop. "Right here."

"Can I open my eyes?" she asked, laughing.

"In just a minute."

She heard him move away from her, then the sounds of the CD with slow country songs—the one that she'd come to love—floated through the air. "Cooper?"

"Open your eyes, darlin'," he said, from beside her.

The living room was once again illuminated with candles and the packing carton he'd used as a table the night they'd danced had been set for two. A platter of bite-size cheese squares sat in the middle of it and two wine goblets with a rich red wine sat at each place.

Turning, she wrapped her arms around his neck and kissed him. "You're the most romantic man I've ever known."

Looking a little embarrassed, he shook his head. "Nah, I just wanted to do something a little special for you."

She didn't think she could possibly love him any more than she did at that moment. In all of their four-year marriage, Eric had never done anything as thoughtful.

"How did you bring all this from the Rocking M without my seeing it?" she asked as he seated her at the makeshift table.

He shrugged and sat down on the crate beside her. "Jenna loaned me a cooler and while you were saying goodbye to everyone, I loaded it into the back of the truck."

"I'll have to thank her the next time I see her," she said, picking up a piece of cheese. Something was different about him, but she couldn't put a finger on what it was.

When she held the cheese to his mouth, his gaze caught and held hers as he took it from her, then nibbled at her fingers with his lips. A tingling warmth filled her and ended all speculation.

He smiled. "I'm the one who should be thanking you for everything you've done around here, dar-lin'." He drew her finger into his mouth and gently sucked on it before letting it go.

"M-me? I haven't done anything but get…in your way most of the time," she said, reaching for her wine goblet. Her hand trembled and she hoped taking a sip of her wine would help steady her voice.

"That's where you're wrong, Faith." He held a piece of cheese for her to sample, then traced her lips with his index finger. "You've held boards, worked to get the house cleaned up and taken better care of Penelope than her own momma would have done."

How was she supposed to concentrate on chewing the cheese he'd given her when his fingertips touching her lips were causing all kinds of delicious sensations to be unleashed deep inside of her?

"I've…enjoyed helping out," she said, breathlessly.

He reached for her hand, then kissed the back of it. "And I've enjoyed having you here with me."

His smooth baritone and sexy grin only added to the warm tingling in the pit of her stomach. But when she gazed into his eyes, her heart skipped several beats and she realized what was different about him. His desire for her was there, as it had been almost from the moment they met. But this time there was also love shining in the dark blue depths.

Her breath came out in soft little puffs. "C-Cooper?"

He took the wineglass from her, set it on the table, then stood up to gather her into his arms. Gazing down at her, he lowered his mouth to hers with such tenderness, her knees failed to support her.

Sagging against him, she gave herself up to his soul-shattering kiss and forgot all about the reason the look of love in his eyes scared her to death. Or that the time had come for her to leave the Triple Bar Ranch.

Eleven

Cooper steadied Faith, then walked over to blow out the candles. Coming back to stand in front of her, he swung her up into his arms and headed for the bedroom.

He'd intended to ask her to share his future, to stay with him and become his wife. But the moment he'd taken her into his arms, the need to possess her, to once again make her his, had become too great a force to resist. He'd never in his life wanted a woman more than he did Faith at that very moment. There would be plenty of time to ask her to marry him after they made love.

Entering the bedroom, he placed her on the bed. His hands shook, but he somehow managed to dispense with their clothing, then stretched out beside her and gathered her back into his arms. He couldn't

get enough of touching her, of feeling her body tremble with need for him.

He wanted to tell Faith how much he loved her,
but incapable of words, he lowered his mouth to hers
and showed her what was in his heart, what was
burning in his soul. She opened for him and the ten-
tative touch of her tongue to his created a flash fire,
searing every nerve in his body, branding him as
hers.

The blood raced through his veins and his pulse
pounded in his ears as her hands slid over his chest
and flanks. It was as if she were trying to learn every
nuance of his body, trying to commit him to memory.

"Easy, darlin'," he said, gently pushing her back
on the mattress. "If we don't slow down, I'm not
going to last much longer."

Gazing down into her luminous brown eyes, he
saw a burning desperation that he'd never seen in
them before. He fleetingly wondered why it felt as if
this would be their final time together, as if they were
saying goodbye. But he threw off the ridiculous feeling and concentrated on bringing her pleasure, showing her with his body what mere words could never
express.

Lowering his head, he kissed his way from her
collarbone down the slope of her breast to the taut
peak. He took the coral nipple into his mouth, teasing, tasting. When she shivered with passion, he
gently chafed her wet skin with the pad of his thumb
as he moved to pay homage to the other tight nub.

"So sweet," he murmured, when she moaned and
clutched at his hair with her hands.

Pleased that she enjoyed his attention, he trailed
kisses down her stomach to the tiny indention at her

waist and beyond. His body throbbed with need, but he ignored it. This was all for Faith, all about showing her how much he loved her.

He smoothed his hands down her hips and legs, then drew them up along her inner thighs to the soft nest of curls hiding her feminine secrets. Nudging her knees apart, he moved to learn all of her, to give her pleasure in the most selfless way a man could possibly give to a woman.

"Cooper—"

The sound of his name on her passion-filled voice encouraged him and he cupped her hips with his hands to steady their restless movements. Bending down to kiss her in the most intimate of ways, he continued the sensual assault until she cried out and shuddered with the ecstasy of completion.

Moving to her side, he held her close and kissed her with every emotion he had coursing through him. But instead of lying passively in his arms as her body cooled, Faith reached out to touch him, to hold him in her hands and stroke him with a tenderness that made him dizzy with wanting.

Her gentle hands caressing him, testing his strength, was heaven and hell rolled into one. He wanted nothing more than to bury himself deep inside of her, to claim her as his own. But he sensed her need to express her feelings for him, to show him the same attention that he'd shown her.

As her lips moved over his chest and belly his pulse pounded in his ears and he had to force himself to breathe. But when she took him into her mouth, time stood still as wave after wave of desire flowed through him. Heat and light danced behind his tightly

closed eyes and his world narrowed to one purpose—
complete release.

''Darlin', I can't stand any more of this,'' he said,
lifting her up to his chest.

Taking deep breaths, he willed his body to slow
down, to relax until he'd gained control once again.
But the feel of her softness pressed to him, the
warmth of her breath on his heated skin, tested him
in ways he'd never imagined.

''Cooper, please make love to me,'' she said, her
voice wrapping around him like a velvet sheath.

He might have been able to hang onto what little
scrap of sanity he had left had it not been for her
softly spoken request. But knowing that she wanted
him as much as he wanted her snapped the last thread
of his restraint and he rolled her to her back, then
covered her body with his.

At the first touch of her moist heat to his insistent
arousal, he clenched his teeth so hard his jaw felt as
if it would break from the pressure. Slowly, carefully
he pushed forward until he lost sight of where he
ended and she began.

Her moan of pleasure and the feel of himself buried deep inside of her created a sensual fog of passion that clouded his brain to anything but the act of
bringing them the satisfaction they both craved.

Thrusting deeply, thoroughly, he felt her feminine
muscles contract around him, holding him tightly to
her, urging him to empty himself deep into her
womb. Gratified by the sound of her broken cries, he
groaned as the whirlwind of sensation caught him in
its grasp and he gave himself to the only woman he'd
ever loved.

Several moments passed before he found the

strength to move to her side, then pull her to him. Brushing a strand of hair from her eyes, his heart stalled at the moisture he felt on her smooth cheek.

If he'd hurt her in any way he'd never be able to forgive himself. "Faith? Darlin', what's wrong? Are you all right?"

"That was beautiful," she said, softly.

He relaxed. She was having one of those emotional female moments that women sometimes had, and that a man couldn't even begin to understand.

Smiling, he kissed the top of her head. "I love you, Faith Broderick."

"And I love you, Cooper Adams," she said passionately. "More than you'll ever know."

His heart soared. She loved him. He felt like he could move a mountain with his bare hands.

"Marry me, darlin'. Let me love you to sleep every night and wake up with you every morning." He raised up to look down at her. "I want to be the man who gives you your babies, Faith. And I want to be there by your side when you birth them."

Tears streamed from her eyes as she stared up at him, then throwing her arms around his neck, she hugged him tightly to her. "Oh, Cooper."

She hadn't said "yes" exactly, but he took her emotional response and the fact that she was holding him like she'd never let him go as a good sign. Content with the knowledge that she loved him, and confident that they'd be getting married in the very near future, he relaxed and felt the exhaustion from their lovemaking overtake him.

"Get some rest now, darlin'," he said, cradling her to his chest. He yawned. "We can start making plans first thing in the morning."

* * *

Faith's tears continued long after Cooper's deep, even breathing signaled that he'd fallen asleep. She'd tried so hard not to love him, tried to keep her distance.

But as impossible as it had been for her not to fall in love with Cooper, it had become just as impossible for her to stay with him.

She'd seen him interact with his nephews and heard him talk about how much he loved being around kids. He'd even told her he wanted a large family. And if ever a man deserved being a father, Cooper Adams did.

But what he didn't deserve was a wife who couldn't give him those children. And as desperately as she wanted to be his wife and have his babies, to be part of the family he so desired, she simply couldn't do it. Her body just wasn't capable.

She and Eric had tried for over a year to become pregnant, but with no success. At first she'd thought it might be something with him. But when she confided her fears in her best friend, Charlotte, Faith had learned that it wasn't Eric's problem at all. It was hers. Charlotte had fallen in love with Eric and become pregnant with his baby, and Faith had not only been forced to face the betrayal of her husband and best friend, she'd been confronted with the devastating reality that she was infertile. They'd both apologized, but that didn't alter the fact that they had everything she'd always wanted, but could never have.

That's why she had to leave Cooper now. She knew him well enough to know that he'd say it wasn't important, that they would have each other and that was all that mattered. But as much as she'd like to ignore the facts and stay with him for the rest of her life, Cooper deserved to have his dream, his family.

And she loved him enough not to take that away from him.

She bit her lower lip to stifle a sob and held him close for a few moments longer. Then kissing his lean cheek one last time, she slipped from his embrace and got out of bed.

Gathering her things, she quickly got dressed and carried her luggage out to his truck. For the first time since her arrival on the ranch, she was glad that she hadn't had a place to put her clothes. Living out of a suitcase had been extremely inconvenient, but it saved precious time that she couldn't afford to waste now.

Taking a notepad and a pen from her purse, she turned on the dome light and with tears blurring her vision, she explained on paper what she didn't have the courage to tell him face-to-face.

She wasn't proud of what she was doing, but she knew that for both of their sakes, leaving this way was the only option. Cooper would try to talk her into staying, and loving him as she did, she'd be powerless to resist.

Carefully folding the paper, she wrote his name on the outside, then placed it on the bench seat beside her. Wiping the moisture from her face, she took a deep breath and started the truck. Once she reached the airport in Amarillo, she'd call Whiskers and have him see about getting Cooper's truck back to him.

KATHIE DeNOSKY   169

* * *

His eyes still closed, Cooper rolled over to pull Faith into his arms, to love her awake. But the bed was empty beside him, the sheets cold.

He opened one eye and groaned. A bright shaft of sunlight was streaming through the window. Damn. He'd overslept again.

Stretching, he thought about the chores that needed to be done, then shook his head. What he really wanted to do was find Faith, bring her back to bed and make love to her for the rest of the day.

He briefly wondered why she hadn't awakened him. They had a lot to do. Not only did they have to take care of the usual chores, they had a wedding to plan.

Grinning at the thought of making her his wife, he swung his legs over the side of the bed and reaching for his clothes, froze. The corner of the room where he'd stacked her suitcases the day after she'd arrived was empty.

Where was Faith's luggage?

Apprehension gnawed at his gut as he quickly pulled on his clothes and hurried down the hall. "Faith?"

The ominous silence in the house was deafening.

When he entered the kitchen, he looked for the CD player, her book, anything that said she was still there.

He found nothing.

Throwing open the back door, he stepped out onto the porch just as his truck drove into the yard. But instead of Faith, Whiskers got out of the cab.

"Where is she?" Cooper demanded. He dreaded the answer, but he had to know.

For the first time since he'd known the old man, Whiskers seemed at a loss for words. He simply walked up to the porch, handed Cooper a folded piece of paper, then shaking his head, started toward the barn.

A sinking feeling tightened Cooper's chest as he noticed his name on the outside. The handwriting was a woman's. It had to be Faith's.

His hands shook as he opened the note, read it, then carefully refolded it and stuck it in his shirt pocket. Anger burned at his gut and he had a deep need to shout his frustration.

He could have understood Faith's leaving him because of the condition of the ranch, or out of fear that he could adequately provide for her. But for her to abandon what they had together because she couldn't have kids was unacceptable.

"Damn fool woman."

Did she honestly think he was that shallow? Did she really believe that he wanted kids more than he wanted her?

He took a deep breath, then another as his words came back to haunt him. After they'd made love last night, he'd asked her to marry him, then immediately started talking about them having a family together.

He shook his head at his own stupidity. He'd just the same as told her that's why he wanted to marry her. But if she thought he was going to let a little thing like her not being able to have a baby stop him from being with the only woman he'd ever loved, she was in for a big surprise.

Pulling his cell phone from the holder on the side of his belt, he punched in Brant Wakefield's number. After he'd explained what he needed, Cooper ended the call, then descended the steps and walked out to the barn.

"Whiskers, I have a job for you," he said when he spotted the old man standing outside of Penelope's stall.

"What's that, boy?" Whiskers asked, his tone cautious.

"For the next two weeks, I need you here to cook meals for about five men."

"That sounds fair 'nuff," Whiskers said, nodding. "What you got planned?"

"I've got a pasture to fence, a house to rewire and plumbing to put in."

Whiskers looked shocked. "That's it? You ain't gonna—"

When the old geezer's voice trailed off, Cooper almost laughed. He could tell that curiosity was about to kill Whiskers. The man couldn't figure out why Cooper wasn't more upset about Faith's leaving.

Taking pity on his old friend, Cooper explained, "After I get this place in shape, I have a little trip to take."

"A trip?" Whiskers's face lit up brighter than a Christmas tree full of lights. "And jest where you goin', Coop?"

Cooper grinned. "I thought I'd take a ride up to Illinois and see if I couldn't find myself a good woman to settle down with."

Whiskers laughed. "I was beginnin' to wonder 'bout you, boy."

"I don't give up that easy," Cooper said, shaking his head. He smiled at the man whose meddling had helped him find the woman of his dreams. "I know what I want. And I'm damned well not afraid to go after her."

Twelve

"**I**'m what?!"

"I said you're pregnant, Ms. Broderick."

Faith stared at the woman in total disbelief. "That's not possible. My ex-husband and I tried for over a year and we never could get pregnant. And I *know* he wasn't the one with the problem. He and his wife have a child now."

"In some cases the harder a couple tries, the less successful they are," Dr. Shelton said, smiling. "Sometimes all it takes is for them to relax and stop worrying about becoming pregnant."

Faith thought back on her marriage. Once she and Eric had made the decision to try to have a baby, he'd started keeping graphs and charts of everything from her temperature to the best time of the month for them to make love. And with each month they were unsuccessful, it added more stress and tension to their relationship.

The doctor handed her a prescription for prenatal vitamins as she rose to leave. ''I want you to cut out caffeine, get plenty of rest, eat well-balanced meals and take these.'' She patted Faith's shoulder. ''Congratulations. I'm sure once the shock wears off, you'll be very happy.''

As Faith got dressed, a thousand different things ran through her mind. She was going to have a baby. Unbelievable!

She'd attributed her feeling lousy for the past couple of weeks to missing Cooper, and of second-guessing her decision to leave the Triple Bar ranch every minute of every day since she'd come home.

A warm happiness suffused her whole body. She was pregnant with Cooper's baby. She wanted to shout it from the rooftops.

Walking out to the car, she stopped in the middle of the parking lot as a disturbing thought intruded. What if he was so upset with her that he never wanted to see her again?

Fear began to take hold. It had been over two weeks and she'd heard nothing from him. Not a phone call. Not a letter. Nothing.

What if he'd decided she wasn't the woman he wanted after all? Had her judgment once again proven faulty?

She took a deep breath and shoved her doubts aside. She may have been wrong about many things in her life and misplaced her trust in several people, but in her heart, she knew she wasn't wrong about Cooper.

In her note to him, she'd asked that he not try to

contact her. Maybe he had just been respecting her wishes.

Getting into the driver's seat of her grandmother's car, she pulled the visor down and gazed into the vanity mirror. She didn't look any different than she had this morning when she was getting ready for her doctor's appointment. But in the past forty-five minutes her whole life had changed. Forever.

She was having a baby. Cooper's baby.

For the first time in two weeks she felt a bubble of hope begin to rise within her.

Cooper pulled the rental car away from the Williamson County Airport and, following a map, easily found the little town of Carterville. He was glad he'd made the decision to fly instead of drive the nine-hundred-plus miles to Faith's grandmother's place. It would have taken him more time than he was willing to waste and been one more day without Faith in his arms.

Less than five minutes after he drove into town, he was standing on the front porch of Faith's grandmother's home, knocking on the door.

When an older lady answered the door, he smiled. "Is this where Faith Broderick lives?"

Her gaze raked him from the top of his Resistol to the soles of his boots before she nodded. "You must be Cooper Adams."

Hoping it was a good sign that Faith had mentioned him to her grandmother, his smile turned to a grin. "Yes, ma'am. I sure am."

"I'm Faith's grandmother, Penelope Hudson," she said, shaking his hand.

"Is Faith home, Mrs. Hudson? I need to discuss some things with her."

She shook her head. "I'm sorry. Faith is gone right now, but she should be back soon."

"Would you mind if I waited for her, ma'am? It's really important that I talk to her."

The woman smiled pleasantly for the first time since he'd knocked on the door. "Why don't you come in and have a cup of coffee, son? It'll give us the chance to get acquainted."

"I'd like that, ma'am," Cooper said as he stepped through the opened door. "I'd like that a lot."

When Faith returned from the doctor's office, a car she'd never seen before blocked the drive. She fleetingly wondered who could be visiting, but as she parked her grandmother's Buick along the curb in front of the house, she forgot all about the visitor's identity. She had more important things on her mind.

She needed to call the airlines and reserve a seat on the first available flight to Amarillo. Then, while she packed, she'd need to decide on what she wanted to say to Cooper when she got there.

Mentally ticking off the things she'd need to accomplish before she left, she opened the front door, dropped the car keys on the antique library table in the living room, then walked straight to her bedroom. She heard voices and the sound of laughter coming from the kitchen, but she couldn't tell who was talking or what they were saying.

It didn't matter. She had too much on her mind to worry about who was visiting or what they were discussing. At the moment all she could think of was getting back to Cooper, trying to decide what she would say to him, and hoping that he loved her enough to give them a second chance.

But first things first. She had to find her datebook with the phone number of the airline so she could book her flight. Searching her desk and nightstand, her impatience mounted. It was nowhere to be found. Where could she have put it?

Maybe she'd left it in the living room. She hurried down the hall to search the end tables. No luck there.

"Nana, have you seen my datebook?" she called as she pulled out the couch cushions to see if it had slipped between them.

"Is this what you're looking for?" a rich baritone asked from behind her.

Whirling around, Faith gasped. She couldn't believe her eyes. There stood Cooper casually leaning one shoulder against the door frame, his arms crossed over his chest. In one hand he held her datebook.

"When...did you get here?" she asked, feeling as if she might hyperventilate.

He checked his watch. "About half an hour ago."

Her heart thumped against her ribs and she took a deep breath in an effort to calm herself. His presence dominated the room, and although she'd have never believed it possible, he seemed even more overwhelmingly masculine than ever before.

"Faith, honey, I'm going to the library," her grandmother said, breezing past them on her way to the door. "I just remembered that I promised Phyllis that I would help her sort through some books for the book fair." Turning to Cooper, she smiled. "There's plenty of coffee left if you'd like another cup."

Faith watched Nana scoop the car keys off the small table by the door and walk out, leaving her alone with Cooper.

What was she going to say to him?

She'd thought she'd have several hours to plan what she wanted to tell him first, to prepare herself for seeing him again. But with him standing there looking so handsome, so undeniably male, she could barely remember her own name.

"I could use more coffee," he said, handing her the datebook. He turned to go back into the kitchen. "You want some?"

"No, thank you," she said, remembering the doctor's warning about caffeine. Feeling completely off-center, she tossed the planner onto the couch and followed him.

She watched him walk to the coffeemaker on the counter beside the sink. Pouring himself a cup, he leaned back against the counter, crossed his feet at the ankles and took a sip. "You look tired, darlin'. Why don't you sit down?"

Her knees turned to rubber and her heart skipped a beat at his use of the familiar endearment. Deciding it might not be a bad idea to sit down before she melted in a puddle at his big booted feet, she sank into a chair at the table.

Not knowing what to say, she asked, "How is Penelope?"

He shrugged. "She's doing pretty well, all things considered."

Alarmed, Faith sat up straight. "What do you mean? Has something happened to her?"

"No." He shook his head, then pinned her with his piercing blue gaze. "She's doing fine if you take into consideration that she's been abandoned twice."

"Twice?"

Nodding, he set his cup on the counter, then walked over to stand in front of her. "The first time couldn't be helped. Her momma got stuck in the mud and died before anyone found her. But the second time was an entirely different story.''

Faith gulped. ''I...I'm sorry. At the time I didn't think how it would affect Penelope.''

He pulled out the chair across from her and sat down. ''There were a lot of things you failed to think about, darlin'.''

Leaning back, he looked deceptively relaxed. But she could detect the underlying tension in the tone of his voice, the tiny lines at the corners of his eyes.

''I did what I thought was best,'' she said, defensively. ''I know how much you love children and I didn't want to deprive you of—''

''You don't know squat,'' he said, cutting her explanation short. ''Where do you get off deciding you know what's best for me? Don't you think I'm capable of making those decisions for myself?''

Taken aback, she stammered, ''Well...I...I—''

Sitting forward, he reached across the table to take her hand in his. ''What makes you think I'd rather have children than have you, Faith?''

Speechless, she shook her head.

His smile was so tender it took her breath. ''Don't you know that you can't miss what you've never had?'' He rubbed his thumb over the back of her hand, sending a shiver up her spine. ''But I have had you. And I can't live without you, darlin'.''

''But—'' For the first time since she'd seen him, the hope that had formed earlier when she was leaving the doctor's office began to grow.

He shook his head. ''No 'buts' about it. As long as I have you, it doesn't matter to me if we can't have kids. It's you and your love that I need. Kids would have been an extension of that love, but it wouldn't have been the reason for how I feel about you." He smiled. "If you'd like, someday we can check into adoption. Or if we feel the need from time to time for some real chaos in our lives, we'll borrow Jenna and Flint's kids for a day or two."

"There's something you need to know, Cooper."

She watched his jaw tighten and his eyes narrow. "Do you love me?"

"Yes," she said without a moment's hesitation.

"Then there's not another damned thing that matters, darlin'," he said firmly. "I love you and I want you with me for the rest of my life." He lifted her hand to his mouth and brushing her palm with his lips, added, "I came to take you back to the Triple Bar Ranch where you belong."

Tears suddenly flooded her eyes and ran down her cheeks as she left her chair and hurled herself into his arms.

Cooper wasn't sure whether to take her emotional outburst as a good sign or not. But at the moment she was in his arms and that was all that mattered.

Holding her close he stroked her hair and murmured what he hoped were soothing words as her emotions ran their course. When her sobs quieted, he lowered his head to kiss her, but leaning back, she shook her head.

"You're wrong, Cooper."

"You won't go back to Texas with me?" Was she reluctant to return because she thought life on the ranch would be as primitive as it had been two weeks ago? "If you're worried about the living conditions, you can stop. You wouldn't recognize the place now.

For the last two weeks I've worked my butt off to get it into shape.''

"Cooper, darling, I'm not worried about that." The smile she gave him just about knocked his size thirteens right off his feet. "There's something else we have to discuss," she said, placing her hand on his cheek.

"What do you want to talk about?" he asked huskily. The feel of her soft hand touching him, caressing him, sent a shaft of desire straight through to his core. He'd like nothing more than to rip their clothes off and prove to her that they belonged together, to once again make her his.

"Since I left Texas, circumstances have changed."

Fear jolted him out of his sensual daydream. "You want to fill me in on what's different?"

He watched her take a deep breath before meeting his eyes. "I told you that I'd been married before."

"Yes, but what has that got to do with—"

She held up her hand. "Let me explain."

As he nodded that he would keep quiet, the fear within him intensified. Was she trying to tell him that she had reconciled with her ex-husband?

"When Eric and I were married, we tried for over a year to get pregnant with no luck. Then just before we were scheduled to go in for testing, I confided in my best friend that I thought Eric might be sterile." She shook her head. "That's when I found out that my husband and best friend had been having an affair and he wasn't the one with the fertility problem."

"He'd gotten her pregnant?" If Cooper could have gotten his hands on the jerk at that moment, he would have cheerfully choked him for hurting Faith.

She nodded. "Eric said that he never meant for it

to happen, but since it had, he wanted to marry Charlotte so he could be with the child I obviously couldn't give him. That's why I quit teaching. We were all teachers at the same school. I just couldn't face being with them day after day and not think about what they had that I couldn't.''

Anger burned in Cooper's gut at the betrayal Faith had suffered at her husband and best friend's hands. But he didn't understand what that had to do with circumstances changing between them. ''What has that got to do with us, darlin'?''

She rose from his lap to pace the floor. Something had her as nervous as a priest in a harem.

''Since it was clear that I was the one with the fertility problem, I didn't see the need to keep the appointment for the testing.'' She bit her lower lip. ''At that point in my life, I just couldn't face having a doctor confirm what I already knew.''

He nodded. ''That's understandable.''

Taking a deep breath, she turned to face him. ''But I was wrong, Cooper.''

His scalp tingled and he sat up straight in the chair. ''About what?'' he asked, slowly.

She laughed nervously. ''It seems I'm not only capable of becoming pregnant, I am pregnant.''

He left the chair so fast it fell over backward on the floor. Cupping her cheeks with his hands, he tilted her face up to meet his gaze. ''Darlin', are you sure?''

''Yes. That's why I was gone when you arrived. I had a doctor's appointment.''

Groaning, Cooper pulled her into his arms and held her close. ''I love you with all my heart and it wouldn't matter to me if you couldn't get pregnant.''

He took a deep breath as emotion tightened his chest. "But I'd be a damned liar if I told you I wasn't the happiest man alive right now, just knowing that you're carrying my baby."

Her arms wrapped around him like she'd never let him go, she asked, "Does the offer still hold?"

"The offer?" Confused, he leaned back to look down at her. "What are you talking about, darlin'?"

"You offered to take me back to the Triple Bar," she said, looking hopeful.

"Nope."

"No?"

Shaking his head, he grinned. "It never was an offer. An offer can be turned down, and I wasn't about to go back to Texas without you." He kissed her with every emotion he had welling up inside of him, then lifting his head, added, "And when we board that plane to go home, you can count on it being as husband and wife."

"You sound rather sure of yourself," she said, giving him a smile that made his body hard with wanting.

"I am sure." He pressed himself to her, letting her know what she did to him, how much he wanted her. "Darlin', I can't promise you I'll be with you for the rest of your life, but you can count on me being with you for the rest of mine."

"I'm going to hold you to that, cowboy." She kissed him and he felt like he'd been given the most precious gift on earth. "I love you, Cooper Adams."

"And I love you, darlin'," he said, swinging her up into his arms. "That's something else you can count on for the rest of my life."

Epilogue

"**W**here Mommy?" Dusty asked, looking around. He clutched a pink bunny in one arm, while he rested his other arm on his father's shoulders.

"She's in a room upstairs with your new baby sister," Cooper said, glancing at his son as he carried him through the hospital lobby.

"Baby Kadie," Dusty said seriously, nodding his little blond head.

An overwhelming sense of love and pride filled Cooper. At a little over two years old, Dustin Cooper Adams was talking better than most kids his age. Of course, as far as Cooper was concerned, Dusty was just about the smartest two-year-old there ever was.

"That's right, your baby sister's name is Katie," Cooper said, smiling. "And we're going to take her and Mommy home with us later today."

Dusty squirmed where he sat on Cooper's arm. "Walk, Daddy. Walk."

Cooper set his son on his feet, straightened his little cowboy hat, then took hold of his hand to keep him from wandering off. "Hang on to Katie's rabbit," he reminded as they stepped onto the elevator.

A few moments later, Cooper led Dusty down the hall and into Faith's room. As soon as he saw his mother, Dusty worked his hand free from Cooper's and ran over to where she sat in a chair holding the baby.

"Mommy!" He held out the pink rabbit. "Dis Kadie's."

"Oh, I'm sure she'll love it, sweetie," Faith said, putting her arm around her son to hug him to her side. "I'm so glad to see you."

Leaning down, Cooper tenderly kissed his wife. "How's the two prettiest girls in the Panhandle?"

Faith smiled up at him. "We're doing just fine. And how did my boys manage on their own last night and this morning?"

"We did pretty good." Cooper smiled down at the most beautiful woman he'd ever known. Although he'd have never believed it possible to love her more than he had three years ago, it didn't even come close to the way he felt for her today. "Dusty helped me feed Penelope and her new calf this morning, didn't you, son?"

Dusty nodded. "Penpee eat lots."

Sensing that his son needed time with his mother, Cooper took the baby, then cradling Katie in one arm, lifted Dusty onto Faith's lap. As Dusty told his mother all about his adventures, Cooper sat down on the side of the bed to get better acquainted with his new daughter.

Katie Jo Adams was the most beautiful little girl he'd ever seen, and when she got older she'd have the boys lined up for miles just to see her smile. Cooper's gut burned at the thought. Now he understood why his brother-in-law, Flint, was so protective of his and Jenna's little girl, Molly.

"It looks like Katie is going to be a daddy's girl," Faith said softly as she held her sleeping son against her breast.

"You think so?" Cooper asked, grinning.

Nodding, Faith smiled at the man she loved with all her heart. She couldn't believe how full her life had become since that day three years ago when she'd found herself stranded with the sexiest man she'd ever seen.

"Thank you, Cooper."

He looked confused. "What did I do?"

"You've given me so much." She glanced down at her son, then at her new daughter. "You've given me your love and two beautiful children." She grinned. "And in a couple of years you can give me another one."

"Darlin', you've just had a baby and you're talking about wanting another one?" he asked, sounding incredulous.

She nodded. "I think another son and daughter would be nice."

"Four kids," he said, seeming to mull it over. He looked down at the baby, then back at Faith, his handsome face troubled. "If you don't mind, I think I'd rather have two more boys."

"Why?" He'd been insistent from the time they

found out she was pregnant with Katie that it would be a girl.

He grimaced. "I'm getting an ulcer just thinking about some pimply-faced kid wanting to take Katie out on a date when she gets older. I don't know if I can handle worrying about two daughters."

"You'll do fine," Faith assured him. "So we're in agreement then? Two more children?"

"Darlin', you can count on me to give you as many babies as you want," he said, his grin wide.

Happier than she'd ever been in her entire life, Faith smiled at her husband. "I love you, Cooper."

"I love you, too, darlin'." The emotion she saw in his eyes took her breath. "That's something you can always count on."

* * * * *

Billionaire Boss

MEAGAN McKINNEY

MEAGAN McKINNEY

is the author of over a dozen novels – hardcover and paperback historical and contemporary women's fiction. In addition to romance, she likes to inject mystery and thriller elements into her work. Currently she lives in the Garden District of New Orleans with her two young sons, two very self-entitled cats and a crazy red dog. Her favourite hobbies are travelling to the Arctic and, of course, reading!

One

"**M**s. Meadows, he'll see you now," announced the autocratic voice of the executive secretary.

Kirsten Meadows stood, already feeling like the poor relation next to the chic older woman. She herself wore a black suit from the local mall and a string of fake pearls. There was no competing with the executive secretary's costly designer outfit, but as Kirsten always did, she hid her fear and worries behind a placid expression.

Certainly, on the brighter side, she told herself, the secretary must be well paid to afford such an expensively tailored suit. The job of personal assistant to the boss would be, too.

With that giving her courage, she stepped into the office of the rich and powerful Seth Morgan.

Her bravado abandoned her at the polished mahogany door.

The man didn't greet her; he didn't even look up from his desk. His precisely clipped dark hair and stern chiseled face belied the fact that he was only thirty-three, not even six years older than Kirsten.

She surmised that the stressful lifestyle of the wealthy financier was what put the scowl on his face, even as she prayed it wasn't her résumé that he was reading. It had taken her last dime to fly to Manhattan to interview. If she didn't get the job, she was sunk.

"I've seen better." Seth Morgan finally looked up.

Kirsten was pinned by an icy stare. "Are you speaking of my résumé?" she finally asked, feeling foolish beneath the man's piercing stare.

He nodded and leaned back in his black leather chair to study her.

The Italian suit he wore fit so well it didn't even crease. His tie was ice-blue and only added to the coldness of his expression.

"Fluent in five languages, the daughter of a

career diplomat—it could be anyone.'' He snapped the résumé with his forefinger and then stared at her, almost as if he was daring her to refute his summation.

Kirsten refrained from releasing a defeated sigh. There was no way this arrogant rich man was going to see her beg. He'd done her a terrible disservice by requesting her to come to New York, but if the trip had been a failure, she sure wasn't going to give him, the Wall Street marauder that he was, the satisfaction of knowing that he'd ruined her.

Quietly she lifted her head and stared back.

''I'm sorry if you don't feel I'm qualified,'' she began. ''However, you had my résumé before you asked for an interview. You certainly could have turned me down in a letter without my having to come all the way to Manhattan from Montana. You've wasted all of our time—''

''Why should I give you the job?''

His words came like a gunshot.

Casually he braced his fingers together in a V and perused her.

Against her will she begrudgingly decided he had nice hands, strong and not paper-pusher pale. They suited his harshly handsome face.

Steeling herself in order to draw on her last

reserves, she said, "I could do very well for your estate in Mystery, Montana, because I know it as well as anyone. Yes, my father served as chargé d'affaires for several ambassadors, but every summer, Mother took me back to her birthplace, and after the divorce—"

She paused, still wounded by the memories more than a decade old of costly divorce-court battles her father had waged on her mother. The final cruelty was her mother's impoverished lifestyle after the wealth of an expatriate. The injustice of it had kept Kirsten and her sister alienated from their father to the present day.

"Well—" she cleared her throat "—after my parents divorced, I lived with my mother and my baby sister in Mystery and finished high school there. I know it as well as a native, but with the additional experience of having grown up in many diverse cultures."

"So you feel you would be qualified to handle my affairs in Mystery?"

She might have laughed if she hadn't felt so much like crying. Darkly she wondered how many affairs he was planning to have—hopefully not as many as her father had had.

"Certainly, as your personal assistant, I believe I can handle anything the estate might require. I took accounting in college. I can run a

household. Additionally, my experience overseas will help with the management of parties
and soirees you might have at the lodge.'' She
added, ''I can also help with your wife's schedule.''

''I haven't got a wife.''

Kirsten released an inner sigh of relief. The
man's marital status was none of her business,
but she was applying for the position of personal
assistant, and she certainly didn't look forward
to doing anything too personal—such as covering up anything sordid with an unknowing wife
waiting in the wings.

''All right, Ms. Meadows, you can go now.''

She opened her mouth as if to ask whether
she had gotten the job, but the words didn't
come. Somehow they seemed irrelevant. This
handsome wealthy man was used to saying who
lived and who died in the Wall Street world; her
situation with him wouldn't change by asking
furtive little questions.

Nodding, she turned to leave.

''The lodge is finished, and I'd like to take a
long weekend there to settle in. I'll leave for
Montana this evening and show you what I want
done there.''

Her back stiffened. It sure sounded as if she
had the job.

"The pay issue…?" She broached the subject, turning to face him.

He cut her off. "It's settled. I'll meet your requirements."

"Th-thank you," she stammered, wondering how she'd gone from the despair of failure to total success within seconds.

But he'd already dismissed her. He didn't look up from his desk, or the memo he was reading.

She exited the stifling office, her heart singing.

"Thank you, Hazel, thank you!" she said to herself all the way down the elevator.

Hazel McCallum was the reason she'd even gotten the job. The aging cattle baroness owned almost all of Mystery, Montana. From her ranch she oversaw Mystery Valley as if it was her own personal kingdom, which it almost was. And the seventy-plus-year-old woman thought of every Mystery native as her own kin. It was Hazel who had taken it upon herself to find Kirsten the position as personal assistant to Mystery's newest resident, Seth Morgan.

And Kirsten needed the job. White-collar jobs were hard to come by in cattle country. Her mother and little sister counted on Kirsten both emotionally and financially, and right now neither one was fit to move elsewhere, to some other town where they had no support.

Nothing could repay all that Hazel had done for them. Kirsten would need a lifetime to thank the woman for all her kindnesses, especially to Kirsten's mother, who'd been battling illness and had needed so much more than either Kirsten or her eleven-year-old sister could provide.

Thinking about her mother, Kirsten walked out of the building and went toward the subway, eager to get to her hotel room and pack for her trip back home.

But even as she descended the subway escalator, she was still thanking Hazel under her breath.

Seth Morgan watched the young woman in her inexpensive black suit depart his office.

Kirsten Meadows had been more than he'd expected. Certainly, as Hazel had said, she was qualified for the job. Unbelievably qualified if her résumé was any indication. He had no doubt she would take her work seriously and be an asset to him.

What he hadn't seen coming was the feeling he'd had when he'd met her dark blue eyes. Certainly he was attracted to the woman. He was male, after all, and Kirsten Meadows's face was positively angelic in its beauty.

Yet it was the eyes that had struck him. Eyes dark and deep, like a drowning pool. His defenses had gone up immediately.

He scowled and jammed the button for his secretary.

"Yes, Mr. Morgan?" came the studied melodious voice through the intercom.

"Get me Hazel McCallum on the phone."

"Right away, sir."

He swiveled his chair to face the breathless skyscape of lower Manhattan, of the Statue of Liberty and Governor's Island. The view was magnificent. One could feel as if they'd conquered the world with a panorama like his.

But lately the view had been less satisfying to him. It was certainly a monument to man's achievement. Each building, its architecture and function proclaimed a new conquest.

Yet he wondered if he was getting tired of conquest. There were times when he would stare out at the buildings and wonder if the people inside—the sum of its parts—weren't greater than the whole, not by virtue of conquest, but by virtue of relationships.

Yes, he was growling for something more. But he never quite knew what it was.

Until it was hinted at in a woman's dark blue eyes.

He was pensive for a moment, his own cool gaze darkening with thought. But then his expression hardened and his eyes flashed.

He wasn't going to be tricked, however, and he knew Hazel McCallum well enough to have had wind of her matchmaking schemes to repopulate the town of Mystery with people other than tourists. Her recommendation of Kirsten Meadows had looked fine on paper, but Hazel had known good and well what she looked like, and to dangle her in front of him, well, it was—it was—wicked enough for him to do.

He pushed the button to the buzzing intercom.

''Sir?'' came his secretary's hesitant voice. ''Ms. McCallum told me she isn't taking phone calls from New York at this time.''

''What?'' he gasped. Never had someone refused to take his phone call.

''She—she said that if you need to speak with her, you'll have to do as all the residents do in Mystery. You can call at her ranch.''

Seth's mouth hardened. His eyes narrowed.

''She did, did she?'' He spoke loud and clear into the intercom. ''Well, call that old gal up and tell her I want to see her first thing tomorrow morning.''

"There or here, sir?"

He could tell even his secretary was intimidated by wily old Hazel McCallum.

"There," he spat, exasperated, feeling like a Victorian suitor who'd finally been permitted to call on the boss's daughter. "And get my plane ready for Montana."

He snapped off the intercom and faced the view again, this time taking solace in the fact that while it wasn't cattle baronesses and blue Montana peaks, he'd conquered something in his life.

Something, at least.

The plane's interior was palomino-blond. The shades and hues of it melted together smoothly, as smooth as the buttery-leather chair Kirsten had sat in for takeoff. They were now at twenty thousand feet and climbing. They flew into the setting sun, the subtle cabin lights turning the interior into a rare, shadowy gold.

The clinking of glass and ice made her look over her shoulder. In the corner of the cabin was a wet bar where a short, natty steward was already preparing drinks. Beyond was another cabin, which held the lavatory and—she still could hardly believe it—a bed where Seth Morgan could nap while he jetted to London or Tokyo.

"—the first week. Then if I happen to be at the ranch I'd like to know that you can handle the correspondence with Mary back in New York." Seth Morgan drilled instructions at her like a marine. "Additionally, I'd like you to work closely with Hazel McCallum in finding me the right kind of trail horses. I will have guests and I want good horses for them in the stable."

"I've ridden since I was six years old—Hazel and I work very well together," Kirsten promised, taking notes on the new laptop Seth had provided.

"What can I get you to drink?" the attendant broke in.

"Water," Seth answered, clearly used to being served.

"Iced tea, please," Kirsten answered, again wondering about the man sitting across from her at the table.

She mused that the sparkling water the attendant poured for him might mean he was a health freak. That would go down hard in Mystery, where steak was considered one of the four food groups.

"Here you go," the attendant purred, holding out a tall iced tea.

She took it.

"Sugar?" the attendant offered, lowering the silver tray so she could reach the sterling sugar bowl.

A violent burst of turbulence hit the plane at precisely the moment she reached for the sugar spoon.

Kirsten watched Seth Morgan toss his sparkling water down the front of his perfect Italian suit. She might even have laughed had she not been doused by the iced tea in her hand, then sugared like a warm cookie with the contents of the sugar bowl.

"Oh, dear Lord!" the attendant squealed, horrified at the mess.

"I'm sorry," Kirsten murmured, instinctively licking her sugary lips, desperate to wipe down the expensive leather seat before even thinking of herself.

Seth Morgan sat frozen across from her, staring, a hard expression on his face.

She was convinced he was furious.

"I'll pay to have the leather cleaned," she added, looking for more napkins for the mess.

"Nonsense," he said, standing.

She was trapped, her front so full of sugar she looked as if she'd just been snowed upon.

Slowly he leaned over to her, easing off her black jacket. His hands were surprisingly warm when they brushed her nape.

For some reason she'd expected cold hands from him. He was rich, handsome, powerful. She'd expected cold hands to go along with a cold heart.

"Well, this won't do." The steward tsked.

She looked down. The white T-shirt she'd worn beneath her jacket was transparent with tea. Gasping, she covered herself with her arms, the sticky sugar only spreading. She prayed Seth Morgan hadn't been thinking what the steward had, but when she looked up and met his eyes, she could see very well that he'd viewed everything right down to the color of her pink bra.

"You'll need to change," he said woodenly, his gaze still dark and penetrating, as if he, too, were thinking of sex.

"M-my bag's in the hold below. I didn't think I'd need it," she stammered, shivering.

"You can't fly to Montana like that. We still have hours to go."

"Maybe I can clean up in the lavatory."

He nodded to the steward. "Give Miss Meadows my bathrobe and whatever she needs to shower. When we land, we'll deliver her bag in here and she can change.''

The steward nodded.

Kirsten gingerly rose from the chair, holding her wet front and trying to contain all the sugar. She followed the steward into the rear cabin, her mind captured by Seth Morgan's stare, dark and full of wicked promise.

All she could think of during her shower was that she and her new boss were off to a turbulent start—no pun intended—and she only feared it would get worse. If there was one thing she already knew about her boss, it was that he was a predator. She would need all her faculties to survive around him. After her father's treatment of her mother, the only plan she could count on was never to be the man's prey. That was looking difficult now that she'd been sugared like a warm cookie and served up for his pleasure.

The shampoo bottle slipped from her wet fingers, the clatter jangling her already frayed nerves. But she comforted herself with the thought that he could rattle her all he wanted; as long as he paid her well, and as long as she stayed emotionally invulnerable he could have all the cookies he wanted.

TWO

Now, how in the hell, Seth wondered as he sipped his second whiskey, was he going to get that image out of his mind?

The picture of Kirsten Meadows, wet and sticky, crystals of sugar clinging to her eyelashes like a dusting of snow, well, it was one damn vision no man would ever forget. She'd looked up at him like a lush, sexual, crystalline fairy, and if he'd been infinitesimally less civilized, he'd have made love to her right there in her seat.

He shifted uncomfortably and stared into the blackness outside the plane window.

The steward had taken a seat up front with the pilots. Alone, Seth could still hear running water from the lavatory over the drone of the jet engines.

The woman had thick blond hair, and it was going to take a long, hot shower to get all the sugar out of it. Against his will he thought of his own hands running through her wet hair, scrubbing the sweetness out of it.

He shifted again, and took another deep swig of the whiskey. The side of his hand was sticky where he'd helped her out of her jacket. Without thinking, he licked it. He closed his eyes, savoring the task. Plain table sugar had been made into nectar just by the addition of desire.

He wasn't just randy, that was for sure. Nikki, his model girlfriend du jour, was happy to comply with his needs, especially since he'd bought her a red sports car and ruby earrings to match it.

But something unfamiliar was happening to him. Instead of wishing Nikki could fly to Montana that night for an intimate encounter, he dreaded the planned upcoming weekend he'd promised her. He no longer wanted to show Nikki the new ranch. Now he just wanted to prowl around it on his own so he could size up his new employee.

"May I come in?"

His head snapped around, and he saw Kirsten standing in the cabin door, her small curvy form wrapped in a paisley robe the exact midnight blue of her eyes.

"Take a seat. We've got at least two more hours of flying time."

She cautiously walked barefoot through the cabin, clutching the cashmere lapels of the robe together at her neckline like a spinster. Her innocent gesture charmed him in a way, but not enough for him to stop staring at her like a wolfhound.

Meeting his gaze, she twisted her rose-colored mouth into a rueful grin and said, "I have to say that's never happened to me before—but then, I've only taken commercial flights and they put their sugar in those little packets. I now know why." She laughed nervously.

He laughed, too. It felt good. It released the tension in the cabin and the terrible tension in his body.

"I'll have to tell Ricky to get some of those," he offered.

She laughed again. Her face lit up. "Is that his name? The steward? We hardly got to know each other."

"Yes, well, he got to know you," Seth said,

his words more caustic than he'd meant them to be.

A silence permeated the cabin.

Slowly she rose and went to get her laptop. Flustered, she said, "I guess we can finish now—"

"I'm no longer working." He raised his nearly empty whiskey glass and gestured to the bar. "Help yourself. It might do you good. You seem to be still shivering."

She glanced over at the bar, unsure.

"Go ahead. I won't hold it against you tomorrow. God knows I needed a drink." With that, he emptied his glass and returned to staring out the window.

Warily she stepped to the bar and fixed herself a drink. He was a strange man, but perhaps great wealth did that to a person. And yet there was something about him that transcended the money. Something primeval, earthy. Visceral. She saw it in his stare and in the way he always seemed to be shifting in his seat. Shifting because he couldn't quite seem to get comfortable.

She doubled her drink and wondered if the restlessness was catching. She certainly was restless every time she met that dark, disapproving stare.

* * *

By her second drink, Kirsten was getting over her unease. The silence grew into an exchange of pleasantries, finally to actual talk. Seth asked a lot of personal questions—no, rather demanded answers to a lot of personal questions, but Kirsten didn't mind answering him. She just explained away, the hum of the jet engines strongly comforting.

"There isn't a whole lot more to be said. After that, my mom and my sister moved back to Mystery. And here we are today. Just hunkydory." Kirsten sat cross-legged in her seat, her hand nursing the best whiskey and soda she'd ever tasted. The liquor left her sleepy and mellow. Even as harsh as Seth Morgan could look, she didn't mind it so much now. Now that the ice had broken, and they were talking.

"Why were you so hungry for this job?" His pointed question sent a chill down her spine.

"Hey, I could have worked flipping burgers at the Mystery Diner, but do you know what they pay?" She averted her gaze with a laugh.

"Hazel said you had to have this job. You needed the money."

Depression crept into her like the whiskey. "Carrie's only eleven, and my mom—well— she's been having some health problems lately. She really can't work."

"So everything's fallen on you."

Kirsten fell silent. Finally she said, "I didn't need Hazel to help me find a job, but I confess, if this can work out, I'd really like that."

Desperate to change the subject, she gave the cabin a cursory glance. "I can't believe I just took a shower on an airplane. I mean, how do you get used to all this?"

It was his turn to fall silent. He stared at her for a long curious moment.

Eventually he said, "I used to be hungry for things, too. I wanted the world in my lap, and then I got it. I guess I'm jaded about riches now. It takes a lot to make me want something these days."

"It must be great to have all your appetites appeased," she said quietly. "I just get hungrier and hungrier."

"My appetites are far from sated. And I always get what I want."

His words seemed more like a threat than a statement.

She studied him, a warning tingle creeping down her spine.

He said no more after that.

He only stared into the darkness out the window, dismissing her as if she had grown invisible.

* * *

The plane landed on time. When the steward Ricky brought Kirsten her luggage, she changed into a pair of jeans and a thermal shirt. Seth had a Jeep waiting for him at the airport and in no time they took off for the new ranch.

It was not what she'd expected.

After seeing his office, she figured Seth Morgan's ranch house would be a sprawling mansion tacked onto the side of a mountain. Instead, what she found was a master-crafted log house settled snugly into the land like a bird in a nest. The house was immensely livable. Fieldstone fireplaces graced each room. The ranch house didn't even have an office. Seth explained that he'd bought a ranch in Montana to relax, not work.

Against her better judgment to remain aloof, Kirsten was impressed by the building and the man.

The housekeeper, Viola, was an older woman with close-cropped white hair and high cheekbones that hinted at Native ancestry. She showed Kirsten her room and kindly left her with a tea tray.

Kirsten looked around the beautiful bedroom done warmly in aqua-blue cashmere, then threw herself on the bed and went right to the phone to call her family.

"Carrie! Tell Mom I'm back and I got the job!" Kirsten whispered excitedly into the phone.

She waited until she heard the familiar voice and then continued, "That's right. I got the job! So tomorrow you quit at the diner. No more work. You need to get over the chemo and be happy again. That way you'll be as healthy as the doctor says you are."

Her mom's expected protests fell on deaf ears.

"I've got it covered, Mom," Kirsten insisted. "You should see the room I have over here. Just the fabric of the bedcover is like my best pashmina shawl, so what do I need the rent money for? It's yours. You must quit tomorrow. I'm going by to thank Hazel in the morning, and I'll stop by then to check on you guys."

She listened for a minute and rolled her eyes. "It's done. Accept it. Everything has worked out just the way I planned. Our ship has come in. Kiss Carrie for me."

She hung up the phone, then hugged herself. It had been the best of days. All her problems seemed to be over.

But then she heard the knock and looked up. Standing in her still-open doorway was Seth

Morgan. He wore only jeans and a wool plaid shirt. He'd even kicked back so much that he was barefoot, but by the look of displeasure on his face he certainly couldn't be described as relaxed.

"Your ship would like a word with you about tomorrow," he said.

She rose cat-style from the bed. Her face heated with embarrassment. "I'm sorry you heard that—"

"Miss Meadows, no one knows my net worth better than I do," he said cuttingly. "If you hadn't noticed, I would have thought you stupid."

He gave her a dismissive look. "Now, on to business. I would like to take what Jim, the ranch manager, has in the barn right now and see which horses will fit my houseguests when I have them. I'd like a second opinion on the horseflesh, so tomorrow you can expect a fair amount of time in the saddle."

"Certainly," she choked out, near tears that her precious job might be threatened by another stupid mistake.

"I'll see you first thing in the morning."

"I'll be ready," she said in a raspy voice. "In the meantime, do you need me to do anything for you tonight?"

His long, hungry stare might have shocked her if she hadn't already been so afraid. His cold gaze raked her lips, then dragged down her throat, finally lingering on her thermal shirt and the way it stretched over her full chest.

"I'll see you in the morning, Miss Meadows." He abruptly turned and left.

She walked to the door and shut it. Alone in her room, she breathed deeply, trying to release the adrenaline pumping through her body.

She couldn't afford to offend the man. She would have to be scrupulously careful in the future. Too much depended on her.

But when her initial fears ebbed, her heart still raced with a strange excitement. She closed her eyes and could still see him in her doorway, his face hard and handsome, his jeans shrugged on over bare feet as if he was just anyone, rather than a billionaire.

The signals her body gave her put her into raging denial. Her breasts, her lips tingled just from his stare. She dreaded to think how she would react should he ever try to touch her. Her conflict certainly had something to do with the fact that Seth Morgan was a man, and an extremely attractive man at that. The gulf between them economically was too large to bridge, and more than that, she didn't want to get hurt, not the way her mother had been hurt by her father.

As her father had gained stature as an expatriate, he'd decided to trade up on his wives. Kirsten believed he was on his fourth right now, and this one was younger than she was.

Certainly, if her father who had only some power could do what he had to her mother, then Seth Morgan would be able to put her in a blender.

So he was not worth it and never would be.

Exhausted, she slipped out of her clothes and found her nightgown in her luggage. Sliding beneath the sheets, she was determined to put Seth out of her mind. She would do the job perfectly, and anything else that might be messy she would stay away from. She would keep theirs a straightforward relationship. A piece of cake. All she had to do was be professional and everything would be fine.

But as tired as she was, she still couldn't get the picture of him out of her mind.

And despite how well everything had been laid out in her mind, she hardly slept at all that night.

Kirsten and Seth had been out on the trail for more than an hour. ''Over there is Blue Rock

Creek where I used to go swimming in the summer.'' Kirsten pointed to the west of the trail.

She sat atop a plump dappled mare named Sterling, and Seth rode a tall dark stallion more Thoroughbred than quarter horse, named Noir. Both animals were the best-trained horses Kirsten had ever seen, and so it was a pleasure to venture forth on the trail until they were beyond the tree line and well into high country.

''Did you take your horse up here then? Back when you were younger?'' he asked.

Shaking her head, she said, ''I never had my own horse. We could never afford it, but sure, I trailed here. Hazel was always willing to lend a good rider a horse. Whenever I had a down moment as a teen, all I had to do was ask and she'd give me one of her best barrel racers. And after a long ride up here to heaven, nothing seemed so bad anymore. Nothing.''

She glanced at him and smiled. Still nervous from the encounter the night before, she'd been reluctant to open up, but once on the familiar trail with a good horse beneath her, she was in her element again and she felt in control once more.

''I even saw a grizzly up here once,'' she confessed. ''She scared me half to death. And you know, it was a worst case scenario. The grizzly even had two cubs with her.''

''You were lucky she didn't come at you,'' he said, turning a concerned eye to her.

Shrugging, she dismissed the danger. ''She was on the other side of the creek, and I'm sure she wanted as little to do with me as I did with her. In fact, I can still remember what I thought back then. I thought of my own mother, who was protecting her cubs by bringing them back to Mystery.'' She released a dark ironic smile. ''It's funny. I guess I'm the mother with the cubs now.''

He seemed to freeze in the saddle. Slowly he queried, ''How many children do you have?''

She wasn't sure if she'd heard him right. ''Did you ask how many children I have?''

''Yes,'' came the wooden reply.

''Does that factor into the job description?'' she asked, unsure where he was going with the questions.

''If you have children, I will understand that you may not want to stay at the ranch. I can give you a bungalow instead—''

Laughing, she shook her head. ''Thanks for the offer, but the only child I have is an eleven-year-old sister named Carrie.''

And a mother who's weak from a successful dose of chemo, she added to herself.

"I like children." His expression was scrupulously washed of all emotion.

"Did you come from a large family, then?" The question, she thought, was perfectly appropriate and not out of line.

He surprised her when he laughed. "I was the only child, raised—if you could call it that—entirely by my mother."

"My parents divorced, too," she mentioned, gaze trailing to the jagged purple horizon iced with snow.

"My parents weren't divorced. That would have been too honest." Giving her a penetrating stare, he added, "My father was a successful financier. He was absent from our lives, always away, having too much fun without us."

"I'm sorry," she offered, her hand stroking Sterling's salt-and-pepper mane as if to comfort. "But at least your mother was there for you."

He gave her an amused, jaded look. "You know that old joke about the couple going into the restaurant—the husband sees another woman there and gives her a big French kiss?"

She shook her head.

He continued. "Well, when the couple sit down, the wife asks him who the woman is and he tells her it's his mistress. The wife is furious and she wants a divorce, but then the husband explains that if she divorces him, gone is the winter cabin in Aspen and the house in St. Thomas, no more shopping sprees in Boca, and so on.''

Smirking, he turned Noir around to face her. ''So the joke ends that the wife shuts up about getting a divorce, and then when they see a couple next to them in the restaurant and the man is kissing a woman they know is not his wife, the woman asks who the woman is, and the husband says it's the man's mistress.''

A long pause ensued for effect.

At last he gave the punch line. Slowly he said, ''So then the wife comments, 'Well, *our* mistress is prettier.'''

Kirsten rode silently on, not sure if she wanted to laugh or cry. The joke was awful, but it certainly told of a woman more interested in her shopping sprees in Boca than her son.

''So you see,'' he said, turning Noir around and continuing the rocky trail heavenward, ''sometimes divorce is much more honest.''

They rode for a long time, each in their own thoughts.

Wanting to break the silence, she finally said,

"Hey, do you want to see where I saw the grizzly by Blue Rock Creek?"

He turned and nodded.

They took the fork in the trail that led to the creek.

Once there, she dismounted and haltered Sterling. Seth did the same.

"I think it's downstream from here. Do you still want to see? It might be a bit of a hike." She looked up at him.

Without her heels on, she suddenly realized how tall he was. He towered over her. Intimidated enough by his brooding dark looks and penetrating stare, she had no need for a reminder that he was physically much stronger than she was.

"No problem for me, but it's rocky—that okay with you?"

She laughed. "Hey, this is my childhood haunt. I could do it blindfolded."

"Then show me."

She took a second look at him to be sure it was what he wanted, then she wandered along the creek edge until weeds choked her path and she was forced to walk in the creek.

He followed, his cowboy boots sloshing along behind her.

"It's not far, I don't think." She chewed on

her lower lip. "It's been a while, though." She walked another few steps. Beyond was the clearing of soapberries that had once hidden the mother grizzly bear and her two cubs.

"There it is. I was standing over there—" She turned to the other bank and her leather-soled cowboy boot slid on a mossy stone. She went flying.

A steely arm went around her waist, catching her.

She looked up, wanting only to give Seth a gratifying glance before stepping out of his arms, but he wouldn't let go. She stood there staring up at him. There was nothing around them but silence. Even the crickets, it seemed, were holding their breath.

"Is our mistress going to be prettier?" he asked, looking down at her, cynicism like a poison in his voice.

She locked gazes with him, devastated yet strangely thrilled at the same time. His arm was like a prison, and his eyes pinned her to the ground. His words stung and promised at the same time. He implied marriage and commitment, all the while assuring her of deception and heartache.

Her pulse beat a staccato in her throat, her lips grew dry and she licked them—just as she had done when doused with table sugar. The water rushing at their feet now became deafening.

"There won't be any mistresses in my marriage. I promise you." Her voice was thick with emotion.

He arched one jet-black eyebrow. "What's to stop them?" His own words grew husky. "This?" he whispered right before he crushed her to him and captured her lips with his.

The kiss was molten lava. Almost more than she could bear. It had been months since she'd been kissed by a man with so much yearning, months since she'd allowed herself the sexual pleasure of one deep earthy kiss.

She opened her mouth to him, selfishly taking what he had to offer. He didn't disappoint. His scent filled her. Whereas she'd thought he'd smell of Bond Street cologne and plastic, instead her nostrils filled with man heat and leather. It was delicious.

He pulled her farther into the hard wall of his body, his kiss deepening with his tongue. She released a nearly silent moan, her hands curling against his chest as he penetrated her mouth with lover's strokes. Her legs weakened; her head grew light. Only her yearning remained sharp and hungry, driving her mindlessly toward ultimate satisfaction.

His palm rubbed the inward curve of her waist, then made its way up her torso. She didn't want sanity to intervene, but she knew if he cupped her breast she would be well on her way to sleeping with her boss. And that was unforgivable madness.

Cold logic forced her return to earth.

As if drugged, she pulled back from him, and with a kitten's fury she spat out, "Look, I've heard about you. I know all about your conquests, all the beautiful girls. Hazel told me you're the talk of Wall Street." Her passion rose. "But I don't want to be another conquest, okay? I don't need the trouble. What I want—what I need is this job. I must have this job, and I won't be able to keep it if you and I—well—if you and I—"

Her frustration, sexual and otherwise, choked her. "Well, we won't do it, okay? We just will not!" she cried before she ran down the creek to her horse and galloped all the way back to the stable.

"Hazel, you're setting me up," Seth growled that evening in Hazel McCallum's nineteenth-century parlor. Ebby, Hazel's housekeeper, seemed to sense where the conversation was going and brought over the whiskey decanter.

"You calling me a sneaky varmint? Seth, you told me you needed a personal assistant, and I recommended one. Now look at you! Sitting there accusing me of rustlin'," she said.

Hazel, with her blue jeans and cowboy boots that were the perfect foil for her silver hair with its elegant chignon, nodded to Ebby to pour two stiff whiskeys.

Seth waved his away.

Hazel took hers, unable to hide the twinkle in her famous Prussian-blue eyes. She commented, "I always like a snort before dinner. Gets my blood up, don't you think? Oh, but yours is already up, I guess...." She lifted the glass to her lips.

He resentfully took his whiskey.

"I really don't think Miss Meadows is the type of woman I was looking for to fill the position," he said in clipped tones.

"Why?" Hazel retorted good-naturedly. "Because she's beautiful and smart? She's fluent in five languages, too. I believe you're only fluent in one, if my sources are correct."

Giving her his notorious icy stare, he said, "Yes, but I'm fluent in the only language that counts—money. So that makes me fluent in every language."

"Kirsten Meadows doesn't speak that language. Just you remember that, Seth.'' Hazel turned serious.

His mouth turned into a hard line. ''I've never met a woman who didn't speak it. Besides, that's not what our dear Miss Meadows was saying on the phone about her ship coming in.''

The aging cattle baroness studied him. ''She's not like those other women. You mark my words—she's something you've never dealt with before, son, and God save you if you forget that.''

He said nothing. The line of his mouth grew harder.

Hazel laughed and refilled his glass.

''Now, on to more pleasant talk,'' she continued. ''I meant to tell you that you're hosting next week's Mystery BBQ Sizzle. We have it once a year in the summer, and I usually host it here at the ranch, but it's time the townsfolk got to know the carpetbagger in their midst.''

''Don't tell me, tell Kirsten. I may have to be in New York—''

''I don't give a damn where you might have to be. When I sold you that prized parcel of my land, I told you it came with a commitment to the town—and that means being here.'' She winked. ''Why don't you invite your fancy New

York friends? They might get a kick out of seeing you play ranch hand.''

He finally laughed. ''Hazel, you're in the wrong element here in this little town of Mystery. I swear you're diabolical enough to work on Wall Street.''

The cattle baroness smiled at his flash of white, even teeth. ''Why, this ol' cowgirl couldn't handle them city slickers, and you know it.''

''No, they couldn't handle you,'' he said wryly.

''We'll give them the chance to find out a week from Friday.''

He took another long sip of whiskey. And rolled his eyes.

''Hazel! I just had to get here and tell you! I got the—'' Kirsten screeched to a halt in the parlor, Ebby at her heels.

''Oh, gosh, I'm sorry, Hazel. You have company,'' she muttered, her gaze going to Seth.

''Nonsense. He's family now just like you are, Kirsten. He bought that land of mine and that makes him a native son.''

Hazel got to her feet—she was slower than she used to be, but more spritely than most her age. ''Now that you're here, we're just about to have some vittles. Come take a place at the table.''

Ebby disappeared to add the third place setting.

Kirsten still shook her head apologetically. ''No, forgive me. I should have called....''

''Since when do I answer my phone?'' Hazel harrumphed. ''If you got words to say to me, you say 'em to my face just like in the good ol' days, or you keep 'em to yourself. So now you two pokes come to dinner before your plate gets cold.'' Hazel left the parlor for the dining room.

Kirsten was alone with Seth.

She looked up at her boss, her emotions still stinging from their encounter in the creek just hours before.

Awkwardly she said, ''How do you do, Mr. Morgan.''

''Miss Meadows,'' he acknowledged curtly.

She swore there was a twinkle in his cold eyes. Her cheeks heated.

''I hope you don't mind my barging in like this. I truly didn't realize you were here.''

He gave a wry twist to his lips, the lips she still found wickedly evocative and handsome. ''Not at all. But if we're going to work together, and now dine together, I'd like you to call me Seth.''

"Certainly. And you may call me Kirsten."

He nodded.

Even she could see how stiff they were with each other. The kiss that afternoon had seemed to freeze both of them.

"Drink?" Ebby interrupted, offering Kirsten a whiskey and ice.

Grateful to have something to focus on other than the memory of their kiss, she took the proffered glass and sipped it.

"She's waiting," Ebby announced, a knowing smile on her lips.

Seth rolled his eyes again. "Oh, I know, one thing we don't do is keep the queen waiting."

Both Ebby and Kirsten stared at him.

Then they both burst out laughing.

Ebby finally interjected with, "You know, Mr. Morgan, you're a quick study, and you seem to be getting things a lot faster than most. I think you might fit here in Mystery after all."

Three

Hazel's dinners were famous for their overindulgence, and the current night was no exception. Kirsten was half-tipsy and full to the gills when she and Seth said good-night to the cattle baroness. Having gotten a ride to Hazel's ranch from her mother, Kirsten reluctantly accepted Seth's offer for a ride back to his place.

The mountainous road was no match for her emotions as she sat next to Seth in his Jeep. Playing elk slalom, he navigated the vehicle with skill and precision through the dark rural night.

''You drive like a native,'' she commented.

He chuckled. "I'm no native. I grew up in East Hampton in New York."

"Well, something's clicking with you and Mystery. The tourists are terrified of the roads at night."

"My parents had a ski lodge in Big Sky, Montana. I decided early on that I like the nature of the mountains more than the skiing. Camping made me learn to drive the winding roads."

"That explains it."

He looked sideways at her, studying her.

"You know," he interjected into the quiet automobile, "Hazel told me that next week I have to host the Mystery BBQ Sizzle. I hope you know what has to be done, because I don't have a clue how to go about something like that."

It was her turn to chuckle. "Hazel's so tricky. She loves handing that over to the greenhorns. It's like a test."

"Well, I expect you as my personal assistant to make sure I pass the test."

She nodded. "I know what has to be done. No problem. Consider it a finished deal."

"I'll want to invite some New Yorkers."

"Certainly."

"I'll leave the list for you in the morning. You can find all their numbers in my files."

"Of course."

"I'll want the plane sent for Nikki."

Her heart went thump. She knew who Nikki Butler was. The tabloids loved to photograph the willowy model with her billionaire boyfriends.

Kirsten denied any pangs of jealousy.

The kiss she and Seth had experienced that afternoon was at best an inconvenience, at worst a threat to the job she dearly needed. The emotions that roiled inside her upon hearing this could only be disappointment—disappointment to find out her boss was so shallow as to date an airhead model with an IQ less than her daily calorie intake.

"I'll make sure she has everything she wants."

Including you, Kirsten thought with more bitterness than even she had expected.

"See that she comes in on Thursday so we have some time alone before the big event."

Woodenly Kirsten responded, "I'll take care of it."

"If you have any questions as to her preferences, Mary can help you with them. She knows everything about Ms. Butler."

She nodded, wondering if her face looked as green in the dashboard light as she felt.

"Do you feel all right, Kirsten?"

Her head snapped around to face him. "I feel great. Why wouldn't I? Why would you ask?"

He paused. "Well, we've been parked at the ranch for almost a minute now. You seem pre-occupied."

Kirsten felt as if she was waking from a night-mare.

Suddenly she looked out of the Jeep window and realized they had indeed stopped at the front of Seth's house. She couldn't remember coming to a halt at all.

"No, no. I'm fine. Just a little tired from the long day," she blathered, getting out of the jeep.

"Well, good night, then."

Like an idiot, she kept on blathering. "I'll take care of everything. Don't worry. In two days every preparation will be made."

"Good night, Miss Meadows."

She paused, suddenly hating the formality when before there had been none.

"Good night, Mr. Morgan."

The Mystery BBQ Sizzle was the event of the summer. Tourists and locals alike attended. It was a tradition of Hazel McCallum's that went back decades. Hazel always said you could find out more about a person at a barbecue than you could at a five-star hotel.

Kirsten, watching supermodel Nikki Butler sunning her long svelte self at the ranch's pool, had the sickening feeling Hazel was right. She was going to get a load of Nikki Butler's character that weekend whether she wanted to or not.

"Could you stock the pool fridge with more mineral water?" Nikki asked Viola the house-keeper in a sweet voice.

Viola smiled as she walked past Kirsten.

"Can I get you anything?" the older woman asked, as always, eternally gracious.

"Don't add me to your woes. I'm strictly self-serve around here," Kirsten offered with a smile of her own.

"It's only going to get worse when the rest of the guests arrive. He's got another model and two brokers coming tomorrow," Viola added.

Kirsten almost shuddered. "There'll be a run on Scotch and rice cakes in town."

Laughing, Viola went toward the kitchen.

Kirsten was about to leave also when she saw Seth enter the pool area from the stables. He didn't see her; he seemed to have eyes only for Nikki.

Stepping behind a rough-hewn pillar, Kirsten watched, a sickening feeling in her stomach. She didn't want to get involved with Seth Morgan, but she feared her rational mind was telling her one thing, and her heart and hormones another.

Seeing him interact with another woman was not something she enjoyed, but she couldn't look away. Her curiosity took over.

They were discussing something. Neither seemed particularly demonstrative toward each other, but Kirsten wondered if she herself was putting a spin on that.

Seth seemed to settle an issue, and Nikki, appearing as self-involved as Kirsten expected, simply sat back in her lounge chair and resumed tanning.

Not wanting him to see her, Kirsten darted behind the cabana and walked toward the house. She went to the desk in the large kitchen and absentmindedly went through her list for the barbecue.

"Miss Meadows—"

Kirsten was startled. Seth stood right behind her, studying her with that wintergreen gaze.

"Yes?" she answered coolly.

"Nikki needs to call her agent—would you bring her her cell phone? She said it's on the bed."

She nodded.

He almost seemed to want to smirk. But he added nothing else before he walked away.

Fuming, Kirsten went up the rough-hewn staircase.

Besides her room and Seth's suite, there were three guest rooms at the back of the house. Hoping and praying she wouldn't have to go looking for the cell phone on Seth's bed, she went to the back of the hall.

All three guest bedrooms were unoccupied.

Nikki must be staying with Seth, Kirsten thought.

Strangely disheartened, she went toward Seth's closed door.

They'd shared only a kiss and a few pleasant moments. There was nothing between them, and his girlfriend had every right to stay wherever she wanted while in his home.

Nikki Butler was his girlfriend. His *girlfriend,* she repeated to herself silently.

She was going to have to remember that while Nikki was here—and most especially once the model left. Seth Morgan was dangerous. He played the field and cared nothing of the women he left in his wake.

After what had happened to her mother, Kirsten was doubly appalled that she'd had even a fleeting thought of a relationship with the handsome lout. Her own experience with men had been wary, at best. She'd made her own bad choices. One in particular, James, was even still hanging around Mystery, nagging her for more dates even though they'd broken it off after James had lost his temper one night. She had no patience for that kind of man, and so far she'd met few that weren't like her father—narcissistic.

So she and her new boss had had one kiss, Kirsten told herself. It meant nothing. It was an error in judgment by both of them, and that was all. The fire in her mouth when he'd deepened the kiss was all that seemed to affect her brain lately, but what she'd have to concentrate on was how cold her feet had been with the stream rushing around her boots. The coldness was what she needed to concentrate on now. Just the coldness.

She opened the waxed knotty-pine door to his bedroom.

Her expression froze.

The perfect specimen of a naked man's backside stood between her and the bed.

"Oh, I'm sorry!" she gasped, the blood draining from her face.

"What the hell are you doing here?" Seth snapped, holding his swim trunks—which obviously he hadn't had time to put on yet—in front of himself when he turned to face her.

Speechless, all she could do was stare at him,

her gaze taking in the grid of muscle on his belly and the dark trail of hair that pointed like an arrow to...to...

"Again, what the hell are you doing here? Don't you knock?" he asked, his voice laced with anger.

"I'm sorry, but you told me to get Ms. Butler's phone on the bed. I didn't think you were in here."

A muscle bunched in his jaw. "She's staying in the cabin. Along with everyone else from New York."

"I'm—I'm sorry," she stammered. "I just assumed she was staying up here."

"She's not."

Why not? she wanted to cry out, desperate to make sense of this man so she could protect herself.

But there was no asking questions now. He had no clothes on, and his relationship with Nikki was none of her business. None absolutely.

Kirsten needed to concentrate on coldness.

And it was very hard to think about the cold as she stared at a naked Seth Morgan, his high, tight buttocks reflecting back at her from a cheval mirror.

"Miss Meadows, you're excused." His gaze

raked her. "Unless, of course, you want to come in and lock the door."

Backing away as if from a bee sting, she shook her head and fumbled for the door. His nudity frightened and aroused her, all at the same time. It brought a rush of emotions she longed to repress. Horrified, she wondered how she would ever keep him from her thoughts when she now had him burned forever in her memory.

She took her escape gladly. She ran from the bedroom, his laughter following her the entire way.

"He's being his usual obnoxious self. I mean, he has the nerve to put me in the guest cabin with everyone else, can you believe it?"

Nikki's upset words to her agent over her cell phone registered all too well with Kirsten when she arrived shortly after retrieving Nikki's cell phone from the guest cabin for her. The model was in a difficult mood in spite of languishing by the pool, and Kirsten could almost sympathize with her. That morning she herself wasn't feeling too gracious, either.

"Oh, honey," Nikki called out to her, her hand on the mouthpiece, "can you see to it that I've got a magnum of champagne in the cabin?

Thanks.'' She went back to her cell phone.
''That ought to do it.''

''Certainly,'' Kirsten said, her insides crawling at the name *honey*. To Nikki everyone was
honey—Viola, Kirsten, Jim the ranch manager.
The only one who wasn't was Seth Morgan.

Kirsten got the champagne from the wine cellar and brought it to the guest cabin that was
nestled in the rock just out of view from the
house. Setting a couple of crystal flutes on the
copper counter, she placed the champagne in the
fridge, her thoughts a million miles away from
her task.

In many ways Nikki Butler was perfect for
Seth. She was gloriously beautiful, so much so
that their mistress would be hard-pressed to be
prettier. Nikki would also tolerate any of Seth's
bad behavior to get her hands on the next bit of
loot, and all would be happy.

But for some reason the thought of Nikki and
Seth just made Kirsten sad. Certainly Seth Morgan was one of the most cynical, jaded men she
had ever met. But there was something inside
him, something very human. As numb as he was
to intolerable behavior, at least he was cynical
about it. It showed some kind of fight in him,
some kind of reaction to it all instead of being
blithely accepting.

Hazel saw something in him, too, and one day Kirsten wanted to ask her about it. The cattle baroness never ever sold her land. For her to have given Seth an unheard-of amount of family land meant Hazel viewed him as worthwhile.

Kirsten smiled to herself. Ironic though it was, it was hard to see Seth's worth at times, with all the blinding riches around him.

From the window she watched as Seth arrived at the pool. He took a dive off the board, splashing Nikki. His head broke the surface, and he was all wolfish smile and glittering water. Behind him, the mountains ripped upward, their cracked tops frozen with ice.

His wealth could dig a hole in the ground and build a pool, an unnecessary extravagance in the cool Montana summer, but there was nothing the man could do about the mountains. The mountains were there, untouchable and magnificent. The pool and the mountains—style versus substance.

And Kirsten wanted substance, while Nikki wanted style.

Kirsten supposed that was what bothered her. She told herself she wasn't necessarily falling for Seth Morgan. Sure, they'd kissed, and it had been…well, breathtaking. Like the mountains.

But deep down she suspected that Seth Morgan was more than just style.

Yet Nikki would win. It was inevitable.

And then there would be no more hot kisses, no more cold streams rushing through their legs, no more talks on horseback. There would be no more mountains.

Strangely depressed, Kirsten sighed and gathered herself. She wasn't necessarily falling in love with Seth, but at times it sure felt like it.

Like now, when she watched him frolic with his model by the pool. In truth, Kirsten wanted to rip him away from the whole scene, to ease her jealousy.

To ease the heartache she felt whenever she saw things of substance slip away.

Four

Friday afternoon Kirsten watched the men set up the bandstand for the barbecue.

The two-step band she'd hired was one she knew well. She only hoped that James, the lead singer in Mystery's best cowboy band, would let bygones be bygones.

They'd dated for less than a month, and it just hadn't been right. Their personalities didn't mesh, but worse than that, James hadn't understood her. He'd continually mistaken her reserve and caution for being stuck-up.

It wouldn't have worked with James, but he'd

been sore when she'd told him. She only prayed
he was attached to someone else by now. Otherwise the barbecue could be most unpleasant,
because James had the ability to swill beer like
a good ol' boy.

Pushing her anxieties aside, she watched another group of workers set down a portable oak
dance floor for two-stepping.

All in all it looked as if the barbecue should
be a success. The weather was supposed to be
warm and dry. A beautiful Montana sky full of
stars was the perfect backdrop for waltzing.

She looked away for a moment, suddenly feeling more like Cinderella than the boss's assistant. The fantasy of dancing in the arms of a man
she loved beneath her beloved Montana sky was
too much to resist. But every time the daydream
took hold, the man she found herself dancing
with was Seth Morgan. And that only depressed
her more.

"Have the others arrived from the airport
yet?" Nikki whined, sipping her umpteenth
glass of chardonnay.

Kirsten saw that the model had left poolside
just to speak to her.

"I don't know. Their flight was to arrive by
now, but I haven't seen Mr. Morgan in the
Jeep." Kirsten eyed the tall, beautiful model.

As horrible as it had been to get through last night without thinking of Seth and Nikki together, Kirsten almost believed Nikki was having a harder time. The woman looked caved-in, and she'd been at the wine since way before noon.

Kirsten bit back all the questions she had. Her boss's relationship with his girlfriend was not her concern, but there were so many things going through her head. As it was, hope and despair played a ridiculous game of tug-of-war inside her heart, and she really wanted the torture to end.

"He'd better show up soon," the model sniped, "that's all I know. If he's going to fly me to the middle of nowhere and take away all my fun, then I damn well plan on getting some from Rick."

Shocked, Kirsten at least put together that Rick was one of Seth's friends coming to town from New York.

"Maybe he's just distracted—you know, getting the barbecue together and all." Kirsten wondered why she was even speaking. First of all, it was clear the model didn't want her advice and sympathy any more than she'd want that from a table leg. And if Kirsten were truthful to herself, she knew good and well she didn't want to encourage a relationship between Nikki and Seth. Seth sure as all-fire wasn't getting the barbecue together; rather, that was Kirsten's job, and she had the pulled-out hair to show for it.

"Distracted!" Nikki snorted. "He's the last man to turn down a night of passion. I should know. When I hit the cover of that lingerie catalog, he was all over me."

Kirsten could definitely feel a headache coming on.

"And now," the model rambled, half-drunk, "now he calls me all the way from New York to visit his lodge and puts me in the guest house—the cheating jerk." Nikki looked at her. "So who is the other woman? Has he been inviting someone else up here?"

Kirsten's heart stopped.

Paling, she stammered, "I—I have no idea."

"C'mon. I know you're just protecting the boss, but really, woman to woman, is it that actress he was seen with his last night in New York? Or is he going back to that Parisian as everyone says he will?"

Stupefied, Kirsten didn't have a clue how to answer her. She wanted to cry out that they'd shared a kiss and maybe, just maybe, the man wanted something more in a woman than a size two hardbody.

Kirsten just shook her head and shrugged and asked if she could refill the woman's glass.

Nikki handed her the empty wineglass.

Always the cool one, always the one to solve everyone else's problems, Kirsten brutally shoved aside her hope and went to get the refill. She got to the kitchen door just as the Jeep pulled up in front of the house. Seth was back. And with a bunch of partying guests that Kirsten knew she had to attend to whether she wanted to or not.

"So how can I get a personal assistant just like you, Ms. Meadows?" Rick Conway asked, his wolfish grin disavowed by the twinkle in his green eyes.

"You can't," Seth interrupted, giving Rick a quelling glance as he passed him on the trail.

Kirsten wanted to laugh. They'd been on the trail for an hour. Rick, another model named Skya and a broker named Bob, who clearly had the hots for Skya, rode together with Seth and Nikki. Kirsten had been asked to lead the group, since she knew Hazel's trails better than the ranch manager.

Rick pulled his quarter horse alongside Sterling. "But on the slim chance Mr. Morgan isn't paying you a fair salary for your—ah—services, Ms. Meadows, you know you can always—"

"Ask for an increase," Seth barked.

Rick laughed. "What is she? Your employee or a shareholder?"

"Why don't you harass Nikki instead, you dog." Seth smirked.

"Yes, why don't you harass me, Rick—sexually is preferred," Nikki chimed in from the back of the trail.

Kirsten cringed at the jab to Seth, but he didn't seem to notice.

"Pardon me, my lady." Rick took off his cowboy hat and bowed his head to Kirsten. "But if I'm to be sued for harassment, I'd much prefer Nikki's lawyers than Seth's. Alas…"

He reined in his horse and left for the rear.

Kirsten giggled. Rick was funny, but what made him hopelessly charming was the fact that he made fun of himself even more than others— an unusual trait, she figured, in the mega-ego world of stockbrokers.

"I should have warned you about him. To him, his whole life is one big party." Seth pulled Noir up alongside Kirsten's horse.

"He's fine. Not a problem." She stole a glance at him.

Seth looked like one of the cowboys who worked on Hazel's range. He hadn't shaved, and dust from the trail coated his hat and jaw. From beneath the brim, he met her gaze with a shadowed stare.

She wished she could say that he didn't wear the dirt and grime well, but deep down she had to admit he looked even sexier than when she'd first seen him in his immaculately tailored business suit.

"After dinner we'll be going into town for a drink," Seth said. "I figure you might like a night off before the barbecue."

She nodded. She'd seen her mother and sister only once since she'd returned to Mystery from New York. "Thank you."

He looked as if he wanted to say something more, but then thought better of it.

Then suddenly, as if angry at himself, he jerked Noir around and loped toward Nikki.

Kirsten didn't look back. Instead, she began a monotone travelogue of historical tidbits about the valley for the benefit of Bob and Skya, who looked as if they couldn't care less. But she cared, and she continued motoring her mouth uselessly.

Anything to keep her mind off the boss.

* * *

Carrie, Kirsten's sister, sat next to her on the couch, curled up in her arms. The eleven-year-old recounted the latest inexplicable fashion fad.

"And then you clip your hair up with these glittery ponytail holders and that's it."

"I'm exhausted—and you plan on doing this to your hair every day?" Kirsten asked with a smile.

"But it'd be really cute on you," Carrie offered.

"Not as cute as on you."

"Dinner's ready."

Kirsten looked up. Her mother stood by the living-room door, dressed in a denim shift and sandals. For the first time in ages, Kirsten thought, her mother didn't look tired.

"Retirement agrees with you, Mom," she said, hugging her. "I can't remember the last time I didn't see circles under your eyes."

"Nonsense. I'm going back to work just as soon as my hair's a little longer." Jenn Meadows smoothed the baby-fine hair coming in around her face.

"Viola keeps her hair real short. A few whimsical pairs of earrings and you'll look great."

"Who's Viola?" Carrie asked.

"She's Seth's housekeeper," Kirsten answered.

Her mother looked at her quizzically. "Seth?" she asked.

"Mr. Morgan," Kirsten added hastily.

In a move of self-preservation, she changed the subject. "Now that I've got the income, I just wanted you to know that I called about buying this place, Mom. I think I'd be so much smarter to just own this old cottage and quit throwing the money away on rent."

"But you don't even live here, honey," Jenn protested,

Kirsten winked at Carrie. "Yes, but you and Carrie live here—and who knows, Mr. Morgan may go out of town for months at a time. I might be back here more than you think."

"I don't know about that. As soon as I've had a rest, I'm looking for another job."

Kirsten sat at the table, grateful to be home if only for the evening. "When you feel up to it, Mom, you can get another job, but doesn't it feel great to know you can go out there and do something you'd enjoy rather than just something that's going to pay the rent?"

Jenn seemed overtaken with emotion. She was quiet for a long moment, then she took Kirsten's hand and squeezed it. "That would feel wonderful, darling, but you have to promise me you feel that way about working for Mr. Morgan.

Otherwise, if I found out you were miserable just to pay our rent, I don't know what I would do.''

"I love my job, Mom. Really." Kirsten gave her a smile and quickly turned her attention to her dinner.

There was no way she was ever going to tell her mother about all the complications. In fact, looking at her mother so rested and content, Kirsten only became more determined to make her job less complicated.

She could do it, too. It would take some discipline. She'd have to rid herself of daydreams. But she could do it. Besides, in all probability, Seth would get bored with Montana and go back to New York for long stints. That would make it easier. And who knew. He and Nikki might make up and get married. That'd solve all the complications.

Heartsick, she began to eat her dinner, unaware of her mother's scrutinizing looks throughout the entire meal.

"There's the girl Friday right now! And hey, it *is* Friday!" Rick Conway jumped into Kirsten's path on the sidewalk.

After dinner she'd walked downtown from her mother's place so she could check on a few details before the barbecue tomorrow. James was one of those dangling little knots. She wanted to have a promise that he wouldn't act up if he was going to play with the band. But she couldn't get anywhere now with Rick blocking her path.

"Hello, Mr. Conway. I see you've been enjoying Mystery's many authentic saloons." She wrinkled her nose at the smell of whiskey on his breath.

"This place is fantastic. There's a good old cowboy bar on every corner."

She smiled. "You don't have to try them all tonight—just a little tip, being a native here and all."

"Why so formal? I know you're not as cold as you'd like to be. I mean, c'mon, you get all my jokes. How cold can you be?"

The earnestness on his face made her laugh aloud.

"See what I mean?" He took a staggering step toward her.

"Did your companions abandon you, Mr. Conway? Would you like me to call Jim to take you back to the ranch?"

"Naw. They're right behind me. Just having another spat. So what'd you do to that guy? He's really upset Nikki—I told her she could bunk with me tonight if she's as lonely as she says she is."

"I—I—haven't done anything," she stammered, his drunken comment catching her off guard.

"He's got his radar on you good. So good." He snorted. "And that damn beautiful Nikki can't seem to figure out that the other woman's right under her perfect nose."

"No—no really—" Kirsten protested.

"No—really," he mimicked, then sobered. "Let me tell you, you seem like a nice woman. Seth's one cold jerk, and Nikki's just made for him. Just make sure you don't get yourself hurt." Rick leaned forward and whispered, "But if you do, I'm here. I'd love to comfort you, if you know what I mean."

She stared at him, unable to form any words. Rick's brazenness shocked her, terrified her even. She didn't want to be in a position to have to rebuff one of the boss's friends. But worst of all, his words about Seth's radar renewed the hope that she was bent on killing.

"Thanks for the advice," was all she could say before Nikki appeared, alone, sullen and demanding.

"What are you doing in town, Kirsten?" the model snipped.

"I had the night off. I thought I'd take care of a few details for the party tomorrow." She lifted a manila envelope she held in her hands, stuffed with papers. "So much to do, so little time."

"Well, we're heading back. We'll see you to-morrow."

"Without Seth?" Rick squawked, letting the model take him by the arm and lead him away.

"He wants to stay and I want to leave," the model announced, her every word laced with re-sentment. "Here are the keys to the Jeep. Do I have to spell it out for you, you lucky boy?"

Rick's eyes widened.

"C'mon."

He followed Nikki down the street like a puppy dog.

Kirsten watched them go.

She would even have laughed if she hadn't turned around and smacked into the hard, un-yielding chest of her boss.

Five

"Looking for your ship, Miss Meadows?" Seth inquired, his tone sarcastic.

Cool and collected, she didn't let him ruffle her feathers. "I was in town and thought to check on a few details for tomorrow, Mr. Morgan."

She refused to take his bait. Clasping the manila envelope and her handbag, she made to walk around him on the sidewalk. "So, if you'll excuse me—"

"Tomorrow is a fait accompli. Take the night off." His words were like a military order.

"I think everything should go very well to-morrow, but I still have a few personal errands to run—"

"Personal errands. What kind of personal errands do you have to run at this time of night?"

She stared at him, exasperated. "I can certainly see why you've done so well for yourself, Mr. Morgan, but bullying me will get you nothing but..."

She paused for the right words, but there were none. There wasn't anything she could threaten him with. Quitting would only hurt her at this point in her life.

"But what, Miss Meadows?" he taunted.

"My—my—my displeasure," she retorted.

Even she had to laugh. She sounded like some nineteenth-century schoolmarm.

Grinning, he stared down at her while a couple of drunken young men rolled out of the Roundup Bar and came their way.

Not in the mood to tangle with tourists, she said, "Unless you have a task you need done, if you'll excuse me, this is my only time to take care of what I have to do in town. I've got to go."

"How are you getting home?"

"I don't know, sir."

He laughed out loud. The wolfish grin enticed

her and the spark returned to his wicked eyes. "You still can't walk around town alone all night. I'll go with you—for protection only."

The drunken men passed by, one accidentally staggering into her. The manila file flew out of her hand and the young men walked on, oblivious.

"You need protection, Miss Meadows," he confirmed as he bent and helped her gather the papers.

"Fine. Come along if you have nothing better to do than cause my displeasure," she told him, flustered as she tried to retrieve all her papers.

"Believe me. Your pleasure is the only thing on my mind, Miss Meadows."

She eyed him, glad they were underneath the dim street lamp and not in naked sunlight where she might read all the lust she suspected was in that last statement.

Giving up on conversation, she walked across Main Street, where the saloons were located, to Aspen Street, where most of the businesses had their offices.

The blocks were dark and desolate compared to the rowdiness of Main Street in the height of the tourist season, but she didn't mind. There was virtually no crime in Mystery. It really was pointless for Seth to come with her. She wondered why she hadn't insisted he go his own way and she go hers, but then she forced herself not to study the motivations too closely, because she didn't really want the answers.

She stopped in front of a plate-glass-fronted office named Mountain Mortgage.

Placing her entire file in the night box, she made a display of dusting her hands of it, then said, "Okay. Mission complete. My bodyguard can breathe easy once again."

"Are you buying a house?"

"Maybe," was all she offered.

"Why do you need a house when you live at the ranch?"

"Because this is a free country, and employees may do anything they like after work hours, including buying property the boss may not understand that they need."

She lifted one eyebrow and gave him a chastising look. "Does that explain it for you?"

"No. No, it does not. Does Hazel know you're buying a house?"

"I'm going to tell her if I get the loan."

"I know you think I plan on being in New York a lot, but I'm telling you right now, Miss Meadows, that I plan on spending most of my time in Mystery, and I'll need an assistant at my quarters, not living in town."

"I'm aware of that, Mr. Morgan."

"Then answer me. Why are you buying a house?"

"I'm buying it for my mother and sister, okay?" she finally snapped.

Her shoulders sagged, the stress of the past couple of weeks weighing her down. "Look, I just thought now that I had a pretty good job I should buy the cottage my mom lives in so she doesn't have to pay rent any more."

"Why can't your mom buy her own house?"

"Because she's been sick and worked to death. She needs a break, and I'm going to give her one."

A muscle in his jaw bunched as if he were pondering her words.

Tears suddenly stung her eyes. She didn't know how she was going to handle James at the barbecue tomorrow, and handling Nikki for the past two days had taken its toll emotionally. Right then, all she could think of was that she wanted to get away from Seth Morgan as fast as she could. She wanted to lick her wounds and quell her embarrassment and sort out her lacerated emotions alone.

She turned to leave, but he pulled her into the darkened doorway of the mortgage company.

"I'll buy your mother the house. You don't

have to worry about that," he whispered as if suddenly aware of her desire for privacy.

"I can't let you do that," she protested, her throat thick with tears of exhaustion. "In fact, I won't let you do it. It would be improper and perhaps even unethical."

"I want to do it." His hands cupped her face.

She couldn't see his eyes in the darkness of the doorway. She couldn't tell if he was the Seth Morgan of substance or style at that moment, and she wasn't about to trust herself either, not when his strong touch sent an erotic rustle down her spine like the scattering of aspen leaves.

"It would take too long to pay you back," she said, the tears beginning to well in her eyes, her strength for protest dissipating.

"Don't pay me back, then."

She looked up at him in shock. He stared down at her, his expression urging.

Soon the tears streamed down her face and onto his knuckles, which caressed her cheeks.

A strange moment held between them.

Her exhaustion and despair were getting the better of her, and she knew it. It was getting harder and harder to think with his warm touch on her face.

But he seemed undone by her crying. His face was a hard mask of marble, his eyes shadowed and piercing. She knew he wanted something, and it was frustrating him being unable to figure out how to go about it.

Slowly, he drew his tear-dampened knuckles across her mouth.

Her emotions raw, she was aware that now was not the time for a kiss, because she knew she couldn't protect herself from her protector.

But the kiss came anyway. And in the end, she wasn't even sure who kissed whom first. All she did know was that his lips were on hers once more, feeding her soul. And she held his mouth to hers as desperately as he held on to her.

Moaning, she allowed the kiss to deepen. His tongue licked fire into her mouth, and his arms trapped her like a cage as they moved around to her back and crushed her to him.

The want built in her like a pressure cooker. When his hand slid between the buttons of her blouse, she had no thoughts of pushing him away. She thought only of giving him more and more until she had satisfied her own growing hunger.

Another button popped open, then another and another. His hands were experienced at undressing a woman; their warmth and dexterity was enticing. Slowly he slid down her bra straps,

leaving her breasts barely held in the pink lace
bra cups.

As if she was weightless, he pushed her
against the plate-glass door, his hands eagerly
taking their fill of her generous female flesh.

She swore she heard him groan, but her heart
beat so hard, she couldn't discern any other
noise. His lips took hers in a taut, intense kiss,
and she felt her very being meld with his with
just the union of their mouths.

Breaking the kiss, he let his tongue trail down
her tearstained cheek to her neck. He licked the
sensitive hollow of her throat, burning her and
leaving her only with a need for more fire.

Her breath came fast when she felt his thumb
caress the lacy line of the bra cup along her
breast.

His mouth hardened as if he was somehow
trying to hold himself back.

But it seemed no use. His hand slid between
her jean-clad thighs and roughly caressed her, as
if readying her, as if she needed readying. All it
would take was his mouth on her nipple and she
would be his.

"Don't worry about that house again, baby,"
he whispered, his breath an erotic musk on
her skin.

His words rained down on her like needle-sharp hail.

With an intake of breath, she suddenly seemed to snap awake.

She saw with crystal clarity what the hell she was getting into.

He was going to help her buy her mother's house, all right, and the price was going to be way more steep than the mortgage company's. And it might even take longer to pay. And the worst of it was, she had just about done it.

Just about.

Quickly she covered her breasts with her hands as they nearly fell out of her bra.

Trembling, she pulled out of the doorway.

"What happened?" he snapped, his own urges clearly setting him on the razor's edge.

"N-nothing. And nothing ever will happen. Un-understand?" she stammered.

"That's not the message I got," he shot back.

"Well, you got the wrong message, got it?" she said defensively, the tears streaming down her face once more.

He actually seemed dumbfounded.

"And I don't need you involved in my personal business." She backed away, her hands still covering her chest. "I plan on working for you because this is the best job I can get right now, but you need to know I want other things out of life—*other things*—''

''The house wasn't enough?'' he interrupted, all his acid cynicism filling each word.

She stared at him, unable to comprehend that a short walk could produce such emotional damage.

''Are you forcing me to quit? Is this where this is going?'' she asked, defiantly wiping her tears with the back of her hand.

He released a cold laugh. ''Yes, Miss Meadows, this is the rich guy's diabolical plan, don't you see? I get the whole blasted town to come to my ranch for a barbecue tomorrow with you running the show, and I force you to quit the night before the fiasco. Brilliant, isn't it?''

He walked up to her and roughly buttoned her shirt. ''Let's go,'' he said, taking her arm.

''Where?'' she asked, heartsick and exhausted.

''Back to the ranch. You've got a lot of work to do tomorrow for me, Miss Meadows.'' He gave her a caustic glance, one that sent a shiver of fear through her bones. ''And if you plan on continuing as my employee, don't forget that I demand perfection.''

''I can handle perfection,'' she answered in a small but cool voice.

He looked at her. His face lit up beneath the street lamp on the corner, and she swore he took her words as a challenge. The expression on his face was filled with smirking doubt, and the light that gleamed in his eyes gave no assurances.

She looked away, stumbling as she tried to keep up with him.

Certainly she could handle perfection.

But the flawed, magnificent male animal that he was—well, even she had to admit she had her doubts.

Six

JJ James and the Outlaws played a lively two-step, children chased each other through the elated crowd, parents ate spareribs and there wasn't a cloud in the deep azure sky.

"It's the best danged Mystery BBQ Sizzle we've ever held," Hazel declared, the cattle baroness with her usual noblesse oblige drinking a beer in a bottle like her own cowhands behind the bandstand.

"And it's the last one I'll ever put together," Kirsten announced, her emotions still raw from the night before.

Hazel took a long, hard look at her leaning against the tent pole. "Something wrong, missy?"

Kirsten shut her eyes, exhausted. "Hazel, believe me, the last thing I want to do is look like an ingrate. As usual, you've done too much for me. I mean, you even helped with Mom's medical bills, but..." She sighed. "I don't know. I think I'm in over my head with this crowd. I don't understand any of them."

"All you've got to understand is your boss, Seth Morgan."

"I know. I know," she affirmed. "And yet he's the one who's the most confusing."

"Is he giving you mixed signals? Now, why would he do that, do you think?" Hazel suddenly came to life like a bear who'd found honey. She all but rubbed her hands together in glee.

Kirsten almost laughed. "Nope. Trust me. The signals are all too clear."

"Well, what kind of signals are they?" the old gal demanded.

A terrible thought suddenly occurred to Kirsten. "Hazel, this job—I mean—you didn't plan on this being some kind of matchmaking scheme, did you?"

"Certainly not! What kind of friend do you

think I am, cowgirl? You said you needed a better job, and I figured Mr. Morgan's offer ain't hay, so I threw you to it.''

Hazel did an excellent job of looking affronted. In fact, Kirsten almost believed her.

''It doesn't matter, Hazel. I'm not accusing you of anything. Nothing's going to happen between me and my boss in any case, because I can guarantee it won't. But with that issue aside, the job is still difficult.''

''How so?'' Hazel took another beer from the cooler, looking suddenly a bit deflated.

''It's just—well, it's just that when Dad left, I knew I wanted more out of life than what my mom had. She settled for something less than love for the lifestyle and security, and she ended up with nothing. I'm not doing that. No matter what. It's all or nothing for me.''

''Good girl,'' Hazel confirmed.

''But this Wall Street crowd.'' She shrugged. ''I'm out of my element. I don't understand any of them. It's so easy for them to go from bed to bed. Nothing means anything to them, not even love. I guess when you have so much to fall back on, you don't need life to mean anything— but not me. I just don't work that way.''

''Sounds like this is turning into more than a

job to me," the cattle baroness prompted, her Prussian-blue eyes suddenly aglitter.

"No. It's just a job. I guarantee you." She studied the older woman. "But I do want to know one thing, Hazel. Why did you sell to him? I mean, of all the people in the world who'd love a piece of your ranch—why him? What made him so worthy?"

The cattle baroness took a long sip of her beer. She seemed to contemplate her words good and hard.

"You know me, Kirsten. The best way I can explain it is I've never been able to see a person go a-wanting. I couldn't let him go a-wanting, either."

Kirsten gasped in disbelief. "Wanting? The man wants for nothing. Nothing."

"It wasn't the land he wanted. Hell, he could have gotten a ranch anywhere. And I didn't have to sell to him. You know that. I've sent bigger wolves than him back to the city with their tails between their legs after they ask to buy me out."

"Then why?" Kirsten asked, nothing making sense now.

Hazel met her gaze. With a wisdom that was beyond even her seventy-plus years, she said, "Sometimes a person can go a-wanting most when he has everything. Sometimes city folk are

the loneliest people on earth, but it's not from
having no company—too much company there,
if you ask me. That's why I'll never leave Mystery.''

Kirsten wondered if she understood. ''Are
you telling me it's something bigger than the
land Seth wanted?''

''Maybe. What do you think?''

She wasn't sure.

Her hesitation and uncertainty must have
shown on her face, because Hazel said, ''He's
only your boss, cowgirl. You don't have to answer the question, just work for him. In fact, I'm
wondering—just a little, mind you—why you
want to know all these things?''

A sly smile tipped the corner of the cattle baroness's pretty mouth. ''Unless, of course, you
want to figure him out—but then there go all
your guarantees, right out the barn door with the
pony.''

''Hazel, you're wicked, you know that? Just
plain wicked.'' Kirsten nudged her. ''But then,
you haven't gone up against Seth Morgan either,
and I don't see your schemes working there.''

''Never underestimate age and treachery, my
dear.'' The famous blue eyes winked at her. ''I
make eight seconds every time.''

Kirsten laughed at the woman's bull-riding metaphor.

The only thing she could think to say next was, "Gee, I'm way overdue for a drink."

Grabbing a cold beer, she left Hazel to her machinations and surveyed the crowd once more to see if anyone needed anything. The band was on break, but the crowd seemed to have enough ribs and cold drinks not to notice.

"Kirsten."

She turned around, surprised to find James standing there. He was staring at her, a hungry look in his brown eyes she knew all too well.

"Band on a break?" she asked, hiding her surprise beneath a pleasant tone of voice. "You guys really sound good, by the way."

"I didn't look you up, girl, to get your opinion of the band. I want to know how the hell you are." He crossed his arms over his chest.

She smiled, another ploy to cover her nervousness around him. "Fine. Just fine. And how are you?"

"Wondering why we aren't married by now," he answered sourly.

Inwardly she groaned. When she'd hired the band to play for the barbecue she'd hoped they wouldn't have to go there. "I thought we'd settled this—"

"You aren't dating anyone else here in Mystery. So why not me?"

"How do you know I'm not—"

He interrupted her again. "I know. I'm from this town, remember? My friends keep me informed."

Exasperated, she said, "Well, your friends might be wrong. Thought of that?"

He grabbed her hand and tried to pull her to him. "C'mon, little lady. You just think you're better than everyone else here 'cause you went to fancy schools and all, but deep down you know I'm good enough. Maybe even too good."

She closed her eyes, desperate to keep her temper. "James, we discussed this. We're just not right for each other—"

"Is this not right?" He bent to kiss her.

She pulled away.

He tried again.

"No. I said no," she protested, trying to wrench her arm free.

Suddenly he was pulled from her and thrust aside like so much trash.

"The lady said no," Seth growled, his sea-colored eyes as frosted as his expression.

"And who the hell are you?" James shouted, his temper flaring.

"I own this place, that's who I am. And you happen to be manhandling my employee."

Suddenly James's eyes narrowed. He looked Seth up and down, assessing him. Then he turned to Kirsten and spat out, "Ah, I get it now. You refused me 'cause you knew there were greener fields out there, didn't you? And everyone in town knows your kind just like 'em green with money. That's right, green with money, not like our fields that just have good old honest Montana grass."

He bent and picked up his straw cowboy hat that had fallen off when Seth shoved him aside.

He gave her one long poisonous look and said, "So long, Kirsten. When he divorces you, or better, never marries you in the first place, give me a call sometime. If I'm not busy, I'll see if I can fit in an extra bronc ride or two for you."

He stomped away, glaring at Seth.

Seth didn't give him another look. Instead, his gaze was fixed on Kirsten.

She opened her mouth to protest, to refute, to say anything that would prove what James had said wasn't true. But every denial seemed so pointless.

She covered her face with her shaking hand. After a moment she resumed her usual cool demeanor and said, "I'm sorry you had to hear that. James and I dated for a while. I guess he's still sore it didn't work out. I had hoped hiring him for the barbecue wouldn't turn into a scene, but I guess I misjudged him."

Seth said nothing. His hard, cynical expression said it all.

Those same old tears stung her eyes, but she would be damned if she'd let him see her cry again. She was not out for any man's money, but there was no way to convince Seth Morgan of that when every woman he'd probably ever known knew the worth of his bank account and never bothered to assess the worth of his character.

But that was beside the point now. She and Seth Morgan would never have a romance. They were doomed from the beginning because it was love she wanted, and if she had to look long and hard to find it, if she had to marry a man who mowed grass for a living, she'd do it. Good old Montana grass was fine by her as long as it came with a kind, honest man who loved her.

"Your ship came to say that I'm leaving for New York tonight. I've had a crisis at work that can't wait. The guests can stay here until my return, but I'll need you to get out some faxes before the plane takes off."

His words contained nothing but dry, accusatory indifference.

She withered inside. Just looking at him made her ache. He thought she was something she wasn't, and he had every right to in his situation, and there was nothing she could say to convince him otherwise.

"I'll be right there, Mr. Morgan," she whispered, her voice hoarse from withheld tears.

"Viola has the stack of papers. See that it's done."

"Yes," she choked out as she watched him turn and leave, her heart shattering.

The party was over—a great success if the attendee count was correct.

Staring out across the fields next to the house where the barbecue had been held, Kirsten sipped on a chardonnay, feeling very much like Nikki at that moment.

Gone was the wide-eyed wonder of her kiss with Seth in the stream. To Seth, she was now right up there on the list of models and actresses and women who prowled the Wall Street scene just to catch themselves a millionaire.

She could tell by the expression in his eyes that she'd now been reduced to gold-digger status.

And no matter how hard she thought, there seemed no way to change that image.

But worse than that was the fact that he was now doubly dangerous to her heart. If before he was dabbling with her, discovering what she was really like, there had at least existed the possibility he might find something that he could respect.

A relationship with him was doomed. She would never be anything more than Nikki was to him, and despite her jealousy of the model, Kirsten didn't want the same relationship with Seth that Nikki had. No, she wanted her own, on her own terms. She was not like Nikki, who when things didn't work out with one man would just hop in a different man's bed. Kirsten was almost certain Nikki had spent last night with Rick.

Now that the barbecue festivities were over, she couldn't wait for the houseguests to leave, but she didn't set the schedule—Seth did. And he was making no effort to have his New York buddies return home.

Reminding herself over and over again, she told herself she had to have this job. If she feared there was even the remotest possibility that she might fall in love with Seth, she knew she would have to leave. It would prove a disaster to everyone. Just everyone.

But mostly it would prove a disaster to her. Because she knew in her heart that if she ever fell for Seth, she would fall hard, and there wouldn't be a place on this green earth that she could go that would exorcise him from her heart. And then, like her own mother, without even knowing love she would be finished with it. Forever.

She glanced down at the empty wineglass. Feeling downright morose, she watched Nikki and Rick romp in the pool, cooling off after the hours in the sun at the barbecue. Their laughter chilled her, and the only thing she could think of that might help the hole in her soul was another glass of wine and a long, bitter soak in the bath very far away from anything relating to Seth Morgan.

Seven

Kirsten was surprised by Seth's quick return. He was back in twenty-four hours. She was even more surprised by his foul mood. However, he wasn't any worse for the wear, because of his private jet.

"I want all of the letters cc'd to Mary, and I want the originals for my files," he dictated, his imperious self sitting at the large oak desk in the living room.

He reminded her of a gruff old bear, one that had a thorn in his paw. Kirsten wrote carefully, making sure she got everything he told her.

"And I want—" he growled.

She squelched a giggle.

He drilled her with his stare. "Is there something funny, Miss Meadows?"

She adamantly shook her head. "Nothing. Nothing at all, sir."

But it was a fib. She found even their conversation ridiculous. They spoke like two strangers when they were not strangers at all.

The more irritated he looked, the more she wanted to laugh.

"Please share the joke with everyone, Miss Meadows."

Her self-control melted. He'd sounded like her junior high school geography teacher.

"Forgive me, I've just got a case of the giggles, I guess." She hiccuped, holding her mouth tight against any further laughter.

He assessed her, his expression dour. "When you're through with this, that will be all for the night."

She stood. "I'll get it done right now."

"Fine." He dismissed her and watched her go, those icy eyes hooded and inscrutable.

She went into the utility room where the office machines were hooked up. Within ten minutes she had written the memos and faxed them. When she returned to the great room in order to go upstairs for bed, she saw Seth through the large windows. He had already mounted Noir and was going down the road at a lope.

He was taking an evening ride—without her.

She swallowed her annoyance and resentment.

Her feelings were entirely irrational, she told herself again and again. Her status in the household meant she held fewer rights than Viola, and she certainly didn't see the housekeeper pining to go for an evening ride with the boss.

Depressed, she went to her room, bathed and slipped on her comfortable old flannel robe. Thinking she might borrow a book from the great room, she walked downstairs, made herself a cup of hot tea in the kitchen and went to find a book to take upstairs.

Nothing interested her. The books were all dry-as-dust tomes on the bond market.

Disappointed, she sat down on the couch, sipped her tea while it was still hot and made a pledge to go into town the next day and buy some novels and magazines.

Chilled, she sat closer to the fire still burning in the large fieldstone fireplace. Curling her bare feet beneath her on the couch, she made a mental note not to get too comfortable.

She didn't want to stay too long. Seth would be returning any minute from his ride, and she didn't want him to catch her cozying up by the fire. *His fire.*

But the tea warmed her, and soon her thoughts drifted. Unable to summon the energy to crawl back up to her bedroom, she closed her eyes for a few seconds, just enough to regain her momentum.

Before she knew it, she was fast asleep.

Dust laden and worn-out, Seth walked from the stable to the house in only the moonlight. Jim had been waiting for him and had taken care of Noir.

It'd been a long ride, and both man and beast needed a rest.

The galloping had been good for Seth. He'd needed the burst of energy. It was better than anger, more satisfying, more healthy. In truth, it gave him equilibrium.

When he'd tiredly dismounted, he'd realized that Hazel might be manipulating the situation, but her manipulations were just that. If he so chose, he would forgo the ranch and find a place elsewhere. He didn't need to be the cattle baroness's puppet.

But his frustration was caused by more than just Hazel. Kirsten frustrated him. He was nothing more than a means to an end for her.

Granted, she'd made that clear from the beginning. Her mother was ill and needed care. But it infuriated him to know she viewed him no differently than had the rest of the bank-account gold diggers who'd been after him in the past. He wondered if he would ever find a woman who could see the man behind the money machine.

But her less-than-sterling motives didn't take away the fact that he had a wicked attraction to her.

Perhaps he was drawn to her merely because she was good at hiding her true motives. If he hadn't overheard her on the phone talking to her mother about their ship coming in, and if he hadn't heard that old boyfriend of hers confess to what a climber she was, he suspected he'd have fallen for her, fallen hard. She seemed to be everything a man could want in a woman— she was smart, graceful, feminine. She had a come-hither look he'd first seen in the jet, and it was so well rehearsed that she seemed completely unconscious of how it had been manufactured to drive a man crazy. And more important, when they were alone and not under the guise of "work," he felt somehow that she saw him. *Him.* The man, not the bank account.

He pushed open the heavy pine front door to

the house, his cowboy boots softly clicking on the flagstone.

Before him, in the great room, she lay on the couch asleep, as enticing as a fairy-tale princess.

Her blond hair formed a halo around her face, the wheat color glistening with gold highlights from the fireplace flames and the rich background color of the burgundy sofa.

She lay slouched back against the pillows, her frayed, raggedy pink flannel robe parted slightly, playing a sweet game of peekaboo with the lush, generous curves of her breasts.

He stood stock-still for a long moment and just stared at the picture, unsure whether he should reprimand her or go to her and slip his hand deep inside the part in the robe.

Slowly he walked up to her.

She didn't move. Her breathing was deep and even, her face an angel's in repose.

The whole thing was a setup. It was so obvious. Fall asleep in the ranch's great room, and then when the seduction was through, make a great gesture of dismay at how he'd taken advantage of her.

As he bent down to the sleeping beauty, he wondered what she wanted out of it.

Kirsten would want more than just a little jewelry, he had no doubts about that. And maybe that was what made her so powerful. Unlike any other woman he'd ever known who was happy with just an account at Tiffany's, Kirsten wanted more. She wanted his soul.

Kirsten sensed the feather-soft caress on her cheek well before she felt it. In her dream state, nothing seemed real; everything was accepted. Even a touch could morph into some crazy plot that made sense only to the dreamer.

The stroke came again on her cheek.

Fluttering open her sleepy eyes, she looked and found Seth, his face so close a kiss was only a breath away.

It seemed as natural as rain to let him kiss her then. He knelt by the couch like a prince. The fire licked golden light across both of them, urging them on, drumming the rally call to their primal instincts.

She wasn't dreaming. He was truly there, kissing her, taking her chin in his hand, his other hand slipping familiarly between the part in her flannel robe and squeezing her breast.

Neon signs should have flashed by then, telling her she was getting in over her head.

But the warnings never came.

Perhaps she was lonelier than she admitted even to herself, perhaps she was truly falling in

love with him. She didn't know. All she did
know was that she'd woken from a beautiful
dream only to find the dream had substance. Her
deepest, darkest fantasy was coming true and
leading to a nightmare. And she had no power
to fight it. No power at all.

He slipped out of his shirt and cowboy boots.

She lay on the couch watching him with
heavy, need-filled eyes. When he unzipped himself out of his jeans, her breath caught. He was
more than she'd bargained for, and yet her
thighs quivered with the harsh emptiness between them.

No words were spoken. The understanding of
the moment was upon them.

He tugged on her frayed flannel belt and
pulled the robe aside, revealing all of her. By
instinct, her hands went to her chest, but he
pushed them aside, taking in every detail like a
man who'd been starved.

His mouth caught her large hardened nipple.
The sensation made her delirious with want. His
hand roughly cupped her other breast, and he
moved to that nipple, unable to get enough of
her.

Her hands swept down his chest. The cool
night air made his nipples hard and flat, but as
he lay atop her, his back warmed by the fire, his

body was a delicious study of temperatures. Cold and hot—just like his eyes, just like his expression.

He kissed her, his teeth nipping at her tongue, his own tongue licking fire down to her soul. His hand stroked her face, then her vulnerable throat, his thumb sweeping the hollows with dark, sensual sweeps.

His passion, however, was nothing less than white-hot. He groaned his readiness, his hips grinding instinctively into hers. She drummed the rock-hard muscles of his waist, driving him on to the end they both knew was coming. Cradling his head in her hands, she proved her own hunger by allowing him to sink between her thighs.

Before she could take in another deep kiss, before she could breathe in his scent of horses and leather, he dived deep inside her, filling her to gasping.

With any other man she might have protested the swiftness, the totality of his possession. But there was nothing to protest when her willingness to surrender transcended his plundering.

He moved against her, slowly at first, his face mirroring all the sensations that she drank in. But soon his hunger got the best of him. His demanding nature won. He pulled on her lower lip with his teeth, his tongue thrusting in and out of her mouth much like his manhood, tempting, promising, fulfilling.

Her desire built until she was at the precipice, his every movement painful in her need to hold back.

But then the dam broke. Grabbing the arm of the couch, he slammed himself inside her as if he wanted to crawl in there himself. He groaned her name against her hair, his hips grinding possessively into hers.

She tumbled into his honeyed oblivion. Taking all he had to give, she held him to her, her last coherent thought the terrible possibility that it had all been a dream. And would be no more.

Eight

The phone rang on her line. Thinking it was her mother, Kirsten rolled over in her bed and picked it up, her voice groggy with sleep.

"Kirsten? This is Ms. Halding from the mortgage company."

"Of course." Kirsten became wide-awake.

"There's a problem."

She tried to focus her sleep-puffed eyes on the receiver. "I don't understand. A problem?"

"Yes, well, it's the strangest problem I've ever encountered in the thirty-five years I've worked in mortgages—"

"What is it?" she asked, frustration constricting her chest.

"Your financing has been rejected, Ms. Meadows. The title company researched the loan as a purchase, and they've put a halt to it. I'm sure there's been a misunderstanding. I told them you weren't double-dealing anyone, but I have to admit, in their defense, it does look fishy."

Kirsten felt as if she were in a bad dream.

"I—I don't understand," she stammered, sitting up in bed, suddenly aware she had no nightgown on. "I applied for a mortgage. The owner of the property agreed to sell—"

"But the title company came back and said you already own that property, Ms. Meadows. You bought it cash. The title's in your name. You can't purchase a property you already own. However, if you really just wanted to cash out, I can get you in touch with our equity arm...."

The room seemed to spin.

The woman's voice dwindled to background noise.

"Did you hear me, Ms. Meadows?" the woman asked again into the phone.

"Yes," Kirsten croaked. "I guess I'll have to get back to you. Thanks for trying, though."

She put down the receiver.

A flood of memories of the night before rushed at her like a freight train.

Chagrined, she recalled the hours on the couch, how she'd wanted more, and then more, and how Seth had given her everything she wanted until they'd both fallen asleep, spent, in each other's arms.

Somehow he must have carried her to her bed, because she didn't remember waking and going to her room. He'd spared her the embarrassment of Viola finding them on the couch, but she couldn't help but feel a twinge of disappointment to wake alone in her own bed after a night of such soul-piercing abandon.

Now she was going to have to deal with the realities of her irresponsibility. The realities and the consequences.

Stumbling to the shower, she knew she was in trouble when she didn't want to step into the hot spray.

His scent clung to her hair and body like rare perfume. She didn't want to wash him away. The musky male scent was stirring, even comforting to her senses, but life had to go on. Obligations had to be met. Denials that their night meant anything to her had to be made.

She slathered shampoo in her hair, closed her

eyes and scrubbed. The shower did revive her, and the cleansing renewed her good sense.

She would have to face him like his personal assistant and no more.

The first thing she had to do was to confront him about her mother's house and tell him how she would pay him back.

She was still rattled that he'd bought the house right from under her. She'd asked him to stay out of it, begged him not to get entangled in any way. Now she was in it up to her ears.

Refusing to think he'd orchestrated the house purchase just to get her into bed, she decided the timing wasn't right. Besides, just the thought that that was what had happened would make her too angry.

And, in the end, leverage hadn't even been necessary.

Now she just had to be sensible, get out an equity loan and pay him back. Then the fact that they'd had a little sex wouldn't hurt so much. It wouldn't leave her so vulnerable and hoping there might be more.

Comforting herself, she knew she could be the queen of denial. They'd had a little sex, and it was no big deal. It meant nothing. No obligations on either side.

She closed her eyes and let the water run

down her. Of course, she was fooling herself. Their night together had been the kind she would comfort herself with when she was old. Indeed, she'd finally known what it was like to be fully a woman, to make love with a man who neglected neither body nor soul.

A small moan escaped her lips. They hadn't used any birth control. There might be repercussions beyond just the two of them.

It seemed unimaginable that she could have Seth's child, but it was a possibility. Nature was something that had a will of its own. And if she did become pregnant, she knew she would have the child. He would be very much like Seth, yet untainted by money and cynicism.

She shook her wet head, letting the drops spray across the marble tiles.

No, starting now, she was the queen of denial. She wouldn't think about all the consequences right now. She just really needed to focus on what she was going to say when she saw him next, how she would act, how she would smile and shrug off the most magical night of her life as no big deal.

Queen of denial. Queen of denial, she kept repeating to herself like a chant.

She saw Seth out in a paddock working on one of his barrel racers. Coolly observing his expertise on the quarter horse, she walked up to the fence and perched on it.

He spied her and loped toward her.

"Howdy, ma'am," he said in his best cowboy accent. He took off his hat to her.

She smiled. He always looked particularly roguish and handsome in jeans and a flannel shirt.

Losing her control, she imagined how wonderful it would be to have come to the paddock, given him a kiss and told him how much last night had meant to her....

Queen of denial. Queen of denial.

She let the smile freeze on her face. "I just wanted to see if you had anything you needed me to do. I have to go to town this afternoon. To take out an equity loan to pay you back for Mom's house."

"Don't bother." He studied her, his eyes hooded beneath the straw brim of his hat.

She shook her head. "I told you, I can't accept the offer. It's out of the question."

"I thought now was different. I mean, after last night I really don't see the need to pay me back."

His words cut into her heart like a dull, serrated knife.

He clearly thought she'd slept with him to get the house. She'd told him she wasn't about to pay for it with her body, but from his point of view, he'd ponied up the cash and right after he'd paid, there she was, waiting for him on the couch, as pliable and complicit as a spoiled mistress.

Choosing each word with care, she answered, "Last night changed nothing. I will pay you for the house."

"Changed nothing? Or meant nothing?" he demanded gruffly.

"Of course it meant something. I had fun—didn't you?"

Her tone was light, her words breezy. Inside she was anything but that.

She couldn't believe the conversation. It was breaking her heart. But she had to remain collected. She had to save herself.

Queen of denial. Queen, queen, queen...

"Fun?" He repeated the word dully, as if he didn't understand it.

"Look, I want to be gracious about the house, but I can't accept the help, and I *will* be paying you back. I don't want any strings. I said that before, and I'll say it again—no strings."

His face took on a rock-hard cast.

She could have sworn he said, "Holding out

for more, huh?'' but before she could ask him to speak up, he simply nodded and cantered away.

Heartbroken, she was dismissed.

Three days passed. Three days of living hell as far as Kirsten was concerned. She and Seth were barely on speaking terms. Desperately she wanted to demand why he was so closemouthed, but she was afraid of facing the answers as much as she was lonely and confused.

Worse than that, she needed her job now more than ever in order to pay back the huge loan she was taking out on ''her'' house. If she were fired, there was no way she could manage those payments.

Frustrated, she told Viola she was going to take Sterling for a little exercise. Seth had gone to town, and he'd left no work for her to occupy her time.

The mountains always worked to clear the mind and free the soul. Determined to cleanse both, she took off toward the high country, the late-afternoon sun slanting red-gold lacquer onto the granite face of Mount Mystery and the Continental Divide beyond.

Choosing the horsepacker's trail in order to find solitude and really think, she loped Sterling easily through the foothills, her thoughts as dark as the thunderheads in the distance.

She had to get over Seth.

It would be difficult, to say the least, but she had no business falling for him in the first place. He was way too powerful to wrangle with, and even if she could make demands on him, he would never bend to her terms. The warning signs had been fluorescent, and she'd wilfully ignored them. He was a rich man, used to manipulation and getting what he wanted. The sale of her mother's house proved that. She was out of her league pretending she could be his match, out of her league in thinking he could be more than James or her father, men who viewed women as compliant dolls. Men who rebelled at the first sign of will in a woman.

Her gaze grew clouded. Even the beautiful stag that jumped through the field ahead of her didn't take her mind from her woes.

But that she was falling in love with Seth was without question. The other night had only cemented her growing feelings. Certainly she was no virgin, but the night with Seth, even on the confines of the couch, had meant more than all her lovemaking experiences combined.

But loving him wouldn't make him love her back. And there had never been any talk of love with him. His cynicism with Nikki was enough to make Kirsten never, ever broach the subject. She knew she wasn't strong enough to take the answers.

She got to the steep path that ultimately led to the pass and the Continental Divide. Guiding Sterling expertly along the narrow rocky ledges, she was so immersed in her thoughts, she barely took notice of the rain until heavy plops of water began to pockmark the dust on the trail ahead.

The wind picked up. The sun hadn't set, but it might as well have, given the opaque black clouds that hid it.

Sterling held her ground even when a spider vein of lightning cracked across the sky, followed immediately by earsplitting thunder.

"What a gem you are." She soothed the animal, patting Sterling's dappled neck.

Kirsten knew if she headed back to the ranch she'd just get soaked and perhaps even break Sterling's leg in a mud slide, given the storm's sudden downpour.

Her better judgment told her to ride it out. There was an old miner's lean-to along Blue Rock Creek. It was still ten minutes away, but it was the best she could do under the circumstances.

Turning Sterling around, she headed down the path to Blue Rock Creek.

"Viola, I'd have thought you'd have gone to bed by now. I've never seen you up this late. You're pacing like a caged bobcat. What's wrong?" Seth asked, having come down from his suite to pour his own coffee from the coffeemaker on the kitchen counter.

Viola looked hesitant. Her gaze flickered from the storm to her boss.

"What's going on?" he demanded.

"I don't know, sir. I don't know what to think. Maybe I should inform Jim—"

"This is my ranch. So tell me."

"I'm sure everything's all right." The woman hugged herself and stared out at the storm that lashed the kitchen window.

"What is it?" Irritation sounded in his voice. From his expression it was clear he would brook no more wavering.

"It's just that Kirsten decided to take one of the horses out. Now with this storm, I'm a little worried she didn't get in yet." Viola smiled, but it didn't budge the worry in her eyes.

She waved aside her anxieties. "Oh, I'm sure she's stuck having to listen to Jim's tall tales in the barn.'' Her gaze slid to the window and the wall of water that pummeled it on the other side.

Seth picked up the phone. Pounding in the speed dial, he barked into the phone, ''Did Kirsten and Sterling get back yet, Jim?''

The grim silence gave the answer before he hung up the phone.

His thoughts tortured him. She couldn't be in danger. He wouldn't allow it. He cared too much. He realized he'd gone too far to lose her now. *And he would not lose her.*

Viola returned to staring at the window. ''I know she's an experienced rider and Sterling's a reliable mount, but still, I'd hate to think of her going through this on top of the mountain.''

Seth was already pulling on his slicker.

''I'll be happy to call for help from Hazel's ranch, sir, to look for her,'' the housekeeper offered.

''I'll find her,'' was all he said before he donned his black felt cowboy hat and headed out into the storm.

Nine

Kirsten shivered against the lean-to. She was at least out of the rain, but the temperature had dropped severely and she was soaking wet. Chunks of ice rained down on the tin roof.

It had to be forty degrees now, and when she'd left, the late-afternoon temperature had been almost eighty. She hadn't even taken her polar fleece. Her only covering was a wet pair of jeans and a T-shirt.

Huddling next to Sterling for warmth, she tethered the animal while it ate what little straw was left from the last person who'd occupied the three-sided shack.

The storm would pass and she would be on her way soon, she told herself, her teeth chattering so loudly she could hardly hear the thunderous rain and hail pounding on the corrugated tin roof.

She hadn't told Jim where she was planning on riding, but there was no point in wondering about that, because she didn't need a rescue party anyway. She just needed the rain to end so she could safely see her and the horse's way home.

Slowly lowering herself against the side of the cold metal lean-to, she hugged her knees and wiped the water from her face.

It would be only a matter of minutes before she could be in the saddle again and heading home.

Just a matter of minutes, she told herself, a strange feeling of comfort and warmth overtaking her thoughts and tingling through her soaked and freezing body.

And her mind was feeling sleep run through it like a narcotic. Maybe just a little nap would warm her....

When Seth found her, he could see hypothermia was taking over. Kirsten hardly roused when he shook her. Her lips were a bluish color and her clothes were soaked through. She had nothing on but a T-shirt and jeans in the forty-degree weather.

He tethered Noir, quickly took a blanket from his saddle pack and pulled aside his slicker. Treating her like a rag doll, he tore off her wet clothes, bra and panties and all, and pulled her cold nude body against his chest, covering her with his own chamois shirt and the blanket.

"I'm—all—all—right. I—I—I'm all r-r-right," she protested groggily, her teeth clacking away as she spoke.

"When you're warm we'll get back to the ranch. Until then, just relax." His arms encircled her farther, wrapping her as close to his body heat as possible.

"Why did you take my c-c-clothes off?" she stammered.

"You would have frozen."

She looked up at him with those dark blue eyes that drove him so wild. Prudishly she said, "You really shouldn't have, you know."

He chuckled.

Tiredly she leaned her cheek against his chest.

"You know," he mentioned wickedly, the rain still pounding the sides of the lean-to, "the professional wilderness rescuers would recommend that we have sex right now. It would really get your blood flowing quickly.''

Her hand shot up. She took a weak kitten swipe at him, but missed altogether.

He laughed and tucked the slim chilled arm back inside the chamois shirt. ''I guess you're warming up just fine.'' He slouched against the cold sheet tin siding.

Wrapped up together, they waited for the rain to end.

''I'm fine, Dr. Saville. Really I am. I just didn't know the storm was going to be so severe.'' Kirsten sat up in her bed. The handsome young town doctor had been waiting for them when she and Seth had arrived back at the ranch, having been called by a frantic Viola.

Mortified at her state of undress when she'd dismounted—Seth hadn't allowed her to put on her wet clothes—she had gone right upstairs with Viola, shrugged out of Seth's chamois shirt and steeped in a hot bath.

Now, with a bowl of hot chicken noodle soup in her belly, all she really wanted was a nap and some privacy.

''Hypothermia's nothing to fool around with, Kirsten. Everyone thinks it's the snow and ice that will kill you, but more people die from cold exposure above thirty-two degrees than below. The body can't get warm while wet." Saville wrote out a couple of prescriptions. He gave them to Viola.

"I'll check on the patient in a few days. Call me if she seems to be coughing or catching a cold."

Viola nodded.

Kirsten thanked him. "And how is Rebecca?" she inquired politely about his wife.

"She's due the end of September. Number two, you know." His face flushed with pleasure. "I don't know how she does it. She's a miracle worker."

Watching him go, Kirsten wondered .if her own husband would be so totally in love and devoted to her as Saville was to his wife.

Dr. John Saville and his wife, Rebecca O'Reilly, had been the talk of Mystery during their courtship. The rumor mill had it that they were one of Hazel McCallum's famous matches. So far it had proven to be a blazing success.

Kirsten slouched back in the pillows.

Tomorrow she was going to have to begin again with her boss; she would have to forget that he'd rescued her from sure death, forget that every kiss, every caress was like food to her hungry soul. Seth Morgan had become less and less like a boss and more and more like a lover.

Yet she was fooling herself that she could ever manage a detached attitude. They'd gone too far. They'd been through too much.

And besides, she was in love with him.

She almost laughed piteously with the thought of it. Yet it felt good to admit it. The queen of denial was dead. It was like the old saying: Now that there was no hope, she felt much better.

He would never return her love as she required it. He was too rich, too powerful, too controlling. He wasn't the kind of man who could raise a passel of children and look forward to making love to his wife, night after night, through a lifetime.

Sighing, she closed her eyes, exhausted. She hadn't realized how fighting cold could wear a person out.

Within seconds she was fast asleep, nestled beneath her eiderdown comforter, dreaming she was wrapped in the warm steel arms of the man she loved.

Seth stoked up the fire in Kirsten's bedroom fireplace. Viola had gone to bed, but he couldn't without first checking on her.

He stepped over to the mound curled up in the middle of the large pine bedstead.

Leaning over, he listened. Her breathing was even and clear. A golden twist of hair peeked out from beneath the comforter. Lovingly he stroked it, amazed at its silky texture.

She moaned and turned beneath the covers. A hand slipped out, perfect and feminine.

He fought the urge to squeeze it, to make her aware he was there. Right now she needed to recover. She could even have died out there if no one had found her.

The thought made him physically ill.

Straightening, he realized how much he'd changed in the few weeks since he'd arrived in Mystery. The old superficialities had no lure for him any longer. Now all he wanted was a warm fire and a good woman. Kirsten. Forever. And ever.

He looked down at the sleeping, vulnerable woman.

He was thinking too much. That was certainly not him where women were concerned.

Maybe Mystery really was changing him. Or maybe it was his friendship with Hazel.

Or maybe it was the beautiful girl asleep in the bed.

All he did know was that the financier in him

couldn't accept failure. And yet Kirsten Meadows was dangerously close to having the power to make him fail. His sure thing, his money, seemed to hold no sway with her. And so he was left bare, unable to understand what might win her.

With that dark thought he silently let himself out of her bedroom and went right for an ice-cold shower

Ten

"**E**veryone's made too much out of yesterday. I'm fine. Really. Just embarrassed." Kirsten blushed answering Seth's inquiry into her health.

"That was foolish of you to go alone," he said, looking ominous even while he relaxed on the couch. *Their* couch.

She handed him the current faxes and opened her laptop. "I just wanted a ride. I won't do it again. I realize it was a terrible inconvenience to you. I'll ride at Hazel's from now on."

"If you want to ride the horses here, I just insist that someone go with you. You know the trails better than Jim does, but the ranch manager here's an experienced mountaineer and you're not. I don't want to ever hear of you going out alone again.''

He gave the faxes a cursory study.

She watched him, thinking he looked less rested than she'd ever seen him.

Against her better judgment, she wondered what had kept him up last night and wished desperately it had been a longing for her.

But that couldn't be. She'd made a total fool of herself yesterday. And even if she hadn't, his words at the paddock the other day had made it clear that their relationship was based on sex and money, and nothing more. She could never go along with that. She wanted love, and not even a skyscraper would be an adequate substitute for it.

Viola came out from the kitchen. ''Your mom's here, Kirsten—oh, am I interrupting?'' She looked at Seth.

Seth scowled. ''We're finished.''

As was his manner, he went back to his faxes.

Kirsten left the room with Viola.

''Mom!'' she exclaimed once she got into the kitchen.

She made the formal introductions between her mother and Viola, then made her mother comfortable at the huge pine table in the middle of the kitchen.

Viola poured some soda while Kirsten chatted with her mother.

"You look great, Mom. Love the earrings," she added, thinking the whimsical flamingos at her mom's ears not only flattered the pink in the woman's cheeks, but also made her short hair look chic.

"So, does Carrie like the art camp?" Kirsten chattered on. "I always thought she had the talent in the family."

"She wants to make jewelry, so she's definitely got the expensive talent in the family." Jenn Meadows rotated her head slowly, modeling the earrings. "These are your sister's creations. Not bad, eh?" She laughed, then accepted the soda from Viola.

"Well, I've got Jim waiting for my opinion on the pool flower beds, so I'll leave you girls alone to visit." Viola left through the kitchen door, but not before asking to buy a pair of Carrie's earrings.

At last Jenn turned to her daughter. "You, on the other hand, young lady, don't look too well. Are you eating right? Are those dark circles I see under your eyes?"

Kirsten wasn't sure how much to tell her mom

about yesterday. Dismissing her appearance, she said, "I had a long day yesterday, that's all. But I'm fine. Really."

"Is the boss working you to death?"

Laughing, Kirsten said, "Hardly. In fact, I have so little to do, half the time I think he should let me go and save his money."

Her mother winced. "I hope that doesn't happen. But if we need to sell the house to take care of that mortgage, I'm ready. I'm really starting to feel great. The relaxation is doing me a lot of good." A furrow developed between her brows. "But you know, Kirsten, you should never have bought the house. It's one thing to give me a rest—it's another to take on too much responsibility."

Right there was another thing over which Kirsten knew she hadn't bothered to go into detail with her mother.

"Look, the house is good for you, and especially Carrie. I can afford it, so let's not talk about it again." She looked down at her soda.

"Fine. But promise me one thing. You'll come to dinner tonight for a housewarming. Carrie's had me shopping and cooking all day so we can show you our 'new' home."

"I'll have to check with Seth—" Kirsten

closed her mouth. "I don't know why I said that—I meant Mr. Morgan."

At that terrible moment Mr. Morgan walked into the kitchen.

Her mother stood up to greet him, a smile beaming on her still-beautiful face.

Kirsten made the introductions. "Oh, there you are, Mr. Morgan," she announced nervously. "Mr. Morgan, I'd like you to meet my mother, Jenn Meadows."

Jenn extended her hand and smiled more.

Seth shook it warmly.

"It's so nice to finally meet you, Mr. Morgan. We were so excited when Kirsten got the job," she said.

The old hardened cynicism was written all over his face as he glanced at Kirsten. He clearly remembered the conversation that first night when Kirsten had declared that her ship had come in.

"She's been invaluable to me here. I'd have to go back to New York constantly without her taking care of things on this end," he added with unusual graciousness.

"How kind of you to say so." Her mother's smile broadened.

"I hope you don't mind my visiting with

her?'' Kirsten asked. "She lives in town and just came out to see me for a minute.''

"Take all the time you want,'' he answered.

Her mom piped in. "I just came to invite Kirsten to the house for dinner. We're having a housewarming for her, Carrie and I. We just purchased the house we live in.''

"Really? Congratulations.'' He looked coolly at Kirsten.

Kirsten's heart stopped. The last thing she wanted her mother to find out was that Seth had bought the house outright for them. That would open so many floodgates, she wouldn't live long enough to close them all.

Desperate, she tried to change the subject. "If you haven't got much for me to do this evening, I'd like to go to dinner with my mom and sister, but of course if there's work to be done, we can always make it another time. Right, Mom?''

"Certainly,'' her mother enthused.

"There's nothing for you to do tonight. Go right ahead.''

He stood there, not moving. Eventually he leaned against the granite counter, proving to Kirsten he was enjoying her discomfort way too much.

"Well, th-thank you,'' Kirsten stammered.

"D-do you need anything right now?" she asked him. "Otherwise—"

"Of course, we understand that you might have other plans, Mr. Morgan," Jenn interrupted, "but we'd love to have you come to our little celebration, too, wouldn't we, Kirsten? After all, it seems only proper to have the boss to dinner every now and then."

Kirsten froze.

There was no way she could get through a family dinner with Seth at the table.

Convinced he'd decline, she tried to hide her nervousness behind a pleasant smile. "Mom, I'm sure Mr. Morgan has better things to do than accept our last-minute hospitality."

"I'd love to. What time and where?" Seth announced.

Kirsten just stared at him.

"Oh, about seven. And the address is—"

Kirsten had had all she could take. "Mr. Morgan can get the address, Mom. We'll be there."

Jenn grabbed her handbag and keys from the kitchen table. "I'd better be going, then. Lots to do before company arrives!" she said before breezing out the kitchen door.

When her mother's car was safely out of sight, Kirsten turned to Seth and said, "It was very gracious of you to be so kind to my mom, but really, you don't have to come tonight. I mean, it won't be fancy or anything. Our idea of a feast is pizza.''

''Don't you want me to come, Miss Meadows?'' Those aqua eyes of his laughed.

''Of course you're welcome to come, but I don't see how you'd ever have a good time—''

''Don't worry about my good time.''

She stared at him, speechless.

''Will you be ready for six-thirty?'' he asked.

''Yes,'' she answered, sure somehow she was being set up, but not quite seeing the scheme.

''How do you dress for dinner at your house, Miss Meadows, if I may ask?''

''Pizza casual.''

''Do I detect sarcasm?'' He lifted one dark eyebrow.

She studied him. None of it made sense. Unless he just wanted to check out the property he'd bought.

''You know,'' she mentioned, ''you can see the house any time without having to sit through a family dinner. And I am paying you back, so really you won't have anything to do with the property as soon as I get the loan I've applied for.''

''You've made all of that perfectly clear, Miss Meadows. Now if you'll excuse me, I have to go down to the wine cellar and pick out a nice bottle to bring to your mother.''

She watched him open the door past the kitchen table. There, with its own staircase, was the wine cellar.

''Red or white, Miss Meadows?''

She rolled her eyes. His motives always caused suspicion in her. Perhaps it was just wisdom. He was not the kind of man one could control. But he had to know that ultimately he would not control her, either.

''Whatever you like,'' she offered, her voice sugar sweet.

''Then we'll bring both. Good choice.'' He smiled, then disappeared down the stairs.

A dinner had never taken so long in Kirsten's entire life.

Fearing any subject might lead to something she did not want to talk about, she stayed animated through the entire meal, so that she could turn the topic to her own liking should the need arise.

However, she needn't have bothered.

Her mom and Seth seemed to have taken an instant liking to each other. Jenn talked of all the places they'd lived overseas while Kirsten was growing up. Seth, the world traveler, naturally found it all fascinating.

Naturally.

But the worst one was Carrie. The preteen girl seemed to have taken one look at Seth Morgan and developed an incurable crush on the man. When Carrie showed him the jewelry she'd been making and he complimented her on her originality, Kirsten thought Carrie would swoon.

It was all too much. And too dangerous.

Kirsten didn't want her family attached to Seth, too. It was hard enough battling her own feelings after all they'd done together. She sure didn't want to answer to her mother's and Carrie's feelings, as well. It was too much like...

Well, it was too much like being entangled.

"Seth, have you ever been to the Devil's Elbow?" Jenn asked, serving dessert warm from the oven. "That's the old part of Mystery where Carrie and I picked these blackberries in the pie. It's not the most magnificent view, but if you walk far enough, you'll come to the old grist mill. You can swim there, and if you bring a bucket, you can get all the blackberries you can carry home."

"I haven't seen that part of the valley yet. I'll have to saddle up Noir tomorrow and take a ride out there."

"If you need someone to show you, I know how to get there," Carrie offered, her blond ponytail bobbing up and down in her eagerness to please their guest.

Kirsten tried damage control. "Surely, Carrie, Mr. Morgan doesn't need our—"

"Can you ride?" he interrupted.

The ponytail bobbed again. "Hazel taught me."

"I've got a good cob in the stable you can take. His name's Plat—short for Platinum. Looks just like your sister's horse, Sterling, only a hand or two smaller."

"My sister has a horse?" Carrie exclaimed, amazed.

"It's not my horse. Mr. Morgan just meant that I can ride her, but it's his horse." Kirsten suddenly realized she was exhausted. Monitoring conversation was worse than mountain climbing.

"Your sister's free to ride Sterling any time she wants," Seth said, accepting Jenn's second helping of pie. "And you feel free to come and ride Plat. I'll tell Jim, our ranch manager, that you have special permission."

Carrie looked at her mom, her blue eyes dancing with awe.

Being virtually fatherless, Carrie had had very

little male attention in her life. It made Kirsten's heart ache to see her so eager for Seth's attention. To be made to feel this special was something the girl was not used to. And Kirsten dreaded the moment when it might end.

"Well, that was a wonderful dinner, guys, but if you'll excuse me, I think I'm feeling a little under the weather so I guess I need to get going." Kirsten stood.

"So soon?" Jenn asked. "I thought you haven't been sleeping well."

"But what about our ride tomorrow?" Carrie added.

Kirsten didn't want to burst her sister's balloon, but these things, as she herself knew from personal experience, were less painful popped earlier than later.

"We'll have to see about the riding, Carrie. Mr. Morgan's a busy man. We don't want to inconvenience him."

"Oh," the girl said, suddenly deflated, as if realizing how foolish her enthusiasm had been.

"Miss Meadows, I want you to take me to Devil's Elbow tomorrow and I want you to have your sister come along, also. The boss, if you pardon me, has spoken." Seth's words were a command.

Kirsten was silent. No one was cooperating.

And there was only so much she could do to intervene if they didn't help her.

"Certainly, Mr. Morgan," she said, hugging her enthralled sister goodbye.

"Come back again soon, won't you, Mr. Morgan?" Jenn held out her hand. "We don't have anything too fancy here, but when you've lived everywhere in the world, you certainly know about hospitality."

Seth squeezed it. "I'd be honored to be invited again. Thank you."

They got into the Jeep, Kirsten silently fuming the entire way out of town.

"Your family's wonderful, Kirsten," Seth said in the dark car.

"Thank you." She didn't know what else to say. Her family *was* wonderful. Which was why she was so insanely protective of them.

"Did you know my parents died when I was in college? Car pileup on the autobahn in Germany."

"I'm sorry," she said, watching him.

He gave a wry smile. "Maybe we could have been a version of a family, but it would have required getting to know one another, and that wasn't something either of them wanted. In the end, I suppose it made it easier for me to adjust to not having parents anymore, since we weren't close.''

Silence permeated the car for a long moment.

Finally he added, ''You know, I always thought you couldn't miss what you never had. But lately I don't think that's true. I don't think it at all.''

She agreed, her voice soft with empathy. ''That kind of emptiness is far and wide. But when you've had something and it gets taken away, well, I've got to tell you, that emptiness goes pretty deep.''

Her thoughts spun to her father, and then to Carrie. The girl would get so worked up every time her father called that Kirsten and her mother had begun to wish he'd just stop calling.

Just the thought of it now made Kirsten realize she couldn't allow Carrie to get attached to Seth.

''So I guess if I sell the ranch back to Hazel, that'd be worse than never having had a ranch at all.'' His words seemed to come out of nowhere.

''Why would you sell the ranch back to Hazel? You just built it,'' she blurted out, confused.

''Hazel didn't sell me the land without attachments, Kirsten. There's always the provision that

I'll have to sell back to her if I don't meet the contract.''

''What do you have to do to meet it?''

He slid his gaze to her, then back again to the night road. ''It's complicated. Something the lawyers drew up. I just don't know if I want to meet the provisions.''

''I see.'' She turned her focus to the road. The ranch gates lay ahead, an artful crossing and weaving of twisted pine.

The impermanence rattled her. Having moved so much as a child, having had her parents break up, she'd always longed for something she could count on. Now, when she worried about whether or not she and Seth Morgan should be lovers, she should have been more worried about what she didn't know, like his contract with Hazel.

Releasing a dark little laugh, she commented, ''Life is so ironic. Just when you think you have everything by the horns, something comes up behind you.''

''What do you think you have by the horns? Me?'' he growled, suddenly becoming the confrontational Wall Street financier.

She shook her head, still smiling. ''I'll never have you by the horns, Mr. Morgan, thank you very much.''

"What's that supposed to mean?" he demanded.

"Nothing. Nothing at all," she said, still laughing at herself and her pathetic little hopes that kept springing up despite how severely they were crushed.

The car stopped in the front driveway, and she got out. Walking toward the stables, she paused when he grabbed her arm.

"Where are you going? Not out for a midnight ride, I hope?"

Freeing her arm, she said, "I just thought I'd go for a short walk. Just some thinking time. Do you need me for something back at the house?"

"No," he answered.

"Then I guess I'm off. So I'll see you later."

She left him in the driveway, wondering if she had been a little harsh, but she was getting overwhelmed. If he sold the ranch, she'd have no more job. No house. No retired mom. No stability for Carrie.

It all weighed on her like Atlas holding up the earth.

She walked behind the stable to one of the short trails that led to a nearby meadow. There was a full moon, and the path was lit as if by electric lights. Once in the meadow, she sat along the hillside and watched the moon slide behind the mountains.

"It does clear your mind, doesn't it?" Seth said, taking a seat on the grass next to her.

She wasn't surprised he'd joined her. It was just like him, to read her thoughts, to sense her yearnings.

"How could it not clear your mind?" She lay back against the padding of grass on the hill. "You can't see those stars just anywhere. Those are Montana stars."

"Kirsten, I'm not a fortune-teller," he said, clearly something on his mind. "I can't see into the future, but more and more I realize how much I want to stay here."

"Sounds like the choice is yours," she commented.

"It's not all up to me. I've realized some things have to work out on their own. They shouldn't have a puppet master." He was silent for a long moment. "Do you understand what I'm saying?"

She nodded, tears stinging her eyes. Having been flung far and wide by her puppet-master father, she knew all about such things. Her family had been thrown to the wolves all in the name of her father getting his own way. But Kirsten also knew about living on the edge of chaos, when everything depended on a razor-thin edge of luck and there was not one damn thing she could do about it.

Seth was saying he might keep life as status quo. Or the roulette wheel would spin and he'd up and sell to Hazel, pay his accounts and leave town forever.

She would never see him again, because she never had any reason to go to New York. Their time together would be distilled down to a summer fling. One that nonetheless had changed her forever because she had fallen in love.

Pointing up to the sliver of moon that was still visible above Mount Mystery, she said, "If you leave, you'll miss that. That's a Montana moon. You can't get that anywhere else, you know."

He studied her in the moonlight, his eyes never lifting to look at the breathtaking display above.

Hesitantly he leaned over her.

His gaze locking with hers, he said, "You know what else is up there that I'd miss?"

She looked up at him. He leaned over her, his body fitting to hers like an old familiar lover.

With a yearning like none she'd had before, she desperately wished he would fall upon her, kiss her and make love to her beneath the stars.

"What else is up there?" she whispered.

He gently kissed her mouth. "It's up there and all around."

"What is it?" She moaned as he kissed and licked the sensitive hollows of her throat.

"It's a Montana heaven. A heaven like no other."

He poised above her, his weight held up by the corded muscles of his arms.

Knowing if she continued with him she would succumb, she nonetheless wrapped her hand behind his neck and pulled him to her.

In seconds they'd shrugged out of their clothes, using them as a blanket over the crush of fresh grass. The world smelled of spruce and male body heat.

Kissing him, she writhed beneath his chest, which covered her like an armor of warm steel.

Safe and secure for now, she opened herself to him fully. He tasted her as if she held nectar. Slowly, dizzily, she succumbed to his mouth, his ever-thrusting tongue. The moment built first in her belly, then, running her fingers through his dark hair, she allowed the fire to seep into her loins. It exploded with a force that made tears rush to her eyes. And made her gasp his name. *Seth.*

He silenced her moan with his mouth. His kiss tasted of blackberries. He filled his hand with her aching breast, then filled his mouth with her nipple. When she could take the exquisite torture no longer, he thrust inside her, and she found her release almost instantly. And then, as he continued, she found it again and again in rolling waves that seemed to have no end.

He alone made it a Montana heaven.

With Seth, it was the only heaven she'd ever known, and the only heaven she feared she ever would.

Eleven

The next week passed as if Kirsten was in a dream.

Despite her fear and hesitation, Kirsten decided to take one last chance and grab life with both hands. Carrie came almost every day to ride and she, Seth and Kirsten would take off to the horsepack trails of Mount Mystery.

Her little sister was completely entranced by Seth, his quick smile and generosity, but Kirsten couldn't blame her, when she herself was finding herself enslaved by him and her insatiable desire for him.

Nights were spent either in her room or his.

Viola had yet to guess their relationship, and Kirsten noticed both of them were reluctant to reveal it to the housekeeper. To do so would mean they would have to define the relationship somehow. They would have to admit it not only to the world, but to each other. That last night in the mountain grass had changed things somehow. A helplessness had seemed to overtake both of them. Their longings, their instincts, had taken over. But would it last? She tortured herself to find the answer.

There were barriers, and she knew it.

As she lay entwined in his arms one night, sated but unable to sleep, she thought of all the problems they faced.

She had a trust problem because her father had left, but Seth, too, had a trust problem. A woman was either a gold digger or out for sex. There were no other possibilities as far as he knew it. She didn't know if she could ever get him to see that there was more to life than money and carnal desires.

But she would try. She now knew she loved him enough to try.

A soft sigh emanated from her lips during her ruminations.

He opened his eyes and ran his hand down her cheek.

"After that long ride we had today, I'd have thought you'd be exhausted." He smiled, his face boyish from sleep.

"I'm just thinking about the day," she confessed, a wry smile on her lips.

His hand tightened on her bare hip. "I think Carrie had a blast. Especially when we took the horses swimming in the watering hole."

"I've never seen her have such a good time," she admitted.

He studied her. "Is there something on your mind? You seem so quiet."

She shrugged. "I'm great. So great that I wish the day had gone on forever and ever."

"Bull markets don't last forever. I know that better than most." He snorted. "That's why you have to make the most of what you have. Carpe diem. Seize the day."

"I think we did that today without doubt. And we seized the night, too," she added.

Smiling, he nipped at her bare breast. "I think we did, but it's hard to make every moment count when you're baby-sitting. Do you think we can do without Carrie tomorrow? Maybe we could take a picnic and climb McCallum Point?"

"I don't know, Mr. Morgan. You set a child's expectations, they have to be fulfilled."

"But I've given at the office. Can't I have a day off?"

She released a bittersweet laugh. "Oh, I see now—you have a greedy side. You want more?"

"I always want more," he growled, rolling on top of her, pinning her beneath him.

She looked up at him, her eyes filled with love.

But the confession gave her pause. It was silly to read more into it than what might have been meant, but she couldn't help herself. There was so much unspoken between them, so much unconfessed.

Overcome by the weight of her thoughts and the future, she instinctively turned to her side.

"What is it?" he asked, his brow furrowing with concern.

Shaking off his question, she said, "I had a great day. A wonderful day. Let's leave it at that. Why fiddle around with perfection? Why fix what ain't broke?" she said, quoting Hazel.

"But what more is there?" he asked, his hold suddenly turning to iron.

"You know what?" She gave a dark laugh. "I don't know what more there is. Isn't that funny? I know there's more. I know I want it. But I don't quite know what it is."

"Where do you think you're going to find more?" he answered defensively. "You think just any man has what I have to offer?"

A hellish minute went by while she turned and stared at him.

All at once she blurted out, "It may shock you to discover this, but I'm pretty sure I could find happiness with a man of less means than you, Seth Morgan. And I can't help but wonder what you mean by 'offer,' because I know you have money. I've known it from the beginning. I'm your assistant, remember? But what more is there?"

She was silent for a long moment, her expression at once accusing and withdrawn.

"You know what?" she began slowly. "There is a lot more. And if this is all there is, I think you're giving it to the wrong girl."

"You didn't complain a few minutes ago," he rumbled ominously.

"So maybe you should give it to Nikki, because from what I could see, she was pretty darn happy with whatever you threw at her.''

A shield of ice went up in front of him.

Narrowing his eyes, he said, ''I don't know what's eating you all of a sudden, Kirsten, but if you don't see what I have to offer, then you're blind. Blind and foolish.''

She rose from the bed and slipped on her faded flannel robe. ''You do have a lot to offer, Mr. Morgan, but a couple of rubies and a new car isn't what I had in mind.''

She hated the fact that they'd gotten to this awful moment of truth, but it had come and she would have to give in to it.

''I'm sorry.'' Her voice was choked with unshed tears. ''I'm really and truly sorry.''

She thought of Carrie and the disappointment her little sister would suffer once she realized Seth's affections were as fleeting as Kirsten had thought they were. ''Yes. I'm sorry for everything,'' she repeated, tying her robe and leaving for her room.

''Carrie, I'm too busy to go riding today. Can I call you later and let you know what's going on?'' Kirsten held her breath. The morning had dawned bloodshot-red, and she'd seen every minute of it. It was now 9:00 a.m., time for her to cut Seth's ties with Carrie and time for Kirsten to go into her protective shell.

"I've got art camp at noon, so it's no big deal," Carrie said over the receiver.

Kirsten breathed a sigh of relief. "We'll work it out to go riding again, but right now just hang tight, okay? Love you," she rasped before hanging up the phone.

Sitting down, she realized all that she'd burdened herself with.

Her mother needed the mortgage paid; her sister had been promised another long riding lesson. Kirsten would never meet all her obligations while under Seth Morgan's power.

But he could make her live or die just by the wave of his hand. She was, in truth, nothing but a dispensable employee. He didn't need a personal assistant when Mary in New York could take over at a moment's notice and fill the job in the meantime.

She rubbed her eyes and realized the only way to save herself and her sister was to quit.

Seth had made love to her countless times, his soft words and kind deeds had touched her, and every gesture, every caress, had convinced her what she was seeing was real.

But he'd never said he loved her. He'd never offered a commitment. The wealth at his fingertips seemed to be nothing more than a manipulative tool.

His machinations would work with most girls. Most women were all too greedy for the next Porsche, the next trip to the jewelry store.

But truly, Kirsten was not Nikki. If she and James had truly been in love, she could have been the wife of a band singer. She could have lived the life of a roadie just to be near the man she loved, the man who loved her.

But Seth offered none of that. And she was in a dangerous game if she was going to hang around and try to convince herself there was more. If she continued down the path she was going, she would only drag Carrie and her mother down with her. It would be a catastrophe for all concerned, and her mother and Carrie had been through enough.

Startled, she looked up to see Seth at the front door. Sitting in the great room, she hadn't seen him come upon her.

"Jim is waiting to saddle up," he announced, his face taut with wariness.

"Carrie's not coming today. She has art

camp. Neither am I," she added hastily. "I've got a lot to do."

His expression as hard as honed steel, he said, "I'm your boss, Kirsten. I don't remember giving you any work."

She looked around the room—anywhere but at him. "I've got personal errands to run if you don't need me."

"Such as?" he commanded.

Giving him an acid glance, she said, "Believe it or not, I've got a life beyond you, Mr. Morgan. I've got to close on that loan for my mother's house, and I've got other personal matters to attend to."

"What is it with you? Yesterday seemed to go perfectly. Now you act as if I forced you into my bed," he snapped.

"I don't want a contract for a relationship, okay?" she blurted out. "I want a relationship, not a benefits package." Despairing, she confessed, "Look, let's face it, Nikki speaks your language. She understands what it is that you stand for. I don't, okay? I don't," she finished, depressed, and yet driven to speak her mind.

"What are you saying?" He crossed his arms in front of him. Scowling in the open doorway, he looked like a marauder ready to strike.

"We've got to break this off before there's a lot of explaining to do to my mother, Carrie, Viola and anyone else," she said.

He looked furious. "You're an adult and so am I. Why do we have to explain to anyone?"

She knew he wouldn't understand. He was used to getting his own way, to manipulating people. He bulldozed emotion like most people ran over pavement.

But she knew she had to protect her own, even if she couldn't protect herself. It was one thing to disappoint her, it was another entirely to disappoint Carrie. She couldn't allow that to happen, no matter how painful it proved to be to her.

"I'm giving my notice, Seth. I can give you two more weeks, then you'll have to replace me." She looked at him, her usual cool facade covering up the volcano of emotion inside her.

"I don't take well to people telling me what to do, Kirsten."

She stared at him. "Well, this time you're going to have to, because you can't force me, Seth. I'm not a robot. I'm not a slave. More than that, I'm not a fortune hunter who will do your bidding with just the lure of a shiny object. No, Seth, I'm a flesh-and-blood woman who wants more out of life than you have to offer. So I'm getting out of here. I'm going to see what else there is in the world for me.''

She stood and made to leave.

''I don't think I've ever met a woman I couldn't figure out, but I can't figure you out, Kirsten. Not at all,'' he told her, his voice bitter.

''You can't figure it out, Seth, because it's too simple.''

She gave him one last lingering look, then with tears in her eyes she ran up the stairs to her room.

Twelve

When Kirsten saw the New York tabloid the following week, her world stopped. After her announcement that she was quitting, Seth had taken off on his plane to New York. She hadn't heard from him in a week.

Devastated, she told herself over and over again that the parting was for the best. After all, he surely hadn't mourned it. Instead, he'd taken off for greener pastures, if the headlines didn't lie: Fab Financier Seth Morgan to Wed Supermodel Nikki Butler. Wedding Plans Secret, Strictly On The Q.T.

Heartsick, she shoved the paper aside and sank into her misery.

As if she could read Kirsten's mind, Hazel was on the phone a minute later.

"What's all this nonsense in the paper about your boss?" the cattle baroness demanded without even a greeting.

"I guess he's getting married," Kirsten answered dully.

"You mean you're his personal assistant and you don't even know the story?" Hazel snorted.

"He left for New York a week ago, Hazel. He doesn't report to me. He's my boss, remember? I report to him."

"And you haven't reported to him in a week? Darlin', you're to report to him this instant. This instant!"

Kirsten wanted to laugh, but the unshed tears choked her.

"He's my boss, Hazel, but he's not going to be that for long. I'm sorry to tell you this after all the effort you went through to get me the job, but I've handed in my notice. I've only got one more week to go."

Hazel was silent, as if absorbing the information. The sympathy in her next words shocked Kirsten.

"You mean you've only got one more week to endure. Isn't that right, my dear?"

Despite her self-control, Kirsten burst into tears. "Is it that obvious?" she cried.

"I'm an old polecat, dear. You can't fool me when I've spotted someone in love."

Kirsten wiped the tears running from her eyes. "I don't know how it happened. It just did. Maybe deep down I wanted it to happen, but I thought I took every precaution...every precaution...."

"You're pregnant, too?" Hazel gasped. "I'll kill him."

"No, no, no." Kirsten sniffed. "Well...at least I don't think so. But that's not really the point. I'm a big girl, Hazel. I knew what to do, and somehow I did everything wrong. I knew he was all wrong to get involved with, and now I'm going to have to live with the consequences of my foolishness. *All* of the consequences, if need be."

"You want to come live with me at the ranch while we sort this all out, cowgirl?" Hazel offered.

"I told him I'd give him two weeks' notice, and I'm going to do that one thing right if it kills me." She sniffed again.

"He doesn't deserve that," the cattle baroness said in condemning tones.

"Maybe." Kirsten brushed at her wet cheeks. "But it takes two to tango, and I jumped, Hazel. With my eyes wide-open I made the stupid decision to jump."

Hazel McCallum met this news with a far-from-defeated sigh. "Don't you worry, dear. Things have a way of working out. There's still time."

Kirsten laughed darkly. "Yes. There's one more week. And if I'm lucky he won't invite me to the wedding."

Another day passed before Kirsten saw Seth.

He arrived like any other time, quietly, in his Jeep. She was sitting before the great-room fire on the couch where they'd made love. Before she could rise from her seat, the door opened and he was there, looking as handsome and devilish as he had ever looked.

"Ah, Miss Meadows. Fine. I'll need you to alert Viola that we're to prepare for fifty visitors for next Saturday." It seemed to be work as usual for him as he shrugged out of his suit jacket and went to his desk to survey the faxes for the day.

Kirsten couldn't believe the stab she felt in

her heart at seeing him. The very idea of him marrying Nikki left her ill. As Hazel had foretold, she would have to endure the last moments with him, but seeing him now, knowing he was lost to her, suddenly seemed more than she might be able to take.

"How was your flight?" she inquired, her cool facade coming to her rescue.

He looked up from his desk.

Warily he replied, "The usual."

"Congratulations." She forced herself to meet his gaze. She would have her breakdown in private, but in front of him she would never reveal her devastation.

"You wish me well?" He seemed almost taken aback.

"If Nikki brings you every happiness, then I must." She said nothing else. There was no more to say.

He studied her for a long time, his sea-ice eyes searching, probing. "Kirsten, I've decided to stay here in Mystery, to keep the ranch. Come hell or high water, I want to stay in Mystery."

"If you're hell-bent on staying in Mystery, then do what you must," was all she offered.

She herself would not be staying in Mystery. Not with him around. She had roamed the world before when her father had been with the diplomatic corps. If she had to do it again to find her place, then she would drag her mother and Carrie along for the ride. Anything to get away from Seth and the pain in her heart.

She gathered up the book she'd been reading in front of the fire. Departing, she said, "I'm sure we'll be busy the next few days, so if there's nothing more, I'll see you in the morning." Numbly she made for the huge staircase to the side of the great room.

He stared after her, not speaking, his expression full of unnamed emotion.

"Kirsten." His jaw bunched. "I—" His mouth jammed shut.

"Yes?" she asked, her breath shallow and anticipatory.

"I—I hope you sleep well."

He roughly dismissed her with his cool glance.

Wounded anew, she simply nodded and went to her bedroom.

Only when she was alone did she release her despair, rubbed raw by the renewed hope of seeing him again. She wept silently, her only succor the fact that the clock was ticking, and soon she would see him no more.

"This is the strangest thing," Mary said to Kirsten discreetly into the phone from New

York. "Nikki Butler is burning up his lines of credit all over this town to get ready for this wedding, but it makes no sense why he wants to transport all that to that ranch to get married. Especially when she hated that place. Positively hated it. It's all over town how she loathed that visit," the executive secretary confessed.

Kirsten closed her eyes, not wanting to hear any more details.

Finally she offered, "Perhaps he's the one who likes it here."

"Precisely my point," Mary said into the speaker. "If he's so in love with her that he wants to marry her, why do it at a place she can't stand? I'd have thought he'd sell the place, she hated it so much. At least, that's what all the gossips have to say about it."

"Men. Don't try to understand them, Mary. They'll drive you insane," she attempted.

"But," the secretary continued in her conspiratorial voice, "I have a theory. I think he's been involved with someone up there. I think he wants to get married there just to prove a point."

Point taken, Kirsten thought to herself bitterly.

Point so taken it had pierced her heart and ripped it out.

In a modulated voice Kirsten said, "Seth Morgan has the world at his fingertips. Why would a man like him bother to make a point to someone? Especially a point so extravagant?" *And futile,* she added silently.

"I don't know why. All I know," Mary went on, "is that I've worked for the man for over fifteen years. I know him as well as my son and husband. I was with him through the loss of his parents and through the building of his empire...and something's gotten to him, I tell you. I wish I could say it was Nikki, but I just don't see it. I don't see it at all...."

"What do you need me to do?" Kirsten asked, desperate to change a subject that was getting all too close to her.

"Well," Mary mused, "Nikki called, and she said the wedding gown designer will have to do the final fitting in Mystery...."

Kirsten didn't hear a word Mary was telling her.

Like an automaton, she took notes and offered appropriate uh-huhs when necessary. Her mind, however, was miles away, kissing her lover midstream in the creek, seducing Seth on the couch, licking her heart wounds as she forced herself to emotionally prepare to leave him.

"I'll get it prepared," she said to Mary when they were finished.

"Hey, are you all right?" Mary asked, innocently inquisitive. "Your mom's still doing okay? I've been dying to come up there. I can't wait to meet all of you at the wedding."

Kirsten gave a choked little laugh. As if she would put herself through that ceremony.

"Mom is doing spectacularly."

"Good." Mary sighed. "You know, I've gotten quite fond of you, Kirsten. Seth has told me how much you've done for your mom. You deserve the best."

"Thank you."

Kirsten didn't think now was the time to spring it on Mary that she would be leaving in less than a week. Besides, the wedding would speak for itself. Her absence would be noticed by some, certainly Hazel. If Mary put two and two together, she would realize why Kirsten didn't attend the wedding, and there would be no need to explain further.

"Oh, and by the way, Nikki will be calling you," Mary advised. "And she's been Catherine the Great ever since that diamond went on her hand, so beware."

Mary said goodbye.

Kirsten hung up.

Suddenly in her heart of hearts she realized the whole charade was a losing game. There was no way she was going to advise Nikki on her wedding gown. Enough pain was enough, and she was no masochist. Her promise to stay the extra week was null and void, given the latest maelstrom being thrust upon her.

She went to find Seth and tell him the truth— that she would be leaving right then.

But the damnedest thing was, she couldn't find Seth anywhere.

He wasn't out riding Noir, and he hadn't summoned the plane. Without friends in town, he never took the Jeep, but the vehicle was missing just the same, and even Viola said he'd made no mention of needing anything in town.

Frustrated, despairing and trapped, Kirsten did something she never did. She went to the wine cellar, retrieved the most celebrated bottle of champagne there and popped it open in the great room on their couch.

"Do you love her?" Hazel's question shot out as if she was a detective grilling a suspect.

Seth sat in the McCallum parlor, upright on the century-old mail-order settee, looking more uncomfortable and belligerent in Hazel's presence than he'd ever been.

"You said I needed to settle down. I'm doing that. Is love in your sales contract, too?" he parried.

"I'm looking out for your best interests here, cowboy, so don't cross me. You can't marry this twit Nikki Butler. She's all wrong for you. You'll be miserable."

"The tabloids say it's the match of New York."

"Well, here in Mystery we have a different standard of matchmaking, and you and Nikki Butler won't make the grade—let me inform you of that right now," Hazel retorted.

"Why not?" he taunted, his jaw set, his long muscular form dwarfing the settee.

"Because you love Kirsten, and dadgummit, I've never been wrong about these things." Hazel stared at him like an angry badger. "She's your match, son, and if you don't mind my words, you'll pay by losing her forever."

His eyes went subzero. "I am not about to admit an indiscretion with an employee, Hazel."

Hazel snorted. "All this employee-boss political correctness is nothing but cow pie in this case. I don't believe it, and the sooner you admit to loving her, the sooner you can grab happiness with both hands."

Seth seemed to ponder her words long and hard.

Finally he said, "I'll admit Kirsten is unlike any woman I've ever known."

Hazel seemed to sense the chink in his armor.

Craftily she said, "I'll make you a deal, son. Look me in the eye like an honorable Montanan, and tell me you don't love Kirsten Meadows. If you can do that, the ranch is yours, and your marriage is yours to do with what you want."

She studied him with her notorious stare. "But if you can't do that right now, I give you only this advice, son—grab her. Grab her so tight, you'll never let her go."

He lowered his head to his hands. "Hazel, you're killing me, you know that."

"Just a few words and you're free, Seth. Free to do whatever you want. Free to ruin your life if you so desire. So what is it?"

He groaned. "Kirsten is like no other." His head snapped up. His expression hardened with hidden frustration. "But because of that, I don't understand her. And so I've never been sure how to go about...well, I've never figured out how to approach—" He snuffed his last words, clearly censoring any confession.

A soft, slow, knowing smile lit on Hazel's mouth. With her gaze probing, she said, "Sometimes you just gotta wrangle 'em. You get me, son?''

He met the cattle baroness's eyes. By his expression, it seemed that want fought with logic.

At last he confessed, ''What if I wrangle her, and she just says no? Then what?''

Solemnly Hazel nodded her encouragement along with her no-nonsense advice. ''If you love her, son, and she won't have you, then you take it like a McCallum. You leave her be, but don't go running in the opposite direction. That model isn't for you, Seth. Don't fool yourself.''

Seth rubbed his eyes, his only concession to Hazel's words.

''I'm used to getting what I want, Hazel,'' he finally stated.

''Take it like a McCallum, son. State your case, bide your time and you just might be lucky enough to get what you want.''

He leaned his head back against the overly carved laminated rosewood. Several minutes ticked by as he ruminated over his choices, so many of which were beyond his control. Finally, in a fit of pique, he said, ''You know what, Hazel. I think I can handle Wall Street over Mystery.''

Hazel chuckled. ''Greenhorn,'' was all she offered.

Thirteen

***

Kirsten was in her room packing when the knock came at her door. The champagne bottle was more than half-empty and the last of her cosmetics had been tucked into her rollaway bag.

"Well, it's you," she announced, flinging the door wide-open to let Seth in.

"You act as if you were expecting me." He didn't move from the hallway. Casually he leaned on the sinuous pine baluster behind him and surveyed her.

"I wasn't 'specting you, but since you're

here, c'mon in. I want to get a few things straight.'' Her eyes read him, and she swore he smiled. It only made her madder.

"What's on your mind?'' he baited, still not entering her room.

She hugged the doorway. "What's on my mind? Let me give you a piece of my mind,'' she offered, her expression damning. "I, Mr. Morgan, am not the kind of woman who makes jewelry, okay?''

He looked appropriately confused. "What are you talking about?' he asked innocently—too innocently, by her mark.

"I said,'' she repeated, narrowing her eyes, her broken heart buried deep for the moment, "I'm not the kind of woman who makes jewelry, and I don't tolerate mistresses. We, Mr. Morgan, if we had ever married, would never have a mistress, I can assure you.''

He took a step forward.

She held up her hand to say she wasn't finished.

"Now,'' she pronounced. "I'm quitting. So goodbye and good luck. I'm outta here. Have a good life with Nikki, and I hope you live long enough to regret it.'' She went to close the door.

He put his hand on the doorjamb.

She stared up at him.

This time he was only inches away.

"You want to talk about this, Miss Meadows?" he grunted, his eyes amused.

Disconcerted, she shook her head. "What's to talk about? I said I'd stay two weeks, and I can't. So what? Deal with it. Mary can handle all your plans. You don't need me. And if it's the pay you're worried about, hey, don't bother. I've got bigger things on the horizon. I don't need your measly paycheck, anyway."

"You sound almost bitter, Miss Meadows."

She snorted. "What gives you that idea?"

"I'd think a disenchanted employee might be a little defiant, but you sound as if there was more here. As if perhaps we were lovers and not just in a business relationship."

The unshed tears froze in her eyes.

Quietly she said, "We were lovers. I know that, at least on my end."

He uncurled his fingers from the doorjamb and entered the room.

"We are lovers, Kirsten."

Her mind tried to parry his meaning. "If you're so delusional as to think we'll continue our relationship after you're married, you need a long rest at a mental institution."

If she hadn't known better, she would have sworn he bit back a smile.

"Marriage doesn't have to exclude sex, Kirsten. I hear you can have both. It's not impossible."

"Spoken just like your father," she accused, her eyebrow rising.

"Touché," he conceded.

Smugly she continued, "Thank you very much for the mistress position, Mr. Morgan, but I'll have to decline your offer."

"Kirsten—" He tried to grab her.

She stepped away from him. The ice ball that was her heart was beginning to melt every second he was near, and she wanted him gone. She didn't want to lose control until she was out of the house and well on her way to her mother's.

"Why did you quit, anyway?" he asked, still keeping his respectful distance. "Come on, confess. It wasn't really the reason you gave, was it? When I hired you, you told me you needed this job. Then you bought your mother a house and couldn't see her going back to work until she was better—all that a fib, Miss Meadows?"

"Certainly not," she defended.

His eyes narrowed. "It looks like it, because just when things get busy over here, you decide you'd rather fling it all to the wind and work at the Mystery Diner."

Impassioned with fury, she almost struck him.

"My mother worked her tail off for Carrie and me there. And she does deserve a rest, and I'm going to give her one."

"Then stay. No one can pay you as well as I can." His gaze was riveted to hers.

She violently turned away from him. "Look, my mom may have had to waitress at the Mystery Diner, and I may have to do that, too, to keep things together. But you know what?" The tears began to melt. One slipped by, no matter how hard she tried to hold it back, and she cursed herself for it.

Damning him, she spat, "There isn't a person in Mystery who doesn't love my mom. Every customer was treated well, no matter how worn-out my mother was. And I guess that kind of stuff doesn't buy you jets and ranches, but I'd rather be loved at the Mystery Diner than live here without it."

Finished, she zipped her suitcase, picked up her half-empty bottle of champagne and stood waiting for him to move from the door so she could leave.

He didn't budge.

She lifted the champagne bottle. "Sorry about this, but I thought a celebration was in order now that I'm leaving. Just deduct it from my last pay-check."

He shrugged.

She waited.

And waited.

And waited.

Finally she dropped her suitcase on the floor with a thud.

Crossing her arms over her chest, she faced him. "Is there something more, Mr. Morgan? You look as if something's on your mind."

"Something is on my mind, Kirsten."

"And what is it?"

"Nikki," he answered, his face revealing nothing.

Angry and depressed, Kirsten had had enough. She picked up her suitcase, planning to barge right through him if necessary.

But his arms went around her and stopped her.

"Kirsten, don't leave," he whispered, a strange emotion in his eyes.

She looked at him, at his handsome face she'd grown to love, and the wound in her heart broke open. She began to weep, and quickly the tears flowed like the champagne growing flat in the bottle.

Gently he pulled her in to his chest.

She thought to fight the gesture, but there was no better place to weep than against the security of his hard chest. It was too much to resist when she was exhausted and without hope.

"Baby, don't cry," he said against her hair.

"What's not to cry about?" She sniffed, unable to get control of herself long enough to shrug off his embrace. "You won't let me leave, and the only thing on your mind is your fiancée."

He kissed her temple. "She's not my fiancée any longer. I called it off."

Maybe the champagne had really gone to her head, but for some crazy reason Kirsten thought he'd said he'd called it off.

"What?" she demanded, looking up at him.

He smiled. "I called it off. The reason she's on my mind is that I owe her a big apology—maybe even a Lamborghini. I should never have used her like I did, but Hazel said I had to settle down to keep the ranch, and I'm keeping the ranch, Kirsten. I'm not leaving Mystery."

She tried to absorb what he was saying, but none of it made sense. "I don't understand any of this. Just keep the darn ranch. What's it to Hazel or Nikki?"

Pulling her closer, he placed a tender kiss on her lips. "None of this concerns them—just you and me." His expression softened. "When I met you, Kirsten, I was convinced you were just another gold digger. It didn't bother me, because I knew all about those kinds of women. My own mother was one. You know that. So when that's all you know, that's all you expect and it doesn't bother you. Hell, I even figured I'd probably marry one of them one day just like my dad."

Watching the emotion in his eyes go from shielded to yearning, she wondered if she was living a dream.

He continued.

"But everything you said, everything you did, went against my prejudice. Even what James said about you— I wanted to believe you were a conniving social climber, but I couldn't match up what I was thinking to what I was seeing and feeling."

Tipping her face upward, he stared down at her, a new kind of hesitation in his eyes. "Don't leave me, Kirsten. Nothing in this world will be the same if you leave me."

She let the words sink into her mind and heart. For several long moments she still couldn't believe what she was hearing, but then a new reality engulfed her, and she knew she had to be cautious.

"Seth," she whispered, her voice still deep with tears, "I can't stay here and work for you any longer whether you're married or not. It just won't work. I just can't do it.''

"What's changed?" he prodded, his tone gentle.

"I—I—" She closed her mouth and refused to say it. If she had any shred of dignity left, she had to leave without confessing her love. To do so and then find herself just another employee in the morning would kill her.

"You love me?" he asked, his stare dark and probing. "I hope so. Because I love you, Kirsten. I love you and I don't ever want another day to pass where you're not in my arms and in my bed."

She locked gazes with him, unable to believe what she was hearing.

"Will you marry me, Kirsten?"

The words lodged in her throat where the tears had once been.

"Will you?"

"Yes," she gasped, tears springing forth anew, but this time tears of joy. "Yes, I will marry you, Seth Morgan. But not for your ranch, and not for your money." Her voice shook from the emotion. "I'll marry you because you kissed me in the cold brook, and made me feel like a woman. And lastly, I'll marry you because you're more of a man than anyone else sees. I want kindness and a warm hearth and children. Those things seem so within reach, and yet only you can bring them to me. And it will take much more than a bank account to do it.'' She laughed and wept at the same time.

Slowly his mouth crushed down on hers in a long, soul-clawing kiss that tasted of tears and champagne.

Inside she melted. Her heart leaped, but she still worried that it wasn't real, that in a moment it would all be taken away and she would wake as if in a dream.

''I love you, Kirsten, and I'm going to make you my wife if I have to sell everything and live in a shack with you and our twelve children.''

She suddenly laughed.

After those absurd words, all of a sudden she believed.

Epilogue

Hazel looked out over her beautiful Montana valley through the window of her parlor. Her face was placid, her eyes twinkling with mischief, even though Jenn Meadows's words were full of anxiety.

"It's not like her to just call me and say she's going away for a few days." Jenn nervously sipped on a hot cup of tea that Hazel had slipped some whiskey into.

"She's an adult, dear. She has a right to take a few days off." Hazel sat down next to her. "Besides, maybe that boss of hers sent her on an errand to Paris, or such."

Jenn shook her head. "No, she'd tell me. Besides—" her face took on a more troubled cast "—I think there's something going on with that boss of hers. She hasn't said anything, but I do hope they're not fooling around with each other." Her eyes darkened. "I'd hate for her to have to go through what I've gone through—"

"And that reminds me, dear. Have you met Jim, Seth's ranch manager? I know the girls have really enjoyed riding up there. Why don't we have him plan one of those old-fashioned hayrides for us? We'll take along a little supper and have a picnic right by the mill."

Kirsten's mother rolled her eyes. "I've heard all the town gossip on how you like to play matchmaker, and I can't even begin to imagine you'd be up to those old tricks with me, Hazel. I'm too old and too ugly."

"You're a beauty, my dear, and there's no such thing as too old for romance. Besides, this isn't some kind of scheme of mine. Jim's a fine man. Lost his wife to cancer four years ago. Never remarried and never even thought about it, I assure you."

Jenn sighed. "A hayride sounds like great fun, Hazel, but all of this is beside the point. I just can't get it out of my head that something's going on with Kirsten—"

"Who's coming, Ebby?" Hazel asked, her sixth sense picking up on visitors even before the dust of the vehicle could be seen in the distance.

"I don't know," Hazel's housekeeper mused, going to the window. After a few moments she said, "Looks like a Jeep. I think it might be Seth Morgan's Jeep. Yep, looks like his, all right."

"Maybe it's Kirsten," Jenn announced, going to the window.

Sure enough, the Jeep came to a halt and Seth jumped out of the vehicle. He went around to the passenger side to help Kirsten out.

"Something's different. I can see that from here," Jenn mused, her forehead furrowed—now not with fear, but rather curious expectation.

Ebby went to the front door and opened it.

Quickly the couple was inside, with Jenn admonishing her daughter.

"Kirsten, I know you're an adult and all, but really, I just want a phone number, anything, if you decide to take off like that. What if something happened?" she said, giving her daughter a hug.

Seth cleared his throat, but didn't intrude.

"I've something to tell you," Kirsten said, looking at her mother and Hazel.

"Should we sit down?" Jenn asked, caution all over her beautiful face.

"Nonsense," Hazel huffed. "Can't you see that sparkler on her finger, Jenn? Your daughter's gone run off and got herself married."

Jenn's gaze fell to Kirsten's left ring finger. There was a pink-lavender diamond surrounded by two others on a thin platinum band.

"Kirsten?" Jenn gasped. "Oh, Kirsten." She hugged her laughing daughter.

When they parted, she added, "But you should have told us. Carrie will be beside herself that she missed you getting married."

Kirsten sat them all down, her hand locked with Seth's as she took her place next to him. "We wanted to tell you, but it was very sudden. And when Seth decides something, come hell or high water, it's going to happen."

"When did you both decide this? I didn't even know you had a romance," Jenn commented. She turned to her new son-in-law. "And I thought you were engaged already to some woman in New York City."

Seth released a wry grin. "Entirely my mistake. Because when I took one look at Kirsten, I knew she was the one I wanted and no other would do." He squeezed his bride's hand. "And once I got her convinced that I loved her and this was forever, we saw no reason to make a circus of it like Nikki'd been doing. We flew to Greece and got married shipboard.''

''But we're going to have a small ceremony here,'' Kirsten added hastily. ''Because I do want Carrie to be my maid of honor.'' She leaned over and took her mother's hand. ''And I want you to be the second woman at the reception to dance with your new son-in-law, Mom.''

It took a few moments for Jenn to absorb all that was being explained to her.

But finally, when she had regained herself, she stood and gave Seth a big hug. ''Welcome to the family, Seth,'' Jenn said.

He gave her a big bear hug. ''I'm honored, Jenn. You three make the best family I've ever seen.''

Jenn smiled. ''We all love each other. That's all a family needs, right, Kirsten?''

''That's all you need,'' Kirsten agreed, looking at her husband with love-filled eyes.

''Now that that's settled,'' Hazel interjected, ''when are the babies coming along? No sense in wasting time. You've both seen the world. I say settle down and get to doing what God put you in this green valley for.''

Seth laughed. ''Hazel, you're too much.'' He

looked at his bride and said, "Should you tell them or should I?"

Kirsten shrugged helplessly. She faced the other two women and said, "We don't have it completely confirmed, but let's just say don't be surprised if the baby comes along sooner than later."

Tears glistened in Jenn's eyes. "How amazing. All of this. How wonderful," she uttered, beside herself.

Kirsten went to be by her side.

But Hazel was on to the next challenge.

"We've got to have a couple of parties celebrating this here thing," she announced, mostly to Ebby, who was in the background making notes on all that had transpired.

"We don't need much, Hazel," Seth added.

"Not much! You're talking Mystery people here. We need to pull out all the stops!" Hazel admonished.

Her eyes twinkled. "And the first thing we should do is go on a hayride! Doesn't that sound like fun? We could pack a nice supper and Jim—he works for you, Seth, I believe—why, he could take the whole family here for a celebration."

Jenn recovered from her happy shock just long enough to say to Hazel, "Hey, I know what you're doing—'' before Seth and Kirsten and Ebby interrupted, each with their own contributions to the idea of a hayride.

In the ensuing fracas, Hazel returned to look out her parlor window.

Mystery Valley lay like a blanket of emerald moss beneath the majestic snow-covered peaks of the mountains. The sun was sinking, painting Mount Mystery a ruby-red. In the far distance a stag was chasing a doe across the golden fields. The cattle munched peaceably, their fat bodies casting long, lazy shadows across the hay fields.

''You can count another happy couple off your matchmaking list, you sly girl,'' Ebby said, standing next to her boss in the window. ''So are you resting on your laurels?''

The cattle baroness put that thought to rest. ''Certainly not,'' she said.

''So what are you thinking now, Hazel?'' Ebby asked above the excited din.

Hazel couldn't repress the twinkle in her Prussian-blue eyes.

The only thing she said was, ''Next!''

*   *   *   *   *   *